HOT PURSUIT

She had gorgeous breasts. They were big and high, very firm, with large full nipples. Her waist narrowed sharply. Normally her figure was obscured by her lab coat so she looked lumpish and plain. But her body was glorious, a full riot of flesh, narrow at the waist and flaring at the hip. She shimmered before Jake's staring eyes and a fierce eroticism imbued her every movement.

She bent over to remove her panties and her breasts swung forward, hanging down, the shape of the nipple and aureole perfect in profile.

Jake knew he had misjudged her. The erotic power emanating from his transformed laboratory manager was frightening . . .

Hot Pursuit

Nadia Adamant

HEADLINE

First published in 1993
by HEADLINE BOOK PUBLISHING PLC

10 9 8 7 6 5 4 3 2 1

ISBN 0 7472 4266 6

Typeset by
CBS, Felixstowe, Suffolk

Printed and bound in Great Britain by
HarperCollins Manufacturing Glasgow

HEADLINE BOOK PUBLISHING PLC
Headline House
79 Great Titchfield Street
London W1P 7FN

Hot Pursuit

Prologue

It was a wonder he'd never been rolled before. Part of him, the part that found his downward slide funny, was cynically aware through the fuddle of drink that his time had come. The punk was going to have him.

The boy must be desperate. It was no night for a mugging, the wind whipping the rain into solid sheets of wet misery that bent round corners and soaked his coattails, sticking them to his legs. He was propped in a doorway and he had time to wonder whether he could find his wallet to hand it over before the kid knifed him.

He could see the knife blade, the light flickering along its shiny length. A spurt of laughter was like vomit in his throat. The kid was using a serrated edge. Stupid kid. No professional this.

A pale moving blur drew his erratic attention. Even his mugger held only minimal interest for him. He looked up the street and saw her.

She was good. Hourglass, that was it. Out of date today but very much to his own taste, in the days when his interest had been more than academic. In the days before drink became his goddess, his whore.

She came towards them, the rain glistening on her naked skin and the streetlights her halo. She glowed. She shone.

The punk was speaking but he took no notice. The woman came closer. Parts of his brain lurched into action. Thirty-ish. Big breasted. Long hair, colour hard to identify because it was wet and slicked back. High cheekbones. Strong jawline.

1

A lovely swaying action to the hips. It was beautiful, the way the rain gathered in her moving hollows and made tiny cataracts off the peaks and points of her body.

Another part of his brain, the part the drink never touched, told him this was it. It wasn't just his night to be mugged. It was his first dose of the DTs. Naked women don't roam the night-dark London streets looking like something out of a Bond movie.

The punk turned round at last. His mouth fell open and he backed into the doorway so that, absurdly, he stood by his victim, as if for protection. His knife hand dropped. The two of them watched the hallucination.

The woman approached them. Riley's journalistic mind attempted a description of her face, of her expression, and failed. Horny. That's how she looked. Really horny.

A moment later she was with them. The light slid over the wet planes of her body. He saw her wide mouth was smiling. The punk next to him gurgled slightly. She lifted her hand to his face and he shut his eyes.

Warm velvet. Spices. A curious smell, exotic, unplaceable. His body trembled and unbelievably he felt himself stir.

He couldn't do that any more. Drink was his chastity belt, alcohol his moral guardian. But he stirred, he felt it, and warm as sin the blood ran through his veins lifting and lightening him so that for a deluded moment he thought he could, he might . . .

She kissed him. Now he knew he was definitely erect. He felt her hands at his groin. His mouth rejoiced, he had forgotten the sweetness of a woman, and a moment later she had his flesh in her grasp. It flashed through his mind he had lost too much, going on the booze, this was too sweet a pleasure to have abandoned.

His knees sagged apart. She came on tiptoe, kissing him, rubbing her skin against his clothing, enveloping him in her

2

strange smell. She caught his hand and lifted her leg, making him hold it up. Now, balanced, she wriggled against him and a moment later he felt himself slide into her.

His shaft was full, gloriously full and firm. Her body cradled it, squeezing it, milking it with firm strokes, sucking him in a slow pavanne of pleasure. His hips jerked and shuddered. Her liquid acceptance, the slight resistance of her flesh, fired him. His eyes were closed still, he had no knowledge of how she did what she did, but her delicious grip and slide was a warm embrace that persuaded him he could come back to the land of the living. That it would be easy.

He could feel her thigh, cool silk in his hand. He felt his cock begin to swell. He felt her hotter, tighter, her flesh rippling on his. His head dropped down so that he rested it blindly on her shoulder. The smell of her filled his nostrils. His body was a sweet powerful machine and he felt its glorious surge with a kind of humble gratitude that this experience was vouchsafed him. He pumped hard, wanting to laugh. She took his fierce swoop of pleasure deep within her loins. She held him, she shuddered on him, and then she too was done.

There was a moment while the world returned, wet and cold. Then she drew away and he opened his eyes. Cool air rushed into his groin. A great sweetness lay over him. He twisted his head slightly to look at her, to let his eyes spell out his gratitude. There were still good things in a bad world. He saw she had the punk.

The kid had dropped his jeans. His sex was up, as pale as the woman herself, a naked shaft in the night. Her long fingers rolled around it, teasing back the hood. It was like a monstrous finger itself, fat, bluntly questing, worm-blind but determined. The kid got a hand onto her naked breast and lifted it. She bent her head in and pressed her mouth to his neck. For a moment Riley thought numbly of vampires.

She placed her two hands behind the kid's neck and walked up the wall. The boy thrust between her parted thighs. To say it was impossible was an understatement. The whole thing was impossible. He must be dreaming. He must be nestling in the sweet oblivion of booze.

The boy thrust and thrust, his body tilted back against her pulling weight. She was balancing herself against the wall, pushing off it like she was about to abseil. She thrust out, she slammed back, so that her driving body weight rammed the trapped sex up into the heart of her.

The boy cried out, wailing a long moan of shuddering ecstasy. Riley saw his face screw up and knew he was coming. The woman had her head back, her wet hair hanging in sodden strands behind her. There was a little mole under her chin like a living piece of the night attached to her skin. The wind caught at her hair and moved it as though it was under the water, like it was seaweed.

She leapt down. She looked at the two men, Riley blankfaced, the boy gasping still with buckled legs. She moved back away from them. The rain, the streetlights, made her skin pale plastic, shiny cool. She swayed slightly, smiling. Her face was horny. She looked horny. Then she was gone.

One

Jake had had a steak at Punchinello's and should have been headed for home. Instead he decided to swing by the works. His business meant a lot to him. It was more than work, more than a means to earn a living. It was part crusade, part wife, part family. He loved it and it drove him mad. He found it hard to keep away.

The perimeter fence gleamed in the lights sweeping the parking lot. Not a big one, he didn't employ many people, but his security had to be tight for obvious reasons. One scandal, one slip-up, and they were done for. He would lose the entire project, and with it, frankly, most of his reason for living.

He fed his card into the slot at the gates and waited while it read his code. The lock released and he passed into his little kingdom. Behind him it clicked shut, a solid reassuring noise. Here he was safe.

He entered the single building through its security locks and felt the whole ambience surround him. The warm air hummed, alive. The corridors were dimmed for the night, the offices dark, but light spilled from the vatroom and control centre through the glass dividing wall.

Jake moved quietly along the corridor looking through into the vatroom as he did so. Sonia was on duty tonight, his most senior operative. He stifled a smile. He knew what the boys called her. He didn't care, it meant nothing to him. He valued her for her loyalty, for her reliability. It didn't matter to him what she was like as a woman. Part of him was amused that she so obviously had the hots for him. It was useful.

5

He stopped at his own office door and lit a cigarette. It was a rare luxury. He leant against the door enjoying the feel of his own business successfully at work around him. You didn't hear the hum in the daytime, too much else was going on. That was why he liked it here at night. He could feel the systems working smoothly. He had a friend, Paul, who did a lot of scuba diving. Paul had told him that one of the turn-ons of the sport was the feel of all the equipment you carried working, down there, a hundred feet under the surface. The suck and whoosh of the air through your demand valve. The dials and gauges, steady, safe. The heavy tanks, weightless. Your own body shrunk within its protective neoprene in flight over the seabed. You could twist and turn with the fluid grace of a cat, swoop like a bird. There was nothing like it, Paul said. And just the whiff of danger to keep you alert.

Sonia moved through the vatroom like a goldfish in a bowl. Her gracelessness was less apparent than usual. It was scandalous, Jake thought lazily, that he should lean here in the dimness of the corridor watching her. He was the boss. He should announce he was on the premises. He shouldn't spy.

His meal was comfortable in his belly. The half bottle of good French wine he had drunk with it warmed him. The smoke from his cigarette curled in his nostrils. It was a pity he had no woman to go home to, now Gloria had gone. It would be nice to think that soon his hands could curl around warm, full flesh, that his lips would feel the cushioned softness of a woman's mouth, that his prick could dive deep, deep into a woman's hot welcoming embrace.

For a moment he let his mind dwell unkindly on the thought of Sonia. Would she be eager? Was he just a sexual dream for the poor woman, or did she honestly crave for the reality? She didn't seem to be the sort of woman who would relish a man's hands touching her intimately. On her breasts. Between her thighs. Jake snorted. The thought was mildly disgusting. She was a heavy lumpen woman with an adolescent passion for her boss that would rapidly crumble if he dared to lay a hand on her. Not that he would be brought to such an extremity. The world was full of bimbos and if you were an attractive man with money in your pocket, it was no problem to fill your bed.

How strange Sonia should make him think of sex tonight. She was the opposite of sexy, yet watching her move around the vatroom, touch herself, stand pensive, aroused a train of ideas quite alien to who and what she was. The truth was, he needed a woman. He needed someone naked in his bed, he needed to ease the burden of his loins.

Jake dismissed his thoughts with an effort. He would have to do something eventually. Gloria had been gone three months and he was no natural celibate. *Not yet,* his mind pleaded. *Not while it hurts still, the bitch, going off with that bloated fart of a real estate . . .*

He saw Kemps, the night watchman and guard, was in the vatroom with Sonia. So they chewed the fat, did they, during the long night watches? Jake grinned to himself. Kemps was notoriously surly and Sonia, so the boys said, didn't need to sign on. She was already processed, a frozen lady with plasmogen instead of blood in her veins. What the hell could those two misanthropists find to talk about? He wished he could hear.

He was just about to go over and say he was in the building when he froze, unable to believe his eyes. Sonia had her hands on Kemps's shoulders and was staring into his eyes. She was a tall woman, full-figured, and she commanded the wiry figure of the guard. She took her hands off him and began to unbutton her lab coat.

Jake kept still, watching. He couldn't hear them, the vatroom was soundsealed, but the glazing started at hip height and he had clear vision from his position in the corridor.

Sonia removed her lab coat. Now she unbuttoned her cardigan. Kemps watched her, not moving himself. Sonia undid each button on the clumsy garment with such an intensity that Jake felt her mood through the glass. She removed her cardigan and dropped it on the lab coat. She was blazing. The whole thing was queer. Now she slid down the side zip of the shapeless tweedy skirt she wore. She pushed the skirt down, wriggling slightly to ease its passage. It was lined and she wore a full length slip under it. She dropped the skirt and stepped out of it.

Kemps watched. Jake watched. The woman wasn't undressing. She was emerging, as if from some pupal state.

Now she opened her blouse, button by button. It was a cream-coloured thing, quite tasteless like all her clothes. Yet her action was intensely erotic. Each fastening released was a promise. Her image seemed to swim. She was metamorphosing. Revealed in her underwear she was not a pretty sight yet Jake had the feeling something rare was being exposed, something marvellous. Something sexy, though his eyes denied it.

She wore white and plenty of it. The slip was unrelieved by lace and extended high over the bust. The bra partly seen beneath it was a solidly constructed object in elastic webbing. A vision of Gloria came into Jake's mind, all warm tones, lace edges, silky textures, absurd scraps that clung to her body to tantalise the eye and ravish the mind. Gloria in her beauty, a tanned warm body lovely to behold, to hold . . . His lost wife. The woman who'd rejected him.

He couldn't move now, dammit. The pair of them had him trapped. The situation was excruciatingly embarrassing. Two of his employees were going to fuck in front of him and he didn't think it was going to be a turn-on.

Sonia removed her slip and her bra.

She had gorgeous breasts. They were big and high, very firm, with large full nipples. Her waist narrowed sharply.

Normally her figure was obscured by her heavy clothes, her lab coat, so that she looked a lumpish plain woman. But her body was glorious, a full riot of flesh, narrow at her waist and flaring at her hip. She shimmered before Jake's staring eyes. No longer was she an ugly, pathetic thing. She was a queen, savagely splendid. A fierce eroticism imbued her every movement. Jake felt himself cringe slightly. The power emanating from her was almost frightening. She held her hips, tilting her head back, eyeing the man in front of her. She swayed heavy-lidded and sensuous. Her breasts jutted proudly. She caressed them, rubbing her thumbs slowly over the large nipples. Now she bent over before the unmoving Kemps to slide off her plain briefs. Her breasts swung forward, hanging down, the shape of the nipple and aureole perfect in profile like a Mandelbrot image.

Despite himself, Jake felt his loins stir. Christ, he had misjudged her. What would it be like, putting his shaft into her powerhouse? Would she grind him to bits? The thought of her attached to his own body via his most sensitive place was at once terrifying and enthralling.

He heard his own thoughts, remembering who he was and who they were. Damn them, damn them.

Now she unclipped her solid pink suspenders and removed that garment too. Its grotesqueness served to emphasise her regal sensuality, or rather to reveal it yet more. She had been in disguise. She bent again, rolling her thick stockings down. She had beautiful legs, the one thing Jake already knew.

She stood straight, looking at Kemps. She appeared to be entirely naked. Jake could see the mouse-brown triangle of hair at the apex to her legs. It was still a little flattened from her confining underclothes. It would take a moment to spring out. Jake knew these sort of details about women. His loins ached. He wanted to finger her sex.

She lifted her arms and began to unpin her hair. Normally

it was wound unattractively about her head, pressed flat. Now it fell in heavy hanks, slipping and sliding free till she shook her head and loosened it. She took a step forward. She grasped Kemps's shirt and pulled.

Jake found his chest hurt. He had been holding his breath. There was something in what he was witnessing, some element beyond the obvious. He had seen a plain woman strip. It hadn't been awkward. It hadn't been coquettish. It had been powerful. The woman had removed her clothes and as each ugly utilitarian garment fell away, she had gained power. Jake had felt it through the glass wall. He was shivering under its impact now. What the hell must it be like for the little Kemps, in front of her? Was it for his benefit? Had she done this before for him? Jake's mind struggled. The answers ought to be yes or she wouldn't have had the confidence, Kemps wouldn't have stood so still. Lizard still. Yet things didn't add up. The feel of the thing was wrong. Again he was aware he was watching not so much a stripping as a transformation. Something new had appeared.

Sonia reached forward and took the material of Kemps's shirt in her grasp. She tore it off his chest and pushed it and his uniform jacket back over his shoulders so that his arms were pinned. Kemps staggered under the assault but made no move to prevent her. For a moment she was still. She swayed forward and kissed the revealed chest, then she tore the tie off him and opened his trousers.

Jake felt hot and sick. Did they do this every night when Sonia was on duty? It must be hellishly expensive on shirts. He had seen Kemps's shirt tear, it was beyond being a matter of buttons being sewn on.

Sonia pushed his trousers down. His sex stood out, quivering. Suddenly she almost lifted the man bodily, moving him backwards. He fell but behind him, where Jake hadn't noticed it, was a high lab stool. The man bent over backwards, the stool supporting his buttocks. His feet and now his head were out of sight for Jake but, grotesquely, his erect penis stuck up from the fluffing of dark hair, and Sonia was climbing aboard.

How she managed it, how she kept the man bent over backwards in place, how she rode his erect prick, how she lifted herself up and down on that quivering shaft, Jake hardly knew. This was passion with a vengeance. No doubt the woman was thwarted and if Kemps was willing, it was none of his business how they did it together, though it was his business when they did it in his time, the time he paid them for. The woman was a demon. Her breasts rose and fell, her thighs strained, her body flushed – Jake could see as she rose the gleaming wetness of Kemps's sex. Hell, she was juicy there. Jake could see her stomach muscles going. His mind stalled at imagining what she must be doing to that trapped male shaft with her potent woman's muscles. She took the man between her thighs like he was a bronco she had to master. She was rearing high up, lifting herself, drawing the man up into her, and then Jake saw it, he saw the convulsion in the man's body, the shuddering of his flesh as his tortured sex exploded upwards to fill and satisfy the lustful succuba who had his body at her mercy.

She climbed off and Kemps fell from his stool. For the first time Jake noticed the air within the vatroom was slightly clouded. The woman stood there with her legs parted, her breast heaving and her head thrown back in triumph. Droplets seemed to hang in the filtered air so that tiny fogbanks blurred his vision. He wiped his eyes but they remained. He wanted to fuck her.

No alarms were sounding. Jake couldn't see the control desk and he still was desperately reluctant to admit his presence before they had their clothes on again. He folded himself quietly into his office, using his passcard again, and shut the door behind him with a soft click. Not that it mattered. He couldn't hear them and they couldn't hear him through the sound proofing. It was more that he didn't want a sudden movement in the shadows to attract their attention.

Kemps, on the floor, used and discarded.

Rapidly he fired up his systems and accessed the control desk. To his horror a mass of flashing red lights indicated some gross failure, so gross he actually felt his mind jump away from it, attempt to refuse the information. Damn being scrupulous about their modesty. There was a crisis, an emergency going on.

Jake took a moment to sort out the source. Tank one was open to the atmosphere. The seals were broken, that was for sure. The temperature was rising sharply. So was his own. After things were under control he would sack the bastards. Then he would sue them for negligence.

He ran to his office door. As his hand reached the handle he felt a soft puff that hurt his ears. Now the building alarms were screaming. He began to turn the handle, frantic to get to the tanks and protect them, with his body if need be. His analytical scientist's mind broke through the din of panic clanging in his skull. Fire. Explosion. Don't open the door. Don't open the door.

He could hear it, a dull roar like a distant sea. It wasn't distant, it was the other side of the frail wood barrier he stood against. Even as he stood there, he felt it warm. Smoke curled slyly from under it.

Jake turned back into his office. He unlocked his desk. Working with frantic haste he pulled out a drawer and emptied it. He scooped as much software as he could and shovelled it into the drawer. He took another drawer and emptied it onto the carpet. He smashed the window and knocked glass out of the way. He put the drawer he had saved with its contents through the window and stepped after it. As he did so his office door imploded and a blast of hot air threw him out across the parking lot.

He staggered to his feet and turned to stare in disbelief at his life in flames. The fire roared through his office window, greedily gulping oxygen. If the tank had been secure it wouldn't have mattered, he thought dazedly. It was fireproof, they all were. He didn't know what had gone wrong before the fire started, but the events couldn't be unconnected. His cargo was at risk, dying, dying twice over and he might as well go and join it, for all the good his life would be to him after this.

He went across to his car and reached in to find the phone. He dialled nine, nine, nine.

Two

'You some kind of weirdo?' The police sergeant was aggressively rude. Jake would have been mad, only he was too sick with misery to have space left over for anger.

'You freeze the dead, yeah?'

'Yeah.' Jake lit another cigarette from the stub of the last. That way he'd have a reason for the sour taste in his mouth.

'They pay you for this?'

'Yeah, they pay me. While they're still alive.'

'And it's legal?'

Jake didn't bother to answer. He sucked smoke and hated the world.

The sergeant rocked back on his chair and considered his pencil. He looked at Jake, grinning. 'So tell me why you went to your place of business tonight.'

'I told you. I felt like it.'

'Do you feel like it often?'

He made the question sound salacious. Unbidden, the image of Sonia plunging on the Kemps's body came into Jake's mind. He rubbed his eyes tiredly. 'I guess,' he said quietly, 'I go maybe once every couple of weeks.'

'You've got no home to go to?'

No, you bastard, nothing I'd call a home. 'Yes.'

'Doesn't your wife get mad?'

'We're separated.' The words were sawdust in his mouth.

'Since when?'

Jake shrugged. 'Three months maybe.'

'Maybe? You aren't sure?'

'Three months. I don't count the days.'

The sergeant deliberated. 'Can you think of anyone who might have a grudge against you?'

'Me? No. Why? Do you think it might be arson?'

'Early days, Mr Connors, early days. Your wife have a boyfriend?'

'Yes.'

'Is he mad at you?'

'Should he be? Surely I should be mad at him.' Jake bared his teeth and abruptly the sergeant set his chair straight.

'Take me through it again. You let yourself in with your security card. There was no problem, I take it? Nothing had been tampered with?'

'It worked fine. I let myself into the building. Everything felt fine. There were just two people who should have been there, Arthur Kemps the night watchman and Sonia Lafferty who was on the control desk for the night shift. We monitor the tanks continuously. That is, there are three, but only one is in operation at a time. They are never unattended.'

Unless the staff feel like a screw, he thought bitterly.

'You spoke to them.'

'You know I didn't. I went along the corridor, it was dimly lit, between the locked offices and what we call the vatroom, where the tanks are. I saw Miss Lafferty through the glass wall. She was in a brightly lit work area, you understand. Then I saw Mr Kemps. They were talking. I went into my office.'

'What were they talking about?'

'The vatroom is sealed for sound. It's sealed against external air. It's a closed environment.' Jake repeated it all, wearily.

'Did you indicate that you were in the building?'

'No. I would have, of course. I don't spy on my employees and I don't generally feel a need to check up on them. Sonia is very reliable.'

Damn it, he must control his tongue. The business about spying, he needn't have said that. He was stupid with tiredness.

'Why did you go into your office?'

'I switched the computer on and looked at one or two things.'

'Looked? It was a TV camera?'

'No, no. Files. Work.'

'Then what?'

'I felt an explosion. The alarms went off. I went to my door and realised the fire was on the other side of it. I broke my office window and climbed out.'

'You didn't attempt to get to Miss Lafferty or Mr Kemps?'

'Get to them? How?'

'Round the building, I don't know.'

'The vatroom is sealed from the outside. It is impregnable, or as near as dammit. The only way in is through the airlocks from the corridor.'

'You got fire regulations on that?'

Jake stared at him. 'Theoretically,' he said softly, 'a fire couldn't start there.'

'A fire did.'

'You don't know that yet. You don't know the seat of the fire, do you?'

'Do you, Mr Connors?'

'No. Have they found the bodies yet?'

'I'll find out for you.'

Abruptly he had peace. He almost fell asleep. He had spent an hour with the firechief helping with a strategy to handle the emissions from the ruptured tank. His senior chemist, Pete Morrison, had been roused from bed and brought to the scene and was still there, helping and advising the firefighters. Meanwhile the boorish sergeant had taken him over and over his futile evidence. He didn't know what had happened. Pete, on site, would understand the need to preserve anything from the building that might give them a clue as to what had gone wrong. There might come a time when he had to admit to what he had seen, if it became clear that simple neglect of the system monitors was at the heart of the problem. But alarms must have sounded at the control desk. Sonia would have heard them. How could she turn them off, let the whole thing go to hell, in order to screw Kemps? It didn't make any sense.

They let him go home to bed. No bodies had been found yet though the fire was under control now. His car was at the police station and it was a final irony that when he turned the key, it refused to start.

It was a BMW, a nice car. A boss's car. It was a car that wouldn't start. He sat slackly in the driver's seat thinking about taxis. Someone knocked on his window.

'Can I help?'

He looked up. She was young, a hat pulled over curly hair and her coat collar turned up. 'Open the bonnet,' she said.

He opened it, unable to argue. Several minutes passed. 'Try it,' she said, reappearing,

It started. The engine settled to its familiar almost inaudible powerful thud, waiting for his command to get rolling.

'Thank you,' he said, amused despite himself.

She shrugged, smiling. 'No problem. Good-night.'

She was off, out through the gates and into the dark rainwashed street beyond. As his electric window whirred up, he heard the clip clop of her heels on the pavement.

He rolled the big car forward and took a left onto the road. There she was, hands in pockets, shoulders hunched, walking along at a fast clip. He drew level and put the passenger window down. 'Can I offer you a lift somewhere?'

'I'm going to the taxi rank round the corner. My car has broken down.'

'You can't fix it?'

18

'Gearbox,' she said and smiled.

'You work at the police station?'

'Yes.'

'You're not a policewoman?'

'No.'

'Where do you live?'

'Hendon.'

'Come on. That's near me. I'll give you a lift. After all,' he added slyly, 'you fixed my car.'

She hesitated a moment. Jake indicated the phone. 'Use it,' he said. 'Tell someone you're with me. Will that make you feel safer?'

She got into the car. 'That's not necessary,' she said. Her voice was soft. 'I know who you are. You're Mr Connors. It's your factory that burned down tonight.'

Jake liked driving at night through the city. He liked the long streets, the orange lights, the blind buildings, the secrets sleeping behind closed doors. He liked his warm, small, luxurious world in the car. His car. His little kingdom. His part of the war against anarchy, against chaos.

She was very quiet in the drugged warmth of the car. 'What's your name?' he asked after a while.

'Sally. Did any of your employees get hurt tonight?'

'There are two missing, presumed dead.' And five fried corpses, his mind added.

'I'm so sorry.'

The silence grew again. He was aware of his heavy eyes, his stiff limbs. When the explosion had taken him, he had been bruised. His lean flesh was so vulnerable, frail around the toughness of his mind. He thought of Sonia, resplendent in her gloating nakedness, burning, burning.

'Was it chemicals you manufactured? I heard something . . .'

'I'm a cryobiologist. I freeze people for a living. You

know, entomb them in liquid nitrogen so that in a hundred, a thousand years' time they can be revived, have their cancers cured, have their brains and personalities switched on. Some people think I'm a conman. Others simply think I'm mad. What do you think, Miss – Sally? What's your opinion?' The car swung erratically as a drunk lurched suddenly from the shadows.

'I think you're tired and in shock and maybe I ought to be driving.'

He slammed the brakes on. The car screamed briefly, slewing to one side and narrowly missing a bollard. Water hissed from under the tyres. Jake put his face in his hands and rubbed it. He could feel where the seat belt had dug into his chest. On his retina was the after-image of a naked woman walking down a dark street between two lines of streetlights. A pale naked woman like a dim flame dancing between parked cars and overfull dustbins. Sonia, about to fuck a little middle-aged man three-quarters her size. An Amazon, gulping her partner, engulfing him in flame.

He pulled himself out of the car and walked round to the passenger side. He saw the girl's thigh briefly as her skirt rode up as she moved across to the driver's seat. He opened the passenger door and saw her face turned to him in the car's interior light.

She was beautiful. His sex stirred.

He got in and slammed the door. She inspected the controls and put the car into drive. They slid forward. A taxi came the other way, a police car went round a corner, a couple walked together along the pavements past the boarded up shop fronts screaming their last, their closing down sale.

'What's your address?' asked Sally.

Jake told her and fell asleep.

Gloria had intimated gracefully he could wait to sell the

house, when property prices revived. Then she would have her half. Alternatively she would accept half the pre-recession evaluation, a third more than its current value. That assumed he could raise the capital. He had decided against this.

It was quite a large house and though he had been against buying it, he had grown fond of it. Now he sat in his car in the drive with Sally.

'You can take the car on,' he said. 'Call me tomorrow, huh?'

She got out and came round to his side, opening the door. They went in together.

It was fine inside. He had a cleaning lady twice a week and he was not an untidy man. They went to the kitchen and for a moment he was powerfully reminded of his lost business. The kitchen was warm and bright and clean, humming faintly with obedient machinery.

Five capsules. Five frozen bodies in a tank awaiting the millennium, the future. Five freshly frozen corpses newly dead, a scandal in the newspapers, horrified glee across the nation as the grotesque nature of what had happened tickled their jaded fancies. His business forever gone. Who would freeze with him now, when they might be turned to ashes after a careless employee got randy?

Dammit, how did the tank begin to leak? How could a fire have engulfed the place? The system had been near-perfect. It was an accident that couldn't happen.

No accident, then. Malice aforethought. They guarded themselves almost paranoically against vandalism from without. Had the enemy been within the walls all the time? Had Sonia gone mad and bust the place deliberately?

'Coffee?' said Sally.

He caught sight of himself in the blank black window. His long lean face was longer than ever, fatigue and failure digging deep into its planes. His chin was blue with his coming beard. He pushed his black hair out of his eyes and looked at the girl.

She had taken off her raincoat. She wore a jumper and skirt. She had high firm breasts and a lovely swell to her hips. Her legs were long and slinky, encased in smoke-dark stockings.

His eyes moved up. He was sitting at the table. Her heavy chestnut hair was released from the black hat she had crammed on against the weather. Now its luxuriant masses swung on her sloping shoulders. Her nose was pert, turned up at the tip over a short upper lip. She became aware of his scrutiny and turned to look at him, her green eyes dark-lashed.

For a moment he thought she looked sly. Her brow creased. 'What is it?' she asked archly.

He was too tired to hide his vulnerability. He put out a hand. She set down the mug she was holding and came over to him, taking the hand. Hers was soft and warm. She stood by him, looking down. Slowly, he leaned forward till his face was in her jumper feeling her body warmth through the soft material. He rubbed his face gently against her. He put his arms round her and then allowed his two hands to cup her buttocks swelling taut under her tight skirt. He remembered the flash of thigh as she slid across the front of his car. She was maybe fifteen years his junior, young and supple and available. He knew nothing about her save that she was built the right way, the way he liked them. He wanted to make love to her. Soon.

He smelt her fragrance. He smelt her skin, warm and feminine. He let her go and she bent down and stroked his hair, smiling into his face.

'I'm so sorry about your business,' she said. Her soft voice stroked him. 'Will you make love to me?'

She didn't wait for his tired dizzy brain to check and recheck what he had heard. It wasn't that she hadn't already told him as much simply by being there. He was used to older women, subtler women. This girl was full-frontal. Now she put her lips on his and ravished his mouth gently, slowly.

The kiss went on for ever, explicit and voluptuous. She knelt by him, tilting her face up, holding him with her fingers in his hair, on his neck, her mouth questing into his. He began to drown. The clamour in his mind eased. Her mouth was honey. He put his own hands into her hair and felt its silky warmth, its living weight. He needed this.

They stopped and looked at each other. 'I need a shave,' he said ruefully. 'A shower, I guess.'

She stood up and took his hand again. She slid it under her jumper so that his palm was against her naked skin. 'Whatever you want,' she said.

They went upstairs into the master bedroom. Then she turned and began to slip the knot of his tie down until she could undo the top button of his shirt. Her hands were on his sides, on his chest. She undid some buttons and felt his skin. He kissed her again, unsteadily now, and suddenly she ran her hand down over the front of his trousers where he was hard.

She pulled out of his arms and took her jersey over her head. Under it she wore only a tiny fawn silk camisole, the lace cupping her flagrant breasts. She slid out of her skirt and he saw the tiny matching panties, a red curl escaping to hint at the silky tangle beneath.

Her thighs were milky white, her dark stockings no blemish but a promise of knowledge, of experience.

Jake took off his jacket and tie. He went over to the bed watching her. It was like watching a whore. He didn't care. He slid off his shoes and stripped his shirt.

'Sally.'

'Yes.'

'Come here.'

She came to him, swaying on her high heels, a little smile

teasing her mouth. He put his hands on her waist, on her skin, so that the lace edging of her camisole top brushed the backs of his hands. He slid his hands up and down a little. Then he drew her to him, where he sat on the bed, and kissed her belly, her hip, her navel. As he did so, one hand moved up to slide under the cup of her garment. He caressed her breast. He felt the nipple harden in his palm. He pulled her quite gently down onto the bed. With his hand still on her breast he looked into her cool green eyes. Then he looked down her body. He ran his hand down until it reached the top of her panties. He slid his fingers underneath looking all the while into her eyes. He saw them grow hot. She was crazy for it. He bent over her and kissed her mouth. As he did so he slid his fingers between her lobed peachy flesh and felt her vulva.

She made a faint mewing noise, her lips held by his, her mouth at his mercy. He moved his fingers, stirring into her as his tongue wound round her tongue. He felt her little hooded clitoris and released it. He touched it, feeling her jump slightly in his arms. His body was pressing against hers. He commanded her mouth. His fingers opened her body and preyed within.

She had her hands on his back, in his hair. He felt her arch up into him, trying to press her body against his. He lifted away from her and stripped himself naked. Then he eased her panties off and opened her legs. You hot bitch, he thought helplessly, looking into her sex.

She was gorgeous there, softly pouting, aroused, gleaming in her expectancy of pleasure. For a moment he bowed his head and kissed her, tonguing her clitoris, feeling her writhe as his black hair mingled with her tiny fox-red curls. Then he came up on top of her and prepared to enter.

She pulled herself up onto her elbows to watch. She wanted to see his shaft slide into her body. As it did so he kissed her and she let her head fall back so that he kissed her neck and caught again her fragrance, the secret smell of her.

Her cunt was a hot honey squeeze that took his ripe cock and massaged it as he fucked. The fire in his shaft spread till all his belly was hot spice, his hips molten power, and he fucked in and out on a rising tide with his face in her big luscious breasts that moved and swayed with her body's surges.

She was calling out things, wordless noises of lust as her climax came on. He felt her belly shudder and a thin runny warmth bathed his urgent cock. He felt her juiciness, her liquid lust, her pulsing inner flesh and he came himself in a series of hard blows, releasing every part of himself into her in an endless stream of hot pleasure.

They lay cuddled, half asleep till he roused himself drowsily. 'What do you want to do?' he said into her ear, kissing it as he spoke. 'Will you stay with me? Do you want to go home?'

'Do you want me to stay?' Her voice rumbled softly like a cat's purr.

'I'm not done,' he said crudely.

She laughed, 'Good.'

He felt he was a steam engine and she offered a whole lot of track.

'I'm going to shave and take a quick shower before coming back to bed,' he said. 'Do you want anything? A drink? Coffee? Alcohol?'

She ran long slim fingers down the crevice between his buttocks. His skin jumped and he felt his sex harden. She grinned naughtily at him and dropped her lashes. 'You mean apart from more?' she whispered. She laughed again. 'I'll make us each a whisky, yeah?'

'Yes.'

'How do you like your Scotch?'

'Straight. Room temperature.'

'What a coincidence.' She swung herself off the bed.

She stripped off the camisole, her garter belt and her stockings. Totally naked, she had a luscious, primeval quality, as though she was a ripe fruit ready to be plucked. He suspected she knew this. She had done this with other men. She enjoyed displaying herself.

He didn't care. She was good to look at, good to plunder. He wanted to sink his teeth into her. He wanted her juice running down his chin. He wanted the slightly earthy taste of her, the near-fermenting musk of her body in his grasp. He wanted it and he would have it.

He looked at himself in the bathroom wondering why such a luscious girl should bother to seduce a man like himself, almost forty, blue-chinned, with tired blue eyes set under a black thatch of hair. Raven, they'd called him at school. Not a bad name for one like himself with a sharp harsh face and blue-black hair. He shrugged, Perhaps she was tired of younger self-obsessed men.

They were sitting cross-legged on the bed facing each other when the phone rang. He had two fingers slotted into her sweet cunt whilst his other hand cradled a heavy breast. Her two hands held his re-awakened prick, a firm full column jutting from his groin.

His answerphone did its business. The caller spoke: 'This is *The Globe*, Mr Connors. We understand your cryobiology plant burned down tonight. If you would consider giving us an exclusive interview we could guarantee a sympathetic treatment of the story and we would be able to keep the other papers at bay, especially the tabloids. We appreciate you won't like us, Mr Connors, but honestly we are your best bet. Call us when you pick up this message. David Jaynes is the name. I'll be on the newsdesk when you want me.'

Jake took a swig of whisky and lay on his back looking at the ceiling, his hands behind his head. Sally lay beside him, propped on one elbow.

She ran a finger through the hair on his chest. 'What are you going to do?'

'I hate the bastards,' Jake spoke through his teeth. 'Vultures.'

'You must be used to PR. You have to advertise. You know it's a sensitive subject.'

'The dead?' He looked at her with hard eyes, a vivid angry blue.

'The dead,' she repeated. 'Dead twice over. Did you have no protection against fire?'

'Of course,' he said wearily. 'I don't just mean sprinkler systems. The tanks were fireproof. Even if the whole building went up in flames, there should have been no problem. They're kept at minus a hundred and ninety-six degrees Celsius. That's the boiling point of nitrogen. We keep it liquid, you see. If all the external connections to the environment are ruptured, the tanks self-seal. Like blood clotting, really. We would have a considerable period before their temperature began to rise and even then it might be a while before that rise affected the inner capsules and the nitrogen.'

'Why aren't they safe now, then?'

'Only one was in use. It could have been ruptured before the fire started. The whole system was already in emergency.'

'What? How do you know?' Her little-girl voice had sharpened.

He looked at her. He needed to be having this conversation with Pete, his senior chemist. 'You work for the police?'

'I'm not a policewoman. I'm an independent person. Jake . . .'

'What?'

'This is the wrong time for you, I know that.' She was soft again.

He was silent, watching her.

'Something's happened for me. Tonight, I mean. I can't

load you with it.' She stroked his forehead. 'Please don't think I get into bed like this with every man I meet. With just any man.'

He turned his head away. As a matter of fact it was close to what he did believe. But if she was telling the truth she was right, he couldn't handle a love affair starting now. If that was what she meant.

Deliberately she changed the subject. 'Did you tell the police about this?'

'No.'

'Do you intend to?' Her voice was lazy. Her fingers were doing things.

'I expect so. I went into my office and accessed the control desk. That's the system that monitors the tanks at all times. I saw that it was screwy, really off beam, a major leak. Alarms should have been screaming. I began to go across to the vatroom, to Sonia, to see what the hell was going on when the place exploded. I got out of the window and that was that.'

'Sonia was in charge, was she?' Sally lifted and teased his balls.

'It was her turn for nights, yes. We don't just monitor it by machine, we monitor it with humans constantly. Nor do we double up on the nightwatchman. Arthur's duty was to guard the place from outside trouble, you know, vandals, jokers, thieves. Sonia watched the system inside.'

'Foolproof.'

'It seems not.'

'You're insured?' She kissed the tip of his cock.

'To an extent. That hardly matters. They all signed something so we can't be sued in the event of an accident that leads to their defreezing. But who else is going to come along, Sally? Who'll trust me now? I'm unemployed, lady, as of tonight. Last night. Jesus, it's almost morning. I wouldn't bother getting the hots for me, Sal.' He was mocking. 'It's going to be all the way down for the rest of my life. I might make it as an industrial chemist somewhere when the recession lifts. Not in a position of trust, I suspect. I'll sell this place and buy a nice little flat somewhere. Luton, Enfield. You know.'

Her mouth was over his, opening it, raping it. She was astride him, he could feel her dew-wet vulva pressing on his slack sex. She rubbed him there, masturbating him with her sex while her hair caressed his skin and her breasts rubbed his chest and teased and aroused his skin with a thousand small electric shocks. His hands were all over her, as greedy for her as she seemed to be for him. She had him up in no time, he was hard erect and full of desire, aching for her new-familiar hole so that when she lifted herself and allowed the fat end of his cock to press against her swollen wet flesh he found the agony of the momentary resistance irresistible, superb. He slid in. The pressure, the resistance, increasing as he pushed, as she lowered herself, and then he was through the narrowing, the obstruction, and sliding deep, deep into the heated length of her clinging passage which was sticky-slidy-sucky close about his cock, squeezing it, stretching it, pulling it till it grew and burst like a dark flame in the volcano of her cunt, their juices swirling and stirring ever more sluggishly as they cooled and he slept. In her. Eased.

He woke to an empty bed. He felt gritty and hopeless and he had a thousand things to do. Not the least of them was to see Pete.

It didn't surprise him that Sally was gone. She probably felt a morning after the night before would be unfortunate. He must have slept very deeply, that was a gift of grace from her, and he had little doubt she would be in touch. Her body was divine, a sensation, she was a magician in bed and he had truly needed her magic like a thirsty man needs water in the desert. But she had the rights of it. He couldn't clutter his life. The last thing he needed was a little girl (what was she? Young twenties?) at this crisis in his affairs, when he was still in love with his bitch of a wife, when his business had just literally exploded. She would become, whatever she said to the contrary, all demands, all clinging demands on his time and his attention. She would be full of the petty jealousies of youth and the grosser stupidities of inexperience. No, however silken her skin, however tantalising her perfume, however seductive her sexual skills, he was better without her. Later, perhaps, would be OK for him but by then he would have lost his temporary glamour. He would be a man heading for middle age with the accumulated bitterness of a failed marriage and a failed business. No, not for him a lively young bimbo, all optimism and petulance.

Pete looked terrible and had no words of explanation. They talked in a desultory way at the police station while the police told Jake they had found no bodies. No bodies at all. They hadn't found Sonia, nor Arthur Kemps, nor the five frozen clients. The tanks were all empty.

The police, he was honoured by an Inspector now, the aggressive sergeant presumably home in the loving embrace of his wife, wanted to know all about how you froze a human body. They were consulting experts, the Inspector said, kind of implying that Jake and Pete (who had an impeccable academic history) were rank amateurs out to make a quick unsavoury buck.

'You begin by cooling the body down,' said Jake patiently. He was used to explaining, he did it for potential clients. 'You know, an ice-bath, heat-exchangers, nothing complicated.'

'In terms of technology, that is,' said Pete. He was quiveringly angry, Jake was aware. He wondered who had wound him up.

'We use a heart-lung machine to keep the blood circulating

and to administer oxygen.' Jake looked up and met the horrified gaze of the police Inspector. A certain gleeful, destructive joy invaded him. 'We inject drugs,' he said, leaning forward with his elbows on the table. He fixed the Inspector's eye 'Not us personally, not Pete and me, you understand. We inject the corpse. Don't we, Pete?'

'To reduce the metabolic demands of the body,' grunted Pete obligingly.

'Then we take the blood away,' Jake relished the words, imparting as vampirish a construction to this as he could.

'It gets too viscous as it cools,' said Pete. 'You know, thick.'

'We use the stuff they use for organ transplants instead,' said Jake. He licked his lips. 'Then we really get going.'

'The problem,' said Pete ghoulishly, 'is to retain as much of the tissue architecture as we can.'

'Freezing destroys it,' explained Jake.

'You know, water expands when it freezes,' said Pete.

'And you are about eighty per cent water, Inspector.' Jake smiled. 'We take about two days to cool the body to the temperature of dry ice—'

'Minus seventy-nine degrees Celsius—'

'Then we inject more drugs, eh Pete?'

'Cryoprotectants. To minimise tissue damage.'

'Could someone have broken in to steal some of these drugs?' asked the Inspector, trying to regain control.

'Glycerol. Sorbitol. Glucose. I don't think so, somehow, Inspector. Then we pop the body into a Dacron-wool sleeping bag. We drop the temperature further to minus a hundred and ninety-six degrees Celsius which is the boiling point of nitrogen, Inspector. All biological processes stop. The bag lies in a capsule containing liquid nitrogen, you see. We pop the whole thing into a tank, attach a great many monitors, and that's it. Till someone figures out a way of bringing these bozos, these patients, back to life. In ten or a hundred years. Or a thousand years.'

'Or not at all, in your case,' said the Inspector stolidly. He knew when he was being given the runaround. 'So how come we can't find any bodies? Would these people simply melt when they were heated up suddenly?'

'Reverse evolution,' said Pete with interest. 'An amino-acid soup boiling off in the burning building. Perhaps we have some monsters loose, Inspector.'

'People have died. Do you think you ought to be joking, sir?'

'I need to talk to my insurance people and I need to talk to my employees,' said Jake abruptly. 'I take it we can go for now?'

'We'll be in touch, never fear. You definitely saw Mr Kemps and Miss Lafferty moments before the explosion? You'd swear to that?'

'They were out of my sight for five minutes only. Seven at the most.'

'They could have left the building in that time.'

Not dressed, they couldn't, Jake thought silently. 'Let's hope they did,' he said and went out with Pete.

They took both cars, Pete following Jake, until they could turn into a pub car-park. Seated in a quiet corner of the pub they began to discuss their problem.

'Check the small ads for work,' said Jake.

'You reckon it's finished, then.'

'Don't you?'

'I guess so.'

'I'll give you a damned good reference. There'll be no taint from this disaster, I promise.'

'Thanks. Have you any idea what happened?'

'You aren't going to believe this.'

Pete nodded in satisfaction. 'I thought you were holding something back.'

'I went there for no reason. You know that. You know me. I just do, especially since Gloria fucked off.'

He had never referred to this before though they all knew his wife had left him. No one had had the nerve to refer to it. Jake could be a very offputting man when he felt like it.

'So when I get there, I saunter along the corridor, enjoying it, kind of.' He fell silent again. Pete knew this too. Knew Jake really cared. That's what made him good to work for.

'Then I see Sonia in the vatroom. Then Arthur. Then get this, Pete. She takes her fucking clothes off.'

'What?'

'Shhh. She faces Arthur and strips naked, smack in front of him. I'm at my office door, sort of lounging, yeah. I haven't said I'm there. I'm about to, but I'm just finishing a smoke. But Sonia takes off her lab coat and all those awful clothes, a layer at a time, and Arthur does nothing, says nothing as far as I can tell, just stands there and watches.'

'Jesus,' said Pete.

'Well, it's fucking embarrassing. I'm the boss. I don't care who screws who. But they're in my time and they have work to do. Still, I say nothing. Then she has him.'

Pete snickered. 'This is too much. Sonia? Our ready-frozen biologist?'

'Sonia. What a body, Pete. White, yeah, so not so nice that way. But big plummy tits, a good little waist and a flat belly. She climbs aboard our Arthur and rogers him till he falls over. Then I notice the air is kind of funny in the vatroom. Something's condensing in it.'

'Nitrogen? You mean nitrogen's escaping. No, of course not. Condensing, you said.'

'Right. It has to be water vapour, doesn't it? Something's cooling the place down and precipitating water out of the air.

There's nothing else it could be.'

'But the alarms?'

'Give me time. I'm getting there. I slide into my office, anxious not attract attention. I last see them naked, post-coital. I switch on and access the control desk data. Everything is red, Pete. It's all screaming. The tank is leaking, the temperature is rising, it's near total disaster. I run for the door and feel the explosion. Just in time I register what it is and I don't open the door. I can hear the fire. I shovel some stuff into a drawer, smash the window and jump out as the door explodes. I phoned from my car.'

'Where's the stuff you saved?'

'In the boot of my car still.'

'How much of this have you told the police?'

'I edited out the sex scene and the water vapour. I said I just fiddled in my office till I felt the explosion. Otherwise I told the truth.'

'Why didn't you tell them everything?'

'I might have to, Pete. But can you see the papers? Employees screw while frozen corpses melt. Sex orgy while the dead revive. I won't mention it if I can avoid it.'

'But Sonia would have heard the alarms whatever she was up to with Arthur. She wasn't wearing earmuffs, was she?' Pete giggled involuntarily.

'What if she switched them off?'

'Why?'

'I don't know. Nothing made sense there. Her behaviour was weird.'

'I agree it isn't nice, Sonia and Arthur, but weird is a bit strong, Jake. You know, the bees do it, the birds do it and so on. I always thought old Sonia had a thing about you, actually.'

'It *was* weird, Pete. He was like a rabbit, mesmerised. She bent him backwards over the lab stool and stood astride him.'

'Kinky.'

'More than kinky. Then all this other stuff. She must have flipped her lid.'

'She's dead, Jake. She's paid the price.'

'And damn-well brought me down with it. Are they sure about not finding any corpses?'

'Very sure. They know their job. I was impressed, Jake, really impressed. The tank was open and empty.'

'Five minutes. Ten at the most. They had no clothes on. How could they get out in that time?'

Pete was fascinated. 'You don't seriously think Sonia and Arthur are wandering about naked with five rotting corpses, do you? Any vehicles missing?'

Jake buried his head in his hands. 'Is this going to get worse?' he moaned.

'Hi.'

He looked up. Water in a desert was unfair. She was caviare. Chantilly cream. Malt whisky. Armagnac. The ultimate fix. 'Sally. This is Pete. He works, he used to work for me, when I had jobs to offer.'

'Hello, Pete.' Sally sat down. Pete's pale eyes slid over her slowly. Then he looked at Jake.

'She's admin at the cop shop.'

'I don't work there now.'

Jake was surprised. 'Since when?'

'I've been thinking for a long time it would be a conflict of interests. I'm not with them.'

'So you're out of work, too.'

'I'm all right. I've plenty by.' She smiled, long lashes, green eyes and foxy red hair.

'She fixed my car last night.'

'Your car?'

'It wouldn't start when the police released me. Sally here fixed it, so I gave her a lift. Her gearbox is shot.'

'What was wrong with Jake's car?' asked Pete.

'High tension lead a bit loose. Did you get in touch with that journalist, Jake?'

'Journalist?'

'The one who phoned and left a message.'

Pete's eyes flickered between them again.

'No. The police woke me and I came straight out with them.'

'I see.' Her eyes danced. They both had pints. 'Breakfast.'

'Do you want one?'

'White wine. You two gentlemen want another each or a short one?'

'Not for me,' said Pete. 'I'm away home to make up on sleep.'

Sally put the papers she had been carrying under her arm on the table. 'There you are,' she said. 'It's starting.'

It was a small report, just that there had been a fire with considerable damage at Timegate, a private firm that specialised in preserving dead bodies until they could be regenerated.

'How did you know Jake was here?' asked Pete.

'The car. I recognised it in the carpark. I drove it last night.'

After I saw a naked woman up a side street, thought Jake, and knew I shouldn't be behind the wheel.

'Have they found the bodies?' she asked Jake soberly.

'No. As it happens, no bodies at all.'

'They could have got out? That's marvellous.'

'So where are they?' asked Pete. 'Our lady biologist and night watchman. Where are they if they got out?'

'Mugged? Murdered? It happens, you know.' Sally looked earnestly at Pete. 'Someone escapes from a rapist and goes for help to another one. I mean, there are enough bad people around to make those sort of coincidences possible. Did you ask the police if any unidentifieds had been brought in during the night?'

The two men sat very quietly. After a moment or two Sally said: 'What's the matter? Have I said something I shouldn't?'

Pete looked at Jake. 'Pillow talk?' he asked gently. Sally licked her lips.

'Did you leave the police so suddenly because someone made you a better offer?' asked Jake. He had the feeling he was navigating through a minefield.

'No one's made me any offers. I don't know what you mean.'

'You made me one hell of an offer last night, Sally.'

'We went to bed together. So? People do it all the time.'

'What if I was to give David Jaynes a bell, Sally. Take him up on his offer.'

'David Jaynes?'

'The journalist with *The Globe* who wanted an exclusive and offered me protection and sensitive handling in exchange. Am I being handled sensitively, Sally?'

She stood up. 'You will need protection,' she said. 'You're going to have to learn to know who your friends are.'

Jake began to tremble. 'Don't give me advice, you bitch,' he said. 'You whore. You fuck-for-money whore.'

Sally went scarlet and then she went white. She swayed suddenly as though she would faint. 'That's not true,' she said. Suddenly it was a little-girl voice.

'Go away,' said Pete. 'Can't you tell when you're not wanted?'

Jake looked down while she went. Pete said: 'I need to go home, boss.'

'I'll be in touch. There'll be money owing. I'll get it sorted out, Pete. Thanks for everything.' He continued to look down.

Riley shambled into work about eleven. A few heads nodded

in the newsroom. He was a familiar if grotesque figure. It was reckoned he was kept on as a staffer to be an Awful Warning to the younger members of the profession not to let the drink get too strong a hold. Riley hadn't filed a story for three years and it was rumoured he hadn't mastered his word processor yet. It was a miracle the man's kidneys held out.

He went over to have a look at what had come in during the night and the earlier part of the day. He sifted through it all with unusual persistence.

'Wozzermarrer?' asked Kevin, the new white hope of the rottweiling classes, doorstepper extraordinaire. 'Checkin' yer stocks and shares?' He snickered.

'If even I can smell a shit, it must be a really smelly one,' said Riley in his rich full elder-statesman public school voice. The rest of the newsroom tittered at Kevin's put-down. He was ghastly to work with, they all hated him. But he got the goods.

'Anyone have any naked ladies in the night?' boomed Riley across their startled heads.

'The subs all wear Snoopy T-shirts,' volunteered a hack.

'I didn't mean Us,' said Riley grandly, 'I know you all poke the night hours away. I meant in the big outside not-Us world, where ordinary people live and have their being. Any naked lady sightings?'

'Two Ufos and a green twigman. Twigalien,' said Monica.

'I've got one. The Strand. Reported to Bow Street nick.'

'Yeah, an' another at the Elephant.'

'D'you see her, Riley?' There was an expectant silence.

'See her? My dear madam, I had her. Or to be more accurate, she had me.'

Someone snorted with laughter.

'Where and when?' asked Monica, ever the professional.

'About the bottom of a bottle and half past the next one. A lady who likes a challenge, let's admit it.'

'Is this for real?' snarled Kevin.

'I rather suspect I'm the last person who could truthfully answer that question, dear boy. One would want independent evidence, wouldn't one? Whereas I am not even sure I was there.'

'I dunno,' said Kevin, suddenly cheerful. 'I like it the way it is. Let's run it past the boss, Riley. This could do you some good.'

The newsroom heard Sam protesting as Kevin led him along the corridor of power to the editor's cubicle. 'But I hate having good done to me, don't you understand-'

Jake went home, or tried to. The ratpack were out in force, filling his drive and camping on his front lawn. He drove past until he came to a phone box which he used to phone his lawyer. Then he went to see him. It was about time he got advice from someone who had his interests at heart. And that included dealing with the press.

The press. Members of the ancient order of journalists. She was young, he knew that. He knew her soft flesh was both firm and tender. He had seen her rosebud breasts, rosebud nipples on the gloriously full firm roundness of her. The taste of her mouth was with him still, her fragrance in his nostrils. He could feel her hair. His hands remembered her body held between them. She was pliant, graceful, urgent and willing. Between her legs, velvet heaven, spiced honey, the milk of paradise.

His sweetheart, his I've-fallen-for-you-sweetheart. His I-don't-usually-get-into-bed-with-men-like-this liar. His fuck-for-money whore, doing her job. Getting the story. He wondered which paper she worked for. Presumably not *The Globe*.

Bitch.

Three

No one could say afterwards how it started. There was a lot of embarrassment, not at the time but afterwards when people tried to make sense of it, tried to explain it. How can you explain such a thing? Mass hysteria? Hardly. Mob behaviour? Of a very specialised kind.

It was a Saturday night in Terry's, a discotheque Hammersmith way, and it looked like a dead normal night. A bunch of girls were having a hen party. The usual lager-heads were in, drinking themselves senseless. The rest were genuine couples come to dance or single-sex pairs on the hunt for a quickie with a pack member of the opposite sex.

Normal.

Generation Gap were running the disco and might have been expected to see what was going on but they joined in too and were as lost as everyone else when it came to the post mortem. They were popular, playing the best pop music from the last thirty years, as their name suggested. The heavies employed as chucker-outs were no good and the best evidence was to come from Alfred, the head barman, whom nature had rendered impervious to female charm.

At eleven thirty or thereabouts, it seemed a kind of rustle went through the crowded room. A whisper zigzagged uncertainly. Those sober enough produced broad unbelieving grins. The crowd shuffled, separated, and came together again. The music boomed. The crowd swayed.

It came again, like a squall over smooth water, a cat's paw of wind signalling something bigger to come.

The Stones came on. *I can't get no satisfaction.* The crowd did a communal bump and grind. They were determined they would get satisfaction, and no mistake.

From the centre the crowd began to draw back as if repelled. A space appeared, incredible in that crush, and people faced inwards at what they drew back from.

A girl was stripping. She was good, jerking her body salaciously at the sweated-up, boozed-up crowd. There was a lot of good humour about and people were laughing.

She had long hair, probably blonde but so sweat-soaked it was dark. It was knotted on top of her head and the topknot worked loose as she stripped, so that a pony tail waved about.

She was heavily made-up and her mascara had streaked. Oddly enough, the dark smears under her eyes emphasised her sexiness rather than detracting from it. She had begun in a shirt and jeans but was now down to a vest and pants, the vest a black sleeveless T-shirt that clung to and cupped her small fierce breasts.

Jerking her body violently to the music, she stripped the vest off. The crowd roared. Her naked breasts were painted at the nipples. They shook up and down as she threw her arms up above her head, grinning and sweating as she bucked her hips at the men around her. She wore a g-string now, just a little cover for her pubic zone. A thread of material ran up between her buttocks. Her bottom looked naked. It also looked firm and sweetly rounded. Her thighs were narrow, very thin, so that she had a wide area at the top of her legs. It was very inviting.

Somehow, after removing her jeans, she had put her thigh-high boots back on. They were black suede, soft, and so she danced, naked-arsed, bare-breasted, her vulva covered but only just, in those long black leg-hugging boots.

She was gesturing now, inviting a partner. The crowd found one and he shambled into the ring, blue jeans, Doc

Martens, crewcut and a bellyful of lager. She made him kneel down and bite the flimsy scrap of cloth away. The crowd roared when he succeeded. Now she threw each leg up in succession so that little glimpses of her pussy were given. Her hair was fair here, and there was very little of it.

She began to dance more or less on the spot, standing with her knees facing outwards and well bent. She bobbed up and down, her breasts bouncing, her hands in her crotch holding it open. She threw her head back and rolled it about, flicking that tassel of hair like a professional flicks tassels on her nipples. Her jerking up and down meant only one thing now.

Someone stumbled into the cleared space, the ring, pulling his jeans down. She had him in a moment. At the first touch his cock sprang up hard. He had fallen backwards but was lifted off the ground, on his arms and up on his feet, crab-fashion. His cock stuck straight up. His jeans were round his ankles. The girl straddled wider. She kept up her harsh jerking movements. She lined herself up and began to approach the waiting body, the erect shaft. She was a little like a limbo dancer only she was going on top, not underneath. She moved astride him so that he was between her legs, bent back, watching her approach his sex. The crowd were screaming encouragement. She jerked and his cock brushed up between her parted legs as she bobbed up and down, the tip touching her vulva.

The crowd were chanting as they clapped. *Do it. Do it. Do it.* She did. She came down on the body below her and they all saw, those who had a view, they saw her take the man's shaft and slide it into herself. She began to bob up and down again, only now she had a cock in her. As her body went up and down in the dance, so her cunt slid up and down the man's sex. She held her own breasts, stroking them, caressing her hard lipsticked nipples. She bobbed up and down and he pushed up, his face crimson with exertion. He was loving it, there was no doubt.

He came moaning and gasping and collapsed flat in the ground. Then another man was there and again she caressed his cock till it was hard and they were doing it. Now a girl and man in the crowd turned to each other and he put his fingers in her pussy and she moaned, trying to climb onto his cock and not succeeding until the crowd helped her, lifting her and holding her legs open so that the man could stand there and fuck, in and out, like they were dancing.

For some of those present this was to be the commanding image of the night, the mental picture that came back, not disagreeably, to haunt them. The girl was held almost flat by willing hands. Her body strained and writhed in her sexual ecstasy, she pulled up her top and fumbled her breasts, moaning with pleasure. The man pumping her held his hands high above his head, his eyes screwed shut in his intensity of feeling. His hips jerked, his buttocks taut with muscle. As he came, as the girl screamed in orgasm, a man by her bent over and sucked one of her nipples.

A girl at the front of the crowd straining to watch, felt her skirt lifted from behind. A cock began to push into her. She pushed back down on it to help. She didn't even know who the man was, fucking into her.

Other couples began to screw together. People fell over and continued, hips bucking. Soon they were all on the floor, writhing, hardly knowing who they were with, it not mattering just so long as they could satisfy the blessed urge to screw and screw. They were like demons. They ate each other, kissing and sucking and being sucked and kissed, connected at different ends to different people till the whole disco was one huge moan and surge of lustful pleasure. They were one creature with a thousand orifices, a thousand penetrating organs, fucking and fucking in a huge orgasm of blissful fulfilment.

Alfred, alone unmoved, put the sprinkler system on. He only just beat the police who arrived because the noise level had crept up unnoticed and someone in the neighbourhood had complained. Suddenly three hundred and fifty people were hauling up their jeans, adjusting their skirts, their suits, crimson with embarrassment. People stood up and stared round themselves, not believing it already. Had it happened? Was it a figment of their imagination, a filthy figment? Yet here were the police, angry, uneasy, and here they all were, not properly dressed.

Rumour oozed out into the night. Couples sidled away adjusting their clothing. People talked, or rather muttered. A hack heard and took the rumour to Wapping. News editors shook their heads over it in amusement. Silly season stuff. Now, if it had happened in one of the posh nightclubs, where the latterday darlings of society congregated, that would have been different. With money and glamour added, it would make a nice little sex story. But Hammersmith. Terry's. Where? Who cared if the hoi polloi did it in public. It was what the rich did that counted, as far as good copy was concerned. The poor could fuck in peace.

There was an incident in Southwark. No one could get a handle on it. Something to do with a table tennis club, a women's aerobics class and a local Freemasons' lodge. Regretfully Wapping gave it up as a bad job.

At last Jake got home with police protection. His lawyer contacted *The Globe* and arranged an exclusive for the following day. The pressure should ease after that though of course Jake's aims and *The Globe*'s were diametrically opposed. *The Globe* wanted something ghoulish concentrating on the corpses. Jake wanted to be as boring a put-off as he could. No bodies had yet been found.

Sally had left messages on his answerphone. She wanted to

see him. To explain. It wasn't how it looked. Please.

Gloria had called and Jake called her back.

'Darling,' she said. 'Is the business truly kaput?'

'I think so.' He was ridiculously pleased she cared, she had got in touch. Her image was painfully sharp in his mind, the laughing eyes, the generous mouth, her peachy skin. She wore her hair in a loose knot so that silken blonde tendrils escaped to frame her face. Everything about her was invitation. She made a man feel thrilled. She said nothing that mattered, yet every word was like a pearl. You felt honoured by her attention. He had seen men again and again bewitched by her, growing glossy in her presence, responding to the half-hinted invitation in her laughing eyes. And she was dynamite in bed, no false promises there. She put her heart and soul into it and she took her man with her, into paradise, all the way.

'You didn't fire it yourself?'

'Don't be silly.'

'Because if this is a cheap way of trying to gyp me out of my share of the house, I warn you, I won't have it. Roger told me you were clever enough to pull tricks. If this is a trick, Jake darling, forget it. I want every penny I'm entitled to and I've seen my lawyers today. You're getting an injunction slapped on you, Jake, so you can't sell up the house to meet creditors' demands. Don't sell the car, either, or you'll be in contempt of court. When you've settled with me you can do as you please, of course. Not that you'll have much left.'

Simon Greening, his lawyer, was composing a judicious letter to send to the relatives of those Jake had frozen and subsequently lost. Since most of them regarded him in the light of a cats' home, stealing their rightful inheritance for a freakish whim, he was anticipating trouble from them. Simon told him not to worry, the legal angle was sewn up unless negligence was proved, which would amount to fraud in this case. Since that hadn't happened, Jake was fine. Just fine. The police continued to investigate the cause of the fire and the absence of the bodies, all seven of them. Channel Four wanted to interview him for their cryobiology programme. ITN wanted to interview him confronting distressed relatives. The BBC had sent some heavy-weight journalists who were urging him to face the facts and wanted to investigate his accounts (his auditors had been on the line) and the insurance company said they were reserving judgment pending the outcome of the enquiry. The police were mute, his secretary was in tears, Mrs Kemps had been on the six o'clock news trying to hint at ghoulish goings-on rendered to her by her Arthur when she still knew where he was. Mercifully she failed, as best Jake could judge.

Sonia Lafferty's aged mother had a mild heart attack and went into a geriatric ward in hospital.

Simon Greening and Jake's accountant, Parker Fane, got the injunction quashed and told him he would weather the storm, not to worry. They advised against liquifying any assets for the time being, however. Gloria was going to be trouble.

Sally phoned and begged him to get back to her. She could explain.

He fell asleep hungry and tomorrow was a new day.

It was a terrible night. Again and again he lay with a beautiful woman, laughing, happy, generous with her body, inspired. He was brought to new heights of pleasure. He was sucked and kissed, tongued, ravished by fingers placed where never he had felt them before. His body was on fire, endlessly powerful. His rampant cock was decorated, masturbated, sucked, engulfed by sweet cunts ripe as peaches, warm as summer sunshine, oiled, clinging, fermenting, musk-sweet. He lay sprawled whilst women adored him, gave him their breasts, wiped him with their hair, licked him, kissed his mouth – and their skin peeled off so that they were monsters of horror, hag-haunted faces grinning as they smeared him in filth. They stood over him shrieking as green vile-smelling sludge dripped from their cunts onto his crawling skin. He cowered naked as they beat him, as they flayed him, and he woke . . . he woke . . . sweat-soaked, exhausted, paralysed with fear, his heart racing, his body trembling . . .

And morning came, equinoctially cold and dank. He had a bath and washed the night's fear out of his black hair. He looked haunted, horrible. He ate eggs and toast for breakfast and sicked it up. David Jaynes was coming at nine. He sat trembling, drinking black coffee, knowing he looked the picture of guilt, knowing he had done nothing wrong.

What had happened to his life? Why had it fallen apart like this?

His post and his paper came. He had a dozen abusive letters, foul in varying degrees but mostly on the Burke and Hare theme. He had several applications for a place in one of his tanks, some with long explanations as to why the applicant deserved to be treated differently from the rest of the human race and given a preferential chance of survival. He had a letter from a medium who explained she could tell him where his corpses were. He had a bastardised version of the Gospels sent him from a small religious faction noted for its evangelical fervour. He didn't know if it was a coincidence or not, but the Right to Life anti-abortion people were lobbying him to join their cause. And he had a letter saying simply: THEY WEREN'T EVER THERE. YOU'D ALREADY DUMPED THEM. I KNOW AND I'M TELLING THE POLICE.

This was a deduction so chillingly rational he shivered for ten minutes together. Had Sonia removed the corpses before he arrived? They could have been dumped weeks before. A terror gripped him. Proving a negative was notoriously difficult.

The phone rang and he heard David Jaynes on his

answerphone. He was round the corner. He would be at the front door in two minutes for their interview.

Jake pulled himself together. Today he must tell the police what had happened that night. It could hardly make things worse.

Jaynes was a man much his own age, genial in manner and carrying a slight permanent air of harassment. He fluttered about with tape recorders and sheets of paper and seemed not quite socially sophisticated enough to handle his coffee cup. Jake was not deceived. He reckoned he was dealing with as shifty a professional as ever he had come across.

The interview began very steadily, Jaynes taking him through the science of the thing, how cryogenics worked, what the drawbacks were. It was soon evident that Jaynes had done his background reading. He knew all about tissue damage, bursting blood vessels, collapsing cell membranes. Though he led Jake to tell him, he also knew of examples from the animal world where nature supplied natural antifreeze to some species of frogs, caterpillars, spiders, ticks and mites. Jake felt himself lulled. He was talking to a man who knew, an intelligent man.

The discussion moved on. 'Do you just do whole-body preservation?' asked Jaynes guilelessly.

'I don't do neuros, no.'

'Neuros?'

'Head or brain preservations.'

'Some people just have their heads preserved, or their brains?'

'That's right. In America, that is. Not in Britain.'

'It must be more expensive to cryopreserve the whole body. It must present more problems.'

'The whole situation is iffy. The point is,' said Jake settling comfortably, 'people want to be defrosted as themselves.

They want to retain their personality, their sense of who they are. Unless their body is grotesquely diseased they want it along, it belongs to them, it's part of their self-image. It's the ultimate possession.' Jake grinned. 'We have to assume that if a future generation has solved the problems of defrosting preserved individuals, it has also solved the problem of restoring damaged tissue and malfunctioning organs. That's the hope Timegate offers. You come back to life as yourself with your cancer removed and cured. Your body might be perfected, or made as perfect as would satisfy anyone brought up with the sort of ideas we have currently about health. The very old don't cryopreserve, Mr Jaynes. It is the man or woman who feels their life is being cut short, that they haven't had their entitlement if you like, who is willing to take a chance. After all, they can only be wrong. I can only be wrong. No one has deprived these people of even one hour of life. They have nothing to lose.'

'Except eighty thousand pounds.'

'Except eighty thousand pounds,' agreed Jake. 'It's a better risk than being a Lloyd's name in these troubled times. You buy an option on the future. It may come through. Technological development is exponential. Medical research is poised on the brink of a colossal breakthrough, Mr Jaynes. Molecular biology is a fantastic growth area. I don't think the layman can imagine the riches around the corner when we start to reap the rewards of biotechnology, of genetic engineering. We are controlling our own evolution already because we control the external environment in so many ways. Soon we will be able to control the internal environment, our own DNA, our master plan.'

'You don't see any danger in this?'

'There's danger in everything. It's the spice of life. I see it as less dangerous than the car, for example. In terms of human life, I mean.'

'But in the hands of a bigoted man, we could have a holocaust, an upsurge in racial destruction the like of which we've never seen.'

Jake hesitated. 'Our humanity is essentially a social artefact,' he said. 'I believe it's part innate, genetic if you like, and part operated on by the immediate cultural climate of the individual. Natural selection selects for it on the whole because where it fails, whole societies, whole empires die. If we misuse the power we are about to have, we'll go under. I was a biologist before I was a chemist, Mr Jaynes. It doesn't trouble me. I'm Darwinian enough to be objective about the survival of the human race.'

'This is strange from a man who gets well paid to preserve a few individual bodies.'

'My employment satisfies a basic and healthy human desire to survive. I see no conflict there. I believe I'm on the side of the good guys.'

'You don't see yourself as shaman, as witchdoctor, as conman, benefiting from the real fears of suffering people when your grasp of science tells you that you are attempting the impossible?'

'I don't see it that way at all.'

'Can you tell me about the individuals you've lost?'

'I had five suspensions. Four men and one woman. It doesn't seem ethical to me that I violate their privacy by telling you things I know only from my professional relationship with them.'

'But they're dead.'

'They are preserved. Their loss isn't established yet and until it is I can't assume they are beyond salvation. They might be revived in our lifetime. And they have relatives.'

'Are you being sued by any of those relatives?'

'No.'

'Now that you are no longer doing what you were paid to

do, are you going to hand the money back?'

'I don't know what caused the fire,' said Jake steadily. 'The police are investigating. I cannot see my way forward till I have more information.'

'Then you might repay? Are you insured?'

'I carry insurance but I am making no statement either way about reimbursement of relatives. My legal agreements were with the preserved persons, not with their families.'

'You call them preserved persons, not dead people. If your neglect has turned them into conventional corpses, would you consider yourself a murderer, Mr Connors?'

'I feel,' hissed Jake through clenched teeth, 'a level of personal responsibility for the preservations in my care such that if you felt one tenth of it concerning the copy you wrote, you and your brother and sister hacks, the media in this country would undergo a revolution. What I am saying is that you don't know what you are talking about!'

'Then you'll have to tell me, Mr Connors, won't you?' said David Jaynes pleasantly. 'I only want to know when is a corpse not a corpse.'

Jake spent part of the afternoon at his ruined workplace, picking through the cold debris and making plans to protect the tanks. It was here that Sally caught up with him at last.

There was a chill autumnal wind blowing. She had rosy cheeks and her tiptilted nose was pink on the end. Her hair glowed like fox-fire. She was as delicious and as edible as meringue.

She held his sleeve. 'I slept with you because I wanted to,' she said pleadingly. 'It wasn't a ploy to get information from you.'

'You're a journalist.'

'Yes, yes.' She shook her head in irritation. 'I waited for you at the police station having jimmied your car. I pretended

I worked there, though in a sense I do, I get information from the police routinely. I did want information from you. I lied about my own car being broken down. But I slept with you because I wanted to. Because you're a beautiful man. You are fantastically sexually attractive. I can't be the only one. Women must fall for you all the time. Don't pretend with me. Don't be so damned self-righteous.'

Jake resisted the urge to pull back. She was a child, for all her hard-boiled hacketterie. She was dirty little contaminated girl who didn't know what sex was for, who had to frill the essential act into a meaningful relationship to make her urges acceptable to herself. The girly liked to fuck.

He couldn't admit to himself that he needed her, that she had got to him. He couldn't be reduced to this sugary sin. He couldn't accept the relationship on her terms.

She was so tasty, so skilled in bed. Rejecting her was to give her too much importance. She must know she was delectable. He might as well benefit from her vacuous promiscuity while making sure she didn't fool him again. He needed sex. She could provide it in a pretty package.

He took her home with him, running the gamut of the ratpack doorstepping him, Wapping escapees. She flashed her press card at them and grinned as she went indoors, flaunting her tail at her failing colleagues.

Immediately within his front door he turned on her. He crushed her mouth under his, feeling its vulnerability, its tenderness, its sweet freshness of youth. His hand came up within the tangle of her clothes till he found and cupped one beautiful breast. He squeezed it, its warmth a benison in his palm, its ripeness a glorious swelling against his harsh flesh. He kissed her neck, forcing her head back, feeling her hair brush against him. She smelled divine, warmly fragrant.

His other hand was down now, running up her leg and lifting her skirt till he felt her firm thigh. She gasped slightly.

'Can't we go upstairs?'

'I want you here,' he said, biting her earlobe. His hand was right up now. He could feel the heat from her sex. The silky encumbrances made him fumble for a moment. Then his blunt fingers were in her vulva, rubbing in her juicy places, finding her clitoris and teasing it.

She squirmed against the wall. 'Jake, Jake,' she cried out, her blouse half open, her hair mussed, her skirt hitched up. Jake laughed and dropped to his knees. He had her skirt right up now so he could see her belly, her underwear pulled to one side. He could see little tantalising glimpses of rosy flesh protruding as she wriggled in excitement. He kissed her belly, pushing her legs apart, invading her with his fingers. She moaned and came down on him. Half squatting she masturbated herself on his hand, sliding up and down the wall.

Jake looked round. Eyes peered through his letterbox. The round black nose of a camera was thrust through. Keeping his fingers up inside the moaning girl, he reached into his jacket pocket and took out a little electrical screwdriver he kept there.

Sally had her eyes shut. She held her skirt up and panted as she rode on his fingers. Jack leant back from her and with a sudden stabbing gesture speared the lens of the camera with the steel of his screwdriver. The letterflap jerked shut. Jake pulled his fingers out of Sally and picked her up. He carried her into the ground floor room he used as an office and laid her on the carpet. He unfastened his trousers and came on top of her.

She had her legs pulled as open as possible, her clothes all rucked up about her middle. He paused for a moment and looked into her sex. Moist and inviting, it softly pleaded for him to violate its emptiness. He obliged.

Big and thick, his hard cock slid between her labia, thrust

through her crenellations of erect flesh and entered her slit. He drove home hard feeling her lift beneath him to aid his access and to make his penetration deeper. Her cunt was glorious, utterly divine, softly tight and squeezingly firm. He felt lapped, sucked, squeezed and nibbled. She moved hard on him, thrusting to grab her own pleasure from his body. He began to stroke into her, powerful surges that brought his cock an agony of pleasure.

She was a magnificent screw. All her young flesh was active, energetic, demanding. She ravished his cock with her inner muscles. She tore her pleasure from his shaft, shuddering around him, pulsing on him, so that exquisite ripples of pleasure kept catching him and giving him little wavecrests of joy.

He could hold back no longer. Lust shot along his cock until she was bulging with his spunk. It frothed out around his still-thrusting stalk. Her sex bit down on him so hard he groaned involuntarily.

Panting, he pulled out of her, enjoying even this, the slide out of glory.

She lay sprawled, her face slack and lazy now she had had what she wanted.

'You're marvellous,' she said, gazing at him through lowered lashes. 'You're a marvellous man. You fuck beautiful. I adore you in me. Jake, I've missed you so terribly. I want you so much. I need your body. You have to need me.' But there was complacency in her voice.

Jake stood up and did himself up. 'Who do you work for?' he asked with mild interest.

'*The Daily News.*'

'Any of your friends out there?' He gestured towards the front of the house.

'No. I'm assigned to the story.'

'What do I owe?'

'I beg your pardon?' She began to sit up and pull herself straight.

'What do you need in the way of details for your paper, now that I've been paid?'

She stood up and slapped his face. It stung but Jake thought it funny. She was a pleasure to insult. Her clothes were still untidy and her hair was mussed up. There was a lipstick smudge in one corner of her mouth. Her green eyes were slitted with rage. She was a furious slattern, adorably sexy. She tried to hit him again but he caught her wrist and kissed her, pulling her angry body in against his with effortless strength. She melted into his arms. She must feel something, then. He could feel her rage turn helplessly to lust. Her hands were in his hair. She pressed against him. He saw her eyes were half-closed and her lips full and soft.

'Take me again,' she whispered frantically. 'In the bedroom. Let me take you. I can do it, I can make you come.'

They went upstairs. The bed was unmade, it wasn't one of the days his cleaning lady came even had she been able, and the bedroom was pale and gloomy in the poor light of the heavily overcast day. Rain lashed the window.

Sally moved swiftly round the room. She drew the curtains and put on the bedside light. She found where she could put music on and took a moment to select something. Jake undressed, watching her with amusement. It was pleasant being seduced. He liked it.

'Aren't you, ah, rather advertising to your colleagues outside what we are up to?' he said. 'Pulling the curtains, I mean.'

'They know what we are up to,' she said briefly. 'I wouldn't put it past them to appear at the window up a ladder and they could well be upstairs in a house opposite with a telephoto lens. I know how they work, remember.'

'Being one of them,' said Jake helpfully.

'Yes.' She gave him a dubious glance. Then she stripped.

As each layer came off revealing more and more of the lovely lines and curves of her body, Jake felt his interest revive. Her confidence grew in inverse relationship to the amount she wore. She began to dance a little, to sway to the music she had put on, weaving her body sensuously to and fro as she parodied a professional stripper.

She came closer to Jake where he lay nude on the bed. She pushed her breasts at him, squeezing them together, trying to lick her own nipples. She turned round and bent over, straining her panties tight between her buttocks so that fox-red curls made little wisps round the taut material. She faced him and split her legs wide, playing in her vulva with her fingers, teasing her labia till they hung down. She climbed on to the bed and knelt astride him. She lowered her body over his face, touching him gently with her sex. Then she pulled her panties aside and held herself there, begging.

Jake put out his tongue and ran its tip along the length of her sex. She shivered voluptuously and mewed slightly in ecstasy. He touched her with little darting movements of his tongue so that she was stabbed again and again, arousing her even more. She lowered herself further, pleading for him to penetrate her, to be rough with her.

He licked her, long and hard, from arse to clitoris. He licked again and again, making his tongue as rough as possible. Then he caught her pendulous labia between his teeth and bit them gently, pulling on them whilst she squealed with pleasure. He began to bite her clitoris, to suck it and push it about with his hard stabbing tongue. She rocked and moaned above him. He lifted his head and placed his mouth over her entrance. He sucked hard and then he inserted his tongue. He fucked her like this, tongue-fucked her, and then he sucked hard again.

Her flesh pulsated. He felt it judder. Suddenly he was bathed in her juices. He heard her sob. Her vulva writhed in his mouth, her thighs trembled and she bent down over him.

She wriggled down the bed a little. She had tear streaks on her cheeks. She kissed him, letting herself taste her own climax in his mouth. She rubbed him, half crying, touching his firm cock and kissing his eyes, his mouth, his chest.

She turned round on him so that he looked straight into the cleft between her buttocks. Her pearly flesh was full and cushiony. There was a little down between her cheeks. She tore her panties and threw them away. She bent over his groin touching his balls and his prick with her tongue. She reached behind her and opened her buttocks wide. He saw the little pursed chestnut-coloured hole. It fluttered slightly, open and shut.

She laid her cheek on his shaft, her head to one side and all her hair spilling in silky confusion over his thighs and belly. 'Enter me,' she whispered urgently. 'Enter me there, Jake. Please. With your finger.'

He slid a finger into her hot bubbly pussy and then he pressed the blunt finger end against the reddish-fawn valve. She moaned again and he pressed further. His finger slid in. Her heat enveloped him. She squeezed and he slid further.

Slowly, carefully, she impaled herself by sliding backwards down his finger until it was all within her. Now she turned her attention back to his cock. Delicately she drew the foreskin back over the bulging head. Her sweet full lips parted. She began to draw him into the hot cavern of her mouth. She began to suck.

She was very good. As cock-sucking went, she was the tops. She took him gently through layers of pleasure seeking some dark core of excess. She fingered his shaft in mysterious ways, as though her probings and grippings were patterned to draw from his erect sex a response on some more primitive plane. She had accessed a code somehow and she spelt it out on his cock so that the whole shaft trembled, brought to a bursting peak of pleasure but held there, forbidden to tip over into orgasm.

Her mouth was satin, sometimes twisting tight over his inflamed organ, sometimes caressingly soft. His balls seemed to bulge with lust, stirred, stroked, teased, tugged and separated into two glowing globes of volcanic desire. His very tendons fired up, thrilling with sexual surges kept incomplete till she should release him. She sucked him, she bit him, she licked him, she squeezed him and all the time he finger-fucked her ravishingly pretty little arse.

He put a hand under her vulva. He felt it swell and subside as he fingered her, as she sucked him. Soon his hand was wet. She was in continuous orgasm.

Something new was happening to his cock. It was pillowed, crushed, cooled and rolled. She had it between her breasts and she was masturbating him with her own breastflesh. Then she sucked him again.

Suddenly her hand was like a vice round the roots of his shaft. She frigged rapidly, her mouth holding the swollen head, her tongue flickering madly over the engorged surface of the bulging glans. His balls were squeezed and his whole body jerked violently as he started to come, slamming upwards again and again, shooting into her mouth, feeling her convulsive swallowing and sucking and frigging while all the time she rode down on his finger, extracting the last possible ounce of pleasure from the body she commanded.

Now it was his turn to lie slack and foolish with glut. His body felt turned inside out. She lay across him, his finger still within her body, and he felt, dimly, the faint after tremors of her immensely prolonged orgasm, her rear pulsing soft and slow around his invading digit.

After a while she turned round and crawled up his body. He saw the green eyes, the long lashes drooping, the face prettily flushed, the swollen lips. She murmured, touching him with her lips, kissing his ear, his neck, his jawline, the edge of his mouth.

'I adore you,' she whispered, 'I'll do anything for you, anything you like. I'll tie you up, I'll let you tie me up and beat me. I love to be whipped and I'd love you to do it. I'll let you go the whole way up my rear, I'll let you force your cock up there. I'll let you take me anywhere, in a car like a whore if you want. I'll masturbate you in a cinema if you want, in a taxi. You can bring your friends round to watch. I'll bring another girl. Would you like that, Jake, two girls to adore you, to bring you to the heights, to assault you and conquer you and to make your body melt? Maybe you'd like to watch her suck me. Or me suck her. Jake, darling Jake, anything I can do for you I will, I swear it. Only let me be near you again. Don't keep me away, darling. Take pictures of me and wank over them when I'm at work. I want to be part of you, inside you. I want you inside me all the time, stuffing me all the time. Jake, darling Jake, it's never been like this for me.'

He sat up and lit a cigarette. She lay on her side smiling, stroking his hip with one long nipple.

'I did the interview with *The Globe* this morning,' he said casually. ' He said it would be in tomorrow.'

She went white. 'Exclusive?'

'Yup. So you see, I know you want me for my body, not my story. Don't I?'

'You told him everything? All about what happened?'

'I bared my soul,' said Jake. 'Nothing left unsaid.'

'All that about the tank being ruptured before the fire, before anything started?'

Dammit, he had forgotten he had been blabby with tiredness and shock the night it had happened. He hadn't told her about Sonia and Kemps, though, that was one mercy.

This was serious. Now she reminded him, he realised he had told her too much but his mind had not retrieved the information, had not made use of it. It was playing him false. What else had he said or done that he had conveniently forgotten about?

'Of course,' he said, smiling at her.

'You bastard. You could have saved something for me. I've invested a lot of time on this story.'

'Like the last hour.' Jake spoke lazily. His body felt marvellous. Nor did he doubt her promise to him. If he had something left to offer, she would be as deviant as he pleased.

'No! That was real. I thought you understood. I'm crazy for you, Jake. You have to understand that. No, I've done a lot of poking about trying to get background. I haven't doorstepped you because I knew it would be pointless. I wanted to see you properly, like this.'

'Naked?'

She kissed his wet sticky cock. Then she looked up at him seriously. 'Jake. Stop confusing business with pleasure. I fuck with you for pleasure. But business is business. I've got my way to make. They only made me a staffer four months ago. I'll be sacked if I don't produce a few plums. It's a cutthroat world I live in.'

'You have some advantages,' Jake drawled. He ran a finger over her nipple and then flicked it.

'Ouch. Don't do that. Well, not just now. I have to think.' She frowned furiously.

Jake roared with laughter. 'You silly little bitch,' he snorted. 'How you delude yourself. You've given me a magnificent fuck, I grant you that. But you've missed the boat. I get to check the copy they're putting in about me but I don't give any other interviews. That's the deal.'

He reached over to the phone and flicked off the answering machine. He dialled out. Sally watched him intently, her lovely breasts hanging disregarded. She was crosslegged with her heels almost in her pussy. Jake watched it with pleasure as he was connected. It drooled slightly. She was a lovely poke.

Jake asked for an extension and got it. Sally couldn't hear the person at the other end, much to her chagrin. 'Hi,' said Jake. 'It's Jake Connors here . . . that's right. Thank you very much . . . Look, this is to tell you something. I have sitting beside me right now the most juicy little hackette in Wapping. She's totally nude on my bed. So am I, for that matter. Well, David, she's given me her considerable and sensational all but I've just explained the nature of my agreement with you. She's a bit mad, you understand, but I want you to be reassured I haven't reneged in any way. If she writes anything, none of it's horse's mouth stuff. Not one word. She's made it up or got it from other sources.'

There was a long silence while the phone chattered at Jake, He smoked, leaning back on his heaped pillows, very relaxed. Sally was white, her mouth agape.

'Certainly the ratpack are still outside,' said Jake. 'I'm hoping you'll see to it they disappear quite shortly. You needn't vanish Sally here, though. I don't mind being doorstepped by her. She says she loves me for the sake of my beautiful blue eyes, nothing to do with recent events at all. Isn't that nice, Mr Jaynes . . . I thought you'd agree.'

Jake put the phone down and grinned at Sally.

She hit him hard. This time he wasn't having any and he rolled her over and smacked her bottom hard. Viciously hard. She gave an indignant scream and held her flaming rear. 'I hate you,' she said passionately. 'You are a horrible man.'

'You begged to be here,' said Jake cruelly. 'And it's a lovely bum.'

'I thought you were kind. I thought you were a decent man. Now I know better.'

'Yes, you do, Sally. See yourself out, huh?'

She pulled her clothes on, too angry to do up the little

buttons and fasteners. Before she left the room she glared red-faced and furious at Jake.

'I have a certain power, you know, I'm well skilled at writing innuendo, you won't get me with a libel suit, Mr Connors. I'm going to follow your future career with great interest and I have considerable resources at my disposal. I'll smash you, you see if I don't.'

'What if I want you to make love to me again?' said Jake provocatively. 'You're very good, you know.'

'Consider yourself dead. You'll wish you were by the time I've finished with you.'

She flounced out. Jake reached for the phone and dialled *The Daily News.* He asked for the newsdesk.

He found himself speaking to a woman who introduced herself as Monica Cavendish.

'My name is Jake Connors,' said Jake.

'Oh yes, Mr Connors. How can I help you?'

'You could find seven bodies for me, for a start.'

There was a silence. 'I see,' said the woman softly. 'That Mr Connors.'

'That Mr Connors, indeed. Look, I've just said goodbye to one of your sister hacks, a young lady with red hair named Sally.'

'Yes,' said the voice cautiously.

'Sally gave me a very delicious time between the sheets, really something to remember, telling me she had fallen for me in a big way and it was nothing to do with her employment or my recent claim to fame.'

'Yes, Mr Connors. I'm with you so far.' Was there amusement in the woman's voice?

'After it, if you see what I mean, after this sensational mutual experience Sally and I enjoyed, I told her I had given an exclusive interview to David Jaynes of *The Globe* this morning. I have promised not to give interviews to any other journalists. You understand the sort of arrangement I mean?'

'I do,' said Monica Cavendish. Her voice was definitely quivering. 'We do the same sort of thing ourselves, Mr Connors.'

'Sally seemed unaccountably cross when I told her this.'

'Did she now.'

'Then she threatened me.'

'How?'

'Hounding me with the resources at her disposal, making sure I never recovered reputation, business confidence, that sort of thing.'

'Naughty Sally.'

'As you say, naughty Sally. Could someone there take her in hand? Explain to her the likely outcome of using her body to get a story. Explain to her that if she uses her sex to get a story but the man takes the sex and won't talk, she should think twice about setting out to pursue him vengefully. She might ruin the rest of his life, she's certainly threatened to ruin mine, but it won't leave her much time to pursue her profession. Vendettas take time and I doubt your readers care either way about me in the future.'

'I so agree, Mr Connors. How refreshing it's been to talk to you.'

'Thank you, Ms Cavendish. Bye for now.'

Delicious though the revenge was, it made him no happier. Maybe he should have played along with Sally. She was a fantastic fuck and he didn't think she'd be back. He was the loser after all.

Riley's naked lady stories were accumulating. Every time one turned up the others put it on Riley's desk so that the ageing soak soon had a fine collection. The others were mildly surprised at how many such stories there were, especially in a cold and wet autumnal season. It was like UFO spotting, they decided. The things came in clusters.

Terry's, the disco where an orgy was rumoured to have taken place, was burned down. It happened at three in the morning so no one was hurt, but the building was beyond repair. It was arson, the firemen found the petrol source soon enough. Some speculated a fundamentalist religious group had attacked the place as a den of vice. Others thought the neighbours had got sick of the noise. Most thought it a random act of violence in an increasingly destructive age.

There was a fire in Southwark, too.

Sir Marcus Wright and his wife Lady Jessica were holding a party to celebrate Marcus being promised a particularly safe seat at the next election. At the moment he had a very slim majority but he had rendered the PM a considerable service recently and now he had word of what his reward was to be.

They didn't live in their constituency, they had never intended Marcus's association with it to be longlasting, and so were entertaining from their rather nice home in Surrey. There was a marquee in the garden, open on one long side housing the band. They would have used indoors if the weather had been frightful but actually it was a fine night, cool and starry, not at all cold and wet despite the time of year.

Coloured lanterns were strung along the terrace. Uniformed servants kept the drink and food flowing. The right people had come and Jessica was deeply and quietly happy.

Rosie and Tim were late for the party and Rosie's dress was rumpled. They explained the car had broken down en route, just a flat, but Tim had decided to change it himself rather than wait for help. Rosie had wandered up and down while Tim went about his mucky business.

She had come back to the car excited and strange. The minute they were safely inside she kissed Tim and told him she wanted him now, immediately, in the car.

65

'Don't be bloody silly,' said Tim, half-laughing.

Rosie lifted the stiff folds of her full-skirted dress. 'Now,' she said hoarsely. She reached into Tim's groin and touched him.

He gasped. His cock stuck up so stiffly within his clothes it hurt. He fumbled it free and they both went into the back of the car. Tim sat with his trousers open and Rosie got astride him, facing him, having thrown her panties away.

She mounted him and clinging to his neck she rode rapidly up and down. Tim puffed and gasped and tried not to dirty her dress with his still grubby hands. Her pussy was gorgeous. She hadn't been as fired up as this in years. She had seemed perfectly normal while he was tyre-changing. Maybe she was excited by his manly behaviour, getting his hands dirty rather than paying someone to do the job for him.

They stopped. She looked round as if only suddenly aware that they were semi-public. She sighed.

'Rosie. That was lovely, Are you wearing a new perfume, darling? Something quite, er, spicy. Strange.'

'No. Just my usual. Come on, Tim, let's arrive.' Rosie was writhing slightly as if she itched.

They moved into the front of the car again. Tim looked at his wife.

'Not satisfied, old girl? Want to go home and have another session?' As he offered, Tim's heart momentarily quailed. Their sex life had been a bit dim for some time. Was he still up to a big session? He remembered the feel and smell of his wife whilst they were joined. Yes, he could make it again. She did smell different, too.

'The party,' Rosie said. She tapped the dashboard with her long red nails.

They introduced themselves to Jessica and told her about the hold-up when they arrived. They didn't mention the sex. Rosie then vanished into the throng which was fine by Tim.

He washed his hands, got himself sorted out with food and drink, and began to gravitate towards Sir Marcus and his pals.

Rosie touched one of the waiters on his fly. The pair of them went quietly into the bushes where he penetrated her immediately and with considerable vigour. Meanwhile Jessica, whom Rosie had dutifully kissed on arrival, found her husband's male secretary, Andrew Wollenfold, and took him up to Marcus's study to help her find something. There she opened her bodice and let her breasts spill out.

'I say, Lady Jessica. I mean I can't,' said the unfortunate man, backing away. She repelled him.

'You certainly will.' Jessica's eyes were flashing like her diamonds. She came right up to the boy, he was barely twenty-two, and pinned him against the wall.

He groaned and buried his face in her corsage. She stroked his hair. She was trembling. She began to lift up her long skirts in their heavy dull crimson. 'Here,' she said, panting slightly, 'On his desk. Now.'

She swept papers, pens, photographs off the leather-covered surface. She climbed up frantically, opening her legs. 'Now,' she gasped. 'Like this.' She turned onto her hands and knees, pulling her skirts up over her head. She had already removed her panties. She crouched now, naked rear up, face down and hidden under her clothes.

Andrew pushed his hard erection into the waiting hole. His own tumescence astonished him. He felt like he was screwing his employer. It felt good too. It felt wonderful, in fact. Lady Jessica was astonishing, juicy, soft and sort of sucky-squeezy. He felt marvellous, kneeling on Sir Marcus's desk, screwing his wife among the penholders and letters from constituents. He felt marvellous full stop.

She wore a strange perfume, not exactly nice, rather pungent in fact. But it added to his excitement. It was part of it.

In a fat glorious moment he was done, thrusting more feebly as he emptied his cock into the woman who had hitherto had only sharp or sarcastic words for him. He sat back on his heels and waited for her to emerge.

She pulled her skirts back into place, did up her bodice and walked out of the room without saying a word. She had a bland blank look on her face, as though she didn't know him, as though nothing had happened. It had, though. He chuckled to himself as he did up his clothes and tidied the desk. It had happened and it had been very good. Whistling, he went back to join the party.

Sir Marcus turned and looked across the heads on his half-dark lawn. Something was puzzling him. He was tall man, broad to match his tallness, and his body was starting to tingle. Something was going on.

He saw Julia, his mistress, but she didn't see him. She had her hand on the man she was talking to, a local magistrate. A moment later they had vanished from his view.

He felt restless. There was a certain amount of whooping and shrieking coming from over by the heated swimming pool where his two daughters and a collection of their friends had gathered. A moment later he was sure he heard a splash.

'Excuse me,' he said to the man in front of him, an exceptionally boring civil servant he often shared a carriage with on the train up to town. 'I think those young fools are getting a little high-spirited. It's fine in July but we mustn't have any of them coming down with pneumonia. It's almost October, after all.'

By the time he reached the pool the tingling he had been faintly aware of, had become a fairly desperate desire for immediate sex, a situation so extraordinary that he failed to notice Zandra approaching him. She was his eldest daughter's closest friend from Benenden. Zandra was in bra and pants and as she reached him she took off her bra.

'Oh, Sir Marcus,' she cried and flicked the bra round his neck, pulling the two ends so that he bent towards her.

She kissed him hard on the mouth, opening his stiff lips and winding her sharp pointed tongue round his. There was a split second where he remembered her age, eighteen, and his own, fifty-two. He remembered his position as an MP and the seat he was going to be given. He remembered the state of his bank account, the nature of the recent payments into it, his wife, the press and the public nature of where he was. Then he pulled Zandra's pants off, opened his trousers and scooped her up.

She swung up into the air clasping his neck, kissing him still. Her legs wrapped round his paunch opening the place between them, at the top. His huge hard cock lifted, pointing straight upwards. Zandra wriggled, moaned and took the tip between her sexual lips. Sir Marcus jerked up. Zandra jerked down. He was in her, she was bobbing up and down and he was fucking, gloriously, out in the open in front of all his guests and at least one gossip columnist from London.

He hadn't felt so good in years. His blood roared and sang in his ears. Zandra's mouth was divine, though her perfume was novel. Not sweet, not musky – odd altogether. Her sweet young pussy was tight round his mature man's organ. She went up and down, his cock slid in and out, someone was clapping, no, there were lots of them, he was surrounded by a ring of clapping people.

He puffed, snorted, humped and finally came. He shot upwards what felt like gallons of juicy spunk. Zandra, bless her, was squealing and squeezing by turns, her head thrown back now as she revelled in her orgasm.

She climbed off him. Dazedly he looked at all the people watching him. He fumbled his cock away and saw Zandra grab the dull civil servant he had abandoned before coming over to the pool area. He was watching gape-mouthed. He fell to his knees and Julia (Julia!) pulled his trousers down. The women roared with laughter, clapping. Zandra wriggled underneath the man, whose cock was hanging down stiffly. He began to fuck her.

Everywhere he looked, Sir Marcus saw his guests falling to the ground, hoisting their clothes out of the way and indulging in public sex. He tried to find his wife but when he did, she was riding the gossip columnist bareback around the garden, using his hunting whip. A woman he didn't recognise, some dim county neighbour, was scuttling alongside masturbating the man's dangling sex.

There was an interruption while Marcia Mainwaring threw herself at his feet, took out his cock (hard again!) and sucked him till he fired great gouts of spunk. She knelt on the grass, her face pressed into his groin, gobbling his sex till he came. After this he got himself into the marquee where the music had long since stopped. Three women were servicing the five bandsmen. It was a group enterprise and it was hard to see where one body ended and another began. For a moment he was able to see straight between a pair of female legs. Projecting from her body was one of those egg-whisk things drummers use, the fan of nylon hairs sticking out from the wooden handle which was deep in the woman's vagina. It shook about as her other end engaged in frenetic activity. It was an interesting sight.

Sir Marcus removed his trousers and sat down. By and by he was visited. He began to lose count of the number of times he obliged some frantic woman. He was proud of his superb virility. He must have done it six, seven times. Eight. He felt fit to go on all night.

Had someone spiked the champagne?

The house was connected to the local fire station. When the alarm went off, the men assembled rapidly. It became clear it was an MP's house. The firemen cheered up. It was less likely that there would be deaths to deal with and more likely that they would receive a thank you for not saving the Renoir. Important people often needed to liquify (in this case, oxidise) their assets at short notice.

When they arrived they found that a party had been in progress. The police had beaten them to it and were wandering around in shock. There was no suggestion anyone was still in the house which was well ablaze. Even the family borzois were on the lawn.

It was easy to tell the police apart from the party-goers. They were still dressed. Almost everyone else had stripped naked and was cavorting in the balmy warmth of the blazing house. As Steve Janes, fireman, pointed the first hose he became aware of a disturbance around his groin. The jet of water began to waver.

Little of the house was saved.

Four

Riley approached Monica Cavendish's desk in something of the manner of a Cunarder docking.

'Hello, Sam,' said Monica absently. She was patching together a story about a Skye terrier dog who had been watching a television advert for hair shampoo. He had then rushed and jumped into the bath. Every time he saw the advert he did the same thing. He turned on the taps and attempted to bite his way into a shampoo bottle. So the owners claimed, anyway. It was an entry for the pet story of the year competition that the paper ran.

'Did you hear about the Surrey fire?' asked Sam.

'Mmm. Vaguely. MP's place, wasn't it?'

'Yes. That's not the interesting thing, though.'

'You tell me.' Monica smiled at the ruinous old hack. She was fond of Sam Riley. They had had a steamy affair together about twenty years before. She remembered it now with a faint shudder of horror at passing time.

'The suggestion is that they were all starkers when the police arrived.'

'The family?'

'There was a party going on. Orchestra hired, marquee in the garden, gallons of lovely bubbly, the county cream.'

Monica considered. 'On the whole I'd sooner believe my dog story,' she said. 'It watches this advert . . .'

'Himself takes it very seriously,' said Sam, referring to their editor-in-chief. 'He's sent Dave Carne and Willie Leavis to probe in the village and to bribe the servants.'

'Dope?' asked Monica.

'Could be. Naughty goings on in the pool and then a match too far. Only . . .'

'What is it, Sam?'

'There's been a lot of arson cases in the last few days.'

'They set each other off,' murmured Monica. 'If you see what I mean.'

'And there are my naked lady reports.'

Monica watched him, brown eyes alert.

'And reports of orgies. Improbable orgies.'

'Details, Sam?'

'That disco in Hammersmith. Something in Southwark. There was a funfair just off the M25. Now our least favourite MP, at Colnefleet. First of all, or the first one I can fit into the pattern, was a factory in north London. No, it was that ghastly freezing plant, where they had human bodies preserved.'

Monica burst out laughing. 'It's wonderful, Sam,' she crowed, wiping her eyes. 'I love it. You really had me believing it till you tacked on the walking dead. Off you go now, there's a love. I'll get back to little Towser and his lust for personal hygiene.'

The ratpack were gone. The front of Jake's house was peaceful once more. He began to eat properly and arranged for the demolition people to clear the site of his plant as soon as the police gave the word. The foundations might yet prove intact and he needed to get temporary structures over the tanks which were worth thousands in scrap alone. They were undamaged as they were designed to be. Despite that he could not see how he would be able to set up in the same business again. He negotiated salary settlements for his redundant staff from the insurance company using the tanks as collateral. If gross negligence should be proved as the cause of the fire the company would eventually refuse to pay under the terms of his policy. They would repossess his tanks.

His telephone rang and he answered, the machine being switched off because he had been working from home.

'Is that Mr Jake Connors?'

'Speaking.'

'My name is Lana Grayson, Mr Connors.' She had a low voice, very intimate in intonation. There was the faint suggestion of a drawl. 'Does that mean anything to you?'

'I'm afraid it doesn't, Ms Grayson. Should it?'

She gave a throaty laugh. 'You sent me such a nice letter, apologising for your little accident with my husband's body and delicately hinting any legal proceedings on my part would fail.'

'Grayson? I had no one of that name.'

'No, it's my name. My husband's name was Jeremy Barlow-Smythe.'

'Please accept my sincere apologies, Ms Grayson. I've really been under a considerable strain these last few days. Of course I sent you the letter. I'm sorry also about the legal bit. My lawyer insisted.'

'I do so understand. May I make an appointment to see you, Mr Connors? If you're not too busy.'

Jake cursed silently. 'Naturally I'm at your disposal. I appreciate that events have been unfortunate, to put it mildly. When would suit you?' He flicked through his appointments diary as he spoke.

'Tonight?'

'Uh, yes. Sure. Perhaps I could take you to dinner. It might make a difficult situation easier, if you don't find the suggestion offensive.'

'Where would you suggest?'

Barlow-Smythe. Paralysed in a car accident. Neglected by overworked hospital staff. Gangrene. He was a psychologist, a professor recently back from a spell in the States when fate had so devastatingly overtaken him. The whole thing had been set up fast.

Posh, then. She would be used to a certain amount of gracious living. She certainly sounded like a woman who knew of the good things in life. She also sounded American.

'The Capricorn,' he said rapidly. 'Greek Street. I'll book the table and meet you in the bar at, er, eight? Would that be all right?'

'That'll be just fine, Mr Connors. Until eight, then.'

He was isolated. He had his back to the wall. He had active enemies. He was very close to going under. Jake sat at the bar in The Capricorn restaurant and thought about his life and the ruination of it.

None of it mattered when Lana Grayson came into the bar.

Jake was on his second drink, having been careful to arrive early. When the woman came into the bar he felt the light soften, the music swing a little lazy and the barman begin to look like a friend. She was kind of smoky, smoky with curves, and a low ache started deep in his belly because he wanted her and he knew he wasn't going to get her.

She wore a dress in Jersey silk that acted like it had been painted on, but softly. Over it was a chic jacket that emphasised the real woman, shoulders, breasts, narrow waist, slanting hips. Her clothes served her, emphasising her not themselves. Incredibly, she had some fur round her neck. Jake saw its silken flutter against her skin before she removed it and knew he wanted to see it again. Her hair was a lush gleaming black, black as his own but full of lights and strange colours like a starling's breast. She had wide narrow eyes, very bright but veiled by her long lashes.

She wasn't young. She must be approaching his own age. Jake thought her the most perfect thing he had ever seen.

She looked round the bar after entering it. Two men in

business suits stopped their earnest conversation and watched her for a moment. A couple turned away from each other to look at her. A heavy man alone wearing a dark blue suit eased himself on his seat.

Jake stood up. She saw the movement and turned. She came over to him, walking with a swinging confident grace. He had never seen a woman like her, not off the big screen.

'Mr Connors?' The throaty voice was warm and caressing. There was a hint of laughter in her eyes, in the way her mouth settled.

'Jake. What would you like to drink, Ms Grayson, or shall we go directly downstairs?'

'I guess I'm not that hungry. A gin and tonic, please.'

'If you sit down I'll bring it over.'

The conversation was banal. Jake tried to get a grip on himself as he bought their drinks. She was really something and she looked clever as a cat. She must know she came over like dynamite. He must be careful. She would be used to her effect on men and he had no doubt she exploited it.

He wished his guts didn't hurt so much, just looking at her.

He watched her sit down and slide along the banquette. She had none of the fussiness of some women he knew, who struggled to manage their skirts, their coats, their bags and umbrellas. The jacket and dress fitted her like a glove. She carried a little black suede pochette with a gold clasp. There was her fur. That was it.

He saw her legs as she sat. He was too far away to hear the rustle as she crossed them at the ankle and laid them neatly to one side, but he could imagine it. He carried their drinks over, aware that the barman eyed him with a new respect. It wasn't every customer met a lady like this, loaded with everything a woman needed with some left over spare.

She was sitting peacefully, apparently relaxed when he arrived.

'Thank you,' she said. His insides gave a little lurch. Damn you, he thought. You know what you're doing.

'How can I help you?' he asked, deliberately cold.

She took a sip of her drink. Then she looked up at him. 'Oh dear,' she said softly. 'You're going to be difficult.'

There was the faintest suggestion of an American accent. 'Not at all,' he said stiffly, feeling absurd.

'I had no objection to what Jeremy chose to do, Mr Connors. We should be clear on that from the outset. He was a free man and it was his choice. However, with what has happened I find I can't quite shrug the matter off.'

Jake waited for the sting.

'I have a need to know what happened to my husband's body. He isn't laid to rest. He isn't cremated. He isn't preserved. I feel very unsettled, if you want to know the truth, and I feel responsible. So I've come to you to help me.'

She fell silent.

'There were no children,' said Jake. He was remembering details of Jeremy Barlow-Smythe's application.

'We had been married two years.'

'You're an American?'

'Yes. We met in the States. He was a visiting professor at Berkeley, initially for two years but it got extended. He was a popular man. Respected.'

'You must have wished he never came back.'

She shrugged. 'He could have been run over if he stayed. No one knows the future, Mr Connors.'

Over the black dress she wore an amber necklace. Her neck was very graceful, her jawline firm and youthful. Yet he was convinced she wasn't young. Her manner was too assured, too intelligent for youth.

He looked into her eyes, meeting them directly. 'It's a complete mystery to me at this time, Ms Grayson. The police are investigating and so is my insurance company. It is an accident that couldn't happen. We had excellent security. We had a committed and concerned staff. The building had substantial fireproofing and the tanks, there are three and only one was in use, are bomb proof. No bodies have been found.'

His voice had flattened and he sounded angry to himself.

She leant forward, resting her chin on one hand. He caught the elusive aura of her perfume.

'My name is Lana. I'm not about to sue you. I have a need to know. Now stop bullshitting me and tell me what you know.'

'I was there,' he said and stopped.

'I know.'

'You've been to the police?'

'Yes.'

'I was in my office. I heard an explosion and then a fire started. If my door had been open I wouldn't be sitting here right now. I broke my window and got out.'

She sat back. 'Do you have a wife, Mr Connors?'

'I'm married, yes.'

'She's a very lucky women.'

'She doesn't think so.'

Their eyes met again. Her mouth started to tremble. 'Oh dear,' she said and smiled guiltily.

Jake suddenly relaxed. 'I didn't want her to go,' he said, 'But I guess I'm well rid of her.'

'Shall we go downstairs, Jake?'

So they went.

They talked about American art, English museums and international tennis. Jake didn't remember what he ate. He saw her back to her hotel feeling the hairs rise on his arm as he took her elbow. She walked with conscious grace, he knew she had been a tennis pro once and she had that athlete's command of her body. She knew where her edges were. So, tantalisingly, did Jake.

At home he was met by the police. They escorted him to the station and put him in an interview room. It was very late and he was tired, tired and dazzled by his evening. He wanted a late drink and his bed.

'Mr Connors,' said the inspector. The room was too bright, the light harsh and unforgiving. Jake rubbed his chin. He could feel his beard coming though he had shaved twice that day.

'This is a hell of a time to bring me in,' he grumbled.

'To invite you in.'

Jake eyed him sardonically, It was a subtle difference as far as he was concerned.

The inspector flourished a smudgy copy of the next day's *Daily News*. 'There are allegations in tomorrow's paper that you were aware that something was wrong before the explosion, before the fire. The reporter, Sally Trenning, says you told her something was wrong. You knew the tank in operation was ruptured. Is there any truth in this, Mr Connors?'

There was a long silence. Jake lit a cigarette and inhaled it. 'The tanks can each contain five capsules,' he said. 'The capsules are full of liquid nitrogen. We have to keep them topped up so the tanks are designed to be opened. Essentially we have a deluxe freezer plant in operation. Everything is monitored, of course, and the results are fed into the control desk. It was Sonia's job that night to watch the control desk and if necessary to top the capsules. She had done hundreds of such night shifts. She was not a gifted woman intellectually, but she was a sound and reliable employee. Very loyal. I had total faith in her.' He stopped. A plain woman, in love with her boss. He had known her pathetic little secret. She would blush sometimes when he spoke to her, an ugly flush ascending her skin. It embarrassed him dreadfully, this awkward sexless dumpy-looking creature, having feelings about him. He had ignored it, mostly. The revelation that her sturdy body was shapely and rich had been astonishing. He could still see her in his mind's eye, heavy-breasted, wide-hipped, narrow-waisted. The way she had taken Kemps half-appalled him. She had been voracious. The little man had been assaulted, though he had made no protest and done nothing to stop her.

'In my office that night I accessed the control desk. It was a routine. Something I often did. The readings were crazy.'

'You're telling me something was going wrong?'

'I don't know what I'm telling you. I never got to investigate. I had just seen the vatroom. Everything looked fine. If what my computer told me was true, sonic alarms should have been screaming. I never heard an alarm till after the explosion. Then it was the fire alarm, not anything from the monitoring system.'

'What did you do after you saw the screen said something was wrong?'

'I stood up and walked over to my door. My ears popped and I felt something through my body. I still didn't understand. I didn't hear a bang, you understand. I didn't hear things being smashed apart. There was a colossal pressure change, that's all. I had my hand on the door when I heard the fire alarm. I almost opened it. I felt the wood warm, it was like I was flushing, warmth beat against my face. I hesitated and saw smoke come in under the door. I could hear the fire then. It's just like I told you. I turned and ran for the window. If I'd opened the door I would be dead.'

'You knew something was wrong,' insisted the inspector. 'Before the fire. Before the explosion.'

'Fuses might have blown. Have you ever had a car warning light on? It can be a small electrical failure, a short circuit, not your brakes or whatever at all. At that stage I was assuming this was a short circuit, if you like. I told you, I'd just seen the vatroom. If the readings had the rights of it, the place would have been howling and the tank would have been ruptured.'

'You're telling me you don't think anything was wrong?'

'Something was wrong. There was an explosion. I'm sure we're dealing with an electrical failure of some kind here, not a chemical explosion. The laboratories where we prepare the bodies are at the far end. We know they weren't the seat of the fire. But whatever it was wasn't in the vatroom.' Jake lied steadily.

'Why didn't you tell us this before? Why did you tell it to the reporter, this Sally Trenning?'

Jake's face hardened. 'I was shocked that night. I was confused and deeply upset. I also know that laymen get the wrong end of the stick very quickly about science. They don't understand, and so if you want to tell them anything, you have to be sure as hell you understand it first. If I'd given you wrong data, data you would have interpreted wrongly, you would have gone off chasing hares instead of properly searching for the truth. By the time I had it clear in my own head, I knew it was trivial. If the explosion was caused by an electrical failure, the fire report would find it.'

'You told this reporter. I fail to understand that.'

'I told her that night. She was waiting for me in your car-park and I offered her a lift. She damaged my car so it wouldn't start and then she fixed it. I was pole-axed, too tired to think. She pretended she was a civilian, working for you. I didn't know she was a reporter. She began to pump me. She took me home, went to bed with me and got what she could. Since I found out who she really is, I haven't been very cooperative with her. I gave that interview that was in *The Globe*, a rival paper to Sally Trenning's. She's getting revenge. A woman scorned.'

The inspector's face was impassive. 'You withheld information.'

'Trivial information.'

'That's for us to judge. We aren't complete ignoramuses,

Mr Connors and our forensic boys have even been to University.'

'I see. I apologise.'

'Are you withholding any other information, however trivial?'

'It's not in my interests, is it? I need this thing settled. I can't get started again at anything till the position is resolved. You think those missing bodies help me? That they are good news for me? I spent tonight with the widow of a man we had in suspension. She's a level-headed woman, but she wants her husband's corpse burned, buried or preserved, not littering the countryside as junk. I respect her point of view, inspector.'

'You can go home now. I'll get a car for you. If I find you haven't told us something else you know, I'll do you, Mr Connors, for obstructing the police. Do you understand?'

'Have you any idea what happened yet?'

'You'll be informed. And make sure you keep us informed.'

Jake stood up. The inspector gathered papers. Looking down at what his hands were doing he asked casually: 'You're certain the bodies were in place that night? That they hadn't been already removed?'

Jake sat down and put his head in his hands. 'I had an anonymous letter suggesting just that,' he said in a muffled voice. 'No, I'm not damn-well sure.'

Pete got in touch the next day to say a reporter named Sam Riley had contacted him from *The Daily News* and he, Pete, had put him onto Jake, refusing to speak. Jake swore and thanked Pete who was going north for a job interview.

It was strange. It was the second incident where he knew something but had forgotten it. He had told Sally things that first night he had put out of his mind and subsequently ignored. And he had filled his car boot with stuff from his office at the time of the fire. There they had sat ever since. Now he unlocked his boot in the privacy of his garage and carried the desk drawer full of what he had rescued in those last horrible moments indoors. It was about time he saw what he had retrieved, however tedious the job.

Sam Riley phoned him while he was working and left a message on his answerphone. He told Jake he might have a line on what had happened to the bodies. Deeply suspicious, Jake contacted the newsroom and asked for Sam.

The fruity rich voice was not reassuring. Sam would tell him nothing over the phone, scorned the idea of telling the police anything, and persuaded Jake to meet him in a wine bar in Aldgate.

Just as he was leaving, Lana Grayson phoned. Jake stood with heart beating, listening to her seductive voice. She invited him for a drink at six that evening. She felt they still had something to say to each other.

So did Jake, only it had nothing to do with her husband or dead bodies or exploding buildings. It was much earthier than that.

He broke into the call before she put the phone down and said he was going into the city now and could come on to her afterwards. They fixed up to meet at her hotel. Jake whistled as he went out to his car. He had never thought he would meet a woman beside whom the image of Gloria became a little cutesy, a little too pink and gold. There was nothing of the doll, of the plastic blonde about Lana. She was pure undiluted woman, burning bright with intelligence and bone-deep in beauty. Yet it was hard to recall her features apart from those light bright eyes, half-veiled most of the time by lowered lids. Jake acknowledged he was dazzled. It wasn't a bad feeling and at least it distracted him from the totality of his wrecked life. For the time being.

He disliked Sam Riley on sight. The man was a haybag,

gone to seed. The drink had broken veins all over his face and his nose was a bloated tribute to a misspent life. The man was overweight in a sagging baggy way, his clothes sloppy and stale-smelling. Jake hated these public school types who made their way on their birth and connexions. He had done it himself using his brains and his ambition. These silver-spoon types dragged the country down, filling important jobs and doing them badly.

Sam said: 'I'm not a real reporter any more, Mr Connors. You should understand that.'

'I'm not with you.'

'I occupy a desk. I collect a salary. On sufferance. I'm a soak, Mr Connors, as I expect you can tell. I'm sliding gloriously downhill and I haven't filed a story for two years and they haven't printed anything by me for even longer, though I had a by-line in my day. In my day.'

Jake was silent, disgusted.

'Recently I had an. experience. As best I can tell, I was drunk at the time, it was around midnight. Maybe a little later. I was, er, Islington way, I think. I like to roam as I drink, Mr Connors. It's my only exercise.'

The plummy voice stopped. Sam looked remarkably pleased with himself. Still Jake said nothing. He thought about Lana Grayson, her long legs, her athletic walk, that free swing of her hips. A generous woman, he thought suddenly. Not a mean streak in her. Not like Sally Trenning. Or Gloria, his wife. A woman happy to be herself with no need to punish those she came into contact with.

'I was about to be mugged. The punk had a knife on me. We got interrupted. A naked woman appeared, it was raining quite heavily and very cold, I believe, though I was too far gone to feel it. She, um, how can I put this, seduced me. Yes. She quite rapidly seduced me there on the street and she followed it up by doing the same to the punk who was goggling beside me. Neither of us resisted.'

The silence stretched. Jake felt the skin of his face tighten with disgust.

'You don't believe me, of course.' Sam spoke softly. 'I don't believe it myself. I've long since stopped having any capacity for sex. Women are quite safe from me, though I never was a tiger. I like to think I had my modest successes. I have pleasures to look back on. But I have to look back a long way.'

'Why are you telling me this?'

'I enjoy the look of contempt I arouse on your face. Not your type, am I? Not anyone's type, really. However, be that as it may, something happened and I had no problem. She vanished, the punk ran off and I went home, a little early for me. And I began to collect, what they call in the office, my naked lady stories.'

Unbidden, a faint image came into Jake's mind. A pale woman like a dim flame between the orange lights on an empty street. The rhythmic whump, whump, whump of his wipers as the picture blurred and cleared, blurred and cleared, blurred and cleared. His car slewing to an abrupt halt. Sally driving it.

'Naked lady stories?'

'They began that night and they are proliferating. It's a little like seeing flying saucers. You report one and it triggers a cascade of reports. It's a familiar phenomenon to newsmen. I was one once.'

'Naked lady stories.'

'That's right, Mr Connors. Hysteria? Stupidity? Wish fulfilment? I was drunk, Mr Connors. I'm not a reliable witness. But the stories grow. And spread south. As do the orgies.'

'Orgies?'

Jake was getting tired.

'And the fires. Naked ladies, orgies and fires. A potent combination, Mr Connors.'

'*The Daily News* is a tabloid,' said Jake brutally. 'You manufacture nonsense. You don't expect me to believe all this crap, do you?'

'No,' said Sam sadly, though he parodied this as he parodied everything concerning himself. He looked like a lugubrious bloodhound, intentionally comic. 'I don't believe it myself, Mr Connors. My colleagues don't believe it and they'll believe anything that will make good copy. But this is too much, too absurd.'

'So why tell me?'

'Because you started it.'

'I started it?'

'With your little freezer plant. What a very sick man you are, Mr Connors, taking money off dying people and freezing their dead bodies.'

'You deserve to have your face punched in,' hissed Jake. 'I'd do it if I wasn't frightened of blood poisoning.'

'Yes.' Sam was delighted. 'I knew you were a terribly fierce and macho man the minute I saw you, all lean and elegant under that lovely tailoring, but oh so tough about the jawline. I bet you bowl the ladies over, Mr Connors. Bright. Tough. Very attractive. No wonder our Sal did what she did, though regrettably she does it in so many places and with so many men. But she must have enjoyed her work with you.'

Jake stood up. 'You old fart,' he said viciously.

'Sit down.' Sam was unexpectedly commanding. 'That's better. You had a fire that night. A naked woman was seen, though the report is unreliable, within half a mile of your plant. I don't believe she is a figment of some latter-day silly season joke. I think she is an arsonist and she began with your plant. If anything I experienced that night is true, she is also the most magnetically sexual woman I have ever met. It should have been physically impossible to arouse me, but she did. She's your culprit, Mr Connors. She's the link. I tell you for what it is worth. My colleagues don't believe me. The police wouldn't believe me. I don't believe me and I can see you certainly don't. God knows what she did with your corpses. She must be a deeply sick woman, though she has done me nothing but good, even against my will. Frankly, I feel marvellous and have done ever since that night. She has a mole under her chin. There's no gin in this tonic water, Mr Connors. I went to my doctor, I felt so good I thought I must be dying at last. God knows I've been trying long enough. My doctor tells me my blood is perfect and my liver has stopped degenerating. I have a fifth of it left. How about that?' He grinned suddenly and for a moment Jake caught the charm of the man, a faint sense of what he must have been like once upon a time, before he decided to enter upon his long and lonely suicide. A worm of curiosity wriggled and was still. The man had a story somewhere.

'I have enough of my profession left in me to know there is something in what I say,' said Sam. 'I don't have the energy to pursue it. I give it to you because you have an interest in finding out what happened that night. I guess your business is finished.'

'Oh yes,' said Jake.

'I can't say I'm sorry. However, this woman is setting half the south of England alight. Perhaps you can persuade someone to look into it though I certainly can't. You look like a very determined man to me, a man used to getting his own way.' Sam shuddered theatrically.

'That's it?' asked Jake.

'That's it. One elderly plonk. One naked lady reported here, there and everywhere. A series of fires where she has been seen. And orgies. Unbelievable, eh?'

'Sex and arson?' Jake permitted himself a grin. 'I can't

think why your paper isn't running it.'

Sam stood up and gathered the skirts of his grubby raincoat. 'It's a very strange thing, Mr Connors. If you spend your life embroidering thin truths into false garments, and something genuinely rich and rare comes along, you are liable to dismiss it as the Emperor's clothes. Goodbye. Thank you for listening to me with a degree of civility.'

Jake unravelled the metaphors and sat for a while nursing his drink. Sex and arson. He was the only person alive, so far as he knew, who had seen Sonia ravish little Arthur Kemps just before the fire. It was a strange coincidence, Sam Riley telling him all this. The man must be half way mad. One fifth of his liver. Yes, Jake knew his physiology very well indeed. It was just enough if you kept to a careful diet to give you a life, though not a very prolonged one.

The old boy must have had an attack of the DTs and resolved to get himself off the booze. All that stuff about wanting to die, the creepy subtext to the man, was showmanship. The man was a clown, an actor. No doubt his lack of self-sufficiency had been his main means of attracting the opposite sex when motherliness was in fashion. Now women kind of liked a man who could manage himself, keep himself together. Sam was out of date and he knew it.

Jake looked at his watch. He would go take a Turkish bath. Then it would be time to meet Lana.

Jake was not a romantic man but he had a vision of the future, even if he rarely articulated it. That night he talked about himself, his work, his ideas with a freedom he had not previously experienced. When Lana invited him at length, after they had eaten, for a late drink in her room, he felt none of the fluttering apprehension of the young. He was sure deep inside himself that she wanted what he wanted, that they were a coming together of equals.

Yet she was a most special lady. In her room Jake gave way to the urge he had had ever since he had met her. He took her in his arms, looking into her face, smiling.

She felt very good against his body. Again, that subtle fragrance enveloped him. He let his eyes sink to her mouth, wide, generous, humorous. He touched it very gently with his lips. He didn't want to rush this at all. There was no need for greed, no place for it here.

Again he brushed her mouth. He felt her body melt and curve into his. Her head began to go back as her mouth submitted. He touched her lips more firmly, a short kiss. Again, and again. Each kiss was a capitulation, a step on the way. Now he kissed her completely, opening her mouth, pulling her hard against him, his arm around her, holding her tight. His hand was in her hair. With his other hand he pressed against her back, feeling the outswell of her body from the hard pelvis to the round full buttocks. She rubbed against his body so that he knew she must be aware that he was roused and ready. But he could wait. He must savour her. He must feel every moment in the slow luxurious climb to the heights of pleasure. This was no woman for grabbing. There was a lifetime of experience in her and he wanted to taste it all.

Her mouth was wise. She must have known many men. He was pleased, her maturity was part of her appeal. He didn't want her any less than she was.

He had a hand on her neck now, at the sensitive nape. He caressed her there and felt her thrill slightly.

Yes. She would be passionate. Excitement of a new sort started to grow in him. He was going to learn something.

He kissed her throat and felt the pulse flutter under his lips. His heart hammered in his chest, deafening him. He felt her hands go under his jacket and feel him, his warmth, through his shirt.

For a moment he pulled back, looking into her face, wanting to hold back the last moment before he fell into bliss.

'Do you know what I am feeling?' she said. Her eyes were crinkled with amusement.

'Suppose you tell me.' Her throaty voice masturbated his mind.

'Your hands on me,' she whispered. 'They make me want to remove all barriers between us. I want to feel your hands everywhere. Everywhere.'

'Yes,' said Jake. He kissed her ear.

'I want to feel your body pressed naked against mine.' Jake kissed her neck.

She stirred against him. 'I want to see your sex. I want to caress it. I want to caress you everywhere, especially where you are most sensitive.'

'I won't prevent you,' said Jake.

'I want to feel your body hard erect pressing into me. I want you to make love to me. I want you in me all night, all night.'

Jake slid a hand up her thigh. He kissed the vee of her breasts and let his tongue go between them.

'The first moment I saw you, I knew I wanted you to make love to me. Is that bad?'

'No,' he said. 'I felt the same.'

'I know. I know you did. I saw it your eyes. You have beautiful eyes, Jake. Unzip my dress.'

'Yes. Jesus. You're so beautiful.'

'You were hard. You were angry with me. But I wanted you to hold me and kiss me.'

He kissed her mouth again and felt her growing excitement. One beautiful breast was free. He cupped his hand over it. He felt the nipple harden and fill the centre of his palm. He felt her tremble slightly.

'Jake. Oh Jake, how badly I wanted you. I ached for you to

touch me. I wanted to be with you in bed, in private. I wanted to explore you.'

He kissed the smooth swell of flesh, her upper breast. Warm and alive, it moved under his lips as she breathed. He opened his mouth and moved down. Now he could touch the nipple with his tongue. He licked it very gently. He kissed it. He closed his lips over it and sucked. He felt the breath judder in her body. With his two hands he eased her dress off her shoulders and dropped it. She drew her arms up out of the way and wriggled slightly, deliciously, as he eased it over her hips. It fell to the floor in a sensuous whisper of sound. She stepped out and he released her breast to look at her, naked but for her peach satin panties, her garter belt and stockings.

He kissed her other breast, delicately tonguing the nipple till it matched its partner. Then he sank to his knees, kissing under her breasts in the shadow there, where her ribs were firm bones under the satin of her skin. He kissed her soft and yielding stomach, feeling the skin jump as his tongue slid into her navel. His hands slid slowly down her back, going into the dip and flowing out again over her broad gracious lines. Now he clasped her buttocks. He squeezed gently as the satin of her briefs slipped over the silk of her skin. He pressed her into his face. Her sexual mound was firm and he rubbed his cheek on it. He put out his tongue and licked the outside of her panties. The material was at once transparent. He could see the wisps and tendrils of her silky black hair. He licked again and tasted the faint musk of her womanly place. He opened his mouth wide and let his lower teeth drag gently under the mound, where she was soft and yielding under its protection. Her thighs trembled against him. His fingers had slid into the crevice of her rear, still outside her panties. He ran a nail over the material and knew she liked it. He knew just what she liked. It was what he liked himself.

He brought his hands to her sides and began to slide her

panties down. As her fleece was revealed, he kissed it, biting it gently and pulling it. He could smell her musk strongly now. He reached with his tongue under her mound and curled it up, questing to find her little sexual soldier, the homonculus who stood guard at the Jade Gate, the entrance to paradise.

'Jake,' she whispered and a sigh went through her like the wind. Her whole body was in sensitive motion like an aspen. A terrifying tenderness gripped Jake so that he felt almost weak. He kissed her thigh above where her stocking stopped, on her milk-white flesh. His finger entered between her legs and he ran it gently along the length of her, seeking her velvet.

Abruptly he stood up and kissed her hard, hugging her to him so that her naked breasts crushed against his chest. Her arms came round his neck and she kissed him equally hard, becoming fierce in her desire for penetration. He picked her up in one easy muscular sweep and took her to her bed. He couldn't prevent himself from coming on top of her, dressed as he was. He needed to feel her nude body under his. He needed to kiss her as his physical weight bore down on her. He needed to absorb her into his texture and then possess her.

She began to undo his shirt buttons. He shrugged off his jacket and rolled off her slightly. She came up on one elbow and kissed his eyes. She kissed the strong tendons in his neck and then she bit his shoulder, pulling the stiff white material out of the way. Her hands were on his chest, pressing themselves flat-palmed against the wiry hair there. They slid down to his stomach and involuntarily he sucked it in. Her long fingers went in under his waistband.

For a moment she hesitated. She drew back slightly. Jake controlled himself as best he could. Then she slid one hand right under, down, till her fingertips touched the firm flesh of his rigid shaft.

For a long moment she was content just with that and no more. Then she removed her hand and undid his trousers.

Jake removed the rest of his clothing. As he did so, Lana took off her stockings. She lay flat on her back, moving very slowly, rolling them down and revealing her long fine legs. She lifted one leg in the air and took off the stocking. Jake slid his hand between her thighs and felt her vulva.

She closed her eyes and arched her back. Then she reached for him and she drew his naked body onto hers.

'Make it now,' she whispered. 'Make it everything.'

He knelt between her legs. He took her other stocking off and removed her little lacy garter belt. He put his thumb into her sex and felt her. She was full and ripe. He put his two hands to her and held her labia apart, forcing them open until he could see right into her sex. She was flushed deep rose and fully aroused. Her vulva quivered in his hands. He saw her pussy flutter helplessly in her sexual need. He kissed it.

She came. He knew it, he could taste her. Her body pushed into his face and she writhed in her ecstasy of orgasm. He tore his mouth away and came up the bed, slotting his full cock straight into her pulsating, orgasming flesh so that he could feel it through his own sex. She was crying out, making muffled noises, so he kissed her, letting her taste herself through his mouth.

His penis was hard in her, held there while her pussy convulsed about it. He had hardly begun to make love, yet they had such pleasure. He had his arms straight on either side of her so that he could look down at her face, her full breasts, her glowing nipples. Her black hair haloed her impassioned face. He had never felt a woman so alive under him and he had had good sex before. Her hands came up his body, feeling his back, his sides, and he drew partly out of her and began to fuck.

Every stroke had a sweetness beyond anything he had ever felt. He knew he was high, he felt she was too. She was arching into him, responding to his every move, her sex sweet heaven, spice-hot and rich. His cock seemed to swell in triumph, his balls were luscious fruits of pleasure. The movement of her breasts as their weight slid about seemed to him to be quintessentially erotic. Her whole body was fluid motion, she was carrying him with her up to the mountain top. He knew absolutely her sexual needs were being met, she was having what she needed and he could supply it, he could satisfy this woman.

Her hands were in his buttocks. She was urging him now. Her pussy sucked him and shouted for climax. His cock was exploding.

Jake grunted as he fucked again and again, emptying his cock into her. He could feel through his own convulsions of lust her rippling cunt going crazy round his shaft. It came to an end at last and he collapsed down onto her. His hair was wet, his skin felt fiery, and a warm glow deep inside him was threatening to uncurl into a fat ball of contentment.

'Jesus,' he whispered.

They lay on their backs side by side, their faces turned to each other. Jake had his eyes shut. Her lips brushed his and he responded lazily. He felt her mouth on his and for a moment their tongues danced together. She moved slightly and began to kiss his face. He lay flooded with peace letting her do as she wished. She kissed every part of his face, his lips, and then she moved down to kiss his chest, the muscles in his arms, his wrists, his palms. She moved down to his groin where she began to lick him like a cat along the length of his slackened penis. Again and again her long tongue licked his cock, till every side of it was licked clean. Then she licked his balls. It was deliciously erotic, simply a glorious feeling. She opened his thighs and licked between his legs, behind his balls. She licked his arse.

He groaned slightly and she licked more. She bit his buttocks and licked between them. Then she kissed his arse, licked it some more, and tried to penetrate it with her tongue.

His cock started to grow again.

'How about,' he said lazily, 'we get some very cold champagne?'

'Are we celebrating?' she asked wickedly.

'That's what you are,' he said. 'A celebration of yourself.'

'I hadn't thought of you as a man with pretty words.'

'Woman, I'm going to make love to you again tonight.'

'Good. That's very good.' Her voice thrilled him, the throaty murmur exquisitely sexual. 'So let's have the champagne.'

He ordered it from room service, paying the boy who brought it so it wouldn't be on her hotel bill. They sat facing one another, each with a long cold flute of biscuit-pale fluid. They touched glasses.

'Tell me about yourself,' he invited. She fascinated him.

'Oh, Country Club tennis, mostly when I was young. Then the circuit. Then rich husband number one. He died of a heart attack. Then Jerry. I guess that's it.'

'Were you very fond of him?'

Her mouth trembled. 'To begin with.'

He stroked her face. 'I'm so sorry about all this business. I'm so glad I met you.'

'Darling. I can't unwish this, can I? Not you.'

'I had a reporter ask to see me today.'

'You said. You met him before you came here. To my hotel.'

'To your body. To you.' Jake kissed her. 'He has this extraordinary theory.'

'About what happened that night?'

'In a way. He thinks there's a naked woman arsonist going round starting orgies and setting fire to places.'

She looked startled for a moment. Then she began to laugh. He had to take her champagne so she wouldn't spill it.

Contentedly he watched her breasts shiver and shake to her laughter.

'I'm sorry,' she gasped. 'That's so far out. Was the poor man totally dippy?'

'Totally. An alcoholic undergoing some sort of cure, I think. No doubt it gave him delusions.'

'Oh Jake.' She was suddenly sober. 'What did happen?'

I think Sonia starting defrosting the bodies, he said silently. I have the computer record but I haven't told the police. I think Sonia threw a loop and tried to bring them back to life.

'I don't know,' he said and kissed her. 'Lana . . .'

'I know. I know. Don't say it. It doesn't have to be said. Make love to me, Jake. Take me there again. Where have you been all this time?'

She took a mouthful of champagne and bent over his cock. She began to suck it so that he felt the bubbles.

Slowly he leaned back till he could unfurl his legs and lay flat, legs apart. The woman hung over him, her face suspended over his sex. Her mouth was a pleasure cavern, a treasure house of erotic delights. He lay totally relaxed, sprawled out, and she took him slowly through dark layers of mysterious pleasure. She investigated delights using his sex as her guide and instrument. Her hair caressed him. Her fingers teased his balls. Her tongue teased his cock. She kissed the tip of his cock with her vulva and then she kissed it with her mouth. She slid the fattened end into her body between her legs, then she slid it between her lips, teasing it with her teeth, wrapping it round about with her tongue. Mouth and cunt, mouth and cunt, she fucked him towards a new climax, a new peak of pleasure. She even pressed him against her rear. She kissed his cock. She sucked it. She put it inside her and fucked it. She penetrated her rear with him so that he gasped with the tightness of her and she fucked him with that part of her, too. She took her hair and wound it round his shaft and abraded the silk of his column with its silky roughness. Again she entered her own arse with him and squeezed him. He lay gasping as his cock suffered sensation after sensation, dragged to new heights again and again. He was between her breasts, between her thighs, between her buttocks, between her teeth.

His breathing came harsh. His chest lifted and he felt dizzy as he hyperventilated. His hips began to jolt involuntarily. Her whole body was snake-like, wrapped about him in every possible way. At the last moment, when he thought he must die, pass out at the very least, she mounted him completely, astride his body.

He was fully within her. Her head was thrown back, her magnificent breasts lifted high and held apart by her posture. He saw her individual ribs, her sucked in belly, her black triangle of damp silk and the roots of his own cock disappearing into her body. She cried out, riding fiercely up and down on him. He drove up into her frenzy and felt her come. He knew total triumph, total mastery and he climaxed as he knew it. His harsh blows as he emptied himself were her final delight, her final consummation.

They drank champagne to ease their dry throats. He kissed her softly, reassuringly as she came back to herself, stroking her damp hair back from her face. She lay with him trustingly, at once herself and his.

He found her perfect. He slept.

Five

BRIGHTON BURNS.

It filled all the news. The television, the radio, all the newspapers. Brighton was in flames.

The television pictures were coy. The cameramen and reporters were being kept well back from the blazing town by a tight ring of police. Within the cordon the army operated. A continuous stream of refugees emerged from the town, mostly unharmed it seemed but shocked and confused. Nobody could get an angle on it. This was reflected in the muddle of reporting.

A television crew flew over the town in a helicopter but it didn't help them. There were several fires and a great deal of black smoke. There was nothing else to see except the army and fire fighters at work, and people being moved out of the town or into safe areas.

Was it an explosion? A bomb outrage? Several bombs? No one knew.

In the news vacuum, strange rumours spread. There were tales of looting, of vandalism, of sexual mayhem as gangs went on the rampage. The sexual theme was particularly resilient, resurfacing again and again. None of the broadsheets used it but the tabloids began to sniff meaningfully. Even they knew they must be careful. The good people of Brighton bought a great many newspapers every day. If one particular tabloid came out with something really gross about them that later was proved to be wrong, its sales might never recover locally. There were precedents.

The police were unable to prevent the newspapermen from infiltrating the mass of temporary refugees, but there was curiously little to tell. No one seemed to know anything, really. People were shifty, shocked, unwilling to talk.

Jake phoned the newsdesk of The *Daily News* and tried to speak to Sam Riley. He wasn't in yet, they said. He usually came late. Jake shrugged. It was just an idea. He would have been interested in what the old newshound had had to comment on the Brighton business. Curious, that whiff of sex about the whole thing. Very unBritish. The way the public behaved in times of crisis was forever fixed by images of plucky Londoners full of cockney humour suffering the ravages of the blitz, what one might call the Vera Lynn/Gracie Fields school of courage. Brighton didn't really seem to fit the bill.

The next few days brought a series of horrors that focused world attention on the south of England. The towns along the south coast burned each night so that from afar, from space, the coastline was jewelled in living flame. The emergency services all but folded under the strain so that all that remained were isolated pockets of officials striving to quench flames, protect property, move frightened people to places of safety.

Parliament sat, ousting the press so they could meet in closed session. The cabinet sweated behind closed doors struggling to analyse the fantastic information as it was fed to them. They couldn't impose a complete press blackout, that way madness lay, but they attempted to censor the reports.

They failed.

The sexual theme resurfaced. Even the serious papers began to report eyewitness accounts of people making love in public, in groups, in the burning towns. There were tales of firemen joining in, abandoning their work. Witnesses claimed neither the police nor the army were invulnerable.

Jake tried to reach Sam Riley several times during those

hectic days. He was not coming into work and they refused to hand out his address. Finally Jake phoned every S. Riley in the London phone book. Sam must have been either ex-directory or one of the dozen who never answered. Jake couldn't trace him.

Meanwhile England burned. Ahead of the flames, managers strove to shut down chemical plants, the army surrounded nuclear-power stations and the countryside filled up with milling vagrants. London was still fairly safe as was the west country. Kent and Sussex and Hampshire lit the night skies. For the elderly of Southampton it was a hideous revisiting of the night of terror when the Germans razed their city to the ground.

The army of refugees flowed north, well-behaved but uncommunicative. A mass amnesia seemed to grip those who had been involved in the disasters.

Then Calais burned. Despite EC regulations the French closed their borders to everyone of British nationality and all Channel crossings stopped, by air or sea. The tunnel was closed.

A siege mentality ruled. The country slowed almost to a halt. Those not involved stayed glued to the news media. The government sagged in despair.

Jake took Lana to his home. He lit candles because one of the increasingly frequent power cuts was in operation. He said:

'Tell me what to do.'

'I don't understand.'

'Tell me it's nothing to do with me.'

'It's nothing to do with you,' said Lana obediently. Then she said: 'Jake, what's happening? I wish I was back in the States with normal, kind of understandable riots. This arson, it's like a disease, a contagious disease. It can't be one person. Why have so many gone so mad?'

'Sam Riley, this journalist I can't reach, he made a connection, see. Naked-lady sightings. Sexual orgies. Burnings. He said it started with me, with Timegate. Then there was a discotheque called Terry's. There were other things, a party at an MP's house, I think. Sam saw a pattern. Now he's disappeared. I've been trying to reach him every day since the Brighton business but he isn't at work and they won't give me his address. I can't trace him without going to all the addresses in the phone book, and what good will that do? If he isn't answering the phone, he isn't there.'

'You think his disappearance is significant?'

'I think it's one hell of a coincidence.'

'You laughed at him before, this business about naked-lady sightings and the arson.'

'Things have changed, haven't they.'

'We don't know about naked-lady sightings any more, do we?'

'No. It's a news refinement that wouldn't surface at the moment, I guess. I gather any amount of women are naked when the flames go up. Who would know about one particular one.'

'Are you suggesting a particular woman takes off her clothes and sets fire to buildings?'

'Yes. I mean, I think it warrants investigation, don't you?'

'But more than one person sets fire to places. That's obvious. Unless she can be in two places at once.'

'But it's like a disease, a plague. You said it yourself. It's contagious. And I've looked at the map. I don't expect the news we're being fed is very accurate, but each outbreak seems to have a core. The fires are like shells of activity, like a dying sun might puff out. It's radial. As best I can see there are only one or two centres a night but they spread rapidly outwards. It could be just one or two people, a very few at the most, acting as a seed, a catalyst. Then others take over.'

Lana was thoughtful. 'I still don't see where Timegate fits the pattern,' she said.

Jake looked at her. She might have been specially made to satisfy his hunger. The gorgeous curves and lines of her. Those bright veiled eyes, knowing and amused. The lush dark beauty of her hair. The generosity of the warm places of her body where she cupped liquid lust and allowed it to spill over till he was full, overfull, and satisfied beyond anything he knew. She was his lady and he didn't expect to have her long, not when things calmed down and he became the poor man that was his future. She wasn't a woman to companion failure. She had too much to offer and she deserved better.

'That night,' he said carefully. 'There was something I didn't say.'

She watched him, her head slightly to one side. He loved the lift of her breasts, the way her legs folded, the sparkle of the jewel in her ear.

'I went into the building just as I said. Unless Arthur, the night watchman, happened to be looking at the relevant security camera, there was no way he would know I was in. I am the only one who could get in past the security locks without advertising my presence. I'm certain neither he nor Sonia Lafferty knew I was there.'

Jake looked at Lana. He would love to buy her diamonds.

'Sonia was a dull woman, a plain woman who hated it. She knew she was ugly but she did little to help herself. She just became angry. But she was a good employee. I paid her well though her qualifications were very ordinary, she had a second class biology degree and little work experience when I took her on. She repaid my trust. I found her totally loyal, dedicated to her job. She was finicky, precise to the point of irritating those she worked with, but very scrupulous. She would never have turned off the sonic alarms.'

'Was she in love with you?'

Jake felt himself squirm slightly with embarrassment. 'I think her loyalty was personal as well as to the firm. But then, I was the firm. There was no conflict. I was completely dedicated myself.'

'I believe that.'

'I think she was a virgin. She had that clumsiness around men, you know? As if they were wild beasts barely restrained. Part of her kind of wished one would slip his leash once in a while. She really couldn't cope.'

'Poor woman.'

'She wore these really dowdy lumpy clothes, cardigans, tweedy skirts, all shapeless and baggy. No make-up. Hair bundled up tight and not washed enough. She had no idea at all, or no wish maybe. Anyhow, I came in that night. It was about ten, maybe. I'd eaten out and come on over afterwards.'

'Alone?'

'Alone.' Jake touched her lips with his own and felt himself begin to rouse. 'The corridors were dim, on a low light. But the vatroom, where we kept the tanks, was brightly lit because Sonia was in there, on her shift. There is a glass wall between the corridor and the vatroom so we can see in. The room is sound and airsealed and you have to airlock in and out of it. Anyone on the outside needs to know everything is OK on the inside, even though we have alarms. Had alarms.'

'A tight system.'

'I thought so. Sonia was in there and moments later I saw Arthur Kemps. Strictly he should have been patrolling the building or watching the security cameras but that was OK. He wasn't actually breaking any rules. I stood by my office door and smoked a cigarette before saying I was there. I have to admit I was kind of enjoying it. All working around me. Do you know what I mean?'

'My apartment in Santa Monica is like that. It's large and airy and very modern. I don't like to work at keeping it clean and I don't like to have my privacy endlessly invaded.' Lana laughed and looked saucy. 'I wasn't born rich. I can't get used to having servants around all the time. So I make it as easy to keep clean as possible with modern technology. It feels nice. And safe. America can be very threatening, you know that?'

Jake said: 'I want to make love to you.'

Her lashes dropped. Jake saw her breast rise and fall. Her voice was a throaty murmur, full of laughter. 'Finish your story. Then I'll see.'

'Before I could tell them I was there, Sonia began to take off her clothes.'

'You're kidding?'

'No, I'm not. I was appalled. I was far too embarrassed to do anything but stay frozen to the spot. She took them all off, and little Arthur Kemps stood smack in front of her like a mesmerised rabbit.'

'Did they speak?'

'I couldn't hear, of course, but I never saw their lips move. Jesus, Sonia did it all. Right down to the heavy underwear and then down below that to her skin.'

'What was she like?'

'OK. I mean, those awful clothes. Another woman with a different temperament could have really done something with herself. Luscious big boobs. Really enormous nipples. Astonishing. Quite a narrow waist, now I could see it for the first time. Wide hips. Sturdy, I guess she was made sturdy. But not inherently ugly. No way. A sun tan and sexy clothes were all she needed.'

'Did Arthur like it?'

'He didn't react. He stood like a fish. Then she grabbed him.'

'This is awful, Jake.'

'I guess it is. She yanked his clothes so that his arms were pinned. She tore his shirt. I remember thinking, this must be the first time, the poor guy can't buy a new shirt every time they are together. He's married to quite a nasty little woman. She would have known something was up. You know, the kind of woman who if a guy comes home and says the trains were held up, phones London Transport to check.'

Lana giggled.

'She shoves his clothes off him. Then she knocks him over backwards till he's bent like boomerang over a lab stool in there. His head's down on one side and I guess his feet are on the floor on the other. I can't see that low down so all I've got in my vision is the guy's cock sticking up, his thighs and stomach.'

'He had an erection?'

'He could have used it as a baseball bat. The guy was stiff as an iron bar.'

'It isn't possible.'

'I saw it done.'

'You try, Jake.'

'What?'

'A kitchen stool. They're padded. Come on through.'

Jake followed her. She undid the buttons of his shirt and loosened his tie. Smiling into his face she undid his trousers and let them slip out of the way. Pressing herself against his chest she caressed his sex. Jake felt himself helpless. Her fingers were magic. His cock hardened and became firm. The knowledge that she wouldn't leave him this way made it harder. He would be inside her soon, feeling her hot velvet close round him.

He sat on the stool and began to lean over backwards. His stomach muscles knotted. Lana helped him as he went out of balance. Finally he was bent right back, his sex exposed, slacker now with the effort he had made.

Lana stood against him so he wouldn't fall off sideways. She began to hitch her skirt up, wriggling to get it over her hips. She slid her panties off. Jake watched, upside-down. She looked gorgeous, her dark stockings ending at her firm slim thighs. The rucked-up skirt was lewdly erotic. He adored this quality in her. Her sexuality was unconfined. She could play whore when she felt like it, and her capacity for licentious behaviour astonished and delighted him.

Her high heels were by his face. She touched his cock, toyed with it. He wished he could see her long clever fingers playing with him. He adored to see her painted nails, crimson-red, in his dark hair, playing with his sex.

She pressed against him. His position was a mild torture. He could smell her musk. She stood either side of his head so her ankles were against his ears. He could see straight up into her swelling, arousing sex. She bent over his cock and sucked it where it jutted up.

His sense of helplessness was profound and peculiar. He was a man who liked to be in charge, in command of himself and in command of the situations he found himself in. This enormously erotic woman masturbated his helpless body with tongue, lips and fingers.

'Did she do this?' asked Lana in a low thrilling whisper.

'She just got astride and went to it,' gasped Jake. It was so good, what Lana did. He didn't want it to stop though he would come soon. Like this, his spunk would jet up into the air, arc across the room. He wanted his cock to be felt like this for ever. He was dizzy with his desire for sex, for satiation.

Lana swung round. She edged her body onto him, as though she were gingerly mounting a bicycle, a penny farthing. Balanced on one heel, she raised her other leg and began to push Jake into her body.

He was tightly strained. He was so fiercely erect she had trouble getting above his cock to slot it in. She achieved it at last and began to edge herself fully onto him so that she sat across his hips, his prick embedded up her body. Both her feet now touched the ground. That was good. She would need that, in order to work his erection to climax. For his own part, he was unable to move.

She began to fuck up and down. Jake's breathing was all muddled now, he gasped and sweated, the blood roaring in his ears. His groin seemed at once separate from himself and yet all of himself. Its fiery state filled him. Lana was moaning as she brought herself to climax on him. She went up and down. It hurt, but the hurt was fierce pleasure. Jake wanted to push himself but he couldn't. Lana had him squeezed. She crushed him with her inner muscles. He felt them pulse and relax. She spasmed again and he knew she was in orgasm. She continued to take him, though. She went up and down, one hand behind her feeling into his balls, stroking them to add to his blind frenzy. It was as if she knew his inability to move drove him almost insane.

He came in harsh jerks. She drew his climax out of him, sucking tight with her vaginal muscles, pulling his orgasm into her. She caught his arms and pulled them. He came up using a muscular agility he had not known he possessed. Now he sat panting, balanced on the stool, with Lana astride him kissing his face and rubbing her breasts into his chest.

'Then what, then what?' she whispered. 'Was it for them like it was for us?'

Jake's face was in her hair. 'She let him drop. I saw the air was faintly clouded. It was a totally controlled environment in there. We have to be able to open the tank to top up the liquid nitrogen so the air is filtered and cleansed. Now water droplets were condensing. A kind of micro-climate was forming. Something was wrong with the temperature or the humidity. I didn't know what. The pair of them were naked in there and I desperately didn't want to catch them at it. I went into my office instead and put on the computer. I accessed the control desk to see what was wrong. Everything was flashing and all the lights that shouldn't have been on, were. The readings were screwy. The temperature of the one tank in operation was far too high. I guess it was carbon dioxide boiling that was contaminating the air.'

'Boiling?'

'Subliming. Solid carbon dioxide, dry ice, evaporates directly to a gas without melting. You need pressure to keep it in the liquid state.' Jake paused, reliving the moment, smelling Lana's hair. 'I went to the door. I was beyond any considerations of taste or modesty. The system was collapsing. At the door I felt the explosion. I felt the door warm as the fire on the other side took hold. Mercifully I didn't open it.' He stopped. Lana took his face between her hands and kissed his mouth. They did that for some time. She sat astride his lap, his soft naked cock in her gentle naked sex, her thighs cool on his thighs, her breasts exposed where she had unbuttoned her shirt, pressed against his chest. Her mouth cooled and calmed him, the sweetness of her filling him.

After this they tidied themselves and went through to the sitting room. They curled together in the smoky candlelight considering Jake's story. The central heating was off because of the power cut so they had only the blue faintly spluttering gas fire to warm them.

'A naked lady, orgies and a fire,' said Lana a little sleepily. She would often doze like a cat after sex, serene and content. Jake adored it in her, seeing it as proof of her trust in him.

'Sonia was naked but that doesn't really count. I don't see how they would have let a naked lady in from outside.'

'Someone set the fire. The bomb or whatever. Did Sonia have time?'

'Not after I saw her. I was only in my office a few minutes.

Maybe the naked lady was on the premises. Unless Sonia set it first and then proceeded to make hay with poor Arthur. Currently they think it was electrical in origin.'

'Poor Arthur indeed.' Lana came as near as she could to snorting. 'You enjoyed it, didn't you?'

'I had you, my sweet. I told you, he was transfixed. Hypnotised. He didn't move himself at all, as far as I could tell. Sonia moved enough for them both, of course.'

'Did you tell the police all this?'

'Not about the fuck. It didn't seem relevant and I thought it might upset Sonia's elderly mother. And Mrs Kemps.'

'And prove negligence on the part of your employees.'

'That too,' said Jake steadily.

'Perhaps you had better tell them.'

'Why?'

'If it is relevant to all this awful business, they ought to know.'

Jake sighed. 'Despite everything, I don't see how it can be. It's crazy, Lana. How can one employee in my place of business flip and the whole country go haywire? The police would treat me as crazy.'

'What if she got out? What if she's still alive? They never found her body, nor the night watchman's. Could they have done it in the time?'

'Only if they didn't stop to get dressed,' said Jake. Then he heard what he had said and fell silent.

'Only if they were naked,' Lana's voice was soft. 'What sort of a night was it?'

'Cold. Rainswept. All over London it was like that. When Sam Riley told me his story, I remember it was the only touch of authenticity. He said how the rain fell on her skin making it shiny like plastic.'

'Did he describe her?'

Jake laughed and kissed her. 'Darling, when a man suddenly

110

has a naked woman in front of him, he generally only notices one or two salient features.'

'So tell me,' said Lana provocatively.

'Well, yes, she was full-breasted with proper hips. Like an hour-glass, Sam said. He's a kind of an old-fashioned man.' Jake smiled down at Lana. 'He said she had a mole under her chin.'

'Did she?'

'You mean Sonia? I don't know. I made a habit of not looking too closely at her.'

'I wish I could meet this Sam.'

'I didn't like him,' Jake confessed. 'I hate it when people give up, let themselves go. He was a drunk and he knew it. He enjoyed it. He was intelligent enough to make some kind of display about it. It made me sick.'

Her fingers stroked him. 'You're so hard,' she murmured.

'No. Not hard. But I know what I want.'

He was silent as the memory flooded in, what he had lost. Lana kept it at bay. When she no longer had that magic, when the problems flooded in all barriers breached, he would put her out of his life. For her, he would offer only the good times.

It was the last flight out of Heathrow. The world was closing its doors to Britain and its strange disease. The Americans had only permitted this flight to get their people home. In New York, where the flight was headed, the National Guard were turning out to meet it. Every man, woman and child coming off the plane was going into quarantine. No one knew what the hell was going on, least of all the Brits. The Americans certainly didn't want it their side of the Pond.

As it happened, there were no children on board. The tourists and visitors had long since fled, mostly from airports safely in the north of the country. It was a flight of business men and women, some minor diplomatic staff being taken home, that kind of thing. It started OK, too, just like a regular flight except that there was an air of tension, of disbelief, of fear.

Gradually the passengers settled down. They were safe. They were away. Heathrow was being closed, anyway, so no one could come after them with the mystery virus and infect them with the desire to set light to their surroundings.

Drinks were served. The inflight movie started. Pillows were handed round where required. Laptops opened on busy knees. Perfume was sold duty-free.

Twenty minutes into the flight a woman in Row G, flying business class, looked at her neighbour from under lowered lashes.

He was a plump man, stockily built with a red face. He had covertly assessed the woman next to him when they boarded. She had been the last person to enter the departure lounge. She had sat stiffly with a glazed look in her eyes and he had not been happy to have her seated next to him. Obviously she was terrified of flying. Her knuckles were white with strain. Now, at last, she softened, audibly sighing. She relaxed back into her seat and smiled. She turned to look at the man next to her.

'Hi. I'm Dulcie,' she said.

'Wayne Lafitte, ma'am. You all right now?'

'I reckon so. Here, let me do that.'

She reached into his lap and brushed the crumbs of crisps off his clothes. Her brushing was firm and deliberate. It turned into something that could better be described as stroking.

Wayne had a window seat. The other side of Dulcie a woman sat with her eyes closed and a headset on, apparently asleep. Wayne felt Dulcie's hand in his groin. He held himself very still while he waited to see if she stopped, if she was embarrassed. When she didn't, he sighed happily.

It had happened before but only once in all the many flights he had made. A hot chick had fingered him where it mattered during an inland flight across America. Now it was happening again. That was great. That was just great. Wayne Lafitte, member twice over of the mile high club.

He shut his eyes as if nothing was going on. That was the fun of the thing, pretending nothing was happening when all the time it was. The woman, Dulcie, slid her fingers under his waistband. He eased himself in his seat. He felt something and flicked his eyes open. She had put a magazine over his lap. That was good. That was clever. Now if an air hostess went by they were OK.

Her fingertips went under the band of his shorts and he felt himself grow a little, expand in the enhanced atmosphere surrounding his prick. Now she was nuzzling him, fingertip to cocktip, teasing, squeezing . . .

Her hand was withdrawn. Wayne opened his round eyes in disappointment. She wasn't one of those screwy dames, was she? The kind who really hated men. They worked a guy up and then abandoned him when he was good and hard, out of spite.

No. She wasn't. Under cover of the magazine she unzipped Wayne's fly and worked his stiffening cock free from his clothes. The magazine wasn't doing much of a job now but Wayne was getting beyond caring.

She began to stroke him properly, her hand clasping his column and working it up and down in a really gratifying way. His plump face got a little redder. He was very happy. She had his balls out too and kept stroking them. She tickled his hair and teased his cock but he stayed happy. She was going to go all the way. This was all right.

He felt the magazine go and for a moment stayed just as he was. She frigged divinely. Then he thought regretfully he had better do something. If someone noticed the airline would ban them, he'd never get to fly with the company again and that wouldn't do at all.

He opened his eyes. His cock stood up beautifully and he gasped to see its perfection as Dulcie stroked the head free from the foreskin, again and again and again. He turned his head stiffly sideways. He would have to cover up somehow. He saw the woman who had been asleep on the other side of Dulcie. She had removed her headset and was leaning forward. She was watching every move Dulcie made. She was staring at his naked prick.

It shrivelled momentarily in shock. Dulcie bent over it and kissed the tip. Wayne almost convulsed. The thing he loved best in all the world, better than the World Series even, was being cocksucked. His rod hardened again and Dulcie gave him a really sweet smile. Then she looked at the woman watching them both.

The woman bent across Dulcie who leaned back in her seat. Wayne thrust himself as far back as he could go, wanting to disappear into the upholstery, The woman bent right over and kissed his cock too.

Wayne shut his eyes again and started to pray wordlessly. Dulcie frigged him, holding his cock low down and working it smoothly. The woman sucked the tip and licked it. He could feel her hair on his balls. He began to mumble meaninglessly in his extremity of pleasure. The Calvinist part of him knew that he was sure as hell going to suffer for this. He would have to pay for it somehow. It was so good, so supremely good, that his business would crash at the least, or his Caddy would get heisted by punks and the insurance prove void.

He was close to eruption now. He felt rather than heard the disturbance. The glorious lips were withdrawn and his cocktip felt a little cool, where the wetness of the woman's mouth evaporated. He opened his eyes again, desperation in them now but a good desperation. He was desperate to come and his only regret was that then it would be over.

He saw the air hostess. She was framing words, come to see what was happening no doubt, with the woman practically lying in Dulcie's lap. He waited for the fury, a fatuous half-apologetic grin on his face. Nothing was going to stop him creaming. The race was run and he was about to breast the tape.

The air hostess bent over as if to get a closer look. No doubt she couldn't believe her eyes. Then she bent right over and kissed his cock too.

He gave a great bursting moan and shot his load. His hips jerked helplessly. Dulcie frigged. The air hostess sucked and swallowed. Wayne slumped back and felt the sweat gather under his chin.

Mistily he saw the air hostess hoist her slimline skirt. She had perfect legs, smooth, shapely, slim. She wore lacy panties and her stockings were the sort that kept themselves up. Standing in the main aisle in the centre of the plane, she took off her panties. The entire deck of passengers watched. She turned to the man in the outside seat in the row parallel to Wayne's, on the other side of the aisle, and sat on his lap, facing him. She loosened his tie, put her lips to his and began to fumble in his groin.

The woman who had been wearing the headset stood up. She took off her jumper and bra and threw them down. She began to caress her breasts, looking along the passengers goggling at her with alert interest. She selected a man who whimpered slightly as she approached him. She laid a hand on him and he was calm. Calm but horny. Wayne could recognise the expression. It was his own when he bought sex off a whore. It was how he looked when he was eager for sex and knew for a certainty he was going to get it. It helped a man, sometimes, to know that.

Dulcie smiled prettily at him and left her seat. She took off her skirt as soon as she was able. She got one of the male passengers out into the aisle and knelt over him. He lay on his back and took what she gave him like a hero.

After a while the co-pilot came back to see why the plane was out of trim. The party was in full swing now and he had to weave past heads and feet sticking out from the seats where those who liked their sex horizontal managed as best they could. His trousers were down in about thirty seconds. Hands reached for his sex. Different hands reached for his shoulders. He was kissed deeply and intimately by one of the female passengers. His cock was expertly frigged by another. A third knelt in front of him with her exposed rear jutting towards him. He sank slowly to his knees, still being kissed, still being frigged, and found himself fed into the waiting orifice. It closed round his freshly woken cock and he began to fuck with the superb and silent joy of the truly astonished.

Premier class and tourist came to see what the hell was going on, the plane was bucking like a bronco, and stayed to play awhile. Then they went back to their respective decks to keep the game going without actually causing the plane to nose-dive into the sea. The co-pilot made it happily and began to fondle the buttocks in front of him. He noticed she was sucking a guy sprawled on the floor, even while he had been poking her from the rear. He staggered to his feet beaming at the busy passengers. Dwight would be wondering where he was. The plane was being flown manually because the trim was so bad, all the passengers freaking out like this. He had better get back and relieve Dwight, the senior pilot. Then Dwight could come back here and have some fun too.

They landed at La Guardia on a runway set apart, the beginning of the quarantine that would be imposed on them till the Brits found out what the hell was going on. No one got off the plane. No doors opened. A certain amount of activity could be seen on the distant flight deck. The pilots had been relatively normal during descent and there was no word of a highjack. The National Guard sidled closer.

Finally a door opened at the top on the steps. Linda, the chief air hostess appeared. She wore her uniform hat and nothing else. She stood there and gave the boys a big wave. Then she began to descend the steps. Another woman grasped her hips behind her, and another behind her. They were all there, every woman who had been on board. Apart from the odd decoration, a hat or a scarf, they were all quite naked.

They conga-ed down the steps and onto the tarmac. The National Guard were frozen stiff, to a man. The women began to snake towards them. They were making the right noises and kicking in time. La la la la la la, ooh, la la la la la la, ooh. La lah, lah, lah, ooh. La lah, lah, lah, ooh. And so on.

Far behind the men, the commander watched in amazement from a jeep. He picked up his radio. 'Water cannon,' he hissed. 'Whatever those Brits have, we've got it now. Close the area. Seal it. And bring the frigging water cannon.'

A wisp of smoke began to ascend from the flight deck.

Sally Trenning got herself assigned, along with almost everyone else on the paper, to the fire 'n' orgy stories, as they were known down Wapping way. There was no other news, really. It all paled to insignificance beside the terrible thing that was happening to their country. For once, the tabloids were almost at a loss. Events had surpassed their wildest imaginings. It was difficult to write extreme and strident copy using half truths when events were extreme and whole truths fantastic. As it gradually became obvious that very few people were being hurt and that all the damage was to property, the papers began to ignore the controls placed on them and print what they knew. It was pitifully little. There was a tendency for hacks to be despatched to the front line and not report back for several hours. Or days, When they did, they sounded uncertain and dazed. Sally was sitting on Monica Cavendish's desk at the moment Jake was put through.

He still tried to reach Sam Riley at regular intervals. On the whole, the phones continued to work very well but many of the hacks had gone back to using typewriters. The frequent power cuts caused their computers to crash and the wiser among them had given up and gone back to an earlier technology.

'My name is Jake Connors. I asked to be put through to someone who knows Sam Riley well.'

'Up to a point that's true, Mr Connors. I do know Sam.'

'Where the hell is he?'

'I really can't say.'

'I need to reach him urgently. You must have his address.'

'I'm hardly going to hand it over to you.'

'Does it occur to you he may be in trouble?'

'What kind of trouble?'

'I don't know. You weren't expecting him to go out of circulation, were you?'

'No,' said Monica cautiously. Actually she was astonished Sam's liver had hung on as long as it had.

'He might be ill.'

'I think he has a cleaning lady, Mr Connors. She would know. He might be in hospital but whatever the situation is, he'll be being looked after. He has family too, who keep in touch. You really don't have to feel responsible.'

Jake sighed. 'Do you know what he was working on when he disappeared from view?'

Monica's voice was kind. 'Perhaps you weren't aware, Mr Connors, that Sam was, is a sick man. It's true he still comes into the office but I don't think he really was working on anything, as you suggest. I'm sorry if he misled you at all . . .'

'He told me he was an alcoholic. He told me he was a

laughing stock, really. I know he was some kind of a joke to you all. But he had some ideas and he told me about them. I think they might matter. I think they might be relevant to this business, you know, the fires.'

'Sam told you something about the fires?' Monica was incredulous. Her journalist's mind worked swiftly. 'Oh no, Mr Connors. That's impossible. He last came in to work before the Brighton blaze. He hasn't been here since. Or are you telling me it was after that that he saw you?'

'No. Before,' said Jake desperately. 'I didn't believe him. He didn't seem to believe himself. It was only after Brighton I tried to get in touch with him again and couldn't. What he said was crazy but it made a kind of sense after Brighton.'

'Nothing made sense after Brighton,' said Monica flatly. Her eyes flicked up. Sally was listening intently. Cogs whirred in Monica's mind. This was the man Sally went to bed with to get a story and he gave it to another paper. He had phoned her when Sally had threatened him. 'Are you the man who had that freezing plant and lost the bodies?'

'Yes. Sam thought it was connected. I had a fire, see.'

Sally scribbled on a pad and held it for Monica to see. *Ask about sex!*

'But there was no sex involved with your incident, was there, Mr Connors?' asked Monica smoothly.

'There may have been. There was some evidence. I rejected it at the time but since all these things have happened . . . Do you know Sam had a sexual experience that night, or thought he had?'

'I do,' said Monica guardedly. 'I still don't really see the connection.'

'Could I meet you? I think it might be worth while.'

Sally was bouncing up and down pointing to herself. 'You met one of our reporters before, Miss Trenning. Would she do?'

'No,' said Jake shortly.

'Do you mind my asking why not?' This was malice. She knew perfectly well Jake had spoken to her before.

There was a silence. 'I don't like her approach,' said Jake.

'Maybe you won't like mine.' Monica was very sweet. She smiled brightly at Sally. What a slut the kid was.

'I'm quite sure there'll be no problem. You're a professional, aren't you?'

'I hope so.' Monica tried not to laugh in Sally's face. The girl was getting her come-uppance in fine style. She had evidently really caught this guy on the raw. In the raw. It would be one to tell the boys the next time they foregathered for a drink upstairs at the 'Tip'.

They fixed a time to meet and Monica put the phone down, well pleased. She looked at Sally who was scarlet with rage. 'I tried,' she said diplomatically. He had been Sally's assignment. Professional etiquette meant that the girl should have first shot on a follow-up. However, if the man refused to speak to Sally, she was clear to steam ahead.

'What's he like?' she asked. It was a professional question. Sally made little attempt to bite back on her rage.

'A shit. A first-order shit. Clever. Good looking. Hard.'

'Mmm. Sounds interesting. Has he an axe to grind?'

'Yes. His business is kaput. He'll be looking to put the blame as far away from himself as possible. You'll be his patsy.'

'Okey doke.' Monica was brisk. 'Run along and interview someone. Keep your chastity belt on. OK?'

'Yeah, yeah,' said Sally in disgust. She hated these faded old slags who couldn't interest a man if they tried.

The commander was commended later for his action. Keeping in his jeep and keeping well clear of the writhing snake of kicking women, he got them trapped and penned by hosing them if they came too near any of his men. He felt sick about what the inside of the plane must be like. The women were herded as a giggling naked bunch into trucks. They were locked up and despatched to the high security compound they had been assigned. Those due to receive them were forewarned they were fully contagious.

The entire nosecone of the plane was covered in foam whilst men in full anti-contamination gear went cautiously aboard. They looked like astronauts, sealed in their cumbersome suits.

Inside the plane it was hazed blue with cigarette smoke and the drinks trolley had long since run out. The men lazed around half-dressed with idiot grins on their faces. They seemed to find the robot-like figures of the suited-up Guardsmen hilarious. They came out of the plane peacefully and full of amicable good cheer. They stood blinking on the tarmac in the warm autumn sunlight. They were faced by a ring of gun-carrying soldiers. Water cannons were trained on them. The commander began to call out to them via a megaphone.

'You guys OK?'

They looked at each other. Some had glasses in their hands. It had been a hell of a party. 'Yeah. Guess so,' one called back.

'Where's the pilot?'

He still had his shirt and trousers on though his tie had long since disappeared. 'Right here. What the hell is this?'

'We've reason to believe you've been contaminated with whatever's sweeping Britain.'

'Hell, no. We just had a party coming over.' The pilot's voice began to waver. He looked at his passengers, at the rest of the air crew. Suddenly he seemed uncertain.

'We're putting you in quarantine. The medics are going to check you over.'

121

'We feel fine,' bawled Wayne Lafitte and collapsed with laughter.

'No one hurt in there?'

'Nope.'

The commander could contain himself no longer. 'What the hell's been happening? You look like you've all been humping the ladies.'

The pilot smoothed his shirt a little. Suddenly he didn't feel so well dressed.

'No sirree,' he called out. 'That ain't it at all. The ladies been humping us. That's about the size of it, gentlemen. We have been humped good.'

'Zowee,' said another of the passengers, grinning from ear to ear.

'You load of bastards,' yelled the commander. 'Get in the motherfucking trucks.'

Jake could put off his duty visit to Sonia's mother no longer. In view of the fact that her disappearance and probable death had occurred whilst she was working for him, he could do little else. Visiting unknown sick elderly ladies who were recently bereaved was not his idea of fun., It was time to get it over and done with.

She had a heart condition which had caused her to suffer a mild shock when Sonia had died. Jake was surprised to find her reasonably alert and communicative. She appeared to bear him no ill will. On the contrary, he found himself unpleasantly reminded of his late employee's secret passion.

'She thought so much of you,' wheezed the old lady, gazing myopically up at him.

'I thought a great deal of her,' Jake said stiffly.

'She admired you tremendously, Mr Connors. She was always telling me things about you, what you had said, what your ideas were.'

This was grotesque. Jake couldn't tell whether she was winking at him or one eyelid was a little palsied. Meaninglessly he repeated that Sonia had been a trusted and reliable employee.

'She's dead, isn't she, Mr Connors?' the wavering voice suddenly said.

'I think it's very probable, Mrs Lafferty.' He was more tender now. It was a shame that this old lady should find herself alone at her time of life. It was a bitter fall-out from the tragedy.

'I have something of hers I think you should have.'

'Oh no. Really.'

'No. It rightfully belongs to you. You can have it as a sort of memorial to Sonia. Such a clever girl. Always so good. She would have made a good wife.'

In the end Jake accepted. It seemed the easier option. It turned out that Sonia had kept a special diary concerning her work. Her mother seemed to believe she was the kingpin of Jake's enterprise and it revolved round her on a daily basis. Her ideas were in the diary and Jake would need them. He could hardly disillusion her in the circumstances.

He had to grub through a bag the old lady had in a cupboard by her bed. It contained things of Sonia's, pathetic memorabilia. The little locked book was there.

A kind of panic to escape was overtaking him. He took his leave. He would put this experience as far out of his mind as possible. It made his flesh creep.

On his way over to his car he flicked through the little fat book having broken the lock with the screwdriver he always carried in a breast pocket.

He stopped for a moment, aghast. His eyes raced over the neat schoolgirlish lines. It was easy to read, horribly easy to read.

Sonia hadn't had a mild mental flirtation with a good-looking boss. What he had in his hands was evidence of the full-blown obsessional neurosis of a repressed and fanatical woman. Every page exploded with the raw ignorant sexual passion she had suffered under. Tiny incidents were developed into landmarks in a relationship that didn't exist, had never existed. She detailed what he wore, how he looked, what she thought and surmised concerning him on a daily basis. Every little attention, almost every word he had said was faithfully recorded.

Trembling with disgust which was partly directed at himself, Jake moved slowly on towards his car. The woman had been totally infatuated, totally unbalanced. Beneath her dour exterior, passion had blindly seethed like worms in warm compost. He felt soiled.

He looked across to his car, orienting himself. Someone was kneeling by it, an arm outstretched beneath it. Thrusting the diary into his pocket he began to run.

He shouted as he got nearer. The man looked up, still kneeling by his car. Jake ran at him hard and they collided as the man got to his feet.

Jake hit him several times, punching low, and feeling himself hit back. They struggled, grappling together, and suddenly there were three more men. Part of Jake's brain told him he had a war on. He was going to lose. The four of them were obviously in cahoots. He fought demonically as they piled into him. Then he was thrown to the ground and they disappeared.

He dragged himself to his hands and knees. They hadn't beaten him to a pulp, as they might well have done. They had thrown him away and made a run for it.

He staggered to his feet, rubbing his neck. His hand touched his car and he steadied himself against it. It rocked slightly.

His car. Why had they run off when they had him outnumbered? What had they been doing, under his car?

He backed away from it suddenly, his heart pounding fearfully. Under his car. Then they had run off though he was easy meat. Even the first man, the one he had attacked, had defended himself rather than attack Jake.

A bomb. A light sweat broke out all over Jake. He couldn't think why he should be the target. But it being a bomb fitted the facts.

He looked round him. Some way away a woman was walking briskly towards her car. Over by the hospital buildings were all sorts of people. How big was the bomb? When was it set to go off? Was it wired to his ignition, or heat-triggered, or on a simple timer?

He waited till he saw a man. He called out to him and got his attention. The man looked at him as though he was mad. Jake smoothed himself, trying to remedy the damage the fight had caused to his clothes.

'I know I sound crazy,' he said hoarsely. 'I believe there's a bomb under my car. Will you go and phone the police while I stay here and stop anyone approaching?'

The man took some persuading but he went off eventually. Some time passed. An official approached Jake cautiously from the hospital. Jake explained what had happened.

A police car arrived. Jake explained again. They called the bomb squad.

Hours passed. Jake sat with a police guard in a small room full of locked cupboards. The car-park was sealed off. Jake could see people being refused access to their cars. The police were everywhere. Jake smoked and waited.

Finally a tall smooth man who introduced himself as a superintendent came to talk to Jake.

'There's no bomb,' he said.

'Good,' said Jake uncertainly.

'Are you a hoaxer, Mr Connors?'

'No.' Jake was angry.

He was taken to a police station where he made a statement. He was threatened with prosecution for wasting police time. He defended himself vigorously. Eventually he was allowed to go home. The whole episode had been stupendously time wasting and he didn't know what the hell was going on.

He was due to meet Monica Cavendish that evening. He took his car in to town and put it in an underground car-park. He came up near Lincoln's Inn Fields, ready to meet with her in a Fleet Street boozer.

He never saw them. They flowed out of the shadows, two of them, and got him one to each arm. He was kicked hard in the stomach and he doubled over with the pain and loss of wind.

They were very efficient. He never really landed a single blow. They hit him in his groin and on his face, but mostly it was his ribs and his stomach and kidneys that took the punishment. They used clubs and boots as weapons and it was a severe and brutal beating, completely silent and dedicated. They were very good at it. They left Jake huddled against the wall of a building. His sore and battered body was doubled over, barely conscious.

He felt terrible. A fitful gust of wind brought rain, black and acid in the night. He was very cold and he felt ill and sick. He couldn't get up and he couldn't speak. He heard some people go by. They gave him a wide berth.

He passed out for a while. He came round shivering and confused. He had to get up, get help for himself. He tried to push himself upright using the wall. The dim world swirled and he fell again. Now weak tears of rage and frustration joined the rain and the dirt on his face.

Someone was bending over him. Fingers probed. A voice spoke.

'I've been beaten up,' mumbled Jake. 'Need ambulance.'

There were hands all over him. He was being mugged, too helpless to prevent it. He cursed inside his head, raging at fate.

Then he was helped to his feet. He had one person either side of him. They were women, shorter than himself. It was hard to see them, his eyes weren't working right and they seemed very dark except for their pale faces.

He stumbled forward. There was car door open in front of him. They helped him in.

He was aware of his blood and dirt and sodden clothes. He wanted an ambulance, one of those warm red blankets and two men and a stretcher. He didn't want two dark girls and an open car door.

He was beyond resistance, too weak to defend himself. The car door shut. Someone sat beside him and the car pulled away.

'I need hospital,' he said. He found talking very difficult. His face wasn't hurt much, it was his insides, his lungs and his ribs that were so painful. This made him very frightened indeed.

'It's all right. We'll look after you. Won't we, Shirl?'

'Yeah.' Shirl tittered.

Jake groaned. He knew something was very wrong.

At the journey's end he was helped out of the car. He shivered uncontrollably. The cold ran deeply through him so that no part of him felt warm. He stumbled down steps, went through a mysterious and incomprehensible building and found himself in a room.

A dim light was offered from a naked swinging bulb. 'Dear God,' moaned Jake. What the hell was going on?

Hands began to help him with his clothes. He sat swaying on a bed. It was a bare mattress. He could smell antiseptic, sharp and clean on the stuffy air. It helped to clear his brain a little.

'Where am I?' he mumbled.

'Safe.'

'I need a hospital.'

'We're nurses, ain't we, Shirl?' This provoked much giggling.

'Been beaten up.'

'We can see that. Lie back, now. Lots of bruises.'

'I'm cold.' His teeth were chattering hard.

'We'll get you warm.'

He was wiped with warm water that made his body sting. At last they wrapped him in blankets. Shivering, huddled, he fell asleep.

He woke up in hell. He had no idea where he was. He couldn't be sure he wasn't dreaming, that it wasn't some terrible nightmare. His body hurt terrifically, amazingly, all over. He was wrapped in smelly itching blankets. He felt very ill and very frightened. This last was a sensation so unnerving that he tried to go back to sleep.

He was thirsty. He cranked his eyes open and looked cautiously around himself. There were stained brick walls showing in a yellow dimness.

He was vilely uncomfortable. He reached one painful arm up and found something round his neck. Shivering, feeling weak and feverish, he made a proper investigation.

Ten minutes later he knew for certain that he was alone in a windowless room, probably a cellar, on a dirty bedstead with three blankets. He was nude and he wore a thick leather dog collar to which was attached a chain. This was fixed at its other end to the metal bedstead.

He was a sick wounded animal, chained naked in a cellar. Either that or he was dreaming. Or he was mad. Jake lay quietly feeling very ill, in horror.

A girl came. She was very short and thin. She wore

something tight and tattered in black material, and over it a studded leather jacket and high black leather boots. Her face was dead white with purple lipstick on her thin lips. The same colour, chipped, was on her fingernails. She wore a mask. Through it Jake could see her eyes, sticky-black with make-up, her pupils pinpricked despite the cellar's gloom.

'You're awake.'

A flat south London whine. 'Yes. May I have something to drink?'

'Yeah. Hang on.'

What he had taken to be a corner was actually a way out of the room. The girl disappeared through it and came back with a cup filled with cold water. She sat on the bed while Jake drank it.

He spilled some of it. His coordination was shot to hell. He felt so weak and ill. He gave the cup back to the girl and huddled into his blankets again. 'Why am I here?'

'To see if you're worth ransoming.'

'What?'

'We picked you up mashed and brought you in when we saw what was in your wallet. Funny they didn't take it. Was they interrupted, or somefing?'

'No. Not as far as I know. I don't remember very well.'

'Right. Anyway, you seem to be loaded. You are Jake Connors, aren't you?'

'Yes.'

'Right. We've got your business cards and that. We're just checking out wifie to see if she can come up wiv anyfing.'

'I'm separated.'

'Oh dear. Perhaps your work will pay up. Hundred grand ain't so much today.'

'My business is bust. There was a fire.'

'You ain't having much luck, are you?' Plainly she didn't

believe him. 'P'raps there'll be an insurance company or somefing. There'll have to be somefing, or we won't let you go. Who d'you think is best?'

Jake shut his eyes. 'I might have internal injuries,' he said. 'Please let me go. I need to be examined in a hospital.'

'You seem all right to us. We looked you over.' She giggled.

'It won't help you if I die.'

'It won't matter. If they get slow to pay we cut bits off you. It'll hurt less if you're dead.'

He opened his eyes and looked at the pinched sharp face. Her eyes were glittery inside the mask. 'No,' he said.

'I wouldn't worry.'

Jake found no comfort in this curious statement. 'Why not?'

'You can't do nuffing about it. You do as we say. That's it. I should lie back and enjoy it.'

Later they brought him food, soup, bread and coffee. Suddenly he felt a great deal better. The pain in his body became an external thing, something added on to him temporarily. It didn't belong any more. It was not part of him.

Sometimes they lengthened his chain. He could get round that blind corner where there was a foetid little washroom. Otherwise he was kept on the bed.

He saw only the two girls though he had the feeling of an organisation, of other people in charge. He had the freedom of his hands though he could do nothing with the chain and collar, they were far too strong for him, but he could see no advantage in attacking the girls.

Time passed. He felt stronger. In a bizarre way it wasn't unlike hospital. Perhaps the food was better.

He had the sense of things happening outside in the world, of himself being shut away in this cellar like a child is closed in by its ignorance, its lack of concern. Only he knew what he was missing.

He asked the girls. They told him nothing, about himself and his future nor about events outside. Frustration and anger burned in him.

They tied him down and shaved him. They stripped his blankets back and sat on him having first strapped his wrists and ankles to the four corners of the bed. Plainly they enjoyed themselves. They were getting a buzz out of his helplessness.

Jake wasn't unaware of it. The tension in them communicated itself to him. He didn't know how to handle it. On the one hand he despised being at their mercy, which he was. Totally. On the other hand, he maybe had a chance to help himself.

'Shall we shave 'is cock?' asked Shirl when they had finished his face.

'Dunno,' said Wendy, watching him with bright eyes. Jake had Wendy sussed. She would enjoy frightening him. 'What if the razor slips?' She sniggered.

Shirl let her eyes walk slowly down Jake's bound helpless naked body. 'It might be a waste,' she said softly.

Wendy touched Jake, flicking his sex lightly. 'There's plenty of that about. We don't need 'im.'

'We don't need anyone,' said Shirl. Her voice was dreamy. She touched Jake.

His cock moved slightly. He shut his eyes. He could feel a sheen of sweat on his forehead. He mustn't smell of fear. He mustn't let Wendy catch the smell of his fear. It would be her trigger.

'No one wants to buy him,' said Wendy, 'He's a waste of space.'

'I wouldn't say.'

'Aw, come on, Shirl.' Wendy was plainly disgusted.

'Look.' Suddenly Shirl was venomous. 'You fuck off.

Yeah? If I want 'im, I can 'ave 'im. See? It's nuffing to do with you.'

Wendy two-fingered Shirl and to Jake's great relief, walked out.

Shirl turned to him. She sat on the mattress and put her hand round his cock.

'Shirl,' said Jake carefully.

'Shut up.'

She continued to handle his sex. Jake shut his eyes again and tried to relax. He imagined afterwards, thinking this scene over. He imagined being the other side of the barrier to his freedom. He imagined thinking about this as an event in his past. A little piece of slum debris was fingering him. She was society's toxic waste, bad, nasty, cruel and vicious. She was a Venus fly-trap. She enticed by a smell of decay. She had no honey to offer, there was poison in her clutches, and yet, and yet . . .

He felt himself stir. She was slight and tough. She would tear her sexual pleasure from him. His own needs were completely incidental to her.

It was a novel experience. He was a man who attracted women easily. This gutter-slut felt nothing for him beyond a passing desire to satisfy her own sexual urge.

His body was responding. She stroked his cock up and he felt it fill and firm. His skin was marbled slightly as the bruising faded, but apart from the discoloration his body was good, arrogantly male, strong.

Shirl stood up. She took off her jacket and her T-shirt. Her body was very skinny. She was white and hard. Little knobbly breasts stuck out. The nipples were pierced and had small gold hoops in them. Jake could count her ribs.

She took off her boots and her jeans. She wore no pants. For a moment she stood looking at Jake, grinning as he looked at her.

The little body was sinewy and scarred in several places. Her tiny breasts were exciting. They invited like cherries. They needed to be bitten. She had a triangle of dark hair at the apex to her legs. She put her fingers into it. Jake could see the purple nails. She reached under herself and opened her sex. She raised one leg and put her foot on the bed. Now she had both hands at her body. She played with herself, grinning at Jake.

She wore only the mask. Her dyed white hair stuck up in tufts.

'What d'ya think?' she asked mockingly, inviting Jake's opinion.

'I think I could do more for you with my hands free.' His voice was husky.

'Why?'

'What?'

'Why should you do more for me? I'll get what I want, never fear.' She tittered.

She touched him again. His cock jerked slightly. Now she climbed on the bed astride him.

She sat across his ribs. She reached under herself again and opened herself wide. She pressed down on his skin. He felt her hot wet exposed places rub on him. She began to croon slightly, rocking on his body and slightly lifting and lowering herself. Her sex stuck for a moment to his skin each time. It was like being kissed. She was kissing him with her cunt.

Jake's hands curled into fists. He couldn't move, except to lift the centre part of his body a little. He could feel the collar on his neck. Like a dog. He was chained like a dog. The girl was using him. She was hardly aware of his presence except as a sexual object. He was cock, nothing else. As a man he didn't matter.

She lay back on him, rubbing her tufty hair into his groin.

His ribs took the slight weight of her. The urge to have sex sharpened. If he lifted his head he could look straight into her vulva.

She was small there too. Like a fat bud, it glistened, winking at him. He wanted to slide his fingers into her and explore her dimensions. She would be tight. But not hard. He could see that. Despite her character, her sex was soft and cushiony. It would open coy plump lips to admit his thrusting cock. His fatness, his rigidness would push and push between those juicy shining lobes until they opened and gave way, stickily, wetly, slidingly. They would squeeze his hard cock and inflame his sexual urge. Her flesh would yield reluctantly and that in itself would be sweet.

She rubbed her head on his cock, it was really nice, and held herself open. Her sweet moist interior beckoned. For a fatal moment Jake wondered if this was it. She might well just bring herself off on him as if he was a centrefold. She might not let him into her at all.

Then she was up and kneeling to one side. She looked into his face. She swung astride him again only this time she had her back to his face. She bent over his cock. He saw her bottom rise up, he saw her sex exposed as a long juicy slit beneath. He saw damp tendrils of hair.

Her teeth were on his cock. He jerked and felt her laugh. She bit down the side of his cock. It was absolutely on the edge of pain. His stomach muscles knotted and he gritted his teeth. It was very good – just. Almost it was terrible.

She drew back his foreskin exposing his head of sex. Her tongue flickered. Jake moaned slightly and controlled himself. He would be better being silent.

She was on the move again. Now she lay between his legs held apart by the way his ankles were tied. She put her feet into his groin, up on her elbows watching what she did. She masturbated him crudely for a moment. Then she came up the bed and dropped herself onto him.

He watched her, keeping his face impassive. She was astride him again, and now she meant to get him inside. She held her sex open and lowered herself till she touched the end of his cock. She arranged it so it stuck straight up. Jake could feel the heat of her sex. She began to push down.

She was very tight. The little body struggled to absorb his big cock. Again Jake was on the border between pleasure and pain. She was very tight indeed.

He thought about the bud opening, bursting between her legs. She forced down so that she hurt him. Then she cried out. She was snarling. He was in her, sliding further and further in. She came steadily down, determined to take all of him.

Jake thrust up hard, stabbing into her. She gasped and stared at him, outraged. This was her fuck, hers to control. He was to have no say in it.

She leant forward. He was fully within her. She slapped him hard across the face.

His cheek was sensitive. They had shaved him harshly and it still hurt. His head snapped over but he had no means of protecting himself. She wore big cheap rings and metal caught his cheek. He felt it sting.

He opened his eyes and looked balefully at her. She rose up and came down on his cock. She slapped his other cheek.

The look of surprise, of anger, made her laugh. She sat back and began to fuck properly.

Jake felt himself raped. His cock stayed obediently hard, she was good inside, but his helplessness and the pain in his face humiliated him. She called the shots. She wasn't going to let him forget it. She was enjoying herself.

It was agony holding himself still. He had never been passive in the sexual act yet that was what she demanded. She was taking herself hard to climax and he didn't matter.

He wondered if he could come early and spoil things for her. He decided not to run the risk. He had no delusions that she would fall for him and subsequently help him. He barely existed for her as a person. She was helping herself to sex from his body like she would buy coffee from a machine. She would connive at his death afterwards with the same lack of involvement.

She was gasping, clawing at his stomach, bouncing hard on him. Her cunt expanded and contracted, feeling soft and liquid. Jake released himself, it had become increasingly difficult to contain himself, and felt her convulse around his jetting cock.

She liked it. She couldn't quite bring herself not to like it, when a man came in her.

He turned his head to one side and shut his eyes. He was done, shrinking in her hard little body. He felt the cold suddenly as she climbed off.

He felt disgusted. Fouled. But he felt eased, too. She wasn't bad. She was a touch violent for his tastes, but she got real enjoyment out of the process. In the end, that was what mattered.

His head was jerked. She had grabbed his hair and pulled his face up.

'So,' she hissed.

'So what?'

'You hated it, did you?'

He stared at her. She gripped his hair more tightly and took his chin in her other hand. She pressed her mouth on his. He felt her teeth, her tongue. She kissed him like she had had sex, cruelly. But she was alive. She had feelings. Jake felt himself respond.

She dropped him and laughed, straightening up and smoothing her hands down her flanks. 'Stupid bastard,' she said, but the tone was softer than the words. She hummed slightly as she pulled her clothes back on.

She left him tied, cruelly bare and exposed with her own sexual juices drying on his body.

He lay in the cellar and tried not to shiver. Time passed. And passed.

They allowed him the freedom of his chain once more. They continued to feed him. Jake felt his time was running out. No one would ransom him. Either they would let him go or they would kill him. He was slightly cheered by the fact that the girls always wore masks. It still mattered, then, that he didn't see their faces properly, that he couldn't identify them.

Often he wondered who had beaten him up. And why. It made no sense. Who were the men at the hospital car-park?

When it occurred to him that he was part of some conspiracy, that events were taking place that he didn't understand and yet was involved in, he decided he was going mad. This was hardly surprising. He thought, but he wasn't sure, he had been in the cellar for five days.

It was a lifetime.

The real world came back to him quite suddenly. They brought him Jane.

Six

Nobody explained anything. As a punishment it was very effective. Nobody told Jake anything because he had no importance. Now they came with this girl and nothing was explained.

Either she was mad with terror or she had been mad before she fell into their clutches. Jake had no idea what purpose she was to serve for them. Maybe she was ransom fodder like himself. Certainly her clothes were expensive. They were also plain and modest. Jane, whoever she was, was no raver.

She was young, too. Maybe eighteen. Not more. She was young, terrified, and strangely distant. It was this last quality that made Jake assume she was mad.

They tied Jane to the bed, The girl thrashed about a bit. Jake felt the rage begin in him. He had defences. He had lived a little. He had a certain toughness. This slight vulnerable creature had none. He was not a protective man but neither was he a brute. He must reassure her as soon as it was possible, however false the reassurance. He took it that Wendy and Shirl would leave them soon.

He felt another feeling also, so strange and so inappropriate he doubted his own reading of himself. His imprisonment must have affected him more than he knew.

Wendy and Shirl settled themselves to stay. They had an air of alert expectancy. Again Jake had the feeling that something purposeful was happening that involved himself. He lacked the key to understanding events, but there was a pattern. It wasn't all random.

Jane whimpered. The air at his nostrils prickled and he quivered slightly. There was a strange smell in the air, spicy, not sweet, not altogether nice. It was compelling. He felt the hairs on his nape rise.

The girl turned to him. She was half crouched, full of tension, like a trapped beast. A wild thing penned. She was, of course. They were both trapped.

Her eyes were large and unfocused. Her skin was pale and pure. Long brown hair slid in glossy sheets. There were tear-streaks on her cheeks.

Her mouth trembled. It was wide and generous. It was vulnerable. The girl had an air of pleading.

She wore a good blouse, a plain skirt. There were tiny pearls at her ears. She had a mouse-like quality, shy and sweet. Terror quivered. And yet.

Jake felt goose bumps rise on him. She reached out one trembling hand and touched him. At the touch of her hand his body physically jumped. The lust went through him like a bolt. His cock was instantly erect. He longed for sex.

She had touched him there. How queer, when she seemed so shy. Yet she had touched his sex.

A tear rolled down one cheek. Through it as the sun through rain an expression of naked passion crossed her face. Her eyelids drooped. Her lips parted. She leant forward to Jake.

He smelt the sour spice of her aura. His own body trembled with desire. She pressed herself against him and murmured deep in her throat. Their lips met and they kissed.

She was very inexperienced. She was also greedy. As a combination it was a total turn-off. Yet Jake was aroused so hard it was painful. He had to have her. He couldn't be stopped.

She must be feeling the same. She was opening her blouse

and shrugging off her clothes, fumbling clumsily because a rope tied her to the bed. She was as eager as him. As desperate. Maybe more so.

With a cold shock Jake saw Wendy and Shirl were watching. Their faces were tight and eager. They had come close, they were staring at the couple groping on the bed. Yet he could not control himself. Their presence, their excited glittering eyes, had no cooling effect. His desperation to push his cock inside the girl remained every bit as potent.

She had her blouse off now and her bra, a schoolgirlish thing. She was unzipping her skirt, panting in her haste to get naked. Jake dragged at his chain. 'Release me,' he begged hoarsely. They didn't, but Wendy untied Jane.

She made no move to abandon him. Jake gave way entirely. He grabbed the girl and crushed her to him, kissing her mouth, her breasts, her throat. He forgot her fragility. The lust ran hot in him. He was as crazed as she was.

Had she known what she was doing it would have been fantastic. Yet her sexual greed was astonishingly at odds with her sexual ability. She appeared to know nothing and want everything.

Jake pinned her hands behind her back. She moaned and rubbed her breasts against his chest. They were both kneeling on the bed. Her skin was soft and silky, perfumed with something young and fresh. Her hair smelt of lemon. Under it all was the strange musky spicy smell that bit into his blood and kept his lust bright.

He pulled his lips off hers. 'Why are you like this? What is it?' he asked urgently.

'Oh,' she cried. 'Oh do it. Make love to me. Please, please. I have to have you. Please.'

He came on top of her. Her legs opened and she thrust up with her body. He felt cold. His fingers went into her pussy and she screamed shrilly.

'What is it?' He kissed her neck. Her hair tangled across his face.

'I haven't done it before. Quick, do it. Now. I want you now.'

The effort of holding back made sweat pour from him. Wendy and Shirl were dancing about and laughing, clapping their hands. 'What have you done?' screamed Jake at them. 'You've drugged her!'

'No, no, we found her like this. Lots of 'em are like this. It's really funny. The men can't resist.'

The girl was moaning under him. Her hands clutched desperately. Jake felt faint. He touched one sweet rounded breast and kissed it. He felt into her vulva and opened it gently. She was crying and laughing. His cock was hard as an iron bar. He began to lever it in.

He came right up on his knees. Lying on her back she came up with him, her legs caught round his hips. She was dry and tight. He felt her tear. He knew he couldn't stop so he put his energies into making it better for her, less fierce. He wanted to be fierce, she urged him to be fierce, but he knew about women. She was a flower. He would bruise her petals. He had no need to crush them, not with his maturity and experience. Not with her ignorance.

She knew nothing about sex, let alone making love. He held her hips and because he pushed down, he was gentler in her. She couldn't drive up, the position was too awkward for her. Jake began to fuck her as gently as his own driving need would allow.

Her elbows were on the bed, her hands under her hips, holding herself up. As he fucked into her, she calmed. A look of terrified peace came over her face. Her breasts swayed gently. Her pussy relaxed and dampened. Jake thrust gently, feeling his cock constrained. Gradually the tightness began to ease a little. Her inner flesh awoke from its virginal sleep and began to melt and slide for him. She rolled gently in a shuddering ecstasy. Jake rose to climax and came in her. She sobbed slightly, the hysteria out of her, and as he lay forward and alongside her on the bed, she was calm for the first time.

She opened her great drowned violet eyes. She stared into Jake's face. 'Where am I?' she whispered. 'Why does it hurt?'

Wendy and Shirl had had their fun. They went away, apparently to tell Tony, whoever that was. Jake was left alone with the girl.

He stroked her hair. 'You'd better tell me about this,' he said quietly.

The fear came back into her eyes. 'It's terrifying,' she said. 'They do it on the streets. Nobody cares any more. The women make the men do it. Daddy said I wasn't to go out but I did. My dog was lost. One of the women touched me and suddenly I had to do it too. I've never been with a man.' Her lip trembled. 'Who are you?'

'They're holding me captive, to ransom me. They can't, there isn't anyone. They brought you in frantic for sex. You made me as bad. Did they give you something? There's a funny smell.'

'They're going to sleep.'

'What? Who's going to sleep?'

'The women. Lots of women. After a while they go to sleep. The news is a bit funny now, it's hard to sort things out. But lots of women are going to sleep. Where the orgies have been. Where the fires have been.'

Her voice softened. She stirred against him. She brought up a hand to stroke his hair. 'You're a beautiful man,' she whispered. 'I can't stop myself. You know that, don't you?' Her lips touched him. Her hands ran down his body gently. 'I have to have you.'

'Have to?' asked Jake. He felt light-headed. Again that sour-spice smell was in his nostrils. His muscles felt strong. He was warm, as if gold ran like liquid sunlight in his veins. He felt his sex tremble and firm. The sweetness was incredible. A mastery rose up in him. He was powerful, potent, inexhaustible. The sweet rose who shivered in his arms was untouched but for him. He must teach her.

He kissed her, using his skill to make her adore him. He knew all about this, how to make women feel weak with need for him. It was a game and he was a skilled player.

He kissed her breasts feeling her gasp and sigh. He was the first, the first to make her nipples erect themselves, the first man to caress those curves, the first man to run his tongue between her breasts and taste her skin.

She was spring incarnate. She was new.

His fingers roved and probed. She blushed and begged by turns. He held her buttocks, he kissed her stomach, he made her lift her legs so he could see.

She was very pale. Her little sexual country had a blind look, like a mole. He nuzzled it and felt her vibrate at the sensation. It smelt very yeasty. He could smell himself. It would be easier this time, his own spunk would lubricate him.

He came on top of her. She moaned with delight as his body pressed hers down.

Her pussy clutched him tight. The sweat stood out on his brow. He pushed in sliding in his own spunk. She was shaking and making little noises under him. He ignored them. Slowly and carefully he stroked in and out savouring her tightness as if it were the manifestation of her greed for him. She didn't want to let him go. Her movements became less awkward, she was learning how to fit herself to him, yet she blushed. Somewhere in her the girl that she had been blushed and was shy. She was embarrassed. It was like making love to two women at the same time, one eager slut and one reluctant virgin.

Jake liked it. The different aspects complemented one another.

He speeded up slightly. She was responding properly now. He found her exciting. All the time his nostrils caught the strange scent of her. When he had a moment free from desire, he would think about this.

Desire held him now. He felt marvellous. His heart thudded strongly in his chest. The gentle body moved under his, stirring him. Her softness aroused him. The need to climax came strong in him and he released himself in thrust after thrust of orgasmic satiation.

He woke sometime later. The bulb had gone out. The cellar was dark and cool. He felt alone on the bed. He could hear something in the room.

Whatever it was snuffled slightly as it roamed. After a while it came over to him. He felt it approach. It stood by him in the dark, breathing. Something touched him.

His skin jumped. He was touched again. This time two hands took him and began to feel their way over him. He caught them at the unseen wrists. She was very slender, whoever she was. Her wrists were so brittle he felt he could snap them.

'You're awake,' she whispered.

'What are you doing?'

'The light's gone out.'

'I know.'

'They keep going out. The power keeps being cut. Everything's falling apart.'

'Stop it. It'll be all right.'

'No. No it won't. It won't be all right ever again. I've got to have you, only first I need your things.'

'My things?'

'Have you got any matches? A lighter?'

'Yes. I don't know where my clothes are. They took them away when I arrived.'

'I think it's time we got out of here. But I need your lighter. Then things will be clean.' She kissed Jake. With a certain feeling of agony he felt the fire of lust go through him. He still felt strong and fit and able for sex. Every second that passed with the girl so close to him in the dark fired his blood more. He wanted her. Her soft curving body was his for the taking. She was murmuring to him, he could smell the lemon of her hair, feel its silky texture. Now her lips were on his skin. Her fingers entered his groin and played with his swelling sex.

It was wonderful. Terrific. A dream come true. But it wasn't him. Or her, for that matter. There was something, some chemical that he could barely smell with his conscious self, that was making him do this. And her. She had been a virgin. Now she was giving herself to him like a crazed nympho. He must have hurt her yet she didn't care. She wanted him. A thought squeezed itself cold into his consciousness. Probably she wanted anyone, any man. It was the need to fuck that was so strong in her. Jake was handy. He was a convenient cock.

Knowing all this made no difference. She was forcing him gently back on the bed, kissing his lips, his chest. 'It can be done this way, can't it?'

The soft schoolgirlish voice might have been asking the sewing mistress how to hem a seam.

'I've seen them on television. She sits astride. It can be done, can't it? It works?'

'It works,' said Jake huskily. He could feel her thighs parted, pressing against him. He could feel the sheet of her hair hanging down, brushing his shoulder.

'I sit on you like this, do I?'

'Yes. God in heaven. Sit higher. Hold me. That's it, come

down gently. It'll force inside you. Don't hurt yourself.'

'It wouldn't matter. What hurts is not having you.'

He was being crushed. She pushed down. He arched his back. Her hands were palm down on his chest. He felt he could lift her entire weight clear of the bed. He had the strength of ten. She squeezed his sex tightly into her body and he felt her pussy shake and ripple around the iron-hardness of his erection.

For a moment she was content just with that, just to let herself spasm around his rigid shaft impaling her soft body. It was so enticing Jake felt he would come, clumsily, too soon, unless he took over. He began to move in her.

She was different again, her body becoming wiser to his each time they had congress.

The light flickered on and off again. Jake saw her still as an after-image on his retina, light in the darkness of his mind. She had her hands up now in her hair, holding it up wantonly as if she was admiring herself in a mirror. Her head was stretched back, her lips parted, her expression one of ecstasy. She had twisted her torso slightly to one side. He saw the hollow of her belly, the vulnerable bars of her ribs, the thrust of her breasts.

She was shameless, self-adoring, given over entirely to the desire of her body. Jake thrust up harshly and came to climax.

She called out, bent over him suddenly, her hair in his face. He felt her pussy tighten unbearably. He gasped himself. Her spasm was over. She had orgasmed.

For a brief while she was herself again, soft and tear-wet in his arms. He knew now that her strange compulsion would not give her peace. Or him. If they remained trapped in this cellar, they would fuck themselves to death. He couldn't help it. She could arouse him at will. His body obeyed her needs, not his own.

'I need your lighter,' she whispered. 'Now.'

No one came for a long time. It remained dark. The silence was profound and disturbing. At intervals Jane roused and tempted and stirred Jake's body. He was unable not to respond. Sex with her was now wonderful though he could feel her restlessness, her mental absence. Despite his increasing hunger he felt powerful. Each sexual joining seemed to strengthen him, to cleanse him. He began to hunger for this feeling like an addict hungers for the fix, for the dope-induced elation.

The water coming through the taps spurted irregularly and smelt bad. Jake knew they had to do something. Their captors appeared to have vanished, at least temporarily. He made Jane stand on the bed.

Though she had her clothes she wouldn't dress. In the dark his hands slid down her silky slim flanks. She moved, only slightly but it expressed everything. Her power over him. Her endless need. His duty to obey, to serve.

'Listen,' he said, controlling himself. He wanted to kiss her belly.

'Mmm.'

'I'm going to lift you. Keep rigid. Above the bed there's a trap door set in the ceiling. I can't reach it because I'm chained.'

'Yes.'

'Chained by the neck.'

'Yes. Darling Jake.'

'You'll have to be careful. They may be up there, in the room above.'

'I will make them love me.'

She said it simply. Coldly. Jake felt the chill right through him. She had no doubts. She saw no problems. There was no feeling involved, no emotion other than the need to have. She had the means to enforce obedience.

Something nagged in his mind. Something didn't fit. There was a discrepancy.

Never mind. Later would do.

'Will your lighter be up there?'

'I don't know. If you find my clothes, you must bring them to me.'

'Of course.'

It was like talking to a child. Jake cursed mentally. He bent, put his arms round the girl's legs and lifted her straight up.

Again he had the golden feeling of strength. Alongside it like a baleful influence lay his hunger, his weakness. He had the feeling he could run till he dropped. When he dropped, it would be for good. He could outrun his own strength.

His face was pressed into her soft thighs. He smelt her sex and almost dropped her, so sharp was the need to slot his cock into her place. His place. His created place, for he had made sex for this girl. He had been her first.

She strained at the ceiling. He staggered and almost fell but she steadied them both, holding the ceiling. 'It's moving,' she said suddenly. Jake could not look up. He hung on. Her weight shifted sharply as she caught the edge and began to pull herself up. Jake pushed. She had lifted the loose-resting trap door from its grooves and slid it to one side on the floor above them. Now she pulled herself up through the gap.

She was free of the cellar. Jake stood looking up. His chain held him from following her. He knew he couldn't break it, couldn't free it from the bedstead, couldn't take the bedstead apart. He had explored all these possibilities in his terrible stretching days and nights.

His heart thumped. He had no knowledge of what she might do. She might simply go off under her strange compulsion and fuck the first man she met. She might find his lighter – his mind shied away from that possibility. Or she might help him.

He heard her moving about. Pale light filtered down,

natural light. It seemed no one was up there.

'Jane,' he called.

She didn't answer. Defeat swelled in him till he felt his chest would burst.

She was back. Something soft and clothy thudded down. Her face filled the square above him plunging him from gloom to blackness.

'Your clothes. I've got a knife. Shall I come down?'

'Yes. Yes, good girl.' Relief made him sit down suddenly. He had more than half believed she would go off.

He got himself to the head of the bed and dressed, finding out by feel what garment he wrestled with. The clothes were stale and dirty. He remembered that long ago fight. This was a suit he would throw away when he had the luxury of a clean one.

Jane landed with a thump beside him. He was aware it was almost time for their regular business. Her body was on a cycle. She needed sex every two hours for about twelve hours. Then the gaps became erratic, longer, until another twelve hours had passed. The biologist in him noted the pattern. His masculinity was aware of the consequences.

There were things in his pockets. His whole character steadied and solidified. He had possessions again. He was somebody. He had definition and meaning.

He came under the square of pale light. Jane held the blade. She crouched slightly, her long hair hanging. The blade shone. She was quite naked still.

'Don't you want to get dressed?' asked Jake softly.

'I don't feel the cold,' she said and laughed.

Jake took the knife and tried to cut at his leather collar. He couldn't do it.

'Jane,' he said.

'Yes.' Her voice was ghostly. She was plunging.

'You must cut the collar for me.'

'You must enter me.'

'Yes. Cut the collar first.'

'I need you in me. Now!'

He lay on the bed. She had only to touch him. It was no problem to be fully erect, hard, his own body demanding the sex she wanted.

She drew his trousers down a little and settled herself on his shaft, allowing it to penetrate up into her body. Now she was happy. She held the knife and leaned forward. She giggled slightly. 'Where do I cut?' she hissed.

'Lay the blade flat to the leather.' Jake was patient. 'Cut the outer layer first. Don't saw through like it was wood. Treat the leather as laminations.'

'As what?'

'Layers. Do a layer at a time. As if you were cutting through a sliced loaf. Cut a slice at a time.'

He almost choked. The blade by his throat terrified him. She rubbed it up and down and as she did so she rose and fell on his cock. He didn't know which activity attracted more of her erratic attention. He suspected he wouldn't like the answer.

Despite himself he began to lose his fear. Her pussy was wet hot velvet stroking his throbbing cock into pure pleasure. He began not to care that a mad girl had a sharp knife at his throat. The gold at his cock warmed and heartened him. She could do things now, tease at him, clench her inner muscles, stroke him into ecstasy with subtle manipulations of her flesh.

'My clitoris,' she murmured.

'What?'

'Masturbate me. While I fuck you.'

He put a finger between their bodies. Now, as she rose and fell, she rubbed herself on his finger. All the time the blade worked at his throat.

Jake's mind began to tumble. The pain was hot at his neck. She had nicked him several times and he thought he was bleeding. Tears oozed from his eyes, squeezed shut. Soon she would go too far. Yet pain and pleasure bloomed with equal heat in his body. His cock ached as it neared bursting. His whole groin was on fire. He thrust hard upwards though he jerked her and felt immediately another little stab in his flesh. Yet he thrust again, his exploding cock and bleeding neck fused into the hot wet pleasure.

He lay still, hating everything. He had no control over himself any more. He was no man. He was a disgusting thing.

His cock slackened peacefully. The sunlight flowed strengtheningly through his veins. His neck stung.

Jane stopped to rest. Gently Jake explored the collar. She had slit it almost all the way through. She would hurt him more now, but she was almost there.

His fingers came away, slippery with blood.

'I'm hurting you,' she whispered.

'It can't be helped. Go on if you can. We don't know when they might come back.'

Two hours till she had what she wanted again. What he wanted didn't matter.

Now they weren't fucking he felt a little more his own man. He could bear the pain though it was horrible. There was even a grim humour in it. He had his shirt back after days, only to ruin it with blood. He should not have had it on.

It comforted him, though. It was good to be dressed again.

'Try it now. I'm almost through. I'll cut you if I go any further.'

Jake laughed. He was well cut already. But the pain was bringing freedom closer and closer. He reached up, feeling the collar. He gripped it and pulled.

The leather tore uneasily. His muscles fired up and he pulled harder.

He was free. He was damn well free. 'Give me the knife.' he said hoarsely.

'Here you are. Why?'

'Nobody is going to stop me now.'

He meant it. He would kill to get out of this place.

He almost threw Jane up through the trap. Then he swung himself up.

The room above was bare and dirty. He screwed his eyes against the weak light, The false strength filled him. Dizziness was close at hand. He had to eat or he would pass out, even if he did feel he could haul down the columns in the temple.

Jane stood slim and graceful, over by the door. She smiled sweetly. 'Shall we go out?'

'Get dressed.'

'Don't you understand yet? I don't need clothes.'

They looked at each other. A smile danced on her face. 'Give me your lighter,' she said, almost laughing. 'I have to make a fire.'

Seven

Nothing had prepared him for what he saw. He had been days in the cellar, maybe as much as a week. In that time the world as he knew it had fallen apart.

For a moment the change was superficial. Things looked wrong. Very quickly the sheer magnitude began to be apparent.

There was no transport. Cars had foundered, stuck at any angle, some in the middle of the road, some parked. There was no power. There were no people. There were the burnings.

It was as if a poison cloud had swept the area killing everyone and everything, before passing on.

Jake was in a small industrial conclave set in a residential district. He didn't recognise his surroundings. No buildings appeared to be occupied. Nothing happened. The city was silent.

No transport roared dully in the distance. There was no noise of trains, of cars, of lorries, of buses. Silence hung suspended over the city. It was dead.

Birds flew and insects buzzed. A cat crept across a road. Nothing was wrong in their world.

After the confines of the cellar the air was cool and fresh. Jake blinked in the dull light of the overcast day. To him it was bright.

Jane leant on the doorway on the building they had emerged from. She looked elegant and sexy in her nudity. Behind her the sour whiff of smoke teased Jake's nostrils. She had lit her fire at last. 'What's happened?' he said.

'There were hardly any services when I was captured.

Shops were closing. Public transport had stopped. There was talk of petrol rationing. The army has to guard the refineries and oil depots.' Jane tittered. 'After they set the Mersey alight. They fired Ellesmere Port, you see.'

'No. No, I don't see.' Jake walked wildly over to an abandoned car. The door was unlocked, the keys still in the ignition. He tried to start it. The engine turned over protestingly but failed to fire.

'No petrol,' said Jane, leaning on the bonnet.

'Put some clothes on!' screamed Jake. Crows whirled into the air protestingly.

Jane laughed and began to dance up the road.

They came out of the industrial estate onto roads and intersections, a shopping street. Jake knew roughly which part of London they were in now, having seen traffic signs.

Now he saw people. A gang of youths, all male, were sitting in the doorway of a pub, drinking and singing. One or two elderly people scurried along carrying bags, looking furtive. Three naked women walked down the street, laughing and talking, looking boldly about them.

Jake stood still. Jane linked arms and stood beside him. The three women changed course and headed purposefully for the youths.

They did it on the street. The women knelt while the youths banged into them, drinking, laughing, screwing and talking all at the same time. Each woman made each of the five youths take her. The boys obliged cheerfully though one fell over afterwards and lay, apparently comatose. Jake couldn't tell whether he was drunk or asleep or dead. No one seemed very bothered.

The women went on. Now they saw Jake. A terrible fear filled him. He felt himself shrink inside his clothes. He would not be able to withstand them.

He looked at Jane. She laughed happily. The women

approached and stopped as they saw Jane.

'Hello, sister,' one of them called. 'Is he in use?'

'That's right.'

They passed on, Jake was left sweating and trembling.

During the next hour Jane saved him from three more assaults. He saw few men except elderly ones. They were left alone. He saw also that older women were apparently free from the contagion. They were clothed, an excellent sign of normality.

It was women. No children. It didn't seem to affect men, except as they had to respond to the women. Women of reproductive age. It looked as though the menopause was the watershed. Women in their fifties and older were safe. Were normal. That left a great many, late teens, twenties, thirties and forties. Thousands of women. Millions. All on the prowl for a man. If they were anything like Jane, they were having sex eight or nine times in every twenty-four hour period. Maybe more. That was probably a minimum.

Jane got restless and they turned into a garden. Many houses were barricaded. Jake satisfied Jane and they went on.

They found a grocer's shop that had been broken into and scavenged for food. All the shops were closed. Some still had steel shutters intact. Others were smashed and looted.

The silence hung like a pall. My city, thought Jake. My home. Destroyed. Broken.

He heard a noise. It was an engine. He began to run. He pelted round a corner and saw it.

A tank.

He ran up to it waving his arms. It came to stop. The top opened and a figure suited like an astronaut looked at Jake. He carried a gun.

'What's happened?' cried Jake. 'Is there nothing left? No one? No authorities?'

'Where you been? The television only went off yesterday.'

'I was held prisoner. That doesn't matter. I don't know anything of the last week.'

He remembered the blood on his neck, his torn and muddied clothes. He must look mad.

'You been fighting them off?' The suited figure laughed. His voice came out through a radio speaker and sounded odd.

'Can you take me somewhere? Is anywhere safe?'

'The men are OK. We've built a wire. You have to queue to get through it. The women are OK the other side of the wire. For now.'

'Where's the wire?'

'Liverpool, Sheffield, down to the Wash. Everything to the north of that is still OK.'

Jake felt the blood drain from his face. Half of Britain destroyed. Lana. He turned round, as if she might be there. What had happened to Lana?

He turned back to the tank. 'What's being done?' he said hoarsely.

'We distribute food. We guard the food trucks. That's it, buster, except for guarding key installations. Someone'll have to find a cure pretty soon, I guess. For the ones still awake. We gotta go now.'

Jake backed dizzily. He wanted to weep but no tears were there.

Lana. He looked round again. The tank was moving along the street. Jane had disappeared. Birds twittered in the trees. He would go to her hotel. Then he would go home. No, home first, to change. To see what remained of his home. There were fires everywhere and evidence of past fires. Then he would find Lana.

She would have succumbed, he thought dully. While he had lain in the cellar recovering from his beating, she would have picked up the contagion sweeping Britain. While he had rutted with Jane, she would have taken any man she came across who took her fancy. She would have the endless craving. She would fire as she went, burning London, burning the world.

Jake began to walk.

It might have taken him thirty minutes by car. Maybe three quarters of an hour in heavy traffic. On foot it took him all day.

He had to contend with certain problems. Landmarks had disappeared. In their place remained blackened heaps of rubble, some still smoking lazily up into the dull yellow sky. The other problem was more mobile.

He was caught twice. The first time he found himself held down by two women while a third did as she pleased with him. She was a big woman with massive dimpled thighs, heavy hips and large swinging breasts. Since his desire rose immediately at her command, he did not loathe the experience while it happened. On the contrary, he enjoyed it despite himself.

She was a faded blonde, a very happy woman. She openly admired Jake's lean dark good looks as she opened his clothes and toyed with his sex. Fully ripe, it sprang up at her bidding. Jake lay with his arms held almost enjoying his captivity. The full soft flesh flowed over him, wanting to please itself but perfectly happy to please him. He had never been so caressed, so flooded with flesh. It was maternal, embracing, kind.

For a big woman she was surprisingly tight. Plump lobes of flesh obstructed the entrance to her sex. Finally her friends released Jake and assisted her to sit, knees drawn up and apart, on a step. Jake came between the fruity thighs and felt them stroking him as he plunged into her recesses, enfolded and soothed. He pumped with long smooth strokes mesmerised by the women softly encouraging him and praising him. One stroked his back. Another reached under him and caressed his balls. Life and strength flowed round his body. The vast pillowy Earth Mother he steadily fucked into held up her breasts. He pressed his face into their full cool masses. They were a world of peace and comfort.

When he was done he allowed himself to lay in against her massive bosom. Her arms held him. The folds of her stomach bulged comfortably against his hard body. His head lay against her neck.

She rumbled with soft laughter. 'You tired?' she asked.

'I'm so tired,' Jake agreed. He put a hand into her sodden pussy. It was nice to feel her fat folded flesh wet with his spunk. Her warmth entered him and filled him.

She cuddled him tighter. 'You can't be a sleeper. That's just the women.'

'Sleeper?' He was nearly asleep.

'That's where we go in the end. After the loving, after the burning. Then comes the sleeping.'

How nice to be young enough to suck your thumb, thought Jake. He took a long fawn teat and placed it between his lips. He began steadily to suck.

'Why are you in such a mess?' she asked presently.

'I got beaten up. Then I was held prisoner. They said they wanted to ransom me. I'm a businessman. But they couldn't do it. Then they disappeared and I escaped. Everything had changed. I was only gone a week but it was all different.'

'Ah. It would be.'

There was a silence. Jake sucked a little, curled into the big woman.

'You want us to look after you?'

'What do you mean?'

'Some of the men give up. They belong to particular women. We don't poach, you see. If you are with a woman already we leave you alone.'

160

Jake roused himself. 'Do you know why you do it?'

'Do what?'

'Um, take the men. Make love all the time. Go about naked.'

There was a long silence. 'It's nice,' she said eventually. 'So what do you think?'

'About what?'

'Do you want to be our man? We'll look after you and you can serve us as and when we want it.'

The cushiony body was warm. Jake was enveloped within the woman. Her cunt was delicious. He felt the stirrings of interest again.

Serving them. Their man. Their thing. Their dog.

He stood up regretfully. Disentangling himself from her had been like climbing out of a vast tangled warm bed where he had been cocooned in bedclothes. 'I have to see someone,' he said.

'Take care, then. They aren't all as nice as you.'

'Then why do it?'

'I always wanted to do it. Now I can. My friends want you now.'

Jake ran.

He learned to keep to the edges so he could escape if he saw women coming. The houses, barricaded or burned, he ignored. Even so he was caught once more.

There were three of them, it seemed to be a favourite number, and they were brash and bold. They were also harshly demanding. They jumped him and dragged him into the back of a lorry. They bent him backwards over the arm of a chair there and each took him in turn, the other two holding him in place.

He remembered Sonia taking Kemps in this position as he was ravished. He couldn't contain himself, he produced the required erection and his hips jolted of their own accord, as best he could in the vile position. It was painfully uncomfortable and the women were rough enough to start his neck wounds bleeding again. They kept him there so that all three had him, laughing and sneering as they made him come back to sexual readiness between each one of them, and then they dropped him like used rubbish. He pulled his clothes together and hobbled out into the deepening night.

He prepared himself for the worst concerning his home. Wearily his mind turned over and over, sorting out what he knew, what he had observed, piecing it all together. He had so expected his house to be burned that it came as something of a shock to see it standing, set back from the drive, its double frontage undamaged and apparently intact.

They didn't burn for spite, he thought muzzily. They burned because they had to, the same way they had to have sex. They fucked and they burned and so it followed no one had been into his house to fuck. Ergo, it was intact.

He slunk between the gateposts and dodged between the shrubberies until he could get round the back. He didn't want to be seen and followed. He would have to barricade it so he wasn't seen at the windows. Then they might leave him alone.

He had his keys still and he used them to let himself in.

And there he was in his own utility room, by his own (nonfunctional) boiler, his kitchen a few feet away. Jake stumbled into it and sat on the floor.

The house was cold. He would have oil in the tank but with no electricity the pump wouldn't work. Jake shivered. The freezer would be off. He might as well take the food before it rotted and eat some. However cold the water, he must wash and change and clean up the sores and wounds on his neck. He could heat water in a pan on the gas. If there still was water. If there still was gas.

Jake dragged himself to his feet and walked into the hall.

Facing him was a totally strange woman. She held a candle in front of her, the flame soft and dancing slightly in a stray draught.

He stood still, dumbfounded. The house had been so still and empty, so intact. He had been sure no one was in it.

The joke was he couldn't attack her. He couldn't throw her out. The moment they touched he would be helpless, jigging and jerking as much and as often as she required.

Bile rose in his throat. He swayed slightly.

'Who are you?'

She had asked him! 'It's my house,' he snarled, 'I own it.' He tensed, ready to flee. If he could keep the distance between them, maybe he could ward off the effects she would have on him.

'You are Jake?' She had a thick hoarse voice. A boozer's voice.

'Yes.'

'Jake who?'

'Jake Connors, for Christ's sake. This is my house.'

'Yes. Yes, I believe you. Look—' She took a step towards him.

He backed hastily.

She stopped and smiled. He couldn't see what she was like in the dark of his hall. The candle threw odd shadows and distorted her face so that her eye sockets were very deep and her cheeks hollowed.

'You're safe from me.'

'How do I know that?'

'Only by letting me touch you. I'm not infected. It doesn't work with me.' For some reason there was a grim humour in her voice.

'Why are you here?'

'Lana helped me. Now I help her in return.'

'Lana!' Jake stepped forward. 'Where is she? Is she

163

safe? What's happened to her?'

'She's upstairs asleep. She's not infected either, but we think she would be if she went out. She stays here.'

Jake thrust forward to reach the bottom of the stairs. The woman stepped back, candle in hand.

He took the steps three at a time. At the door of the master bedroom he caught himself and stopped. Then he gently opened the door and went in.

She was no more than a pale blur on the pillow. The room was hung with darkness like cobwebs. Jake stood still and over the beating of his heart, the rushing of his blood, he heard her breathing.

It no longer mattered whether the woman downstairs had lied. He had to help Lana, if help her he could.

He walked across the carpet softly. He sat down on the bed which gave a little under his weight. He took the hand he could see dimly.

'Peta? What is it?'

'It isn't her,' said Jake unsteadily. 'It's me, Jake.'

For a long second she was still. Then with a rush she sat up and opened her arms.

For a long time they sat like that, their arms tight round each other. At last they had time to talk. As they did so the woman, Peta, slid into the room and listened. She had blown out the candle though the curtains were drawn. They did their best not to attract attention.

Jake had disappeared on his way to a meeting with Monica Cavendish. He told Lana what had happened, how he had emerged from his time capsule and found the devastation around him. He left out the part about Jane, glossing over how he found a knife and escaped. Those sort of details could wait, for ever if possible.

Lana had come looking for him after twenty-four hours, with him not answering his phone and having failed to meet with Monica Cavendish. At that time the streets had still been relatively safe.

She had found his house empty and his car missing. She had not known what to do. On her way back to her hotel she had witnessed some youths beating a woman on a street corner. She had driven on to the kerb and chased them off.

The woman was Peta. She was perfectly frank about the incident. She was a prostitute with a habit. She had been arguing with her dealer. She dealt a little herself to help pay for her habit and there was a dispute about payment. They were beating her up to tell her who was boss when Lana intervened. They had been more or less done, it was only a warning to behave, and so they had been easy to chase off.

Lana had taken Peta back to Jake's, knowing her hotel would not have accepted her. There was no point in going to a hospital, Peta didn't want it and anyway they were very busy with casualties from the fires.

At Jake's Lana had used a tyre lever to break the padlock to his garden shed. She had taken a ladder out and climbed it. She had broken an upstairs window, triggering the burglar alarm. She had found the source and switched it off. No one had taken any notice of all this. She had opened the front door and let Peta in, putting the hire car she was using in the garage. She could get into the garage from the house and unlock it from the inside.

That night the news had begun to explode. The two women, so different, had clung to each other as the full horror of what was happening to the country was finally brought home to them. The newscasters were now urging the population to stay home. The army had been called in. The government had fled north and there was talk of dividing the country in two to contain the plague.

The radio and the television, when the power was on, had continued to issue warnings and directives, no longer pretending any sort of normality obtained. The radio was still on, but the women were conserving the batteries.

They told Jake all they knew. They confirmed there was a barrier built north of the midlands and something approaching normal life still continued above it. In Brighton, apparently, and to an unknown extent elsewhere, women were falling asleep. The government in exile from London said that medical research had failed to establish any virus and the sufferers appeared to be perfectly healthy in all other respects.

Peta made them all some food while Lana took Jake's clothes off and washed his wounds, applying salve to his neck. He washed all over, he couldn't take a bath with no hot water and the house was deadly chill as it was, and put on clean clothes.

They felt marvellous. The women were wearing his clothes too. They had none of their own except what they had arrived in, and they were so cold they wore what they could.

They sat together in the sitting room on the floor in front of the gas fire. The curtains were drawn to stop any light leaking out. They had to discuss what to do.

Peta was not old. She was in her thirties. Jake asked her why she thought she hadn't been affected.

She laughed cruelly. 'Perhaps it's because I hate sex,' she said. 'I do it for money, remember.'

He asked about her habit. If she was a user, she would be in trouble.

'I had a week's worth plus some to sell when all this happened,' she explained. 'I've got that stash with me and I'm eking it out. When that runs out, drop me in a ditch somewhere. Oh yeah, an' I've got some methadone on prescription. Officially I'm coming off H.' She sniggered.

Clear and sharp it came back to Jake. Jane hadn't contaminated Wendy and Shirl. They had brought her in, handled her, and yet not been affected themselves. There had been no change with them.

And they used. Jake didn't know what. But he had known they were doping.

Chemistry. It came down to chemistry. He could smell whatever it was that drove the women in their sexual frenzy. The sour-spice smell was the hallmark of the plague, and neither Lana nor Peta had it. He himself was immune to it direct. He had to be infected each time and it was temporary. The minute the source was withdrawn, he went back to normal. As did other men.

Hormonal. Not much distinguished men from women save for their sexual organs and their production of one or two hormones. Testosterone. Oestrogen. Progesterone.

They went to bed. Peta had a spare bedroom. Jake and Lana went together.

'I haven't been out for days,' she whispered. 'I didn't know what to do. We had food. The water and gas are still on. I wondered if we could wait it out. Peta has been out a little.' Lana giggled. 'She has to take her clothes off though to look as if she is one of them, and it is too cold for her. The infected women don't seem to mind.'

Jake stroked Lana's long smooth flank. Mind and body were in total harmony. 'We've got to get away,' he said. 'Somehow we have to get out of London, north. We must get to the wire and cross it.'

It was strange to make love under no compulsion. Jake could linger with lips and hands over breast and thigh, over the soft warm places of his woman. In turn, she caressed him, feeling his hard male strength between her hands, running her palms over his muscles. She laced her fingers into his hair and arched into him as he kissed her breasts. She wove her legs between his and rubbed like a cat against his sex. She slid down the bed, down under heaped covers, till she could rub her face and hair in his groin. He lay in deep lazy contentment while she kissed his sex. It aroused slowly, naturally and without pain or urgency. Her lips caressed his stalk, nibbled the sides of it, sucked and kissed its length, licked the tip. She drew back his hood of skin with gentle fingers. She kissed the sensitive tip. She took him into her mouth and began to suck.

Jake abandoned himself to the luxury of it all. He came slowly by delicious stages to a peak of pleasure. Lana moved against him and he rolled over with her underneath. Her legs opened in welcome. He kissed her mouth, her breasts, and entered her body.

He moved with gentleness, in full control of himself and the woman under him. He drew her pleasure to its peak and he brought his own there too. He began to thrust harder. He felt her quick response, her need of him.

He drove with all his strength. She responded vigorously. They climaxed together clinging and thrusting, shaken by tremors of lust. Their bodies seemed to melt together.

Jake slept.

He rested for two days. He ate hugely, the defrosted food would soon go off, and they all cooked what they could. Plainly the gas would be cut off eventually. Cooked food would last longer than raw.

He went out on the second day with Peta shivering and embarrassed beside him. He was her serving man and safe in her company as long as she masqueraded as one of the touched.

They began to hunt for methadone.

All the pharmacies were broken into and looted. But Jake knew there were other stores of the opiate. He entered empty and vandalised police stations. Many kept some by so that they could stabilise and question suspects under the influence of Class A drugs. He knew what he was looking for and had the time to search properly. Peta guarded him, trying to control her shivering. He had to succeed. They would need it to get Peta away. Her stash would run out soon. He wanted to save her if he could. Eventually he found some.

The car garaged by Lana a week ago had a third of a tank of petrol. They were going to drive out of London and make it up the motorway to Sheffield. There they would find the wire and seek to cross it. Jake needed to find people in authority. He might possibly know more than they did. He certainly had information to pass on.

Sonia. He had the feeling this business all related to Sonia, that repressed and bizarre woman. If she had lived out the fantasies in her mind, thrown off somehow the shackles of convention, would she have roamed naked, gobbling men sexually as she willed? What would satisfy a woman like her? Total power over men. Would she not want them to be helpless victims of her sexual rapacity, even as she had been a helpless victim of her own unrequited passion for him, Jake?

It disgusted him still. It wasn't that an employee had had sexual fantasies concerning him – the mind was free to roam, though he disliked reading about it. No, it was Sonia herself, and her obsessional secretive nature. Many normal women who enjoyed satisfying and vigorous sex lives were plain, plainer than Sonia if truth be told. Sonia was warped enough to focus her sexual attentions on one person who was, to all intents and purposes, unobtainable.

They packed the car with containers of water, blankets, bedding, food and clothing. There was no way they would be in it for long. They didn't have far to go and the petrol would anyway run out eventually. But they had no knowledge of what it was like in the more thinly populated areas north of London. Their car would attract attention. It was not going to be easy.

They decided Peta would drive. She was the least vulnerable if they were forcibly stopped and could even talk at her window in a way neither Jake nor Lana could. In particular, he wanted to keep Lana safe. His mind revolted against the idea of her becoming a puppet of endless desire, mindless sex. He could not bear to think of her reduced to a mobile cunt ever-seeking to fill its gnawing vacancy.

As if to confirm their decision, the gas stopped that last evening. Now the house was cold, very cold. October lay dank and chill over London. They could no longer cook, heat water, make tea or coffee.

Jake locked the house as best he could, having fixed a board across the upstairs broken window. They warmed up the car in the garage. They couldn't afford to stall or have the choked engine play up while it was cold. And Peta and Lana had to have their top halves naked. It was the hallmark of the touched women, nakedness, but Lana and Peta felt the cold, not being touched themselves.

Jake sat in the car. It was not unpleasant having the bare-breasted Valkyries with him, but he thought it tactless to say so. Both women were very pleasantly built and his eye enjoyed their naked breasts.

Their job was to protect him from the touched women. His job was to protect them from any men who decided the car was too useful to be allowed to pass. For this reason they all three carried knives as weapons. Jake also had a very realistic gun, an automatic, which was in fact a desk lighter of a superior sort.

There was that, too. They took the fire extinguishers from the house. It wasn't only sexual mayhem that was abroad. There was the fire, too.

They worked their way out across London, Jake sitting beside Peta and directing her. She had to weave between abandoned vehicles. On the whole the women ignored them, or waved a friendly hand when they saw the naked Peta driving.

Once they came across an army patrol. The tank lumbered to intercept them and Peta swung the wheel sharply and fled into a maze of side streets. Half of them were one-way but that hardly mattered. There was no one else on the road.

Several times men ran out to flag them down, but when they saw Peta and Lana they slunk away. A man's strength counted for nothing when a woman could render him harmless with a touch. With a caress. With a kiss. Men were crippled by their own sexual urge, and the thing was, as Jake well knew, it was a pleasurable disability. The submission might be involuntary, but it had its good side. The sex was great.

He hadn't told Lana and she hadn't probed. He reckoned Peta knew he had been caught himself. Peta was tough, it would be good to save her from her wretched habit.

Peta was their saviour at the moment. Immune herself, she afforded the very best of protection.

She contained the clue, too. Jake was sure of it. Peta was immune for a reason. Other women would be immune. North of the wire, research must be pressing ahead. Peta was relevant to that. How many other women had gone through this 'wire'? None that were contaminated, that was for sure, if the north wasn't infected yet.

They reached their first serious impediment near Watford Gap. The motorway was blocked from side to side. A jumble of vehicles were drawn up, lorries, cars and so on. As Peta slowed, youths in crash helmets and camouflage gear came into view. They carried rifles. They hefted these meaningfully and flagged Peta to stop.

'Swap drivers,' said Jake urgently.

Peta hesitated. 'They might be girls,' she said.

'No. I think they're male. Let me, Peta.'

They swapped, stopped short of the road block. Jake made Peta go in the back. The youths watched impassively. A thin autumn sunlight lit the scene. It was calm and cool. Crows flapped heavily at the road margins. Their supply of carrion had come to a halt in recent days. They were hungry.

Jake rolled the car gently forward. There was no way to avoid the obstruction. They were in a cutting and the slopes were steep-sided either side of the road.

'Lana, get right down so no one can see you.'

'We can turn round, Jake.' Her throaty voice made sense.

Jake felt his blood sing. He ached for the confrontation. He had a quiet word with Peta, sitting directly behind him. One of the youths swaggered out in front of the car. He waved it down, using the rifle he carried.

Jake rolled his window down. 'What's the trouble?' he asked pleasantly, as if things were normal. As if they weren't being held up by armed thugs.

'What's in the car, then? How many of you?'

'Two. Can we go through, now?'

'Where you going?'

'North.'

'Why?'

'Business.'

'A funny man,' the youth said softly. His face was globular, a swollen black insect head nodding in the sunlight. Jake wondered if the closed helmets really afforded protection from the touched women. He doubted it. 'Now get out of the car.'

'Suppose,' said Jake carefully, 'you make me.'

'I'd like that.' The insect-youth tittered.

'Then my lady'll touch you.'

'Don't matter. It don't hurt me.'

'*Now*,' said Jake. He grabbed for the barrel of the rifle, pushing it. He felt it shudder and explode in his hand. The windscreen shattered. Peta was out of the car with Jake's replica gun pressed to the youth's neck.

Jake's hand and arm hurt. He got out of the car. The youth was standing stiffly, the automatic pressed hard into his neckflesh by Peta. The rifle was slack in his hands.

Jake took the rifle and worked the bolt. He held it up as the other youths came up at the run.

'Now drop your weapons,' he said. He took the handgun in his left hand from Peta and continued to hold it against the youth's neck. He pointed the rifle negligently at the other youths. 'Take off his crash helmet, Peta,' he said.

She obeyed. The pale spiky head of the dazzled youth emerged. He was in his late teens, maybe his early twenties.

Peta took the automatic back. Jake gestured at the others. 'Drop them,' he said. 'He'll be killed and at least two of you. I'm president of my local gun club. I've been practising shooting at man-sized targets for years. It'll be nice to move on to the real thing. Squish,' he added gently. Madly.

They dropped their rifles. Jake took the handgun/desk lighter and slipped it into his pocket. He pointed the rifle at the youth by him. 'Collect up the rubbish, Peta,' he said. 'Carefully, now. They can stand back.'

He made Peta get back into the car with the weaponry. Then he told the others to take their crashhats off.

There was a muttered rebellion. Jake let off one shot which produced a thin scream of terror. They took off their helmets and stood looking shifty and afraid.

'Now, you dismantle the road block so we can get through.'

He lounged against the side of the car while they did so. Peta cleared the windscreen glass as best she could, knocking it out onto the bonnet. Jake dusted it off, onto the road away from the tyres.

Ten minutes later they drove through, Peta at the wheel, Jake holding one of the rifles. He made Peta stop for a moment by one of the sullen thugs. 'You a user?' he asked.

'Who wants to know?' The aggression was automatic.

'I'm a dealer.'

The youth came to life. He started forward eagerly. 'Hey, man, I'm sorry. I didn't realise. We've got plenty of greenbacks. Have you got stuff on you?'

Peta had her foot on the clutch, the car already in gear. She shot forward and they heard the youth's outraged shout as they left the road block behind them.

Ten miles up the road Jake suggested Peta pull over. There was a police stopping place raised slightly behind the hard shoulder. It was one of the places where police cars waited and watched the motorway in the days when it had carried traffic.

They tucked themselves into it, virtually out of sight of the motorway. It had sufficient privacy to be somewhere where police ate their sandwiches before rolling forward to hover over speeding cars.

The women now dressed themselves in Jake's shirts and jumpers. All of them felt there was no need to go on pretending they were touched. Somehow things had changed out here. It wasn't like being in London at all. There was a raw, primeval feel at odds with the placid fields, the yellowing trees. They all felt the thugs were symptomatic of a new order, where the police and rule of law had ceased to operate.

They ate heartily. Jake and Lana took a short walk, leaving Peta in charge of the car. Jake had checked the safeties on all the rifles and shown Peta and Lana how they worked. They were two twos, each with a partially full magazine. Now he took a rifle with him, slung casually over his shoulder.

'Were you really president of a gun club?' asked Lana.

'No – I'm a liar. Are you disappointed?'

'I think we needn't have had that confrontation,' said Lana. 'I know it worked out fine. But you might have been dead.'

'You might well be right,' said Jake quietly. 'It's just that

I think things are going to get worse. I know we haven't far to go but I don't think it will be easy. You might say I needed the practice.'

Around them it was very domestic. The field was neat, decently fenced, with a footpath running along one edge. At its lower side a small stream ran through a deep ditch, with trees and bushes and nettles growing thickly over it. Jake could see a little wooden bridge with a hand rail going over it.

He was staggered at Lana's beauty. In the awkward ill-fitting clothes she retained an animal grace, a svelte shapeliness that made her every movement sinuous and elegant. Her hair gleamed. He put his hand into it. Hesitantly he kissed her, his lips gentle against hers.

'What is it?' she asked presently.

'This wasn't what I intended. Maybe you aren't so happy with things. With me. In the situation we find ourselves in. Maybe I shouldn't presume anything.'

'Make love to me, Jake,' she said huskily.

They sank onto the sweet grass. Jake spread his jacket for Lana to lie on. He undid her shirt, his shirt, and kissed her beautiful breasts, richly soft and inviting. Despite the cool air he slid out of his clothes and felt her body the length of his. Every inch of her aroused him. His eyes feasted on the perfection of her rounded belly, the little silky tangle below it. His fingers slid through her curls and felt the cleavage in her flesh that invited, seduced, enticed him in. She was moist and yielding. He felt drawn in. His finger touched her clitoris and he felt her judder slightly as excitement grew in her. When he moved to place his sex against hers she made a little animal mewing sound, her need was so great. Her legs opened. He came between them feeling the warmth and welcome of her parted thighs. Now his cock began to nuzzle into her velvet ridges and dips. He pushed forward. His cock slid easily into her body. She gloved him, she enveloped him, she surrounded him and as his hips worked, as he pumped into the beautiful body submitting to his fierce plunges, he knew that it was different. He had known many women. Recently he had enjoyed almost endless sex. Yet none of it had been like this.

'Get up.' It was a roar more like a bull than a man. Jake had come and was resting on the magic body below his, content with his world. His head jerked up.

A heavily built man wearing an old tweed jacket, a cartridge belt and corduroy trousers tucked into gum boots stood at a distance waving a shotgun at the two of them.

'Get off my land, you filth.' The shotgun waved threateningly.

Jake eased himself forward so that his body protected Lana. 'Get dressed,' he said quietly. He began to pull his own clothes together. The rifle was half-hidden by his jacket.

'Get off,' the man roared. He had a full fleshy face which was red with rage.

'We're going,' said Jake quite quietly. 'It's OK. We're going, see?' As he spoke he took the rifle in one hand. He hefted it quickly, flicking off the safety and aiming to the left of the farmer. He fired once and then pointed it directly at the man. 'Get the shotgun off us,' he said. The farmer frothed in his frustration, but he lowered the shotgun.

'We're going,' said Jake again. 'I won't hurt you but I won't have you frightening the woman here. You understand?'

'Yes.'

'Good. Ready, Lana?'

'Yes.'

'OK. Keep your gun.' Jake was now speaking to the farmer. 'You may need it. But we are not your enemy, let us go now.'

They walked back up the field and over the small rise. Below them was the motorway. Jake looked back occasionally.

The farmer didn't move, not even to pick up his shotgun lying in the damp grass. He just stood, burly, furious, bewildered, watching them go.

They made a slow and bitter journey of it up past Leicester and Nottingham. It had started to rain and this was so unpleasant in their windscreen-less car that they pulled over for an hour to let the worst of it past.

Jake was increasingly worried, though he said nothing to the women. He had the feeling it wouldn't be easy, getting through the wire to the world north of them, where comparative normality still ruled.

In the late afternoon it cleared, becoming mild and sunny. Jake's spirits rose. They were getting close.

The tank coming down the motorway saw them and immediately crossed the central reservation, crashing over the barrier, so that it was on the northbound carriageway, facing them.

Jake was driving. They took turns because their hands became so cold. He slowed as the distance between them closed.

'They are our friends,' said Lana. 'It's the army. We have nothing to fear.'

'If it is the army,' said Peta.

'I don't feel like arguing.' Jake had almost stopped. The tank lumbered towards them. Then it stopped too.

A megaphoned voice roared over them. 'Leave the car. Get out of the car.'

Lana put her hand on the door. 'No,' said Jake. He was trembling. He opened his door and half got out of the car. 'We're heading for the wire,' he shouted.

There was a long silence. Their engine burbled. The car was very low on petrol.

'Leave the car,' the voice said. 'Cars are not allowed.'

'All right,' shouted Jake. He ducked back in. He slid the

car into first and revved gently.

'Jake!' cried Lana.

The car spun round in a tight circle as fast as Jake could make it. He gunned away back down the road, weaving from side to side so that the girls crashed about in the car.

Five seconds later the road to their right exploded. The car rocked and juddered. Jake pushed it through the debris and smoke. He put the vehicle into a tight arc again. This time they were leaving the motorway. They roared up the slip road leading to the roundabout at the top.

There was no choice. If they crossed the motorway to head east, the tank could get them on the bridge. They turned west to Chesterfield.

The red fuel warning light was on all the time now. Jake turned off the A-road they were on, so that they faced north again. North to Sheffield, Yorkshire and the wire. Safety. Only he wasn't so sure now. His guts were telling him something very bad.

They drove gently for some time on B-roads. For the first time they saw people. They were men, trudging along at the side of the road with packs on their backs or even suitcases in their hands. For a moment Jake thought they were tramps, in ones and twos, in small companies. Then he realised they were refugees.

They were heading for the wire.

Ten miles up the road the petrol gave out and the engine ceased. Jake didn't know precisely how far they had to go. Twenty to forty miles was his best guess. An hour at the most in a car.

Now it was a day, two days. Maybe even three. And the countryside didn't feel safe at all.

They took food and a change of clothing and such waterproofing as they had. Neither of the women wore shoes suitable for tramping, though both wore low heels. Even

Jake's handmade loafers were hardly suitable for a forced march. He took the car rug because he thought the coming night might be bad, he didn't know what shelter they might get. And they took three rifles, leaving two behind. They took all the ammunition and the three of them made sure they could change the magazines on the rifles. Each still held four or five bullets.

Lana said: 'Why so much caution? What have we to fear? People won't want to harm us.'

'I think they might.' Jake was grim. 'You might say there is a power vacuum here now. The police, the army are useless. The whole distribution network has stopped. People will be cold, hungry and afraid. I think they will gather themselves into groups and seek to protect themselves. Everyone will be the enemy unless he proves differently.'

'And the touched?' asked Peta. She didn't speak much. When she wasn't driving she seemed to drift into a unpleasant doze. Her skin was greyish and unhealthy and she sweated slightly. She twitched. She hadn't said if she had run out of stuff but Jake reckoned she hadn't. She was making it last.

'I don't know.' Jake looked round them, worried. 'It isn't like the towns here. I don't understand what's been going on. I suspect we won't like it when we find out.'

They walked along the road in single file, each lost in thought. The countryside seemed vast and quiet. Once, far in the distance, they heard an engine. They decided it was a helicopter.

They rounded a corner and saw a village ahead of them. Vehicles were pulled across the road. As they slowed and hesitated, heads appeared.

A big man stood up on the roof of a post office van. He held a shotgun.

'What d'you want?' he bellowed.

179

'To go north,' said Jake. Peta and Lana came in behind him.

'To the wire?'

'Maybe.'

The big man laughed. He wore a miner's hat. 'They won't let you through,' he shouted.

'Why not?'

'Quarantine camps. And no women.'

It made sense. Jake felt sick inside. He had known something was going to go wrong for some time.

'They aren't touched,' he yelled.

'So you say. We'll take the old an' we'll take kids and we'll take men who promise to do as we say. But we won't take the women. You get me?'

'They aren't touched.' Jake was desperate.

'And we won't be. You tell 'em to keep off. We'll shoot if we have to. As for you, it's up to you. You can come inside or stay out, it makes no difference to us. But you can't have them. They come nowhere near. We got some clean women here and they'll stay that way. Make your mind up, mister. Make it up now.'

They took to the fields. There was nowhere else to go. Now their travelling was really slow.

They heard noise ahead of them. It came on the wind like the cackling of geese. Indeed, Jake looked up at the sky, it was the right time of year, but the skies were empty of everything except some small white clouds. The afternoon was very mild.

They became cautious. The noise was altogether wrong. They had topped a small hill and were dropping across a large field to a line of trees. They entered the wood on a path and kept close together, Jake leading, their guns held up.

Very slowly Jake approached the last trees. It was the thinnest of woods, barely a dozen trees wide.

They stopped. A thicket of holly edged the wood. They eased themselves sideways away from the path till they could stand by the large trunks of tall trees. They looked out at the scene before them.

A wide shallow valley dropped from the wood, flattening in the far distance into indeterminate countryside scattered with villages and farms. A large city could be seen on the horizon. The whole scene was dull and quiet, the grass faded and the trees dulled and thinned by the advance of autumn. Yet near at hand all was lively and animated.

It had something of the air of a Brueghel peasant canvas. A large mass of people were engaged in lively activity together on the shallow hillside before them. Their cheerful shrieks and shouts carried on the still air.

Jake stood quietly watching, his senses alert.

They were playing. Indeed, their activity could be described as cavorting. Jake would not have been surprised to see the hillside ringed with little red figures with forked tails and horns. There was something medieval about the gross carnal indulgence displayed before him. It was so hearty, so abandoned. The players were wholly given over to their lewd practices and nothing else held sway with them.

Men were going about on all fours licking women. They licked where they could, at hanging breasts, at naked rumps, at oozing underparts. Women grappled with each other and fought to get the erect sexual organs of men into their bodies, pulling at each other and at the men in the process. Some women stuffed their mouths with cock, as many as they could get in, so that groups of up to three men were jerking obscenely into one woman's mouth. Hands played among their thighs, clutching at their testicles, urging them on.

Other women tried to get two men to fuck them simultaneously. Some tried in vain to stuff two cocks into one cunt, almost breaking their legs in the process. Others, with more self-control and sophistication, or perhaps with more imagination, got one man to fill their rear while another stuffed their cunt.

A man was busy in a woman, with another woman licking and feeling his rear. In her turn she was poked by a kneeling man whose hips jerked rapidly to and fro. His head was thrown right back because a women stood astride him so that as he rogered the one, he sucked another. The standing woman being sucked had her hands in the groin of another man who was trying to escape so he could get himself and his urgent sex inside another woman.

Like vast balls of writhing pink worms, ejaculating humans rolled in mass congress. Between and among these squirming bundles of copulating humanity ran others, screaming and whooping. A woman knelt on all fours and gave support to another women bent back over her. A man shafted the bent back woman whose arms waved wildly in the air. Another man fumbled her breasts, bending to kiss them. Another man crawled under the woman kneeling on all fours and began to lap her sex.

Men ringed a single woman lying writhing on the ground as if maddened by her driving need for constant sex. They pumped their hips, each one with a woman attached masturbating him, and as they came they jetted through the air to almost smother the writhing woman on the ground. People fell on her, of both sexes, and licked and slobbered over her body, entering it and kissing it so that she disappeared under the throng at her, using her in the unending need to satisfy themselves.

Women knelt masturbating men so that they shot into their open mouths. Some women were so besotted as to try and prod men, entering their rears and ravishing them even as they fucked into another woman. Some women seemed to have lost track of their own sex, as had some men. Men copulated with men in a strange reversal, a woman kneeling to take the cock of the front man whilst another man took his rear. Men placed their cocks into women's breasts and rolled and masturbated them there. Women wrapped their hair around men and abraded their sexual organs into climax, licking them clean afterwards. Women lay furled together, frantically mouthing themselves whilst men came at them from behind and fucked. And fucked.

Like maggots they heaved and rolled and separated and reformed, slobbering, licking, penetrating, climaxing, soaked in every visible manifestation of sexual juice, of sexual frenzy. They sucked orgasms from each other by mouth and penis and pussy and arse. No human orifice, no human projection, was ignored. Everything that could stroke and masturbate and penetrate and caress and engulf, everything was employed in the total abandonment to copulatory excess.

Jake turned away and stared unseeingly back through the thin grove of trees. He stumbled slightly and looked up. Peta stood before him. With an animal cry Jake threw himself on her, tearing her clothes off.

For a moment she was frozen, unyielding. Then, she too was tearing her clothes off. Her teeth were bared in a snarl of desperation. Lana was there, stripping also. With a sob of relief Jake got his hot hard cock deep into Peta. He began to fuck her in a frenzy, as if at any moment they would be ripped apart. He groaned and shouted as he fucked. Lana stood staring for a moment. Then she threw herself down and stabbed a finger into Jake.

He screamed briefly as the digit raped his arse. Then he fucked harder into Peta. One hand groped out till he could catch a swinging breast. It was Lana's. He tried to feed the nipple into his mouth. Peta was almost lifting them off the ground as she thrust up hard to meet Jake's blows. Jake

183

climaxed and fell out of her. His spunk trickled after him. Immediately Lana was on him, licking his cock to clean it of Peta and to bring him back to immediate erection. Seconds later he was in her, on his back this time as she rode him like a horse. Peta bent over his face kissing him and caressing him, swinging her breasts across him as Lana took him again to climax.

They huddled in a barn. A thin rain fell. It had started with the dark and seemed set for the night. They had no hot food or drink and managed as best they could.

'I'm sorry, Peta,' said Jake eventually. 'I think the smell of them must have been carried on the air. Like spores. Because there were so many of them.'

Peta said: 'I don't like men. I earn my living by sex with men and I hate it. I hate sex. All I love in life is heroin, my sweetheart, my lover, my friend.'

'It'll kill you,' said Lana morosely.

'I welcome Death. He is my friend also,' said Peta. 'I can be happy with Death.'

She was silent for a moment. 'But I wanted you too, Jake, when you fell on me. I wanted you in my body and it was good, very good.'

Jake looked at her. They were in the dark and he couldn't see her face or expression. She would hardly be saying what she said as a sop to his male ego. She had shown no signs of wanting to please him. It had to be the truth.

'You were immune in London, ' he said. 'Perhaps it's a threshold thing. We were exposed to a particularly intense sample this afternoon.'

'Perhaps I'm using too little dope to protect me,' said Peta. 'Now there's an irony.'

'Am I now infected?' Lana's voice was sweet and low.

'No,' said Jake. 'You'd be at it all the time. Well, every

couple of hours, anyway. You've gone back to normal, though, so you must be OK. Not a big enough dose.'

'Too big for me and not enough for her?' asked Peta mockingly. 'Come now, Mr Scientist, That ain't so rational.'

'I don't know.' Jake was weary. And afraid.

'How do you know so much about it?' asked Lana.

'How do you think?' hissed Jake, 'I was shut in that damned cellar with one. I knew everything there was to know about how it took her. I can assure you, you aren't infected, either of you. I wouldn't be in one piece at the moment if you were, and you wouldn't be cold. Remember? They don't feel the cold.'

I certainly do,' grumbled Lana and she cuddled closer to Jake.

They had one blanket. The three of them held together as tightly as they could with some comfort, and they tried to sleep.

Sometime in the night Jake woke., His dreams were fitful and troubled. He kept imagining things, hearing things.

He wanted a drink. Something short and strong. He lay trying not to move and disturb the women. Their shoes were almost shot. He had been a fool not to get some before they left London where stealing them would have been easy. Neither of the women complained, but then, they weren't complainers. He grunted softly to himself. A man could do worse for company on a trip of this sort. But he wished they were safe. Especially Lana, however unfair this wish was. She was a woman who deserved luxury, the soft things in life, and he, Jake, would adore to give them to her.

Life didn't pan out how you wanted.

Now he could hear something. An undefinable noise. Getting closer. One of the women stirred.

'Lana?'

'It's Peta.'

'Can you hear it?'

'Yes. Do you know what it is?'

'No. I guess I'd better go look see.'

'Jake.' This was Lana.

'Yes?'

'Careful, darling.'

Bless her for that, thought Jake, blundering clumsily towards the barn doors. They had pulled them to after breaking the lock on them.

He eased them slightly open and peered out. The rain had stopped and behind thin cloud a moon dropped dim light over the hidden landscape.

His noise picked up a scent. Acrid. Sour. His eyes adjusted. The noise was coming closer. It was like this afternoon. It was the noise of a holiday crowd.

They were coming this way.

'Grab everything,' he said hoarsely. 'They're coming. We have to keep clear. They're all infected.'

The girls scrabbled in the dark to collect their meagre possessions. Jake ran back to them, slinging the guns over his shoulder. They were useless in this situation, of course. Apart from the fact that he would be unable to shoot the women, he didn't think the threat of gunfire would stop them. They were beyond fear, beyond reason.

Urgently they collected their gear. Lana limped over to the barn doors.

'Jake!' Her voice was high with fear.

'What is it?'

'They have torches. They're burning.'

He had forgotten the compulsion to fire. Now his forgetfulness might kill them. There was smoke at the barn-end. Some of the women must have been in the lead, quieter than the bulk of their sisters.

'They're here,' said Lana. She shut the barn doors and put her back to them.

The barn-end crackled. A flame, pretty as sin, climbed the musty wooden wall.

'Oh Christ,' sobbed Jake. Outside were hundreds of sex-crazed infected women, surrounding them, waiting to contaminate Peta and his beloved Lana. Waiting to force his manhood into their service.

Inside was the other enemy.

Fire.

Eight

'Peta.'

'Yes?'

They crouched together, the three of them, in the centre of the cleared area. One end of the barn burned strongly and the smoke was choking. At the moment the draught from the main doors kept their air fairly clear.

'Have you any methadone left?'

'Yes.'

'Come on. You know the safe dose. We all have to have it.'

'You don't know it works. You only guessed it made me immune.'

'And the bitches in the cellar who held me. And the thugs who blocked us at Watford. Come on. Quick. I swear I'll get you some more. I'm a biochemist, for Christ's sake.'

Peta fumbled with her clothes. In the leaping firelight Jake could see her eyes were hard and glittering. This was costing her, handing over her future.

The three of them took what she offered. They held each other, waiting as long as they dared to give it a chance to take effect.

Outside the women bayed, maddened and excited by the flames. Despite the heat Jake found himself trembling. He did not want to fall into their clutches. He did not want to end his days fucking himself to death among touched and frenzied women.

A great gout of flame shot upwards and timbers ominously creaked.

'Oh God,' sobbed Jake and the three of them stood, coughing, and made their way to the doors. Jake eased them open. Perhaps the women had passed on and were gone from this dreadful place.

He saw the ring of firelit faces. A great cry went up. They had not known anyone was in the barn. Their compulsion was to burn, not to murder.

'A man,' someone said. Another laughed. The laughter grew and swelled. The ring began to advance.

Jake felt dizzy. The fire beat warmly at his back. Lana and Peta were there.

'Sisters,' cried a joyful voice.

Jake gathered himself. 'Let us pass,' he bellowed. 'We are not for you.'

'Join us. Join us. Join us.' It went round them like a whisper, like a breeze moving through a wood.

'Let us pass.'

Behind Jake something fell from the roof. With a tremendous crackling roar the flames leapt into the night. Sparks flew upwards on the hot air. The women sighed happily.

Jake held Lana and Peta and began to edge sideways.

'You cannot escape us.'

A woman had come forward. She was tall and strong. Down her body, from one shoulder, over one breast, to one side of her stomach and down one leg was a blue painted line. Her breasts were firm, even beautiful in the dancing light. The red glow lit sparks in her eyes. Her hair was wild and tossed. The firelight suited her. She looked bold and fine.

'You cannot escape us,' she repeated.

'You cannot infect us,' said Jake. 'We cannot be touched. See?' He let go of Peta and Lana and gestured them forward.

One either side of him, fully dressed, they stood so that they could be seen.

'Is this your man?' asked the blue-painted woman. Jake saw now that the other women had blue lines on them too, but shorter than the one who addressed them.

'We are equal companions.' Peta was surly. 'Now let us pass.'

'Touch him. Touch them. Touch them,' whispered the crowd.

The woman came forward. Jake went to meet her, his bundles swinging, the guns clanking on his shoulder. He felt stirred and aroused. He felt a strange compulsion in himself. The fire roared upwards madly at his back. The flames lit the magnificent creature in front of him with a leaping dangerous light. It would be wonderful to concede, to relax, to submit. She was worth it. The power here in the women and in the flames was more than any puny thing he was capable of. It would be good to acknowledge that. It would be good to worship her and be her favoured creature.

She reached out with her hands. She was smiling. Her hands invited. She offered all three of them a place in the new order of things.

Jake took her hands and held them, looking into her face. His hands tingled. His groin stirred. He let go and stood back, smiling. Now Peta and Lana stood forward in their turn. Each took one of the women's hands and held it. Then they released her.

'You see,' said Jake gently, speaking directly to her. 'Let us pass. We are not for you but we wish you no harm.'

She stood back, confused. The women started to murmur. The barn crackled and spat flames. Jake held hands with Lana and Peta and moved to one side. The crowd parted reluctantly, looking to their leader for guidance. She gave them none, thoughtfully watching the three she wanted.

'Can you run?' Jake's body was willing, though his spirit was weak.

'You bet,' said Lana.

And they ran.

It was a terrible night. The rain came on again and they became cold and wet. They had to skirt another barricaded village and Jake lost his sense of direction. They blundered about looking for shelter, somewhere to huddle together for rest and warmth, and finally they broke into a caravan parked in a layby. It had served as a fish and chip van. Inside it stank cloyingly of old oil and stale food. It was the best they could do.

'We survived,' said Jake. He had a feeling things were worse than he realised. The methadone worked in him.

'We aren't infected,' said Lana. She leant her head on his shoulder.

'Did you get a tickle?' asked Peta.

'More than a tickle,' admitted Jake. 'But controllable.'

'Me too.'

'And me.'

'We have to get through the wire,' said Jake. 'We know things. We can help.'

All the next day they tramped north across fields, sometimes along roads, but having to avoid villages. They had one excellent piece of luck. They came across a deserted village. Jake reckoned it worth the effort to ransack it. They managed to find two pairs of discarded shoes that roughly fitted the two women. Extra socks helped.

They were frightened of being caught again by marauding bands of women but they took time to wash in an empty house and rest. Each took turns to stand guard. It all used valuable hours but already Jake's sense of passing time was changing as he adjusted to a more primitive time-scale. London to Sheffield – a matter of a few hours in the old days. Now they spent days.

All the food was gone except for some garden produce ripening in the ground. They broke wood and built a fire, heating water and boiling some potatoes. They found tea and brewed it. The hot food heartened them. Their own had nearly run out.

Jake's shoes were sodden and useless. He too found better footwear. They went on having lost half a day but in considerably better heart.

That afternoon they had their first glimpse of the wire.

Sheffield lay to the west of them. Across the countryside the double fence marched. Jake could see no guards and his spirits rose. It wasn't very high. They could climb it. If it was electrified he reckoned he could deal with it.

Later he was puzzled. It looked too easy. Why hadn't the refugees from the beleaguered south flooded over it?

Perhaps they had. Men weren't the problem, after all. Perhaps they guarded it somewhere to the north that he couldn't see.

Perhaps it had been a first defence and was now abandoned. This was a terrible thought. Had they made all this journey, expecting to find friends and comfort and order and government, only to find the mayhem had preceded them?

Perhaps the women didn't want to cross it. Perhaps they were happy with the way things were. They showed little sign of active malevolence, after all. They just wanted to indulge their compulsions and while there were men and buildings enough, the one to fuck and the other to fire, they were content.

They kept away from the roads now. Slowly they came up to the wire.

It had been run up hastily. It was not electrified. The two parallel fences were a hundred yards apart. Now Jake knew why he could see no guards. Now he knew why the fence wasn't especially high, nor was it of razor wire.

It didn't need to be. The gap between the fences was mined. There was no way they could cross it. Signs every hundred yards were pinned to the fence warning them. Jake believed them. Anyhow, there was no way he would take the risk.

Wearily they turned and began to walk west. They knew they would arrive somewhere eventually. And they did.

The checkpoint was hard to see for the crowds. There were tents and latrines and food distribution points all making up the large and busy camp. Red Cross officials worked. The army patrolled the perimeters.

This was how the men went north. This was the filtering process in action. There wasn't a woman in sight.

When Jake was first spotted, men took one look at his companions and then fled to warn the authorities. An army jeep arrived next, the soldiers wearing all-over suits and carrying guns.

'Hand over the weaponry, sonny, and wave goodbye to the ladies,' Jake was instructed.

'They're clean.' Jake was so tired he didn't know what to do. He reckoned it was the after effects of the methadone he had taken.

'So you say. It's them or us. Make your choice.'

'Perhaps if you went ahead and explained,' said Lana. 'We could wait here.'

Jake looked into her white exhausted face. Her beauty shone pale and translucent like fine china. She looked as fragile as china too. She needed safety. He couldn't leave her.

Peta was fighting her private war, her eyes dull, her skin

sagging, sweat putting a sheen on her greasy skin. It was a hell of a way to cold turkey.

Jake put the rifles down. 'I'm a biochemist,' he explained. 'I need to reach the authorities. I have urgent information to pass over that might help sort all this out. These two women bear witness to the fact that I have a cure. A defence. They are not infected and will harm no one. See, I am not touched.'

'The ladies stay away. You can come. You wait your turn, though. Everyone thinks he's special. Everyone wants to get through quick. They all have different stories. It takes a week, OK? You'll be in the camp about a week at the present rate. There's a backlog, see. But the ladies go away.'

Jake bent down. He picked up the rifles. He turned his back on the camp, on the jeep, and began to walk away. Lana and Peta trailed after him.

He looked back only once. The soldiers were lined kneeling on the ground. Every gun was raised to shoulder level, pointing at him and his two companions.

They held a council of war. 'You have to go through,' said Lana. 'We'll wait here until you can persuade someone it's safe for us to come over.'

'You have no food,' said Jake. 'Eventually the women will find you. Peta will run out of stuff and you'll be touched. That'll be the end of it. I'll never be able to find you then. You won't care about me or anything. You'll go about the countryside with no clothes on getting every man you can to poke you. Then you'll set light to things.' He stared at her angrily. 'So get this now. I am not going to leave you here. OK?'

'Can you phone somebody and explain,' said Peta.

Jake stared at her. Since the power cuts had started he had never thought about the phone. But many exchanges, most exchanges were automated. The phones might well still be working, especially this close to civilisation.

Who could he phone? Before starting his business he had worked in cryogenics research in the south of England. Colleagues had come north, though. Who did he know? Who might understand what he said, accept his expertise? Who might listen to him?

Pete. Pete had got a job at Manchester University after Jake's business folded.

Jake barely knew what day it was. It could be a weekend. However, he doubted things were as regular as they used to be north of the wire. It was worth a try.

They found a small hut in some woods. They were on an estate of sorts with parkland around them. Jake left the women there, taking with him a rifle and ammunition and all the money they had. He even had a phone card in his wallet.

He might be caught by women and used to serve them, but he might escape. The infection was local and temporary for him, not the final catastrophe it was to the women. He hoped not only to phone, but also to bring back food.

It was late afternoon. He headed for the big house at the top of the rise. Perhaps it had its phones on.

As he came onto the terrace searching for signs of life in what could only be described as a manor house, a window opened upstairs. Jake looked up and prepared to shout.

He never had the chance. The muzzle of a double-barrelled shotgun stuck out and they shot at him.

Jake ran, conscious of the pain in his shoulder. Another shot was let off at him but this one missed completely. When he was a fair way down the main drive he stopped to inspect the damage.

His shoulder was torn and bloodied, but it didn't look serious. He didn't think much shot was in him, if any. But it hurt to damnation.

He walked wearily now, the responsibility for the women heavy on him. He came to the lodge house.

It was boarded up but Jake saw that phone lines ran to it. It seemed a hopeless chance but he was willing to try anything. He smashed his way in at the back and began to scout round.

There was no food of any description. Jake picked up the phone.

He had never in his life heard such a reassuring, such a welcome noise. The familiar sound was pure music to his ears. He nearly wept with gratitude. There was even a phone book.

It took two hours and seven phone calls. He waited, cold and alone, for people to get back to him. He took this time to read more of Sonia Lafferty's diary which he had carried in his pocket all this while. He had an urge for masochism. It distressed him almost unendurably that he could escape north but Lana and Peta couldn't.

He tried numbers he had been given again and again. When Pete finally came on the line, Jake could hardly believe it.

'Are you south of the wire still?' demanded Pete once he realised properly who Jake was.

'Yes. I'm in a bad way, Pete. I'm near a checkpoint, it's on the A631 near Maltby, but I can't get across.'

'Why not? I thought you just waited till they gave you papers and then you could enter New Britain.'

Jake let this chilling nomenclature pass him by. 'Yeah. That's right. It takes a week at the moment, they told me. The problem is I have two women with me.'

'Oh come on, Jake. You're not serious.'

'I am. I can't leave them. They aren't infected. I have to get them across.'

'I can't help you, mate. What you ask is absolutely impossible. You might as well have carried a rabid fox through customs in the old days. No amount of shouting will get them across.'

'They can go into quarantine. It doesn't matter. They're exhausted and hungry and would welcome the rest. But they have to come with me, Pete. They are clean for a reason. We know how to stop the infection. It works for them and for me.'

'So tell me.'

'No.'

'Why not, Jake?'

'It's my entrance ticket. You know my pedigree. You know my expertise, You know my character. This is no bullshit, Pete. I don't know what the hell your crowd in the north have come up with, but I know how to make men and women immune.'

'So why can't you leave the women safely there, come across and tell us all, and then go back triumphant?'

'Because it requires a certain medication I only have in very short supply.'

'It's not a permanent cure.'

'Not so far. You have to take it, then contact is safe until it wears off.'

'Orally? Injecting? Inhaling? The bloodstream? How's it work, Jake? Convince me.'

Jake swallowed. 'Do you know anyone working on the problem?'

'Don't be fucking stupid. Every chemist north of the wire is working on it. Of course I'm working on it.'

'Right. Stop me when I get it wrong. It's a contact infection temporary for men who have to be in its immediate presence, permanent for women. For men it's purely sexual. For women it alters the metabolism enough for them to go unclothed. They also suffer under a compulsion to light fires after sexual congress. It's airborne, but it can't travel far. It must degrade on contact with air. It smells sour-spicy. It affects only sexually-reproductive women and men, though for men that stretches at least into late middle-age. For women it stops at menopause.

'Go on,' said Pete softly.

'Women appear very healthy on it, though I've heard rumours of sleepers. I haven't come across this myself. It makes men feel great, being under its influence.'

'Have you been under its influence?'

'Yes. I felt I could outrun my strength. Even when I got dizzy with hunger I felt marvellous if an infected woman was by me.'

'Well, I'll tell you this. The Yanks took an infected planeload from us but got them into quarantine. They've been extensively studied. Get this, Jake. No illness. None at all. Three of the passengers had cancer. One had multiple sclerosis. Fifteen had heart conditions of varying seriousness. Twenty suffered from common allergies, either asthma, or skin allergies or hay fever, that sort of thing. Right. Get this. All symptoms have disappeared. Totally. As if they never existed. They have perfect blood, perfect bodily functions, organs in perfect condition. Ageing is reversed, they think, though they haven't had enough time yet to confirm this. There are signs of hair regaining its colour, of new hair growth for the bald. And though the males' sperm counts are very high, not one of the ladies is pregnant.'

'Jesus,' said Jake. 'If we can isolate what makes the feel-good and health factor but tone down the sex and get rid of the burning, we could revolutionise the human race.'

'Meantime the damned country goes up in flames. Look, Jake, don't play games. What is it you have? A hormone therapy? We can't get any luck at all.'

'Nope,' said Jake steadily. 'I don't have a cure, but I have a simple means to provide temporary immunity that is harmless in itself and likely to be a fruitful avenue of research. You wouldn't have to suit up or wear gas masks or anything. You could walk among the touched and be safe. Hands-on contact, the whole thing. I've used it, my two ladies have used it, and we are all OK. I can resist and the women aren't infected.'

'Where are you?' asked Pete. 'I'll have to see what I can do.'

'I'll phone you again tomorrow. I'm not having myself snatched and forced to leave the women behind. I'm armed, Pete, and I swear I'll shoot if need be. They will submit to any sort of restriction after they are north of the wire, we all understand your fears. God knows, we've been living with them for days. It feels like weeks, I can hardly keep track of time. But they've saved my life and I'm going to save them from the degradation of becoming one of the touched. I mean that wholeheartedly. I don't care if the whole damn country goes down the tubes. They come out with me, or what I know stays locked inside my head.'

'OK. I get the message. You always were a passionate bastard, Jake. What's your phone number? I'll call as soon as I can.'

'I'll phone your number tomorrow. Don't let me down. I know you'll have everything set up to trace the call. All I want to do is come over and help. But the ladies come too.'

'It's been great chewing the fat, Jake.'

'Yeah. We must meet for a drink sometime.'

Jake fetched Lana and Peta and brought them to the lodge. It was set up a short drive from the road, only a matter of a hundred yards but enough, he thought, to offer some protection. Men went by from time to time, heading for the wire and eventual safety.

The manor house was out of sight up its long driveway lined with lime trees. As the women came tiredly into the lodge Jake gave them the good news.'

'There's a kitchen garden.'

'A what?' Both women were exhausted. Jake had been grateful to find them asleep in the shed. If they had had more strength he reckoned they might have run off, leaving him free to cross with a clear conscience.

'A vegetable garden. We're such a bunch of townees we never thought. Autumn, season of something something and mellow fruitfulness. Well, we've got spuds and turnips and beans and cabbages and sprouts . . .'

'I thought I hated sprouts,' said Peta. 'Now I love the very sound. Sprouts. Sprouts. It's kind of poetic when you think about it.'

Jake laughed. No one had made a joke in a long time.

'What's a turnip?' asked Lana. 'Is it anything like a steak?'

There was a solid fuel range in the kitchen and they lit it with some difficulty, none of them having any experience in such things. Then they cooked.

The food was hot and though they all missed the meat they craved and the salt, it was very good. They ate till they could eat no more. They all believed they were close to crossing the wire.

Before they slept Jake reread some of Sonia's diary. He had learnt to ignore the grotesque and embarrassing references to himself. There were clues here, he thought. In that latter period before the explosion Sonia had had certain experiences, conducted certain experiments, that threw a light on subsequent events. It wanted thinking about.

There were things he hadn't thought about, though. He hadn't given his phone number to Pete, but he had given it to various secretaries and switchboard operatives before that. Pete was no slouch either. So they came in the night.

Peta woke Jake. He and Lana, partly dressed against the cold and the damp beds, were huddled together in a bedroom. Peta had elected to stay downstairs near the smouldering range.

'What is it?'

'I can hear engines.'

Jake sat up. Beside him Lana stirred and woke. Peta went over to the window. The upstairs ones weren't boarded. 'I can see headlights,' she said.

It fell into Jake's mind like a stone. Of course. Of course they could trace him. He had even told Pete the area they were in.

'Get ready,' he said roughly. 'We go together or not at all. Give me the guns.'

He ran downstairs pulling his top clothes together. He put all three rifles over his lap as he settled in the kitchen. The girls wouldn't shoot. It was pointless them being armed. He didn't want it on their consciences either.

He heard the engines come closer and stop. They throbbed dully. Not a tank, he thought. Jeeps maybe.

He heard a megaphoned voice. 'Dr Connors. We're coming in. We are from New Britain, north of the wire.'

Jake backed against a wall as the voice spoke on. He ignored it. They would be seeking a way in as he listened.

The boards on the window beside him exploded inwards, the wood ripping into splinters. Immediately, so immediately it seemed one with the breaking wood, a balled figure dived into the room. As it uncurled the muzzles of two automatic rifles were thrust through the ruptured space.

'Stand still and you won't be hurt. Stand still and you won't be hurt.'

But Jake was across the floor and had his own rifle hard against the neck of the figure on the floor.

The man wore an all-over body suit and this had slowed him down. Now he lay quietly, feeling the gun at his neck. A two-two bullet can penetrate inch thick wood at a mile. It would have no trouble penetrating his protective clothing.

'Now,' he said, striving to keep his voice calm. 'Let's stop the schoolboy stuff, huh? I am not a military operation. Come in the door like civilised people and we'll talk about this.'

'Put the gun down, Dr Connors. We have no intention of hurting you.'

'I'm not questioning your intentions, soldier. It's your actions I go by. Now, get away from the window, it makes me feel nervous. Go round to the door and come in.'

The man flat on the floor kept very still. His palms were open and resting on the floor. Jake saw he could spring up at any moment.

His shoulder nagged. He was tired. He could have wept to be given a cup of coffee.

Two men entered the doorway. They were both fully suited and neither carried guns in any obvious way.

Jake was kneeling, pressing his barrel hard against his hostage's neck. 'I resent this,' he said, his voice hissing with anger. 'I resent you forcing me to do this. You bastards, playing your stupid games. I can help, I want to help, and you make me the enemy. You make me a terrorist.'

'We've been told you are an important man. We can do this quite differently. But you have to let my man go.'

'The ladies go with me. I don't go without them.'

'We can discuss that.'

'There's no discussion. Stand still!'

He heard Lana and Peta enter the room. All the men stiffened. 'Watch the window,' commanded Jake without taking his eyes off the man at his feet and the two men in the door. 'They'll distract us and come from another direction.'

'OK,' said Peta in a low voice. 'Point taken.'

'Come here, Lana,' said Jake.

'I'm here.' Her voice was soft and husky.

'Take my knife.'

'Yes, Jake.'

'Cut into this man's suit.'

'No.' It was the spokesman at the door. 'Don't do that.'

'I'm going to damn well prove to you these women are

harmless. Now, Lana. Split his suit.'

Jake stood up, careful to keep the rifle pressed hard into the man's neck. Lana struggled briefly and then managed to penetrate the strong suit. She hacked a jagged tear into it.

'I'll get you for this,' said the other man at the door. 'You bastard.'

'Put you hands in, Lana. Touch him good.'

She did so.

'Now swap with Peta. Watch the window, not us.'

Peta too touched the man through his suit.

'Now,' said Jake. He backed slightly. 'You can get up. And you can take your suit off.'

The strange unhuman figure got slowly to its feet. The suit was all over green. He looked like a baggy soft insect, perhaps a gelatinous sea thing. It was the parody of the human head that was so insect-like. It turned and looked at Jake.

'You have no urge to hump them, do you?' he asked softly. 'You're angry and a little scared and you'd like to throttle me. But you aren't sex-crazed. You don't want to rip off your suit and shove yourself into every pussy for miles. That's what it's like, you know. I know. I've been there. The whole thing. But you don't feel like that at all.'

Slowly the man raised a hand. He released something at his neck. He began to split the helmet from the neck of the suit. Now the seal was broken it came apart with a tearing noise, like velcro.

The room was still. Jake had a moment to think on the fact that the girls had changed. Both were in their own clothes, what they had been wearing the day they went to his house so many days ago. He had seen them cleaning and trying to mend their own shoes last night. He had attached no significance to it.

They wanted to go north as women, dressed in decent

clothes, with some pride and dignity. He couldn't blame them for that. This was squalid, what was happening now.

The soldier looked at Jake, his face blank. His hair was mussed up, he had been wearing a balaclava under the helmet and he had removed this as well.

'How are you, Jenkins?' asked one of the men at the door.

'I think I'm all right, sir.'

'You don't feel strange in any way?'

'No, sir. As far as the ladies are concerned, I feel quite normal.'

The one addressed as sir stepped forward. Jake's gun was loose in his hand.

'Shall I take that now, Dr Connors? I'm Colonel Bullard, by the way.'

'No. Until we are all in the north, I don't trust you one inch.'

'That's a very unhelpful attitude. You can't be surprised that I don't want to put my men at risk.'

'You can't be surprised that I don't want to put two perfectly safe women at risk.'

'Touché. We have a test, Dr Connors. Would your lady friends be willing to submit to it?'

'What sort of a test?'

'Saliva sample. It takes about five minutes.'

'So why all this?' exploded Jake, 'If you knew you could test them, why treat us as criminals?'

'We aren't sure the test is one hundred per cent proof. Our researchers have had very little time to do any testing, Dr Connors. There have been no controlled field trials . . .'

'Right. I see. Sure. Do the tests. Is that OK, Lana, Peta?'

'Of course. We are as anxious as you to prove ourselves clean. Perhaps more anxious,' said Lana and smiled painfully.

'Now,' said Jake. 'Since I don't trust you at all, I will have the Colonel without his suit over here by me so I can point my nasty little gun at him. Jenkins can hop it, then, and pass the good news on the men outside that these women are completely harmless and also unarmed, and that their Colonel will get it in the knee if one of them feels like free-lancing to earn a little honour and glory.'

There was a silence. 'I really do feel fine, sir,' said Jenkins. Lana took his hand and smiled at him. He smiled back and then released himself. He walked over to his Colonel and saluted. Jake danced quickly sideways so that the body of the soldier did not obscure his aim at the officer.

The Colonel strolled forward. What it cost him, they never knew. He broke the neck seals of his suit and released the helmet. He stripped the entire suit off and was revealed as a smartly dressed officer in uniform.

Lana and Peta shook hands with him. He then walked over to Jake collecting a kitchen chair on the way. He reversed this and sat down astride it. Jake pointed his rifle at him.

A certain amount of activity went out outside. The Colonel lit a cigarette and offered the packet round. Peta took one with a trembling hand and sucked it eagerly.

'Do you have any coffee?' asked Jake suddenly.

'Do we, soldier?' asked the Colonel of one of his men now in the room.

'Yes, sir.'

Lana groaned. 'I could die for a cup of coffee.'

'And me,' said Jake.

Pete walked into the room. 'Jesus, Jake,' he said, looking round him.

'This was not the way,' said Jake softly.

'I got them here. I told them it was important. I'm on the line over this, Jake. So I couldn't control they way they chose to do it. They don't control my lab technique, Jake. It was their show.'

'Why are you here?'

'To confirm your identity. I can also run the test on the women.'

Lana and Peta sat down. Pete opened a small case he had with him. He took an oral scraping using a small wooden spatula. He then tested this in a pH meter.

'OK,' he announced. 'They're clean so far as the test goes.'

Lana stood up. She wore her own tight skirt that revealed her superb legs and her shapely hips. Over it she wore a buttoned to the neck tailored jacket. She wore stockings and the rather battered shoes she had worn that distant day. Her hair was glossy and shining. She had used cosmetics with subtlety. Her beauty was refined, sharpened by her hungry adventures, but it was very much there.

She was everything a woman should be. She was beautiful, bold, shapely and wise. Jake's heart went out to her, standing there in apparent peace. She was very brave, too.

And so was Peta, dammit, who had been breaking a heroin addiction ever since they came together. Not a whine out of her, not a squeak. A brave woman too, though an unhappy one.

They climbed into the jeeps. All the windows were tight closed, the doors locked. Sealant was sprayed round the interior afterwards. It smelt rubbery and unpleasant. Holding his coffee, wondering if it was drugged, Jake sat between Lana and Peta feeling the weakness steal over him. They were almost safe.

It was dawn. They were almost at the checkpoint when they ran into a marauding band of women.

The women surrounded them and began to beat on the jeeps, on the windows and the bonnets and the doors. There were maybe twenty of them. Colonel Bullard was in Jake's jeep. He spoke to the others and Jake saw the suited men emerge and physically pick the naked women from under the tyres.

It was grotesque. The women pressed their breasts against the windows at the men. They stroked themselves and preened so that the men could see. They opened their legs and caressed their own sex, pouting their lips and acting as if they would kiss the men. One of the women knelt down and kissed at another's sex, peeping round and smiling as if to invite the men to join her. They simulated sex, bumping at each other. One had a vibrator and she slid it into herself with the men watching. She began to writhe in a sexual dance as it took her, and all the time the men watched.

One even mounted the bonnet of the Colonel's jeep and lay on it, her head to the front, her open legs splayed. Through the windscreen they could all see. She held her vagina open. The cushioned pink flesh was fruity and glistening. It steamed slightly in the cool air. Another woman leant from the side and slid a finger into the pouting sex. She began to frig her friend.

Jake was aware of the restlessness and discomfort of the men in the jeep. They must all have escaped before the touching was widespread. None of them, unlike himself, had actually coped sexually with the ferocious demands of the frenzied women. It was still the stuff of fantasy, total sexual abandonment.

The women were sexy. There was no doubt about it. It was gross. It was extreme. There was nothing of subtlety or delicacy about it. But it was a garden of carnal delights, an invitation to indulge in the far reaches of passion and excess.

The men weren't being infected, either. This was the plain and ordinary sex factor at work. Healthy men like sex. They like to fuck. These women offered unlimited opportunities to do just that.

They got going at last with considerable difficulty. Tear

gas had to be used and Jake turned away from the awful sight. He heard a small noise from Lana.

'What is it?' he said softly. She had a tear in the corner of her eye.

'Those women. Those poor women. I might have been one of them. Jake.'

'It's all right, darling. Everything's all right now. We might be separated for a while in the north, but not for long, I swear it.'

'That's good.' She rested her head on his shoulder.

'As long as you want me, I'll be around.'

'That's very good, Jake. But I warn you, it might be a long time.'

The moment they drove through the wire was one of deep satisfaction to Jake. He had done it. He had brought himself and his to safety.

The new day brought a new set of problems plus the realisation of how desperate things were. Pete had been allocated, there was no other word for it, two rooms and a bathroom that were the property of the University of Manchester. The powers that be had evidently decided that the two men should stay together for the time being, so Jake moved in to this midget apartment. Housing was at a premium. The population of the south in large part was flowing steadily north. Temporary housing, billeting, even tent cities were part of the new order. Winter was coming, everyone knew. They had to have this sorted out within a month, and the problem kept expanding as men were allowed through the wire.

Pete explained. 'They are bastards enough to leave the men south,' he said cheerfully. 'The politicians, I mean. But the long-term strategy is to get the infected women isolated and then gradually retake the south, squeezing and squeezing the women into less and less land. So it actually suits the government to do the moral thing. Sorting the sheep from the goats, we call it.'

Jake was tired and part of his mind worried about Lana and Peta, especially Lana. They had been taken to a quarantine centre. But his ignorance sat heavy as sin on his shoulders. He desperately needed to know.

There was radio and television news. There were power cuts but they were organised on a rota. It was simply that the power demands on the increasingly crowded north could not be catered for all at once and so power was rationed. The university had continuous electricity, though, because of its status as a research organisation. Nothing was being spared in the need to find out what had gone wrong and how they could end it.

Everything was rationed. Jake had already been issued with temporary documentation validating his residence in New Britain, and a book of food coupons. There was still plenty of food but it was felt that people should get used to rationing before real shortages started and panic was allowed in. Mercy flights of food were made south, too, though the infected women hardly seemed to eat. There were still elderly people south, some children, and the men.

Petrol was rationed. Power was rationed. Space was rationed. But the society was working. Everyone had work to do. Only a little cash was paid out but a voucher system to complement the coupons operated. Money lay in bank vaults south, temporarily unreachable, but a kind of parallel banking system was operating as if that money was available. Everyone sincerely believed it would be, eventually. Meanwhile the move to a credit society almost without coin was being brought closer into being.

Pete didn't know much about it, he worked all the time, but he had a feeling imports were a problem. Other countries weren't touching Britain until its little domestic problem was solved. But food was promised if the situation went on too long.

France was succumbing. It was very slow, but there had been leak from the Calais situation. A kind of Maginot line had been drawn up isolating northern France, Paris was mercifully south of it, but it was a great problem. The French spoke of suing Britain. They were very angry.

America was totally under control. They had kept that infected planeload entirely separate from the word go and the full weight of scientific research had been focused on the passengers and flight crew. The men were all fine, seemingly unchanged except that their health had taken a lurch for the better.

The women were going to sleep.

'Tell me about the sleepers,' said Jake, sleepy enough himself and savouring some good whisky Pete had. Pete, as a chemist, was a privileged being in New Britain. The distilleries were in the north, too.

'We don't have the time scale. It might be two, three weeks. It might be more. It might be related to the amount of sexual activity they indulge in. We are very ignorant about it. But the women go to sleep eventually. Hibernate would be a better description. Their metabolism gradually slows till you'd think they had been frozen, Jake. Biological activity barely occurs.'

'Do they wake OK?'

'We don't know. We've had no one wake up yet. Maybe they die. We just don't know.'

'The men don't sleep?'

'No. Not so far. Of course, some have been exposed to more touching than others. What about yourself?'

The silence grew. Jake didn't like Pete, his good friend and ex-employee Pete, having to walk round circles with him.

'Those two women,' he said. 'Peta was a prostitute, a man-hater. The point is, she is a heroin addict. She was repeatedly exposed as the touching spread and it had no effect on her. Lana has simply not been exposed or I think she would have succumbed. Anyway, while I was detained elsewhere, the two women met and took shelter in my house. Peta could go out safely, you see, and she protected Lana. Then I came back. Neither women was touched, I knew straight away. I have been considerably exposed, Pete, if you want to know, and I know all about it.'

'We need everything you know.'

'I understand. I had met up with another couple of women who seemed immune and they were dope addicts too.'

'Heroin?'

'I don't know. Peta, Lana and I decided to make a break for the north, to get through the wire. I helped Peta steal some methadone from a police station.'

'A police station!'

'Some keep stocks to give to addicts when they bring them in for questioning. We then left for the north. We had a car but there was trouble on the way and then we ran out of petrol. I saw some more users who also seemed to be immune. They were men this time. After we lost the car, we were hiding in a barn, Some women came and fired the barn, they had come from an orgy.'

'Jake . . .'

'So we were inside this flaming building. There were maybe a hundred infected women outside. Lana was vulnerable, so was I. We all took methadone and got away safely. We went right through them. I was touched and it didn't affect me. So was Lana.'

There was a silence. 'And that's it,' said Pete.

'That's it.'

'That's very good. It's a start. Opiate receptors. We can do so something with this. It isn't a cure but it's a help.'

'I thought it might be. Peta will be vulnerable now, I think. She's been coming off the stuff for days. She hasn't been well. She's some lady, Pete.'

For a while the two men were silent. Then Pete spoke. 'I see why you had to bring them through.'

'Yes.' Jake was bitter. 'And now they'll be laboratory specimens, yeah?'

'It can't be helped. We have so few specimens, er, people, to work with. It's a plague, Jake.'

'Any idea what it is?'

'Not really.'

'I might be able to help there too.'

They went to the university building where Pete worked. No one offered Jake rest after his broken night, and he didn't ask.

There were things he hadn't taken on board. He was used to a professional objectivity but he had never seen such callousness as this. Perhaps he had been too many days on the road. Perhaps he had witnessed what had happened to the women too closely. Perhaps he was too sympathetic.

They had a woman in a cage. She was infected, touched, and they had scooped her up, south, in a net like a wild beast and brought her here to the Institute to work on her. She had been assigned a fairly comfortable cage with a bed and sanitary facilities, but it was still a cage.

She had no privacy. One wall had one-way glass fitted in it. They could see everything she did.

She was, of course, entirely naked.

Jake stood with several other men watching her.

'We've put clothes in but she won't wear them,' observed Pete. 'She won't read, watch television, listen to music or the radio – she won't do anything. Except the one thing,' he added.

'You handle her?' asked Jake.

'Naturally, We take samples. We monitor her. We analyse what we can. We conduct experiments.'

'Such as?'

'Water dampens her ardour., We know the effect degrades in air. We are assuming it is the oxygen. We've tried oxygen-only breathing but we daren't try it long enough. Specimens are at a premium and we mustn't damage her.'

She might have been a white rat. What she was was a young woman in her mid-twenties. She had flowing chestnut hair, quite natural as they could see by the springing curls at her groin. Her skin was very white as with so many red-heads. She was freckled on her face, across her petite nose and a little across her shoulders and her upper back.

No part of her body was hidden. Jake could count her freckles.

Her breasts were not large but they were beautifully shaped with foxy-red nipples that pointed with pert cheerfulness up and out. She carried no spare flesh on her waist and had shapely hips, long thighs and nice calves. Altogether, she was a nice little honey of a piece and to see her like this, viewed by the lizard eyes of cold men, was a bit rich for Jake's stomach. He felt lousy about the whole thing.

They couldn't be submitting Lana to this, could they?

'So what does she do with her time?'

'She doesn't eat much,' Pete was remorselessly cheerful. 'She plays with herself a lot. We've given her toys, too. Watch.'

A slot opened in the door to the chamber and a tray slid in. There was something on it. The girl stood up in a liquid flow of grace, her muscle tone was excellent, and walked across to it. Her buttocks were perfect, taut, strong and beautifully shaped. She had a panther-like grace as she walked that made her nudity seem completely harmonious and natural.

She picked up the object and smiled. She went back to the bed fondling it.

'She doesn't need the feedback response from a man,' said Pete. 'See.'

The girl took the long object and caressed it lovingly. She arranged herself so that she was on her back, and if she lifted her face she could look down the length of her body and see straight into what was for her a mirror. It was what the men looked through at her. She opened her legs.

Her sex seemed to throb almost visibly. It pouted out as if it was greedy to take something between its curling curving lips and suck it deep into its cushiony-soft interstices. Her fingers played gently with herself. She palpated her sexual flesh. She held it open and rocked slightly from side to side. She forced the lips together and then allowed them to unfasten stickily, slowly, so that the men saw, in great detail, her pussy unleaving and the throbbing pouting centre of the rosebud reveal itself.

Jake felt a little hot.

The bud opened slightly. She was pulling it open now. It was like a rosy mouth being offered for a kiss. It was moist. It was juicy. It was like a bursting strawberry, a rich and lusciously sweet fruit that invited the teeth to ravish its blushing perfection.

She began to feed the object she had been given into her gulping sex. It was a long vibrator, fat, with added parts to simulate the full set of male sexual organs. The girl lay with her knees drawn up and her legs as wide as they would go. The entire obscene length of the thing was plunged into her.

The five men, four in lab coats, stood watching impassively as the girl autofucked herself to climax.

She writhed, she sobbed out words, her pussy convulsed visibly. Suddenly the door opened and three suited men rushed in.

'What?' cried Jake.

'We need samples. This isn't a goddamned sex show. It's scientific research.'

Two of the men held the girl. She made no move to resist them, allowing them to hold her as she continued in her sexual frenzy. The third took skin scrapings, a saliva sample from her open mouth, and some blood from her arm. He packed these neatly. Now he reached his gloved hand down to the girl's groin. He removed the vibrator.

'Watch this on camera,' said Pete. 'You see it better with the zoom lens and under magnification.'

The girl was arched so hard she might have been having a fit. Her legs remained wide open and the two men both restrained and supported her. The third dipped his little wooden spatula into her pussy and took a sample of her sexual juices. Then he stood back.

The camera showed the girl's sex in stupendous detail. Jake stared at the video screen. Her vulva filled it.

He could see the whole thing quivered like an animal. Her clitoris visibly pulsed, the end swelling and shrinking rhythmically. It flushed a darker red as it swelled and became paler as it subsided. It was like a tiny beacon, a lighthouse, bulging and subsiding, glowing and paling.

Below it the crispy rigid flesh that made up the convolutions of her sexual territory throbbed in sympathy. The ridges swayed and rippled. The valleys bulged and subsided. Colour came and went. Jake was irresistibly reminded of a squid.

The whole vulva was in motion. It waved from side to side, it pulsed, it changed colour. Within it the budding flesh of her bodily entrance pushed outwards.

It seemed to reach out and draw back, as though it longed to contact something and draw it into its heated interior. One of the scientists issued a command over the radio to the suited man who had collected the samples. They saw his huge gloved hand descend into the palpitating sexual pit. He prised the vulva open so that the sexual entrance was more clearly revealed. Pete magnified the screen.

Now Jake could see the vaginal entrance was like a pump, seeking to draw into itself something absent.

The male sexual organ, of course. That was what was absent.

It was a process of fascinated horror for Jake. He was unable to forget the sex-maddened creature on screen was a human, a woman. Even as he watched the girl orgasmed.

Her flesh leapt out at them. It bulged as though it would turn inside out. Then it sucked in and almost closed off, save that she was still held open by the gloved man's hand. Several times this was repeated, the outward explosion of bulging flesh, the inward sucking. Then tremors shook the entire vulva. Colour flooded richly. It all shook violently, and then began to calm.

Delicately, thinly, they saw her sexual juices flow. The brilliant flesh was veiled. The juices clung and covered the pulsating organ.

The men released her and began to retreat to the door. The girl rolled over so that she was on her knees, her face down in her pillows, Her bottom was lifted high in the air. Her vagina oozed in front of their eyes.

She reached round behind her holding the vibrator. She began to push blindly. Her vagina throbbed and opened, its flesh bulging out again as if searching for the shaft it so desired. The girl ignored it, going higher. She began to insert the vibrator in her anus.

Jake turned away. She lay with her face to one side, sucking her thumb. The artefact stuck out from her ravished arse, throbbing about its work. Below it the vagina kept up a steady trickle of sexual juices.

Her eyes were shut. She was happy.

'It's pheromonal,' said Pete, following Jake. 'We are analysing the chemistry of the pheromone involved. It isn't one we know about. We haven't got it unravelled yet, the entire structure, I mean. We will, of course, but it takes time. The gas chromatograph separates it for us. The trouble is, we need to sort out the active ingredient by trying it out on women. We don't have many volunteers, as you can imagine. We can't guarantee they won't become infected.'

'Do you know what type of thing it is yet? A ketone? An aldehyde?'

'We think it's a carboxylic acid. We aren't even sure of that. The chemistry's complex.'

Jake said: 'How about an amino acid?'

'Nope.'

'I've got some evidence.'

'I don't believe you.'

'Take me to your office. Better still, convene a departmental meeting if you have such things. The more heads on this one the better.'

'Don't waste our time, Jake. This is wild speculation.'

'No, it isn't. Don't be a dumb bastard.'

'We call a meeting every day,' said Pete grudgingly. 'We brainstorm ideas and report on individual progress so we all know where we are. Speed is important on this one.'

'I know,' said Jake. 'Call the meeting.'

His idea was simple enough. Put crudely, humans are made of protein, and proteins are made up of different combinations of amino acids. There are only about twenty naturally occurring amino acids manufactured by us in our cells. Each contains particular chemical groupings strung on a carbon backbone and all contain nitrogen which is vital for life. Each also has oxygen, carbon and hydrogen attached in specific ways. There are other chemical groups differentiating them, but they have much in common.

Sonia had been playing naughty games in her latter days. The evidence was in her diary.

The tanks contained liquid nitrogen. There was dry ice, solid carbon dioxide around also. There was air, stuffed full of nitrogen and oxygen as gases, though gaseous nitrogen is extraordinarily hard to fix chemically as fertiliser manufacturers know.

As for the hydrogen, humans surround themselves with carbohydrates. We eat it all the time. We call it food and our bodies are skilled chemical factories that break it down.

Jake's suggestion was that Sonia had so interfered with her own chemistry as to accidentally synthesise a new amino acid. A piece of non-functioning DNA might code for it and suddenly begin manufacturing the new molecule, the chemicals it needed being initially supplied by Sonia's dangerous lab games. Then her body would synthesise them. She was no longer precisely human. She was a mutant.

'It explains everything,' Jake argued. 'It affects women. Well, what if it is coded for on the female chromosome, the X chromosome? What if it is therefore able to be eliminated from the reproductive process by the body's natural rejection of the alien. No one gets pregnant. Men are susceptible but can't be infected – the Y chromosome is shorter and offers no locus. What I'm saying is that with women it wakes up a chunk of dormant DNA but it can't do that with men because they don't have that DNA anyway, it's on the female sex chromosome.'

He argued. They argued back. How could Sonia's DNA be affected? They all knew the bulk of DNA apparently codes for nothing, but how could an external event trigger action and carry to other women, just by touch? They talked about viruses, about bacteria, they rushed off and phoned people, they asked to see the diary.

'She was an emotionally sick woman,' said Jake. 'I was her boss. You have to ignore the terrible stuff about me.' He felt incredibly uncomfortable and embarrassed.

Only then did they let him go. He left them buzzing like bees in a hive. He went back to Pete's little flatlet, took a bath, shaved, ate a little, and fell into bed.

He almost slept the clock round. The tiredness was bone deep. But his mission had been accomplished.

Or so he thought.

Nine

He had to find Lana and Peta. It took him a while and he was unfamiliar with this strange new land he found himself in. But he found them.

He was allowed to enter their quarantine quarters having agreed to an enforced six hour period afterwards for 'decontamination.' It was just the word, he thought. Amines were the problem. Amination spread the infection. Decontamination ought to be possible.

He was damned if he could see how or why.

At the moment all he could think about was his woman. He needed to know if she was safe.

She had a little cubicle in a vast building broken down into compartments with minimum space. There were men who worked in the building but as long as they decontaminated after a work session, there was no problem. They tended to do a week of long fourteen hour days and then decontaminate like a diver might decompress. They could re-enter normal life afterwards.

Jake lay on the bed. There was a bed, a chair, a chest of drawers. That was it.

'Bring me books, Jake. Magazines. I can watch television, there is a public area, and listen to the radio there also. But I am desperate for personal music equipment and my own radio. And books. This is very boring, Jake.'

He gave her his phone number at UMIST and told her Pete's full name so he could always be reached via Pete. Then he told her what had been happening with him, the discussion that had raged.

He didn't tell her about the caged living woman being observed for her sexual tricks. He didn't tell her about video cameras homing in on pulsating sexual organs. He didn't tell her of a woman writhing with passion held by three men looking like monsters from outer space. He didn't tell her about samples being taken from living flesh while a woman orgasmed for her audience, on cue, on demand.

The specimen.

He didn't tell her any of these things. He put his lips in her hair and kissed her. He felt her frail in his arms. He tasted her lips. He felt her slow natural rise to a consuming passion, a passion for himself. A passion that he could satisfy. He felt this woman of his, alive and well and safe in his arms, full of a mounting sexual desire for him, for Jake Connors. For no one else. He felt her lips on his, her mouth open under his, her hands in his hair, under his jacket, stroking his body, undoing his shirt, touching his skin.

He felt her palms flat to his skin delighting in him, in the texture and smell of him. He felt her move, her swelling breasts pushed against his hardness, her hips swaying to rub against him. He allowed his hand to slide slowly up the long beautifully shaped leg, to feel where the stocking stopped, to feel the warm thigh, to feel the intimate heat beating down from her inner places.

He allowed himself to enjoy the skirt sliding up in a sensuous rustle, so the beautiful order and elegance of her clothes was ruffled and disturbed to make a readiness for his passion, his need for consummation.

He knelt over her as she lay back on her bed. She smiled, her hair around her head on the pillows like a halo. He opened her blouse, kneeling over her, feeling his welcome into very heart of her body, all of her secret places.

Nothing was forbidden.

Her breasts were lace-covered. He slid the material down, its softness yielding to his strength. He took one ripe full breast and freed it from its confines. There was a delicious lewdness in her now. Her skirt hoisted up to reveal her thigh. Her open blouse, her breast spilling out – Jake bent and kissed the plump flesh of her. His lips sampled her skin. He tasted her femininity. He licked across her nipple and watched it grow at his bidding. She laughed at it, the little glossy column of her sex, her private organ, and he bent his head again and sucked her sweetness into him.

He undid his tie and shrugged off his jacket. He knelt over her lissome and graceful form, so soft, so curving, so yielding. It was in his hands to play with as he wished. It was soft with the desire to gratify him. It lay inviting him, the woman smiling warmly in anticipation, her own special smell ascending to his nostrils.

He was on fire to fuck her and for all her seeming passivity he knew by the gleam in her eye that her passion was as potent, as demanding, as his own.

They were equals. She was crazy to fuck too. She just enjoyed the game.

He left her clothes on. Their slight barrier was no impediment to his invasion of her body, but they gave a hint of it, to fire him that bit more. He looked at her below him as he moved to enter her. Such a beautiful woman, so rich in looks and personality. She was his. As his cock slid into her welcoming body, he knew she was his. For this time, for now, she had become a woman totally given over to pleasuring him. It was in that that she found her own pleasure.

He felt his excitement grow. It wasn't just the velvet tightness of her sweet cunt wrapped with honeyed slipperiness round his hard sex. It was seeing so nakedly the delight she took in having his cock in her. She adored sex. She adored him in her. She yearned for his thrusts.

He felt her move. She gripped his shaft and squeezed it. She sucked it in. His balls were on her cool thighs. Her breasts enticed and ravished his eyes. His belly was on fire. Her eyes had glazed with passion, she was totally given over to the moment. He sensed her orgasm wouldn't be long in coming. Indeed, at that moment he felt her change. She gasped and sighed, her cunt playing the sweetest music on his cock, but then she went on, still in orgasm, her cunt pleading with him never to stop.

He held out as long as he could. When he came Lana bit down on her pillows to stifle her cries. They had no real privacy, the partitions were matchwood and there were people all about.

Jake subsided onto her trembling body. She held him, kissing his face, rubbing it in her breasts, kissing his hair.

'We've got to get you out of this place,' said Jake.

'Yes. Somewhere private. Where I can bite you and love you fiercely.'

Altogether, she was one hell of a woman.

He tried to see Peta but she was asleep. That night he told Pete Lana had to get out.

It took days. On the basis of the meeting Jake had spoken to, all other groups were alerted. They all spoke practically daily anyway via specially appointed co-ordinators. This was one where the government was not allowing a traditional fight for academic pre-eminence. It needed answers and it need them as fast as possible. No one worked alone, no one kept secrets.

The molecular biologists devised a new test. They found the place on the chromosome, the mutant gene that Jake had guessed existed. Now they could check women on a different basis. If the mutant gene was absent, the women were clean.

So Lana and Peta were tested and released.

Lana was a foreign national, an American. She went to her relocated embassy and made her presence known. Few Americans were left. Most had fled before the plague reached them.

She organised having clothes and money sent from her home so she could stay in New Britain more comfortably. She gave Peta her coupons so that the woman could buy some clothes – she had abandoned everything in the south.

She found a little flat, a tiny place with a shared kitchen. Accommodation was at a premium as the southern hordes crowded north. Since she couldn't get anywhere alone, she and Peta shared. At least they knew each other.

Jake was relieved. Women were having a hard time in New Britain. They were liable to be stopped on the street by roving patrols and be forced to show their papers, their residency permits, their certificates of non-infection. It was a humiliating business. Though the news of a totally secure test spread rapidly throughout academia and officialdom, and was published on the news, the ingrained habit of scepticism on the part of the general public meant that they took it all with a pinch of salt.

He had work himself now and he continued to live with Pete, there not being enough room in Lana's for his permanent residency there. But he visited often. Peta had found clerical work. She was as quiet as ever, as withdrawn when he was around. Jake wondered about her happiness, about her drug dependency, but he didn't ask. She would tell him if she wanted to. He had no right to probe.

There were very few sleepers in the north. Those there were were tested as they slept. As they hibernated. They all had the mutant gene. They had lowered amounts of the pheromone but this was probably only a reflection of their almost stationary metabolism. All their bodily functions were severely depressed. They weren't far off an extremely healthy clinical death. Yet they did breathe. They did metabolise. Slowly. Their hearts beat so slowly. Their blood moved so slowly. Yet they lived.

Jake attended his first-ever total conference. Every researcher of any kind and all attendant officials not actually bedridden on the day attended a local hall or conference centre that was itself a television studio. Vast TV screens gave visual and sound access between them all. Everyone was brought up to date on everything known so far.

It was in this way that Jake saw his first map. The south was regularly overflown by helicopters and spotter aircraft. Satellites helped. The results were combined and area maps were shown.

The devastation caused by the burnings was what first took Jake's eye overwhelming all other feelings. It was unbelievable. It was almost unbearable. Only gradually did his sense of shock abate.

The maps were shown as a sequence through time. They were measuring the rate of destruction. A rapid sequence of fourteen consecutive days, one superimposed on the next, woke Jake up.

He had an idea. Something teased at him.

He continued to think about it after the total conference was over. He understood the progress so far. They could identify the symptoms, analyse the chemicals, describe the molecular biology involved. They knew the body's source, on the DNA itself. They understood a little of how skin contact transferred the ability to mutate.

They didn't know how to stop it. They didn't know how to cure it. They didn't understand why there were sleepers and what would happen to them in time. Could Britain afford to lose almost an entire generation of women?

Jake did his assigned work, reported to his peers, and worried and nagged at the half-formed idea in his mind.

Like stones in a pond. Ripples. Seeds of destruction, the effects radiating out.

He'd like to see that map sequence again. He talked to Pete about it. Finally he talked to Matthew Vance, his new departmental head. He was given a day off to go to the Ministry Office newly created to handle the emergency.

It had some official name but the streetwise called it the Ministry of Fear. They were all afraid, even if they didn't say so.

Jake was given a pass and allowed into the map rooms. He sat in front of a terminal all day, forgetting to eat.

His idea might be a goer. He didn't like what it led to, though. It presented a sequence of actions to be undertaken if it had any reality.

He didn't want to know.

He left the building dizzy, not noticing that he was treated with respect, he had status. Word was getting round that he was the man who had made the intellectual breakthrough. He went to a bar and had some peace for a while from the clamour of his mind.

He was drunk when he went to find Lana. He didn't remember too much, only the joy of shafting her, of feeling the glorious rise to climax in her sweet hot body. He had vague memories of feverishly kissing her breasts, her sweet pussy. He ate at her hungrily as if it was the last time they could be together. He spaced out on her sweet juices as he brought her sobbing to orgasm using his mouth and fingers. Her sexual country was divine. He wanted to dwell in it forever.

There were things to do.

He woke in the night and felt her instantly stir. She must have been awake. He nuzzled into her body as his mind turned slowly over, deciding how to take her, how to please his body and hers the best.

'What is it, Jake?'

'I want to make love to you.'

'I know. I know. I want you to. But why are you so desperate? What's happened? You make me frightened. What is it you know?'

He told her how he felt about her. How he had nothing to offer. His business was gone. His income was meagre. His work uncertain. His country plagued and infected, its social order collapsing.

He was at war. She needed to be home in the States. He wanted her but he wanted her away before the mess got worse. Already New Britain had the makings of a police state. If they didn't solve the problem soon, that's what it would become. She should get out.

She was satisfied. Like all good lies, it was built round enough truth for her to believe it. She came on top of him and sucked his shaft till it bulged with the need to climax. She took him with cunt and mouth till he was drained. Then he slept.

He didn't know if she slept and he didn't ask. In the morning he drank coffee, already a luxury good as trade foundered, and said goodbye.

He saw Peta. She looked austere and handsome. She said nothing about her night being disturbed though surely they had made a lot of noise.

Lana was beautiful, even to the shadows under her eyes. Her thick curling hair was bright and alive. The slender column of her neck made him long to kiss it. Her shoulder bones were delicate and vulnerable, inviting his protection. Her breasts were full and womanly, offering peace.

Between her thighs was all a man could ever wish. Hot fire, an explosion of lust, a ripeness of need with the deep knowledge of how to satisfy it.

She wore a long lace and satin dressing gown, more a negligé, that slid and rustled as she moved.

Jake kept the picture in his mind as he left her. The panther grace, the sliding sheen of the material as it caressed her curves. The swell of her breasts. The invitation of her throat. The hidden sex-fire of her velvet cunt.

He went to his boss, his departmental head.

'I think there's a source,' he said. 'A single unitary source. I think it re-infects all the time. Each time it does, the destruction, which is really a measure of the infection, spreads outwards like a ripple on a pond.'

'It's all over, Jake. You know that. It's everywhere south of the wire.' His boss was sceptical but prepared to listen. Jake had got it right before and he had sounded wild then.

'If you study the maps,' said Jake patiently, 'you can see how it spreads. It begins from a point source and is very intense. It spreads out in waves, diminishing in intensity all the time.'

'Where is the point source?'

'It moves. Every day it's different.'

'This is nonsense, Jake.'

'It never moves more than ten miles in any twenty-four period. It's a person. It's a woman. I'm sure of it.'

'A woman? The single source of all the infection?'

'Yes. I think if we knew more about it, we could fit the sleepers into the pattern. We know so little because we all keep clear.'

'For obvious reasons. You are suggesting we send researchers into the field? Doped with methadone, I suppose. We don't have anything else, you know.'

Jake said steadily: 'This is a guess. The maps don't go back right to the start as you know. It took time to get organised, to appreciate the seriousness of the situation. But I think I can guess who the source is.'

'This is a very long chain of conjecture with no proof along the way.'

'I think it's Sonia Lafferty. Or whatever she has become. I think she is the point source and without her, the infection would begin to dry up, to stop. Even if the poor women fell asleep. We could keep them in quarantine wards and go on working. But otherwise we could re-occupy the south and rebuild Britain.'

'So what do you suggest?'

Jake was aware he was being humoured. 'I don't think this is a case for the army,' he said. 'I don't think we drop mortars or bombs on these poor women. But she has to be neutralised. And first, she has to be recognised. And that's where I come in. She was my employee. It was my business. Her neurotic behaviour had focused itself on me. I'm a scientist, dammit. And I feel responsible. I'll take her out. I'll find her. I'll neutralise her. The army can drop me near where she is.'

'How do you know where she is?'

'That's what I've been telling you. The maps give it away. There is a centre from which trouble continuously radiates. She is at the centre. The army has to put me as near as it can. I'll only be ten miles away at the most. Then I have to find her and stop her.'

'How do you propose to stop her?'

'I'm going to need some help there. I don't want to kill her. Murder her. I just want her stopped. Then we can lock her up. I guess we need her, to make sure this never happens again. We have things to learn from her.'

Jake met the resistance he expected to meet. He didn't go to see Lana though he phoned her daily and told her he was very busy, not to worry, things would get better.

He saw people higher and higher up the hierarchy. He attended meetings where his analysis was derided as facile and unproven. He attended meetings where the army asked to blanket bomb Jake's 'centre.'

Experts analysed the maps in the light of Jake's hypothesis.

They agreed with him. There was a discernible pattern. Once 'noise' was eliminated, it became easier to see. It had been obscured before.

Naked ladies. Orgies. Fires. Jake thought about Sam Riley sometimes. He wondered where he was. This was Sam's legacy. It was Sam who had made him connect in the first place.

Had he seen Sonia himself that first night, when he was crazy with shock and Sally Trenning was in his car?

He had seen the naked figure in the rain-drenched street, lit by a sodium glare yet strangely white. A white flame.

Sam had seen a vision, experienced a hallucination. Or a naked woman had assaulted him and used his body sexually.

Sonia?

Had Sonia then travelled south, via Hammersmith, Southwark, the M25, that place in Surrey, and so to Brighton? Was it Sonia who set Brighton ablaze that terrible night?

From Brighton, trouble had radiated out along the south coast, back north towards London, and south across the Channel. Had Sonia caused all that, infecting other women who then carried it away with them, weakening as they went, but still infected, infecting, still burning?

Sonia. Sonia who had nursed a demented and obsessional passion for her boss.

He hadn't said he thought Sonia might kill. He hadn't said he thought Sonia could hardly be human any more. He thought she might recognise him. He might have a chance to get to her.

She had been hot for him. He felt cold at the thought. What was she now?

He had to pursue her. The thought made him sick but it had to be done and he didn't doubt he was the man to do it.

He had known her. He had employed her. He had been present at the first burning. He knew something of her perverted,

231

thwarted passion. He knew what it was like south, he had lived in it, survived in it, as so many here had not. They had got across before the trouble.

It was his idea. It was his risk. It was up to him to go.

There were more high-level discussions. Now they centred on how he was to stop her, aside from killing her which Jake said he wasn't prepared to do. If that was the decision, he would oppose it. The army would have to carry it out. He was offering to get to her and keep her alive. He made no offer to be a murderer.

There was the matter of his equipment, then. Food, certainly. Dry warm lightweight clothing. The molecular boys had come up with a injection of reduced-strength methadone that would mean Jake wasn't actually high all the time, yet still it afforded protection. He would have to carry supplies and inject himself daily.

Jake was taken to see this tested. Post-graduate students had offered to be guinea pigs. It wasn't that any of them working on the problem feared being aroused against their will by an infected woman and being forced to enjoy sex until they could escape. No, it wasn't that at all. It was the knowledge they were being watched. It was one thing to cavort sexually with a desirable woman who could hardly get enough and who would do anything, commit any perversion, in the name of pleasure. It was quite another to be watched by lizard eyes, to have a camera spying, to be recorded on magnetic tape. Most of them were too coy sexually to want to be involved in that.

The students didn't care, it seemed. They had a good opinion of themselves. It was just as well.

There were two women and six men. Three of the men were inoculated, three were not. They all agreed to resist any sexual advance made to them, to the best of their ability.

They entered the chamber. Jake sat in a lecture theatre, darkened, the seats in tiers. The video screen had been rigged at the front. Scientists, government officials, researchers of all kinds watched.

Officially it was called The Venus Project.

The engineers had everything sorted out. For a while the silent audience sat in the dark watching the two women, the two specimens, roam their quarters. Their activity had synchronised and they were on a two hour cycle, roughly. Since they had no men they used each other and the sexual toys they had been given.

They were coming up to their next predictable frenzy. Though they didn't know it, this time they were going to have men-things to play with.

Jake missed Lana. He knew what he would see would affect him sexually, as it would everyone who watched. They weren't dead, any of them. Most of them had wives. They would almost all be sexually active men. This was crazy, watching displays of gross human sexuality in the name of science. As research it was very hot. A hot pursuit of knowledge.

A desperate pursuit. As would his be, when he went looking for Sonia. The women began to get restless. They got off the beds and walked up and down, touching themselves. Jake wondered why they looked so good. It seemed to him that those the plague infected became beautiful. Even plain women began to glow. Breasts were riper, hips fuller, waists narrower. Hair gleamed. Even their features were more regular, more pleasing to the eye.

He remembered their superb health, this curious by-product of the infection. They were perfect sex machines, beautiful, desirable, healthy, cheap to maintain. They wanted no clothes, little heating and little food.

For a moment he grinned to himself. There were men who might say they were being offered Nirvana. Maybe they should keep a colony of these sex-mad gorgeous ladies. A man could drop in, fuck himself slew-eyed and go away.

There were worse solutions to the sexual problems of society.

The six students went in.

They were all naked. They looked like rugby players. They were husky giants with broad shoulders and neat tight hips. Two of them were erect already at the thought of what was to happen.

The audience had no way of knowing which men were injected and which weren't.

One women did a handstand so that she ended up upside-down against the body of a startled man, standing on her hands. Her companion immediately pressed herself against her upside-down friend and took the student's face between her hands. She kissed him and put a finger into her friend's cunt. She put the finger between his lips.

He staggered backwards. The women sprang apart, the one landing gracefully on her feet. The other made a flying leap and grabbed another student round his neck, her legs round his waist, so that he fell back onto a bed. His cock stood up rigidly. She gave a whoop and plunged onto it. Within two seconds she was shuddering up and down.

The original student had backed against the door. The voice-over told Jake he was inoculated. The student on the bed being ridden with ferocious speed was not.

The second woman bent from the waist and fastened her mouth to the erect cock of another student. As she did so, a third ran across the room holding his cock like a lance. He ran it straight into her backwards-pointing pussy. She pushed her bottom out as hard as she could. As she sucked the one, the other fucked hard into her. All three bodies shook to his blows.

Three students now stood back, watching their mates being sucked or fucked.

All three had mild erections. This was hardly surprising. Jake doubted there were many in the audience unaffected by what they saw. As for himself, he was hard. He couldn't help it. The sheer ferocity and appetite of the women was arousing. They offered no threat. They offered endless pleasure.

The first man, the one flat on his back on the bed, had come. He lay spread-eagled, his face fatuous and happy. His cock lay limp and wetly glistening across his thigh. The woman riding him had abandoned him and was advancing on the three at bay against the door and the wall.

She touched one. His cock jerked. She swung one leg straight in the air with a limber grace that a ballet dancer would have envied. She stood on tip toe on her single foot and pressed her open sex against the student's cock.

She was very wet. Very open. Very easy. Very moist. Very welcoming.

He screwed his eyes shut and turned his face away. They heard him crying 'no'.

Several in the audience shuffled uneasily. It was hard to distinguish between ordinary sexual arousal and the response to touching.

The student capitulated. He was fine healthy male. His cock slid into its velvet heaven and the woman shook herself against him in her extraordinary position, apparently suffering no discomfort from the leg trapped up between her body and his. She held him tightly and slammed her body into his. He kept his eyes shut, his knees bent, and his hands flat to the wall either side of himself.

He couldn't resist her, but it was a normal failing.

The other woman stood up. She licked her lips, swallowing spunk, grinning at the man she had sucked to climax. The man at her rear slid out. Spunk dribbled down her thigh. She turned round. She touched both men, the one now behind her that she had sucked and the one now in front of her who had rogered her from behind. Both cocks sprang to attention.

She laughed. She bent over quite slowly and took the cock before her into her mouth. Her rear jutted enticingly. The student she had sucked slid his freshly awoken cock into her damp hole. The scenario was replayed, exact in every detail save that the two men had swapped roles.

The woman with the reluctant student finished her business and abandoned him. She leapt up suddenly at the next in line, gripping his neck. Her feet were against the wall. He braced himself automatically. She kissed him and as she did so she tried to arrange her pussy over his cock.

He was naturally aroused. He wasn't so stiff. His cock didn't seek like a blind worm its nest, its hole, which had eager lips to suck him in.

She had to put a hand down and help him in.

She began to swing herself on him, using his neck and the wall to give her balance. His muscles bulged. He had to lean at an angle to the wall, his feet well forward and his shoulders hard against it, to support her weight.

She took him expertly to climax. Her first inoculated victim retreated as she finished and jumped down. Her second sat down abruptly on the floor.

She turned her back on the third and bent double, touching her toes. He gave his friends a helpless grin and entered her.

The man on the bed sat up. His cock was hard. The woman who had touched him was being taken by the rear. The other woman had a man at each end. He was desperate himself. He didn't see where he could fit in.

He wasn't left alone for long. The woman with a man at each end straightened. Again she licked her lips as if she was pussy and had been stealing the cream. She saw the man on the bed. She went over to him quite slowly, smiling. She turned round and sat across him, beckoning to the others. Now she raised herself and before the astonished eyes of the audience, she lowered herself on the man on the bed so that he penetrated not her cunt, but her rear.

His face took on an expression of idiot bliss. He began to bounce himself on the bed so that he fucked gently into her arse. At her command one of the other men knelt before her. His head was buried in her groin so that his hair was like some vast pubic excess of her own. As she was penetrated in her rear, so this other man sucked her pussy. The other man, the third at her body, bent over her breasts and began to suck them.

The second woman finished with her student. None of the three she had just had, one after the other, was aroused. She gave up on them and went over to the bed. There was plenty of room. She found a cock and made him come hard. She was indifferent to the activity of the rest of the man whose cock she held. She arranged herself so she could slot it into her hole and began to bring him to climax again.

For some time the audience watched in frozen silence, grateful for the shrouding dark. The two women and three men on the bed became one vast multi-limbed sexual animal. Endlessly, in a dozen permutations, orifices were penetrated, breasts and balls were sucked, mouths met and parted, things were sucked and entered and sucked again. At one point, apparently oblivious to what he was doing, one student ravished the arse of the other. The women were at them all the time, caressing, sucking, drawing them in, bringing them to erection after erection, bringing them to endless climax.

The other three cowered against the wall, grateful to be left in peace. It seemed the experiment was successful. After another ten minutes they were allowed out. The women were coming to the end of their cycle. Their activity declined. The three students who had received no protection fell into deep sleep, aroused only to be led dizzily out.

The women watched, seemingly uninterested now that,

temporarily at least, their appetite was slaked.

One further experiment was scheduled. An inoculated man would be exposed to two frenzied women with no other men present. It wasn't just that he must be able to resist them and not degenerate into a mindless plaything. They must be able to lose interest in him if he failed to respond to the touching. This would be the true situation for Jake. He might well find himself with no other men by him to focus the women's attention. Yet he still had to be able to escape. What would they do to a man who only came to erection once or twice at their bidding, who was not inexhaustible? A normal man, in other words.

A smaller audience watched this time. They saw the women with their pulping panting sex take the volunteer and use him. One sat over his mouth, one sucked his cock. They became uncertain as it took him a while to regain his erection. When he did, they made him take one them kneeling on her hands and knees. As he banged into her, his balls and buttocks were caressed and kissed by the other woman. But then he was done.

Jake was deeply disturbed, more so than before. He had witnessed a great deal of 'touched' sex now. It shouldn't be bothering him so much. Then the source of his discomfort became clear in his analytical mind.

He had a personal lust to have two women. He wanted to be ravished by two women simultaneously, not in the gluttonous frenzy he witnessed but all night, all day, lingering in the arousal and satiation of flesh.

He wanted Peta and Lana together.

He controlled his mind and watched the experiment. For a while the women played with their victim. They kissed him, they masturbated him, they wrapped him in their hair, they penetrated his rear. They massaged his skin, they kissed him with their sex, squatting over him to do so.

He had come twice in ten minutes. He needed longer to be ready to come again. They tired of him before he was ready and turned to each other and their toys.

He was left in peace.

Now Jake knew he had no reason to stall. He had brought this on himself because he believed it was the right thing for him to do. He didn't want to do it. He had to do it. The sooner he did it the better.

That night Lana came to see him.

It seemed to him she had never been so desirable. Her slender willowy grace, the beautiful curving lines of her served to emphasise her richness at bosom and hip. Her lips promised delights. Her eyes communicated secrets. Her hands knew things.

He couldn't tell her what he was going to do. He knew perfectly well he would be assaulted at some point. There was no way he would get to Sonia without having first paid his dues to the god of licentiousness who ruled south of the wire. As he pursued her, so he would be victim to her victims. As he got nearer to the heart of the conflagration surrounding her, so his own body would be increasingly forfeit.

He must not mind it. He must be willing like the husky students to fuck for science, for progress, for a return to normality. He mustn't be squeamish about allowing himself to become the sexual toy and plaything of fevered women. He mustn't mind if they ravished him with fingers, mouth, pussy and breast. He mustn't mind if they penetrated his own private places.

He would have nothing, no reserve, no privacy, no control. He would be entirely subject to their gross animal desires. They would plunder him, tearing their pleasures from his body till he collapsed exhausted in a welter of sexual juice.

His only protection was the inoculation that wore off after twenty-four hours. It wouldn't save him entirely, but it would prevent him from drowning in juice-sodden pussies wanting to gobble endlessly at his cock. They would tire of him. They would let him go. He would only have to fuck once or twice and he would be free.

He didn't want to explain this to Lana. He didn't want to tell her he was going south of the wire into no-man's-land. No man's land, but woman's land, where men existed to serve one purpose.

He took Lana to her home and made sweet and tender love to her. When she was sleeping he left her bed and dressed quietly. He went through to Peta's room. He crept over to the bed and woke her gently.

'Peta, it's Jake.'

'Yes, What is it? Is Lana OK?'

'She's fine. Can I have a word with you?'

'Sure.'

He sat on the edge of the bed. She pulled herself up on her pillows and looked at him.

There was no light on and neither of them made a move to change this. A dim light filtered in through the window from street lights outside. He could see Peta pale on her pillows, watching him. She reached to light a cigarette, offering him one. He took it though he rarely smoked. It seemed to be one of those times. As he bent forward to light hers for her, he saw in the small blaze of flame she was naked. Her breasts were above the covers but she made no move to cover them.

For a moment he hesitated.

'What is it?'

He was silent. They were north of the wire. Things were different here from that mad flight they had undertaken together.

She laughed suddenly, softly. It occurred to him he had never heard her laugh or relax. 'You mean because I have no clothes on?'

'Yes.'

She swept the covers back suddenly. He saw the whole pale length of her with the dark triangle at her groin. He smelt her warm womanly smell.

'Does it matter?' she said. 'You don't want me. You're a civilised man. Your woman is in the next room. What does it matter if my breasts or my pussy or my backside show?'

'You're very attractive,' said Jake. He put the covers back over her and leant forward. His mouth found hers. He felt her naked breasts press against his shirtfront. He kissed her.

It was a gentle, lingering kiss. A sexual kiss. When he was done Jake sat back. 'That's the truth,' he said. His voice was soft. 'I know you don't like men.'

'Why are you here?'

'I have something to do. I haven't told Lana. I have to go away.'

'I know she's been worried something was up.'

'I'm going back south of the wire.'

'Why?'

'There's just a chance this whole thing might be being caused by one woman. She used to work for me. I know her. She's a second-rate biologist. A third-rate chemist. We have evidence she did some experiments. We think they went wrong.'

'So what are you going to do?'

'Find her. Stop her.'

'How?'

'We think we know roughly where she is. The army are going to drop me in by helicopter tomorrow night. Then I'll go on foot.'

'But you'll be attacked by the women.'

'We have a mild methadone-based inoculation. I can only be aroused naturally under its influence. I can't be touched. I might have to suffer one or two short attacks, but I won't go under. We've done some experiments. Nowhere near enough, of course, there isn't time for proper field trials. The women lose interest if you fail to respond. They don't attack in any other way.'

'Experiments here, in the north?'

'Yes. In laboratories.'

'Mightn't it be different in the south? I mean, women in bands on the loose might not be so easy to control as women in a lab.'

'There are risks. But I'm only one person and if I succeed, if I'm right, this whole thing can be brought swiftly to a conclusion. If I'm right but I fail, someone else can try. Perhaps more drastically. If I'm wrong, I should still get back alive. There'll be no harm done.'

'Except to you.'

'I think I can stand that, Peta. I know the women can't help it. It doesn't mean anything. It has no reflection on my maleness, my personal sexuality. All that is transcended. You know that for yourself.'

'When we fucked in the wood . . .'

'Yes. We all were a little infected then. I'm glad it wasn't enough to harm you two. There's a threshold to this thing.'

'I liked it.'

There was a long silence. 'Perhaps,' said Jake, 'now your way of earning your living has changed, you might like it in general.'

She sat up and put a hand behind his head, drawing his face to hers. They kissed again. Jake stroked her breast, rubbing his thumb gently over her nipple, caressing it to erection.

'If I come with you, you'll be safer,' she said presently.

'No. I can't shelter behind you, Peta. You must know that.'

'We know the women don't attack if they think a man has someone already.'

'That certainly was true. But it's nearly December, Peta, and the women go naked. You can't do that. You'll get pneumonia.'

She lay back on the pillows putting her hands behind her head so that her elbows stuck out. Her breasts lifted and divided. 'That's true,' she acknowledged. 'Can't you fancy-pants scientists find a way round it? Put me in some transparent body-hugging clothes that'll seal in the heat and keep out the cold.'

Jake shivered with laughter. 'I wish we could. You'd be delectable. You wouldn't be safe from me.'

Peta gave a throaty murmur. 'Perhaps I don't mind so much, if we're going to save the world as we know it. It seems a small price to pay.'

Jake was aware he was definitely aroused and this was precisely what Peta wanted. It was nice to get aroused this way, the old way, by subtle use of body and words. It was all very well being pounced on, it had a certain novelty value, but this was best. This slow gradual excitation as they both played sexual games was the very best of all.

He stood up. 'It was a great offer, Peta.'

'It was meant,' she said. He could hear the amusement in her voice. Which offer was she referring to? The one to accompany him, or the unspoken one, that he enter her bed.

He knelt on the bed and kissed her again, firmly. His hand slid under the covers and snaked down. Her legs opened. For a moment his fingers slipped into the divide. He touched her sex and felt its moist soft welcome.

'I hope it won't be too long before I see you again,' he said. He brought his hand back and raised it to his nostrils. He adored the fragrance of an aroused woman.

'Take care.' Her voice was so low it was hard to hear. 'And I'll look after Lana.'

'Thank you, Peta. I owe you.'

'You certainly do,' she said and laughter bubbled in her throat.

It only remained now for him to sleep and then pack the gear he was assigned. Field rations. A radio so he could call for assistance when he was done. Or if he was in trouble he couldn't handle. His own inoculation equipment with a twelve day supply. A compass. Maps. And what he would use on Sonia.

They sat him well back in the helicopter and he spent most of the journey feeling sick. He wasn't allowed a pill, they hadn't had time to test how the differing chemicals would react.

He was dropped at four in the morning. They had decided, in their wisdom, that activity was low then, the normal metabolic low for humans. It would be dark for several hours at this time of the year, a cloaking darkness Jake could take advantage of.

He was dropped near Dorchester, the last identifiable centre they had found.

The journey had a nightmare quality not just because he was nervous and lonely and travel sick, though these would have been enough. As they went over the wire all lighting ceased. The countryside below was black and mysterious like the open ocean. No towns lit the horizon. No villages gave a small cheery light. Nothing guided, nothing showed life. Nothing except the occasional pinpoint fire, where some building succumbed to the madness of the women.

There was no place for him here, Jake knew. It was given over entirely to madness.

He wished he was safe home in Lana's arms.

He thought again about Peta. Suddenly he was erect.

Ten

It went wrong from the start. He fell as he jumped from the helicopter which was hovering a few feet above the ground. The spotlights shining down dazzled him and he misjudged the weight of what he carried. His ankle hurt but this was such a feeble response to all their preparations that he gave the helicopter the thumbs up and watched it pull up, switch off its lights and veer away into the night.

He lay on the cold grass feeling his wrenched ankle twang with pain. His shoulder hurt too, the one that had been shot during that last terrible flight from the south to the north.

Gradually his eyes adjusted. The night was very dark and still. The forecast was good, dry and calm. High clouds obscured the stars. The chill from the ground struck up through his warm clothes.

He was meant to get up and run as fast as he could away from this point so that if the helicopter had attracted unwelcome attention, he could escape it.

However, he sat there nursing his ankle, feeling a devastating loneliness overwhelm him.

He thought about Peta and had no guilt at the thought. Perhaps he was too fond of Lana. To think of her would weaken him when he needed to be strong.

Peta was a pleasant memory, though. He wondered what sex with her would be like. Good, he thought, on the whole. She was a professional. Would that help or hinder her, doing it for pleasure instead of profit? They had been united once, in that wood, but that was when they were under the influence of the touchers.

What would it be like having her here now? That would be good too, he thought. She would help him up. Clear his black mood. Hearten him. Perhaps, when they were away from this dangerous landing place, they would fulfil the promise they had so nearly made to each other. Her comfort would be welcome. He would enjoy feeling her body against his, feeling his sex in her. There would be a satisfaction too in giving her pleasure when so many men had failed. He could do with a boost to his ego.

He clambered awkwardly to his feet and slung his pack more comfortably on his good shoulder. There was nothing really wrong with the bad one, only a residual bruising. It hurt because he was cold and afraid. That was the truth of it. He was afraid.

He began to limp across the field he was in having checked his compass direction. His map was marked where they had intended to drop him. South of it was a big wood where he could hide and sort himself out and orient himself.

He couldn't find it. They had dropped him somewhere else. Although he couldn't see properly anything close at hand, he could sense it was all open terrain around him for some considerable distance. He could see the sky well enough. There was no wood close at hand.

He stumbled around in a boggy area for some time before randomly choosing a slope to climb. He was desperate for firm ground under his feet. He cursed the night, he cursed the helicopter navigator, he cursed Sonia, he cursed his sore ankle and most of all he cursed his own foolishness and obstinacy for being here at all. He could be in bed with Lana. Or Peta. He might even be alone. It would all be better than being here.

If he was anywhere near his proper drop-off point,

Dorchester was to his north. He presumed the women would congregate in the towns. More shelter. More to burn. Anyway, there was no one and nothing around here. He tramped north. He found himself climbing a steep hill clear of vegetation except for short grass. It was very steep. He came to the top aware of a dim light in the east. He plunged steeply down into a valley. A tiny valley. Minutes later he was toiling painfully up another steep short hill.

This was ridiculous. After several more hills and valleys had been accomplished in this way, Jake sat at the bottom of a valley and used his torch to study his map. After some painful thinking he decided he was in Maiden Castle and he was busily climbing his way through a neolithic earthwork.

He switched off his torch in irritation. This was degenerating into farce. Perhaps he should just get out his all weather sleeping bag and get some rest. In the morning he could sort himself out.

'Who goes there?' a voice called sharply.

Jake froze. A woman. From his left.

He got stealthily to his feet, made sure he had all his gear, and began to sidle along the valley floor to his right.

'Who's there?' called the voice again, strongly and imperiously. Like a guard with the right to challenge. She probably was a guard.

Guard? Against whom? Jake shuffled faster keeping as quiet in his movements as he could. His ankle had swollen and was troubling him considerably. He wanted to ease the lacing on his boots but didn't like to stop.

The valley continuously curved. Of course it would. It was a circular earthwork. If he kept going he would meet his challenger head on, in twenty minutes time or whatever. This thing that he was going round was enormous, maybe even as much as a mile across.

He had to be careful. He was moving east, unfortunately. If

he climbed to his right to escape out of the earthwork, he would be silhouetted against the sky, however briefly.

How many women were here? He couldn't hear them or see them.

There would be an exit, of course, a cutting through which the iron-age owners had entered and left their home. Hadn't they fought the Romans? He didn't know.

Jake slowed down. He crept up the bank to his left, the way into the interior of this thing. It had occurred to him that maybe Sonia was not holding court in some town. Maybe she lurked in this timeless place heavy with its dark history. Maybe she was here.

Would she be one of many? Would she stand out?

Jake didn't know.

He slunk over the hill on his belly and dropped quietly down into the next valley. He went up the next hill even more carefully.

He could hear noises, smell a fire. Now he could see flames. There was a camp here.

He lay watching, mindful he had been spotted and that they might even now be searching for him.

In the grudging light of the cold winter's dawn he could see a large ghost-pale plateau disappearing into the gloom of the receding night. At the end nearer to himself a large bonfire burned. Round it figures were busy.

Firelight flickered on naked thigh and breast. Long hair lifted in the light dawn breeze.

A shiver ran through Jake. There was some atavistic fear here. For all the world these women were the image, the fulfilment of those old woodcuts of witches. Here they were round their fire, planning their devilry.

Had something like this ever happened before? Did these mutants throw up naturally from time to time? Was this the source of all the witchcraft stories, why men could fear women so profoundly they felt a need to burn them and drown them?

The primeval place, the strangeness of the vision, his own fear, all worked in Jake. It was some time before he could bring himself to reason.

This was a modern blight and he had a chance of stopping it dead in its tracks. Primitive nonsense was something he could do without.

He heard a noise behind him. Looking back over his shoulder he saw three women advancing stealthily.

He ran at them. He was between them and the camp. They wouldn't expect him to come towards them, they didn't know he had an immunity. They had no weapon but their touching. Jake ran clumsily through them and panted up the other side of the valley. Unencumbered by gear they came after him, light of foot. He charged down the next hill.

They could have had him but they gave up, they lost interest. This was just as well. His ankle was giving him hell.

He soldiered on across dimly lit fields. The rural desolation of the countryside in winter, dead, bare, cold, damp, seemed to his urban soul to be devastating. He yearned for the warmth and light of a town. When he came to a hedgerow he looked round him. He could see nothing and no one. The sun was a dim red ball behind the thin clouds. He took out his waterproof sleeping bag and burrowed into the hedge. Then he burrowed into the bag. When he was right inside and zipped firmly in with just his face showing, he turned on his side and slept.

He slept well. His ankle had gone down with his boots off and it felt much better. He ate. He felt heartened. He forgot the comforts of north of the wire. He had a job to do, and those comforts he had longed for were illusory. They were under seige up there and just maybe he could help lift the seige.

His mental adjustment was complete. He had shaken off the north and his weakness with it. Jake packed carefully and emerged into the hostile world.

The air was cold and raw but he felt warm in his survival clothing. If he went north west he would hit Dorchester. There he would find out what was going on.

When he came to a road he ignored it, striking out across country instead. It lay bare and empty. The occasional barn had been fired. He rested when he needed to and ate again. His food was simple and untasty but he had plenty of it. The soldiers had warned him he should eat well. It would keep his spirits up, keep him alert, and keep his strength up. They could bring him out if he ran out, or drop more food. He shouldn't hoard it.

It was a timeless day. At the end of it he came to the outskirts of the town. He would wait for dark to enter. He folded himself into the corner of a garden shed and slept.

He entered quietly, keeping to the edges and striving to attract no attention to himself. The first thing he realised was that the once pretty town was unrecognisable. It was razed almost. It might as well have been blanket-bombed. Ruined buildings stood as blackened fangs reaching blindly to a dull sky. Façades gaped like Hollywood stage sets, like false towns erected in the desert.

An open area had crude brick and wood shelters, lean-to erections. Here in its centre Jake saw the men of the south.

They sat round bonfires cooking, smoking, talking together. Jake watched from the shadows for a while. After some time he observed a woman tied to a stake to one side of the camp. She had her hands tied and she was tethered to the stake. She was naked.

Jake watched quietly.

She stood up and became restless. Jake heard her calling. Whether she uttered words or whether she bayed like an animal, he did not know.

The noise round the campfires increased. There was some

laughter. A man stood up and casually walked over to the woman.

For a moment he stood out of her reach. Jake saw her imploring, writhing on the end of her tether. His gorge rose. The woman couldn't help it. This was sick.

The man stepped forward quite deliberately. She touched him. Immediately he pulled his clothes apart. Now the two of them were equally eager. Equally desperate. They fell to the ground together. Seconds later he was in her, bumping away.

He stood up, staggering slightly. He adjusted his clothes. He shambled off.

Another man took his place. Then another. It was a fast-fuck service she offered. She was a canteen queen, offering quick sex like a plate of chips to all who stood in line.

Jake had stopped feeling appalled. He still didn't like the woman being tethered. He had a feeling that certain aspects of the new order were not entirely bad. The woman wanted it. The men wanted it. He knew that such bizarrely circumstanced sex conferred health and strength and immense well-being. Meanwhile it wasn't such a dreadful thing. The very openness of it, so shocking at first, was something you got used to. Maybe it would be nice to have a good satisfying poke just when you felt like it from street dispensers, like getting money out of bank cashpoint. People would be a lot less chewed up if this basic urge was expressed with greater freedom.

When all this was over, maybe people would have learnt something. A relationship could be great but sometimes you just wanted a fuck.

He went on through the night, keeping to the shadows still. He needed to learn how this new society worked. He had to appear to obey its rules or he would be picked up.

He shrank back suddenly behind the ruins of a some shop fronts. He could hear what sounded suspiciously like marching boots.

They came swinging into view, marching in step with arms smartly swinging. Jake was bemused. They looked like an army except that they were not in uniform. Were these resisters?

They carried torches, flaming brands that lit their ordered ranks. Jake reckoned there were at least two dozen of them. He saw now that they carried something. A palanquin. A raised litter supported by the men.

It contained a woman. She rested like an Oriental potentate looking around her as she was carried through the decimated streets of the little town.

Jake began to follow. Here was order out of mayhem. He needed to know how the trick was done. Why didn't the men climb on top of and ravish their fair burden? Were they immune?

He backtracked the way he had come, trailing the little procession. He saw the campsite he had observed before. His blood quickened. This would be interesting.

The procession halted. Someone blew a trumpet. The men of the campsite rose and hurried over. They prostrated themselves on the ground. The woman on the litter stood.

She was high, her feet on the level of the heads of her bodyguard. She stood up surrounded by their burning brands. She was not entirely naked. She wore some kind of bracing or strapping across her body so that her breasts and belly and buttocks were still bared, and they were enhanced by her curious gear. A few filmy pieces of material were attached to places on her leather strapping.

She was awesome. She was mysterious. She was at once commanding, powerful and beautiful. She stood with her veils blowing, metal bosses on her garment shining, and her long hair lifted in the night breeze. All around her men knelt. Then they stood, humbly, with downcast eyes.

Taking her time she looked slowly round them. The torch light was reflected up and down her long gleaming limbs.

Jake wondered why her veils didn't catch in the flame.

He wondered a whole lot of things.

She pointed. The crowd hissed and sighed. A man stepped forward.

Jake had eased forward to join the rear of the crowd. He felt the magnetic attraction of the woman. She was glorious, fear-inspiring.

His heart lurched. He felt sweat prickle on his forehead. He knew her. He knew who she was.

That cheeky little reporter who used her body to get her story. This was Sally Trenning, fox-red hair and youthful beauty all intact.

Jake gaped. She lay back on her litter and opened her legs wide.

The chosen man walked up to the litter. It was still raised on the shoulders of the bodyguard, supported by six men at least.

Sally moved. She drew her knees up. The crowd surged closer.

The man walked between her legs and placed his face in her groin. Before some sixty people, the chosen man began to lap Sally, to lick her pussy, to bring her to orgasm by putting his tongue in her cunt in front of everyone.

He worked at her and she writhed pleasurably. It was gross. Jake remembered the close-up of the squirming sex of one of the touched women. He imagined his face in there, his mouth over Sally's musk, his tongue in her sexual juices.

He had kissed her there in the old days. This public offering made him feel hot and ashamed. And horny. He had no defence against ordinary sexual arousal. Somehow the sight of Sally's cunt being worshipped in this way, before an adoring audience, made his trousers tight.

Sally was calling out, shouting in ecstasy. Then she was done. She lay back sleepily. Then she clicked her fingers. The crowd fell back. The guard reformed. They began to march away.

Dazed, Jake followed, slipping from shadow to shadow, unable to do anything else. He became aware another followed. It was the woman from the camp, the woman who had been tethered. Now she was released and she stumbled along behind Sally Trenning and her pet men. Had Sally instructed this to be so? Jake shook his head. There was so much he didn't know.

Part of him still knew that he was in a little burnt-out town. Part of him still knew who he was, what he was doing. That part of him became dimmer and dimmer. Brighter flames burnt in his consciousness.

He was aware of sex, of the smell of sex, of the adoration of sex, all around him. The figure carried on the litter loomed larger and larger in his awareness. She was archetypally female. She was beautiful. She was womanly. She invited and caressed her followers by allowing them to take part in her triumphal progress. He was uplifted by his nearness to her.

Every so often she stopped and gazed upon the crowd. The men stood humbly round, worshipping her. She would select one and he would have congress with her. Then the procession would continue, eternal through the dark fire-lit night.

A man climbed aboard her swaying platform and knelt between her open legs, slipping his hard sex into her endlessly greedy body. Copulating together surrounded by the burning brands, it was primevally powerful. The man's head was thrown back as he plunged into the woman. It was in shadow and hard to see, almost as if it wasn't there. It didn't matter. Jake thought horribly of the praying mantis. The female may eat her copulating partner during the act itself, beginning with his head. It may even enhance his sexual abilities, since the head contains inhibitory nerves.

What need had a man for a head, for the ability to think, when he served the touched?

Again she chose. This time she was entered from the rear, the kneeling man serving the woman on all fours with her back to him. Jake was closer now. He saw the swaying balls. He saw Sally's firm rounded buttocks. What filled his mind was not disgust but envy. She was so beautiful. She was beyond beauty. She was wonderful, magnificent, awesome, incredible . . .

He wanted her. He wanted to be selected. He didn't stand back now and hide. He pressed forward in the crowd each time she stopped her Pied Piper procession. He was an eager rat. There was honour in mounting her and a blessing to be had. He longed for it.

There were women in the procession. These lesser lights made little local fornications, bubbles of sex in the crowd. They reached and touched as they required a man and so were serviced. The two would break rapidly apart as soon as they had finished and rush on to catch up with the main action.

Jake was caught himself in this way. He was touched and immediately she began to pulling his clothes apart.

For a moment he faltered, coming back to himself. Fatally, his sex softened. It was Sally who aroused his lust, not this nymphet busy in the crowd. She had no power to touch him and so her magic didn't work.

He pulled himself together. He had his identity to hide. He looked over at Sally and let his mind dwell both on remembered and anticipated pleasures. The smell of the scene filled his nostrils. Burning tar. Sweat. Excitement. Sex. Winter-cold air held at bay. All his senses were crazed, his eyes, his sense of smell, his ears – he looked at his toucher feeling the excitement of the crowd in his blood so that he was one with them and glad to be so. This creature before him was ripe and delectable, plump breasts, plump little hips, a pleasing tangle of dark hair below her little round belly.

She lay on her back in the mud and grit of the broken road surface. She squirmed delightfully. Jake knelt and found that mercifully his body was obedient. It would play the game and not let him down.

She was pleasant to shaft. He had been aching for Sally and this was a relief. Her little plump cunt cuddled his cock gleefully extracting such vigorous and hearty pleasure that Jake was sorry it was over so soon. He wanted to laugh. A manic exhilaration possessed him. She had no desire to hang about. The procession was moving on. She stood up and, without a word said, scuttled off.

Jake hesitated a moment doing up his clothes. His thoughts jangled in no logical sequence. He was getting carried away. The girl was quite clean. He was forgetting his mission. Why had she no dirt on her back when she stood up? He was in danger of exposing himself.

He longed to fuck Sally.

The awareness of this hammered in his brain. He was being attacked on a more subtle level that just touching. His protection against that was working fine, he had had natural sex with the mysteriously grime-free girl. Yet he wanted to succumb to Sally. He yearned to be up there on the litter in full view, receiving her strange benediction.

The procession went on. More and more people became attached. Like a long snake they flowed through the broken town. Primitive music played somewhere so that they danced and jigged as they followed the litter.

Did this happen nightly? How come Sally had this superiority over other women? Out of the anarchy and mayhem of the touchers a new order was appearing, a new hierarchy.

Who headed it?

They went on and on. Jake became tired. The music was in his blood. It disturbed his thoughts. It was easy not to think at all. He was the music. He was the night. He was fire. He was in some way a part of the woman who led them. He wanted to join with her and confirm his belonging.

Dawn paled the eastern sky. The torches burned dim. The men stumbled with weariness. Only the guard who carried Sally maintained a firm step. As did the women.

The procession left the town, winding off into the countryside. Now it was all female save for the guard. Men collapsed and lay where they fell, snoring deeply.

Jake stumbled to one side blindly seeking somewhere to hide. He found a wall and sat on it. Once it had divided two gardens. Now its coping stones were gone and all that remained was a crumbling brick structure. Jake sat astride it for weariness and looked red-eyed at the brightening sky. He shivered. He lay back on the wall folding his hands across his chest. He meant it only for a moment but utter weariness overtook him. He slept.

He dreamed dreams of luxury, of spice and aromatic oil, of exotic perfumes and gorgeous materials, of the silken skins of willing women. He awoke to acute discomfort in some areas of his body and agonising comfort in others.

He lay on his wall with a soft winter sunshine spilling over him. There was even a little warmth in the sun. Astride his loins and moving sweetly was a naked woman.

He should hardly be surprised. He had left himself vulnerable for a passing appetite and here it was, feasting on his flesh. Jake felt momentarily smug. He had been accosted in his sleep and sexually mounted. His body had behaved with aplomb. She would not know he was immune from touching.

He must top up his immunity soon.

She rose and fell softly on his sex so that he enjoyed her taking of him. He watched her as she dreamily fucked up and down. She had small pointed breasts that lifted and fell, their tips caramel coloured. He would have liked to suck her nipples. They looked sweet and saucy.

Her hair was honey-coloured. It fell in a heavy mass about her shoulders. The sun caught it and made it flicker gold and copper as she moved. It was lovely.

Her sexual fleece was also honey-coloured. Jake watched it with appreciation as she worked them both slowly to climax. He would like to see the sun glisten on her sex fur. He would like to tangle his fingers in it and gently tug it till she laughed.

Her face was bland and blank, mindlessly smiling. Her eyes were empty of awareness. Jake knew this was a terrible tragedy even though he couldn't feel it to be so. He was disengaged emotionally from the experience. He could as well be having a manicure or a pedicure except that this was so much nicer. It was good to be serviced in this way. She was a sweet kid.

That was all she was, too. Maybe she was seventeen, maybe eighteen. He liked having such a young thing envelop his cock, take him to the gates of paradise. It made him feel good.

Her hands were warm on his hips. Her whole body warmed him. He touched her skin and felt its smoothness. It was as if it resisted dirt. It was not foul in any way. It glowed a rich healthy colour without pallidness or grubbiness.

He felt the living warmth and power of her inner sex. It drew him inexorably towards climax with it. He felt pulses and ripples stroke his cock as it was squeezed and cuddled and caressed. It felt divine. She was superb. Her delicious fruity sexual parts ate his firm column in gulping bites yet left him intact, alive and responsive.

He grunted as he came, shooting up into her.

She smiled her bland blank smile and swung a leg over as though she was dismounting a horse. She lifted herself but before she could move away Jake caught her hand.

'Hold on,' he said. 'Let me look at you.'

He ignored his own hanging sex, still wetly half-erect. The girl sat obediently and when Jake touched her knees, she opened them.

He looked deep into her sexual parts. He saw them slightly swollen and still puffy from their congress. He saw that they were flushed and slightly trembling. He put in his fingers and delicately felt her clitoris. It vibrated, a tiny stiff soldier under his fingertip.

He ran his fingers along her vulva. All her flesh shook slightly. When he let his fingertips enter her pussy, he could feel its aspen-shiver transmuted through his flesh.

She was so alive.

'Do you know what's happening to you?' he asked gently.

She slid forward. His fingers went deeper into her. Her arms wove round his neck. Her soft lips were pressed to his.

Her breasts crushed between them. Her pussy clenched his fingers. He began to frig her.

She moved and wriggled on the little human spit. Her lips were on his all the time, kissing him, murmuring hungrily, mumbling his skin. One time she hung on to his neck and let herself fall back. He twisted his head down and sucked those little nipples. They were as lovely as he had expected them to be.

There was a special pleasure in masturbating a girl with his fingers all the way to climax. She drew what she wanted from him and took her time, enjoying him in her, enjoying his wriggling finger-worms playing in her pussy. She came in a soft yielding bundle of warm femininity, all glossy hair and soft lips, writhing body and pouting nipples.

She sighed, curling against him with her head on his breast. Then she rose and left him.

He watched her dimpled rounded buttocks as she moved

gracefully away through the rubble. He saw a wisp of steam escape, clear on the sharp air. He saw a tiny slick gather down one inner thigh. His juice. Her juice. He remembered the shiver of her pussy as his fingers entered it. He sucked them now and sighed.

He found a place sheltered from spying eyes. He ate and then he injected himself. Now he was safe again. He slept some more, this time in a cellar in his sleeping bag.

He was aware he was making no progress. His mission was failing, he was proving too weak.

He stayed in hiding all day. He emerged with the dusk and began to roam round the edges of the town.

They came with tinkling bells and banging drums. They came dancing lightly over the landscape to which they seemed immune. It could not hurt them. It could not soil them. It could not chill them. The guard marched in step supporting a woman on a litter. Even at a distance Jake could see it wasn't Sally.

Some one else's turn. Could this be Sonia? He was sure she was close, within a few miles of him.

The women attendants did handstands, turned somersaults, and swept into the town with burning torches and bright energy. They had energy for one thing only, Jake knew, but their energy for that was limitless.

He was more prepared now. He stayed clear of the sexual progress knowing its seductive dangers. It enticed, it encouraged, it pleaded that he join it.

He didn't. Instead he watched and waited the long night through, nodding with sleep much of the time.

At dawn he saw them leave. He hitched his gear close about him and prepared to follow.

They left the town going north and very slightly west. They were on the road to Sherborne via Cerne Abbas. Sometimes they stayed on the road. Sometimes they went across the fields, but always they headed north. Chalk downland rose before them. Jake crept across stubble fields, across plough, sliding through hedgerows and copses. He was in crop circle country, he remembered. He spared a grin for the ingenuity of the hoaxers.

If only this sex thing was hoax, a cosmic joke perpetrated on men by women. What a relief all round that would be.

He remembered the sleepers. Where were they? Why were they? What would happen to them?

A slight mist rose from the ground into the colder air. It hung trapped at the foot of the massive ridge rearing before them, catching the weak rays of the winter sun. Through its dim gold radiance Jake saw something loom over him. Something familiar, a known sight.

Vast through the mist the naked man shimmered. Jake's hackles rose. It was a ghost memory, something seen but not believed. It was familiar but terrible. It hovered in the air, the gigantic penis triumphantly upraised, the swollen fruiting testicles suspended below.

The Cerne Giant. One hundred and eighty feet high he towered. Forty-five feet across at his shoulders. The great erect figure striding triumphantly along the downs was either a Romano-British dirty joke on an awesome scale, or a deity to be worshipped. The phallus. The seed-spiller. Man-god. Man-cock.

It had a basic congruity that the women in this locality should gather beneath its chalky protection. No doubt it pleased them to have a cock so graphic about them. They didn't appear to think of much else, and it was surely true that here men had become reduced to their sexual appendages.

Jake cheered up. He didn't know why. It was hard to take the mighty figure as anything but a huge and vulgar joke and that gave him a feeling of kinship with his ancestors. It was, in addition, a relief to see that the women were susceptible to his gargantuan charms. If he felt linked to the past by his appreciation of the figure, so too did it link them with the known, the acceptable, the real. Had he been haunted with a half-held view that they might be aliens? That his beloved home planet might have been invaded? That they had met up with something they could not control?

It wasn't so. The women were aberrant, but as natural as the monstrosity of the hill. His mind could contain them. The problem would be solved.

The whole crazy column entered the blackened stumps of the village tucked slyly at the Giant's feet. Jake lay in a shrubbery and thought.

They did not emerge on the other side. He hadn't expected them to. He had reached some local headquarters, so much was obvious. He would have to investigate.

He ate and rested. He had had a lot of sleep in the last twenty-four hours. That was good, very good. Perhaps now he would have a chance to act.

In the afternoon a new column emerged and began to head towards the town in the south.

He switched on his radio and called up the way he had been taught. He felt a mild surprise that it was successful. This was followed by a cold feeling. They expected him to succeed. Now he was out here, he realised how fatuous his thinking had been, how frail his logic. He felt that understanding was coming closer to him but not a resolution. The problem was too vast, too far gone.

And they hung on his words.

He told them where he was and explained that he intended to get closer that night. They told him how they now saw that there was a population movement towards where he was. By slow degrees people were concentrating. They drifted, they clustered, they came together. Slow but sure there was a considerable build up in his area.

Jake was surprised. He had seen hardly anyone since leaving Dorchester. They had satellite pictures, he knew, and were now watching this area particularly. Maybe they were seeing a focus that didn't exist. Maybe he had done the same himself.

He went in in the dark. The village was empty. Some houses were boarded up. Some were ashy heaps. No one was there. Jake slunk about with all his senses alert. It was most creepy. He wondered if they had all left for the south and would not be back till mid-morning.

He saw a pale glimmer and crouched low. His heart hammered absurdly. Witches. Ghosts. Giants. He was having altogether too many supernatural thoughts.

Mothlike, things glimmered on the edges of his eyesight. Pale things hovered, joined, and moved apart. He smelt a sour-spice smell.

The hairs on the back of his neck erected themselves into little spines. I am descended from something fourfooted, he thought wildly. Otherwise the crest-erecting would be higher up, more on the top of the skull.

They were searching for him. They were sniffing the air. They were hunting him.

He broke cover and ran at them. They offered no physical threat. His nerves were getting the better of him and sapping his confidence. He was afraid.

They laughed as he ran by. It was soft musical laughter. Things fluttered in the air, shadows took substance and then disappeared. His arm was caught and released.

He ran. He came out of the village and saw them ahead of him. The women. They came fluttering and running and laughing, their breasts bouncing, their hair flying. Their arms were outstretched towards him.

He ran, ducking and weaving. They were throwing nets at him, trying to twist him in the webbing and bring him down.

His chest heaved. He didn't know which way to go. There were so many of them. Always they came at him, laughing and throwing their nets.

He was tiring. His legs ached. Around him in the dark they smiled as they hunted him. They were going to get him. He couldn't escape.

He ran at them again. They were solid. He couldn't crash through them in his big boots, stamping on their soft flesh, crushing their pretty rounded limbs, making their breasts bleed, bruising their sweet bellies, their buttocks.

They closed in a ring round him. They came closer and closer. He stood panting, his head lowered like a bull's.

No, not the bullfight. It wasn't that they reminded him of the bullfight so much. He knew what he felt like. He knew what they were like.

He was the male member. He was the erect man. He stood in the circle of womanhood with it closing round him. They pulsed slightly, they throbbed as they came closer and closer to squeeze him in their tight hot embrace. He could smell them.

Had this happened long ago on these chalk downs? Had neolithic women closed around some hapless male and crushed him in their sexual embrace? Was this the re-enactment of some pagan sexual right? If so, he was the victim, the sacrifice.

He was the intruder.

They pressed close. Stifled, Jake cried out. His legs gave way. Their animal smell swept over him. He fell and was absorbed into their heaving mass of naked femininity.

He came round an unknown time later. He woke from sleep, somehow having passed from unconsciousness to this kinder state.

He felt light, limber and free. His body was marvellous. He felt the sunlight flow gently, warmly, through his veins.

He lay at peace savouring his inexpressible sense of well-being.

A gong beat slowly in his mind. A warning bell. He ignored it. If this was a dream then he would enjoy it a little longer. The time to wake up was not yet.

His eyes opened. He was bathed in light. He looked down his body and admired it. It didn't look bad, even with no clothes on.

No clothes on. Was that a cause for worry? No. Not yet. Life was too pleasant to worry about little things like no clothes.

Jake sighed and stretched. He was on a bed. It had some silken material over it which was cool to his body. This was pleasant because his surroundings were warm, very warm. Was he in hell? Jake giggled to himself.

The bed was curtained but the curtains were drawn back and tied. Jake looked lazily to see where he was.

He lay in a large room artificially lit. A fountain tinkled and gently splashed. Music played. It was very hack, like a cheap Hollywood movie. It was also wonderful.

He lay thinking about very little. Some women came in. Veils fluttered from them. One approached the bed.

She was tall, maybe as tall as himself. She had rich brown hair which was coiled about her head. Wide hazel eyes were sombre and thoughtful. Deep full breasts swung as she walked.

She sat on the bed and looked down at him.

'Hello,' he said.

She touched his cock. It stirred slightly but it did not rise. 'Can you explain this?' she asked. She had a deep voice. Jake saw the little tufts of hair at her armpits. Her belly was very hairy low down, a thick glossy fleece of it masking her sex.

'Where am I?'

'Where have you come from?'

'London. I was in London.'

'I see.' She looked at him thoughtfully. 'What's your name?'

'Jake Connors. And yours?'

'Marilyn. Can you explain your immunity?'

'No. Are you a toucher?'

'Yes.'

'How come you can talk? Most of them only have one form of communication.'

'Mmm.' She smiled. 'How have you managed the demands made on you?'

'I'm quite fit. I have a certain natural ability. Otherwise I hid.'

'We find it curious, the equipment you carry.'

'I was a soldier. I treated it like being in a foreign land. One I was at war with.'

'Enemy territory.' She smiled again.

'Was I so wrong?'

'Perhaps not. There is a new order to get used to. You will acclimatise, of course, but it will help if you view us as your friends. Your protectors.'

'I can protect myself.' Jake was nettled.

'Can you?'

The question hung between them.

'Are you a leader?' asked Jake presently.

'Yes.'

'The leader?'

'No.'

'Who is she?'

'She is a mystery.'

'Where is she?'

'Where she wishes to be.'

'Is she here?'

'Sometimes.'

'Is she here now?'

'Who knows?'

'You do,' said Jake brutally.

Marilyn laughed. 'Why don't you enjoy our facilities while we decide what to do with you?'

'You can talk. This place isn't burned. How come?'

'We have control. Some of us, I mean. Those who do are the leaders. It is very simple. Our new ability can be organised to suit us. The weaker sisters are slave to their condition but we help them. In return they obey us. It is so with men, too. Our New Model Army. Perhaps you have seen them?'

'Is your control chemical? I mean, do you take something so that you have control?'

'My, my. What a strange soldier you are.'

Jake was silent. Then he said: 'May I have my things? I'd like to shave.'

'My ladies will shave you.'

'I'd like my things. I'd prefer to be dressed, for example.'

'We wouldn't prefer it. Now be good and your life will be pleasantly interesting.'

'And if I am bad?'

'It will be brutishly nasty.'

She laughed and moved away.

Jake felt curious. Had they used his body while he slept? Could he have climaxed in a woman unknown to his conscious self? Had he been drugged or hypnotised?

How strange to think his body was the property of any passing woman.

Now they came for him. They were so pretty. The veils they wore were attached to little jewelled collars about their necks. The veils fluttered loosely attached only by one corner. Thus when the girls moved all their pretty bodies were revealed in a pleasing nudity. When they were still the veils fell together so that their naked charms were obscured and smokily hidden.

The effect was bewitching. Jake could not help smiling. As if they understood, they laughed and twirled, their arms held high in the air.

Jake's cock stirred.

'Would you like a bath?' one asked. It was hard to distinguish between them.

'A bath, a bath,' the others faintly chanted.

'Yes, please.'

They caught his hands and made him stand up. He towered over them. He was partly erect now. He couldn't help it. They were a ravishing dream.

They led him across the wide mosaic floor. He would have liked to study it. His impression was of nymphs and satyrs at play. They went past the fountain to where there was a deep trough in the floor. This was filled with faintly steaming water, a deep blue because the bath was tiled so. Dolphins leapt joyously around the bath, on tiles, that is.

They walked down steps, three of them, Jake in the centre. Their veils stayed on the surface of the water. Now Jake was able to lie back. His hands came out of their own accord. He touched a breast. He touched a sexual fleece. Legs parted in the warm embrace of the water. His fingers drifted into intimate inlets in convoluted and complex shores. Between their thighs the girls had coastlines of delight, deep fjords, bays and openings. Jake closed his eyes. Hands supported him. The water held him weightless. Lips brushed against his ears and neck.

They soaped him, all of them now in the water with him. The little pool had five women and one man in it. It was full enough so that Jake rolled against their skin all the time. Plump breasts were under his shoulders. Thighs curled round his legs. Everywhere about him hands soaped and rubbed his body so that his skin was cleansed and perfumed and aroused.

Hands stroked his cock, masturbating him gently and teasing him. What a game it all was to them. They washed his hair. They rinsed him. They led him from the bath.

He lay heavy and warm on thick towels. They patted him dry with little caressing movements, interrupting themselves to kiss his skin. They touched him where they pleased. He was languorous and compliant. This was nothing to fight against, even if he could.

His eyes were shut. Now his buttocks were opened. Lips kissed his secret places. Tongues naughtily poked. He heard them laugh. His balls were played with, lifted and stroked and cradled. He felt his foreskin drawn back. The tip of his cock was kissed. His chest was kissed. His throat was kissed. His ears were kissed and penetrated by tongues.

When he was dry they transferred him to a clean towel spread on a high padded bench. Now they massaged him. Oils were rubbed into his skin. He lay slack under their hands. Every part of him felt marvellous.

They shaved him. They dried his hair. They kissed his cock. They led him to the bed.

He lay nested in beautiful women. They tickled him with their hair. They kissed each other, tongue tip to tongue tip, leaning over him so that their breasts stroked his chest while they did it. He lay on his back with his arms and legs open, his palms up.

Two heads bent over his groin. Two sets of lips kissed his cock on its opposite sides. They licked and sucked at its sides gently. A third face pressed down from above. Two women kissed his stalk and caressed his balls. A third kissed the head and began to suck him.

He opened his eyes to watch. It ravished his vision almost as much as it ravished his cock. At either side of him the two remaining girls turned their backs and bent over. They reached behind themselves and held their buttocks apart. They had their rears slightly raised. Jake saw straight into their sexual country.

He reached out his hands. He slid a finger into one girl's pussy. She wriggled and he felt her try to clamp him tightly. He moved the finger in and out. She sighed and squirmed on him.

He licked the forefinger of his other hand. When it was well wetted, he began to slide it into the rear of the other girl who pouted her bottom at him. She gave a delighted squeal. She thrust back on him. His finger slid into her bottom. Below it her pussy gaped and dripped. He put his thumb into it and began to work her with finger and thumb, in arse and pussy.

He looked between the two writhing bottoms. The three heads bent over him. He sighed and let go.

He climaxed hard up into the mouth of one of the girls. All three made the climax perfect, holding his shaft, his tip, his balls, in marvellous coordination.

They stroked and soothed his cock as it relaxed and softened. Jake twisted himself and applied his lips to the pussy of the girl he had put a finger in.

He sucked her lovely musk. He felt her orgasm and tasted her nectar. He licked roughly along her vulva until her throbbing had eased. Then he turned his attention to the girl he ravished by arse and pussy.

He would suck her too. He kept his finger in her rear and sucked and licked her pulsing length, pushing his tongue in, running it round, stabbing her interior with fierce little blows till he felt her come too. Ah, the sweetness of her come, her musk. He lapped her eagerly. She was divine.

If there was something he should be doing, he could do it another time.

They fed him. Grapes were suspended above his face. He bit at them while the juice ran over his chin. They lapped up the juice, their breasts pressing softly into his flesh as they lay against him.

He was fed cubes of freshly grilled steak. Cooked tomatoes, warm and squishy in their skins, were gently squeezed so that they dripped into his open mouth. He was given wine to drink, his head supported while he drank it. He had to do nothing for himself. They did it all.

He ate a marvellous concoction of fruits and vegetables and meats. It was all flavoured with spices and herbs. Later they fed him sweet things and gave him coffee, bitter and strong in a small cup.

There was more wine. Now they crooned over his cock again. Jake was heavy-eyed. He slept.

He woke not knowing the time. His watch was gone. How long had he been here? Soon he would be susceptible. He might be so already.

The room he was in had no windows. Its walls were curious and when he explored, something he felt almost too lazy to do, he found they were of rough chalk with tapestries and hangings over them. Chalk and rock. He was in a cavern. He was underground.

It was a fantasy place, like a fairy castle with its gorgeous hangings, its boudoir furniture, its fountain. Its sunken bath.

He enjoyed the bath again. The girls were there. He was locked in the cavern by perfectly workman-like doors at all times. The girls were admitted or excluded by some other's wish.

They were delightful. Endlessly they played with his body. He was soothed, excited, caressed and massaged.

His mind slipped. He felt sleepy for much of the time. He felt mentally inert and passive. If there were things to do, they could be comfortably delayed. Later would be soon enough. Meanwhile these lovely creatures fed him, tended him, aroused him and satisfied him.

He became unaware of when they came and when they left. Sometimes he would open his eyes from a vague and formless dream and look down his body. Giggling, they would be clustered about him. One would reach forward. He would see some detail that his mind would fix on. Perhaps her fingernails were painted a sugary gleaming pink. He would watch the pink nails come closer and close. Like the brush of a feather, like a butterfly landing, they would touch his sex. Immediately it would spring up. Feeling would ripple through him. His need would fill him.

It was all right. It was always all right. One would immediately push her veils aside and climb on to him. Eager hands would grasp his shaft. The one upon him would hold her sex open. Then she would lower herself. Fingers would tickle his shaft as it vanished into her interior. Hands would cradle his balls. Breasts would brush softly against his ribs, his chest. Hair would slip over him like silk. Lips would touch his eyelids, his mouth, his nipples.

He would lie doing nothing, not one thing. The girl on him would do all the work of bringing herself and him to sexual satisfaction. She would be so good at it. They were all so good at it. So uniformly good.

Each cunt, and there were five to be his constant playthings, was a firm warm juicy hole that sucked his rampant pole eagerly into its cushioned depths. He felt surrounded by cunts. He was. One slipped from his sex to be replaced by another. It didn't matter whose it was. Each was delicious, rosy, squashily tight, electrically alive.

He slid from fantasy to fact and back to fantasy without ever knowing the borders of reality and when he crossed them. He slept and dreamed and woke and dreamed, as they fucked him, bathed him, fed him, cleansed him. Were they his playthings or was he theirs? Was he their pet?

His mind grappled soggily. Was he being drugged? Perhaps

he shouldn't eat their food. He could never escape this jewelled net they had him in. His body must obey their wishes. He had no say in the matter.

A dim panic seized Jake. He had been gone from himself too long. He didn't know where he was or what he was doing. His mind was too tired to work out why he was here or what had happened to him. When he tried to apply it, to think consistently, he would find he was ravished by pretty things. He was adored. His cock was worshipped. It was so much pleasure, such endless pleasure.

How long had he been here? Days, or was it weeks? Steadily the feeling of unease grew. It was hard now either way. It was hard to think. But it was equally hard to yield mindlessly to his playmates' attentions. Their hands were as clever roving his body. Their fingers were as invasive. Their tongues were as naughty. Their lips were as soft. Breast and buttock, hip and thigh, he was continuously assaulted and he liked it, he did. Who wouldn't? But it was no longer enough.

He had no means of knowing the time. He could not tell day from night. The cavern was endlessly bright with indirect lighting. In the end he crouched by the doors and waited.

The first time he did this he fell asleep and they found him there when they came, wrapped in a blanket cloak fashion and asleep on the floor.

The second time he was successful. The doors opened, they came in and Jake threw himself at the gap.

There was corridor outside with women moving along it. Jake shoved hard and found himself outside the doors of his cell. The corridor was the same in either direction. He chose one and ran.

He had had, in common with the rest of the human race, dreams of running through treacle. Running through glue. Dreams where he had needed to run urgently but couldn't for unspecified, horrible dream-reasons.

Now he knew the reality. His body had received only one form of exercise for an unknown length of time. His legs were heavy and stupid. His running was more of a shambling shuffle. He could not get speed and force into his escape. The mists cleared as terror gripped him. His blood ran faster, his mind became sharper, but his legs were leaden impediments and he wanted to fall down and give up.

He could hear the breath rasping in his chest. He passed startled faces. Hands were held out. He was touched.

It had occurred to him foggily that recently he didn't respond quite so quickly to being touched as he had before. Now the familiar thrill exploded from his groin. His cock lifted hard erect. His balls felt tight. His belly seethed. Like a firework exploding, sensation rained in glittering sparks out from his sexual core. It was beautiful. It was thrilling. It was the best high in the world. He needed sex and he was going to have it – Jake cried out in agony.

He mustn't give way. He ran like a winged bird, lolloping along the endless corridor. The faces turned to him were amused now, or sweetly pleading.

Again he was touched. Coruscations of desire flamed through his body. He tripped and almost fell. He needed to sink his cock into something, he needed it.

They caught him. He fell to his knees, held by either arm. His face was down, his chin against his heaving chest. He sobbed dryly.

He was touched and touched again. His cock vibrated stiffly, he needed sex so badly. They held him kneeling there and something was brought.

He felt cold metal. He cried out and was struck across the face. They were bolting something around his hips, touching his desperate cock. He was flooded with failure. The women bent round him. His disgrace was absolute.

They hauled him to his feet. He looked down.

About his hips was a metal belt locked tight. A bar went between his legs. He was reminded of the bit between a horse's teeth. From this bar and also made of metal was a contrivance. It was a tube. His cock had been inserted into this tube which had an open end.

He was in a chastity belt. Despite his erection and his terrible need, it was impossible for him to obtain relief. He could not be masturbated. He could not enter a woman. His cock was inside the tube and it was impossible to touch it except by poking a finger up the open outer end. One could just touch it, fingertip to cocktip, then. But nothing else.

Jake stood shakily between his captors. 'Why have you done this?' he said hoarsely. He hadn't spoken much during his captivity. It was strange to hear his own voice form words.

'You have abused our hospitality.' It was Marilyn. She faced him, stern and queenly.

'You can't blame me for wanting to be free. It's natural.'

'Many things are natural including murder. We forbid them. It is our society. You have no say in the matter. Your opinions are worthless. We are uninterested in any speech you might have.'

They did not take him back along the corridor to his lushly appointed cell. Instead he was led forward. He became aware he was in a building rather than underground. They took him into a room, bare and small. He was chained to the wall and left.

He became hungry.

He was cold and hungry and bitterly uncomfortable in the humiliating object they forced him to wear. Unfed, he found his mind cleared. He had been drugged, then. He had been tranquillised.

Now he was to be punished. It wasn't entirely bad. However vile his punishment and however apparent his humiliation, at least he was master of his own mind again. They had given him back to himself and for this he was profoundly thankful. That was the worst of all, not being able to think. He might as well have been dead.

Meanwhile he had no idea how much time had passed since he was taken captive in the village. Certainly a week, maybe a month. He found it hard to believe it was longer than that.

He remembered that nightmarish run where even his hips had seemed dislocated, his movements were so clumsy. He got to his feet and began to exercise. He must strengthen his flabby muscles.

He was tired and even hungrier. His stomach rumbled. He wondered whether he would be strong enough to refuse food and drink if it was brought to him. He couldn't know whether such a gesture was even necessary. He could think of no good reason for tranquillising him in his present state. He was securely and humiliatingly bound. He was at their mercy. He was due for punishment, not soothing.

They came with food in the end and left it on a tray within his reach. One of the two who came reached into the steel tube in which his sex was encased and touched him.

It was cruel. His cock jerked awake. The need for sex filled his guts and his belly. They giggled and left him.

In these circumstances Jake ate. He didn't see any point to their drugging him, and indeed he felt no tranquillising effects from the meal. Quite the contrary. As his physical strength was restored, he became angry. A fury as naked as his skin filled him. He wanted to throttle someone. He felt his muscles bulge helplessly. He bent over his aching unsatisfied sex and beat the floor.

At least twenty-four hours passed. He had no bed, no mattress, no chair. He sat on the stone floor and shivered. He was chained from a collar at his neck and from the steel chastity belt around his hips, chained to ringbolts in the wall. He became dirty.

They came in and hosed him down like he was a pig in a pen. In a sense he was. They fed him. Then they stood back against the walls. They looked expectant. The door was open. More women filed in and lined the walls. They all waited. Someone was coming. Someone important.

Eleven

Jake felt his body hair erect itself in a primitive reaction of fear. In his youth he had thought that if he were ever to meet something truly strange, he would react with an open enquiring mind.

Now, when it happened, he felt fear.

She was recognisable, just. Whatever this was that entered his cell and stood before him, he knew what it had been before. What it was now was beyond him. The woman-thing was tall and stern. Its eyes seemed to gaze inward. They were not devoid of expression. Simply, they were little concerned with externals. Jake was himself included in those externals.

He could not focus on what she wore. She was certainly not naked as the women who roamed the countryside outside had been naked, and she was certainly not coyly dressed in a few flimsy transparent veils that floated up and away from the charms they mistily hid the moment their wearer was in motion.

She was fire-wreathed. It was cold fire, a flickering greenish light that made flame shapes round her person, obscuring her, making her a glimmering image. It was ghastly. It was superstitiously fearful. It was in the oldest sense, horrid.

She stood tranquil amid her reverent followers.

'Sonia,' said Jake. His voice cracked slightly. He was aware of the degradation of his condition.

Gradually her attention became focused on him. During

the unpleasant few seconds while this occurred, Jake became angry.

'What did you do with the bodies?' he said harshly.

Now he had her attention. Her brow furrowed. Sometimes he saw her clearly, or parts of her. At other times the green fire smeared her image and he blinked to see more clearly.

'Bodies?'

'From Timegate.' Jake shouted. Damn the bitch.

'Ah. I released them. But she would not walk with me.'

'Sonia.' He had his temper under better control. 'You've been damaged. Biologically altered. We can help you. You need to be in hospital.'

There was a long silence. 'Do I?' she asked politely.

Whatever she was, a sense of humour was included in the package. That had to be good news, it was so human an attribute.

'You've destroyed this country. All the towns burned. All the people fled. It's terrible, Sonia. You can stop it.'

'There will be a new order. We are in transition.'

Jake tried to move towards her. His chains rattled. He swallowed. 'I read your diary.'

'My . . . oh yes. My diary. I remember.'

'Your mother gave it to me. She was in hospital. I don't know where she is now.'

'I do.'

It was a lever. She had memory. She had feelings from the old life.

'You loved me,' said Jake. It was his ace. His last card.

She smiled and green fire burned, silent and cold.

'Let me go. I'll return north. For the feeling you once had for me.'

'We can do better than that. I've looked after you for a long time. In the old life. And since. I sent ones to watch you. You fought with them and they lost track of you. Then you disappeared. You see, you needed my protection. You have been foolish.'

She stepped towards him. Two women immediately came to Jake, on either side. The steel brace was removed from his hips.

Sonia stretched out her hand. Jake saw green fire leap from her fingertips. Her hand went down. It pointed at him, at his revealed sex. She advanced a step still holding her hand stiffly towards him, towards his sex. Jake reversed till his back was against the wall. He shivered uncontrollably. She took another step forward.

'No,' screamed Jake.

She touched him.

Green fire flickered in his groin. From its midst his sex projected. His insides burned. He pressed himself against the cold wall in desperation. The heat was terrible. His insides flamed and melted. His eyes were shut as he struggled to control himself against the onslaught of pain.

He gasped as breath whooshed from his tortured lungs. He opened his eyes.

The thing that was Sonia was attached to him like a vast evil proboscis. She was taking her leisurely will with his sex. She had turned round and bent over. Willing acolytes had fed his flaming shaft into her open orifice. Now they manipulated him so that he performed his animal duty.

In and out it went. He saw his own cock sink into her flaming sex. He felt his pain and heat absorbed and made over. He felt the flicker of her will. She had a desire to teach him what he was, what she was. He felt her control on his innermost desires and feelings. He was cupped in her, cured in her, hurt in her. She could kill him.

He knew it. She could kill him like this. With a flick of her mind she could cause his death via the link between her sex and his.

He could not disobey the demand she made on him. Even as his thoughts worked in him, so he continued to serve her as she required.

She was done. She stood up and turned round. Jake sank to his knees on his release. His body was in shock. When he looked up she was gone.

The women filed out. The door was shut. He was alone as before. Now he was chained by his neck only. They had not replaced that hideous belt.

The entire terrifying process was repeated the next day. The third day was different.

The women entered and lined the walls. Sonia entered in flames. On this third occasion Jake dropped to his knees. He was learning.

'Why do you do me this honour?' he asked huskily.

She was silent, watching him.

Jake bent as far as he was able, given the length of his neck chain. He touched the floor with his forehead.

He looked up at Sonia. 'I worship you. I obey you.'

She smiled and gestured for him to stand. Things proceeded as before.

On the fourth day Jake knelt again, touching his forehead. 'You honour me,' he said again. 'You are mighty. You are marvellous. It is my part to serve.'

He did indeed serve her and then she was gone. An hour later they came for him.

He was bathed and perfumed, his hair washed, and he was shaved. The collar was kept on him and he was led on his chain to a set of chambers underground.

Music played. The air was perfumed. A large carved chair sat at one end of the room. Jake was led up to it. When he was close enough he cast himself full length on the ground.

Sonia gestured for him to rise. A footstool was by her feet. She indicated that Jake should sit on it. He shook his head. 'I am your dog,' he said and crawled on all fours. Sonia took the end of his chain and looked thoughtfully at him. He curled at her feet and kissed them.

Women came and went. Things were discussed. Sonia gave orders. Then her need came over her. She bent over Jake. He kissed her feet some more.

Her flame licked hot over his skin. Now he was not so afraid, it hurt less. It was not so much the flame that burned him. Rather it was skin contact with her.

She led him to a couch. Unconcerned by her courtiers' presence she lay back. Jake came up on her. She touched him and his sex leapt at her command. He dropped it swiftly into the fire of her hole. He began to service her. As much as he was able he tried to use technique and expertise from his past. He tried to give her a good time in the old-fashioned sense.

She rose up when she was done. He saw that her ladies were allowed to satisfy their needs now that she was served. Around the chamber, men had been brought in and were doing their duty.

Jake tried to ignore them. He kissed Sonia's feet, her extended fiery palm. 'I live to serve you,' he whispered, looking up at her.

For a brief moment something flared in her eyes. Then it was gone. He curled at her feet again.

He made them feed him in a bowl. He crouched on all fours and ate from this like a dog. When Sonia stood up to walk, he begged her to take his chain and let him come. He crawled along behind her. The women tittered and laughed. They found him very comical.

Sonia rested on a bed. She issued no commands and so Jake began to touch her. He kissed her feet, her calves, her knees. He stroked her thighs, the green light flickering over his skin as well as hers. It was like stroking a stove.

He reached and stroked her breasts. She lay back, allowing

him to feel her body. He kissed her breasts and her throat. He saw a little brown mole under her chin. He kissed it.

He drew her legs apart. She sighed. He kissed her inner thighs. His fingers strayed. He touched her pussy.

'Why?' she breathed.

'It is all I can do to serve you,' he murmured. 'I worship you.'

She sighed again. Jake kissed her sex.

She didn't stop him. He probed delicately with his tongue. The heat lapped him, against his face, even as he lapped at her sexual parts. He saw her little ramparts and ridges, her fleshy protuberances. He kissed and licked them, nibbling them, biting them into arousal.

He drew his flushed face away to cool. He opened her sex with his hands.

The lobed flesh parted. Now it was crisp and full. Colour flooded it. The green fire ran along and around its convoluted dimensions. Jake plunged his face in and sucked.

He felt her come against his teeth. He swallowed her sexfire and felt it hot in his gut. Her whole vulva pulsed fatly against his mouth. He withdrew with a sob and fell to the ground.

He screamed. He was hit savagely across his head. Light splintered his world and he lost consciousness.

He came back to himself feeling very sick and weak. He groaned at the pain in his head. A hand touched his forehead. A cup was held to his lips. He sipped eagerly feeling the liquid spill. He groaned again at the terrible pain.

The next time he came round was not so bad. The pain had reduced to a dull fearful throbbing. With an effort Jake lifted a sluggish arm. He touched his head gently. It was bandaged.

Either his eyesight had been affected or the room was dimmed. Jake stirred and felt someone by him.

His brow was cooled by cold cloth. A sponge was pressed to his lips and he sucked it. 'What happened?' he murmured.

'You were attacked by one of the men.'

'The men?'

'The serving men. He did his duty. He saw you going beyond your duty voluntarily. This angered him.'

Jake made a great effort. 'Where is my mistress?' he asked. 'Is she safe?'

'She is beyond any man's harm.' His informant was amused. 'She is in the Council Chamber. This is her restroom. She is concerned for your well-being.'

'Tell her,' Jake whispered, 'I wish only to serve. If I cannot serve, I am useless.'

'I will tell her.'

'I am her dog.'

'I will tell her.'

'Thank you. Tell her now. Then I can be happy.'

'I will stay here to look after you. When the mistress comes I will tell her what you say.'

Jake looked agitated. 'I must do it myself,' he muttered and began to crawl out of the bed. He had no strength and he fell.

His nurse helped him back into bed. 'You must rest,' she chided.

'Tell her.'

'I will.'

As soon as he was alone Jake got out of bed. In truth his legs were weak and he felt terrible getting upright. He dropped to his knees and began to crawl about the room.

When the nurse returned to tell him his message was safely passed on Jake was lying weakly in bed with a throbbing head. His pulse fluttered. He refused the soup she offered and slept.

When he next woke Sonia was in the room. Immediately

Jake rolled out of bed and flattened himself on the floor.

'This is not necessary.'

'To me it is.'

She lifted him up. Now her eyes were all green fire and she looked at him. 'Did you care before?' she asked.

'I had a wife. I couldn't say till I was free of all that.'

Sonia smiled. She lifted Jake to her blazing bosom. She held him against her. She was very strong. He felt engulfed. 'I can kill you,' she whispered in his ear.

'If it pleases you, you must.' Jake slid his hands between her thighs. His head ached. His cock ached. It stood stiffly, yearning to be gloved in her body.

She lay back and opened her legs. Jake saw her sex pulse. Each throb made it swell outwards. Out and back, out and back. It bulged towards him threateningly. It withdrew with false coyness and pleaded that he follow where it enticed.

Jake slid himself into her. Heat coiled along his veins. Power surged through him. He began to slam into her, shouting as he did so. He fucked with all the energy and enthusiasm in the world, not as himself but as the creature she made him into. His cock was whoremaster, womanfeaster, cuntsucker, sex gladiator. He rode triumphant in a blaze of strength. He came rapidly to climax. He spurted freely into her. He was generous, shooting again and again into her open greedy sex. When he was finally done he hung there, supporting himself on his arms, looking down in triumph on her lying beneath him. He was flushed with heat, sweat running down his body and filming his face.

Honey flowed into his loins. Soft and sweetly nourishing, he felt himself melt and ease. He lay back and wiped his face. A dull throb reminded him of his wound.

'I can do this for you,' she said.

'You command it?'

'I do. I can make you burn. I can make you swell with

pleasure. I can bring peace and health to you. When I am pleased.'

'I wish always to please you. I am your dog, your serving creature, your thing. You do with me as you please. I am yours in body and soul.'

'It pleases me to have you sleep in my chamber. I do not rest much, it is no longer necessary. We will see, dog, how well you do.'

Jake kissed her feet and slunk away.

There was someone with him all the time. He was never alone. He made no demands nor any complaints. He was servilely grateful for everything.

They treated him well and his head felt much better. He was kept cleansed and perfumed, being waited on as before. This time he did not service the girls who tended him nor did they make him. His duty was to one woman only and he must service no other.

He did exercises, explaining that it would make him a better sexual partner. He found indeed that Sonia had sexual preferences. Remnants of normal humanness remained. She was basically conventional. She liked lying on her back with Jake on top. Being kissed between her thighs thrilled her inexpressibly, as though it was something extraordinary. Jake initiated sex when he could and was as athletic as his strength and arousal permitted. He could not have performed such feats naturally. He needed her mutant ability. She hardly expected it to be otherwise.

He began to encourage her to experiment. He indicated his own preference which was to come into her from the rear. When he was stiff after touching he could run across a room and plunge straight into her without either of them being hurt. They both enjoyed the shock of his sudden entry. He would then pump vigorously until he came.

Sonia would lie bent forward over her bed for these occasions. Then when he slammed into her she didn't fall. Jake could see the ring of fire from across the room. His cock would plunge into the black heart till the fire licked all around his own groin. He laughed now when this happened. His fear was gone, though he showed Sonia his awe of her and gave her the obeisance that was her due. He never forgot her capacity to destroy him.

His chain was removed for these occasions, then left off altogether. He still wore the collar and could be chained at any time. He lived in Sonia's restchamber continually now. She no longer had him serve her in the public Council Chamber. He was her private pet and she came to him when she required his services.

He slept in the bed he had been nursed in. He pleaded to keep the blanket, he said he was used to coverings and more comfortable with them. Under these covers was his sole privacy. He had nothing, nowhere else, no possession of his own, nothing. He lived for Sonia and she had made it clear that if it pleased her he would die for her. She had dreamed of such a relationship in her former life and recorded it in her diary. Now it was her reality. He was hers entirely, heart and mind.

Sonia entered the room and sat on her bed. She looked over at Jake. 'You ask me for nothing,' she said.

'I ask you for much.'

'You do?'

'I ask for permission to serve you.'

'You want nothing from your old life? No books. No companions. Nothing to occupy yourself whilst I am running my brave new world.'

'I want nothing of the old life. I occupy myself with thoughts of you, mistress.'

She nodded. Jake thought of the dumpy plain woman. That

woman would enjoy being this woman. Power would be a constant pleasure to her.

'Would my mistress be pleased to have me in her?'

'How?' asked Sonia.

'If you were to bend over I could fondle and caress your rear.'

Sonia shivered so that she was momentarily a shimmer of green fire. This was Jake's latest ploy. He was teaching her that there was more than one way to bell the cat.

She turned and bent over on the bed. Jake ignored the guard/attendant. There was one in the room at all times. Sonia was straddled with her legs wide apart. Her arms were spread wide on the bed, her face buried in it. Jake stood up from his bed.

'Tell me what you would have me do, mistress?' he said. He knelt down and fumbled under his bed. He took something hidden in its springs. His voice was very soft.

The guard stepped forward curiously. Jake signalled her to approach and see. Sonia was telling them in precise detail what she wanted Jake to do. Her voice was muffled, buried in her bedding.

Jake stabbed himself in the thigh. The guard opened her mouth. Jake clipped her neatly under the chin. Her head snapped back. She fell dazed. Jake wrapped her swiftly in his blankets.

'Come now,' Sonia was saying. 'Come now. Come now.'

Jake went across the room. He touched her rear. He opened her buttocks and kissed her. His tongue probed. The body he served shivered. Jake slid a finger into Sonia's pussy. 'Would you have me penetrate you elsewhere?' he asked. He touched her rear. 'As you command, so I serve, mistress.'

Sonia writhed on his finger. 'Yes,' she commanded.

Jake lifted the hypodermic high above his head. There was a spot of blood on his thigh where he had dealt with himself.

He plunged the needle into Sonia's buttock and pressed the plunger home. At the same moment he jerked his finger out of her pussy.

She screamed. So did Jake. He had not been fast enough. The digit that had been in her body was burned.

He clutched the injured hand to him. Sonia stood up groggily and turned to him as he backed away from her.

'What have you done?' she whispered. She took a faltering step towards him. 'What have you done?'

Jake continued to back away from her. His hand hurt like the devil. He saw her green flame flicker and dissolve.

'What have you done?' she screamed.

'It won't hurt you.' His voice was hoarse. 'I haven't hurt you. You'll be OK.'

'My power! My strength!' She was screaming.

Jake had no idea how far she was affected. All he wanted to do was to get out. He ran for the door. Sonia pursued him. He got through first but she touched him.

He had his immunity again. His things had been stored in Sonia's room. He had found them and prepared the one time he had been alone, after the injury to his head. The blessed attack, the one piece of real luck that he could not have arranged, had helped him so much.

Sonia touched him and it had no sexual power over him. But it burned. His flesh sizzled. Jake hit her as he had hit the guard.

She fell. Immediately he went to cupboards set in the wall and pulled out his things. He hauled the trousers and boots on. The radio was there but when he tried it nothing happened. The batteries were flat. He reached for his shirt and saw his bedding heave. The guard was coming round. From the floor Sonia groaned. Jake grabbed his shirt and ran.

This time it was different. He was well fed, well exercised and carrying out an orderly plan. There were no nightmares.

With boots on his feet he ran hard. The women scattered as he came. Some tried to touch him but he was gloriously immune.

He had more knowledge of his surroundings and he had spent long drearily boring days thinking about this. From the moment he had first knelt before Sonia, this whole thing had been in his mind. He could not have planned the details, but he had used his seeming servility to gain him the freedom he needed. He had wanted to vomit over the words he had used and the self-abasement he had shown. But it had been worth it.

It was good to be himself. It was good to run free. It was good to be clothed. Jake's blood sung sweet and fierce. He crashed out through the entrance into the star-thick night.

He had long since lost touch with whether it was day or night. Somewhere in the pockets of his clothes his watch would be. Jake began to lope through the dark. He was on a hillside. He was not aware of being followed. For a moment he stopped to catch his breath.

He was high up in the cold night air. Below him like a thousand jewels camp fires lit the night. As far as his eyes could see to his left and to his right, vast numbers of people were camped along the foot of the hill. Thousands of people. Maybe millions. The camp fires were endless, dwindling to minute pinpricks in the distance. The whole plain below him was filled up with people. This then was Sonia's web of power. For a moment its heart faltered. That was all he had achieved. The plan had gone wrong and he knew he had failed.

He had escaped. He was sure he could get north. But he had failed to bring Sonia out with him. The idea had been for the army to co-ordinate with him so that when he disarmed her, she could be captured.

He couldn't contact the army. His radio no longer functioned. They must have given him up for dead a month ago or more. And he couldn't take Sonia with him. He couldn't touch her because although she had lost her sexual power over him, she was still imbued with the mysterious force she had gained in his laboratory, in his place of business. Now she was actively against him she could burn him. He had disarmed her sex but not her fire.

He turned up the hill. He must go north. They would expect it but there was little else he could do. He had no food and only enough methadone to guard him for a few days. Most of it he had jabbed into Sonia's right buttock. She had had the maximum dose they dared give her without endangering her life.

Jake heard a baying. He began to run again. The hunt was up.

He ran up the hill at as steep an angle as he could. The ground was firm and smooth. He saw vast white lines loom in the night. The hill giant, of course, the Cerne Giant. Sonia had chosen her centre of operations well.

The hill top above him glowed strangely. Suddenly he became aware that women were approaching him from a new direction. He changed course and ran painfully straight up the hill.

He could hear a thundering sound. For a moment he wondered stupidly if the generators within the hill that lit and warmed the underground world were making the whole hill vibrate.

His breath laboured. The women ululated as they came. Jake turned as he ran and looked over his shoulder.

In their thousands they came. They ran carrying torches that streamed in the wind. They ran screaming and wailing and calling. The whole vast encampment from below must be on the move. He could never escape. They would trample him to death. Jake ran with his lungs bursting and his heart breaking. He had never given up, not for one moment in all the long dreary painful humiliating days of his imprisonment. He had known he would get free. He had known he had a personal future.

Now like termites from the mound the very earth spewed up his enemies. On they came in their screaming hordes, in their thousands, so that at his back not one blade of grass could be seen for the rush of feet coming after him.

Sobbing, Jake ran, up and up and up.

He was blinded by light. From the thundering sky came a great bolt of light that picked out his puny figure and lit it for the maddened murderous horde to see. He swam in light but could see nothing himself. His ears were filled with an enormous roaring and through it he could hear the screams of his pursuers rise in volume, a sound so atavistically terrifying that Jake stumbled and fell with the horror of the thing. They bayed for his blood. In their thousands they bayed and the very skies opened and helped them.

He put his arms over his head and knelt, bent over with his back to his death. As he realised this he stood up. He would die facing them. He turned and bellowed defiance in the face of death itself.

Both his arms jolted with pain. He struggled and found his feet were kicking free. He was suspended. He hung. The cold air touched his burning face. Below him women grabbed at his dangling feet, screaming to reach him and tear him apart.

He swung higher. His blood roared in his ears so that even the women could not be heard. The night was bitter cold as he disappeared up into it, sucked into the light.

They hauled him into the helicopter. He lay on his belly looking down. Below him the tiny lights danced. The whole countryside was alight with them. Only in one place was there any dark part, any break in the pinpoints of flame.

Like globules the pattern flowed and reformed. Jake stared.

Someone was putting earphones over his ears but he took no notice.

Below him the women bewailed their crippling loss of power and their lost chance for revenge. As they did so they obeyed forces Jake knew nothing of, would not have believed.

The Cerne Giant appeared. Around his broad lines the women formed. Where it revealed his shape they left the hillside bare. In flame the giant glowed. His entire body was revealed by the height Jake flew above him in the circling helicopter.

There he was, boldly erect, arrogantly male, a vast neolithic joke, a vulgar deity preserved through the ages by a people not entirely lost to their origins.

The women had brought him to life.

Twelve

'Who are you?'

'Jake Connors.'

'Really? Where the hell have you been?'

'I was a prisoner. I escaped tonight. How come you were here?'

'We've been keeping an eye on the build-up of people down there. We overfly a couple of times a week, I guess. We saw you running. You surely stirred up a hornets' nest.'

Jake was silent. He felt shaken. He could hardly believe it was all over. That is, it was all over for him personally. His mission had failed. Sonia would recover. There would be no second chance.

Despite his experiences the thought of the women massed below him being attacked and killed was nauseous. Soon it would be the only solution remaining.

The helicopter continued to circle. Jake's presence was reported to HQ. The men watched what was going on below them.

'Go down a bit, Tom,' said one of them. The pilot obeyed.

'Switch on the light, will you?'

They all watched now. They saw the women fall to the ground. Their legs buckled and they fell. It was like corn being blown over by a wind. In vast ripples the women were flattened. Unlike corn they did not get up again.

The whole thing was extraordinary. They were throwing their torches onto the giant's outline. Then they would fan away and fall.

'Is it a trick?' asked one of the men doubtfully.

'You do anything before you escaped?' Jake was asked.

'I've temporarily disarmed their leader. The source of their power. Maybe she'll be out for a day or so.'

'Do you think this is the result?'

'I don't know.' Jake's tired brain began to work again. 'Go down the hill, will you? She could be captured if her women were being weakened. You need asbestos gloves, though.'

'We're all immunised, Jake. No one flies south without it. We got three months protection in our blood stream. In case of a crash, you understand.'

'The source has a power to defend herself that I couldn't switch off,' said Jake. 'If she is angry she can burn you on contact. See. She got my hand while I was disabling her tonight.' He held up his burned finger. It hurt intolerably.

'Hey, we've got medication on board. Especially against burns.'

The pilot took the machine lower down the hill while Jake had his finger dressed. 'That's one hell of a deep burn,' said the man doing the bandaging. He introduced himself as Leroy. He was on loan from the US. His duty was to report back what he saw to his own people.

'I'm full of methadone,' said Jake and grinned weakly.

'We got something better now.'

'Good.'

'Look, they're all falling down here too.'

They circled discussing what they could see. If the women were really collapsing then it was a prime opportunity to go and get Sonia. They had protective clothing. They could take her.

If the women were somehow fooling them or only in some temporary phase of their behaviour, then the whole crew was at risk.

Urgent discussions were held with HQ. Jake lay back in

his seat with his eyes shut. For the first time in a long time he allowed himself to think of Lana.

He really didn't want to go into the hill again. He did not take kindly to failure but he wanted to relax for the first time in a long time. He wanted to be among friends.

'OK. This is it. We keep in the air and one stays on board with Tom to render assistance as necessary. The rest go in and try to take this lady that burns. You willing to guide us, Jake?'

'Yes.'

'Leroy, you stay with Pete. You can help get everyone back aboard.'

No one commented on this. Leroy was the non-national. When it came to it, the risk wasn't his. It had remained a British problem.

Below it looked as though nerve gas had been sprayed. Jake found he was torn between a fear they would rise up and smother him and a fear that they were dead. The helicopter took them close to the exit from the building built into the hill. The first man went down the ladder and jumped off.

Three of them followed, then Jake. His bad hand made it awkward.

None of the women moved. A rapid inspection seemed to indicate that suddenly they were sleepers. It was as though with Sonia's power muted, the women fell down. She powered them directly, though by what means Jake had no idea.

They found her on her bed. She opened her eyes as they approached. Jake saw that the green fire was still there, locked inside her. Her power was in abeyance only temporarily.

Would all those women arise like a vast clay army and live, when she recovered?

'You,' she said faintly, venomously. She had eyes only for Jake. As she stared at him he felt his inside melt and panic. The men surrounded her. They threw a fireproof tarpaulin over her, a fireblanket they carried on the helicopter. As they did she hissed and glowed incandescent with rage. She did not have the strength to get up, but she could be angry.

Her bedclothes smouldered. Deftly the men bound her. They carried her like a rolled carpet on their shoulders getting out as fast as they could. They all found their surroundings creepy.

The helicopter landed. They loaded Sonia and tied her up near the back of the loading bay, leaving a light switched on above her so that she could be watched at all times. It was like carrying a live bomb.

They began the flight home.

He woke in a white hospital room. He lay comfortably feeling the dull throb from his hand. The window had a venetian blind across it and this was angled so that slatted winter sunlight lay across his bed.

He was warm and at ease. A nurse looked in, nurse Judy Mayhew. He knew all their names.

'Mr Connors. A cup of tea?'

'Yes please.'

She came back with it and smoothed his bedclothes. 'I feel a fraud,' Jake said. 'There's nothing wrong me.'

'Your hand is very bad.'

Jake shrugged. 'It'll get better.'

'I'm sorry it won't ever be right. I mean, it'll stop hurting . . .'

'I know what you mean.' He would be permanently disfigured.

'How did you do it, Mr Connors? We're all dying to know. You're a real hero.'

Jake remembered where his finger had been and how it had suffered what had happened to it. He grinned. 'It's not for your shell-like ear,' he said and drank his tea.

Later he had visitors. Pete came to see him and his boss,

Matthew Vance from the university. Jake was news hungry
and grateful to them.

'They're all asleep, Jake. We don't understand it. We can't
explain it. But they're all asleep and we're bringing the wire
down. We're one country again.'

'Can they be handled when they're asleep or are they still
contagious?'

'We know from sleepers we've had under observation here
that the effect diminishes the longer they are asleep. Their
biology returns to normal.'

'But can they be woken up?'

Pete was astonished. 'Don't you know?'

'I've been out of action for a long time,' said Jake grimly.
It was almost Christmas. Part of his life had vanished under
that hill of the Cerne Giant.

'They wake up. They're normal. They're cold and they
want to get dressed and they're hungry. But they are as normal
as any woman who's never been touched.'

'What do they think of it all?' Jake couldn't imagine.

'They can hardly remember. It's shadowy, dream for them.
It's as though the mind is letting them off the hook.'

Jake lay back on his pillows. 'I still wonder whether
something wasn't released deep in the female psyche,' he
said.

Pete smirked. 'You mean thousands of years of being told
by men their sex drive was less important and somehow less
significant than ours finally blew their minds?'

'Something like that.'

'A whole lot of men are wondering that. Maybe we should
feel guilty.' The men grinned companionably. After a while
Jake said: 'It'll be one hell of a clear-up. Britain's got be
rebuilt south of the wire.'

'It ain't so bad. The rebuilding will cost but it'll be a
terrific boost to the economy. And in ten, twenty years' time

we'll have the most advanced plant and housing in Europe. We can build modern energy-efficient homes and businesses. It's an unprecedented opportunity.' He chuckled. 'Or so the politicians say.'

Matthew added seriously: 'There's a health pay-off too, though we don't know for how long. These women are fantastically fit. They are organically perfect. They even look prettier. The touched men seem in better health, too. We'll be saved millions in health care if the effect lasts. The reduction in the costs of all our major diseases is incalculable. Apart from the improvement in people's personal lives, there'll be much less time lost from work. A healthy nation does more work per head and costs the State less per person than an unhealthy one.'

'What of Sonia?' said Jake uncomfortably. He didn't want to ask. He didn't want to know. Yet he was fascinated.

'Don't know. Our people aren't handling it.'

'Nothing on the electronic mail? No word, no rumour?'

Matthew said: 'It's hush-hush. We ordinary folk aren't being told.'

Jake was outraged. 'I brought her out. That is, me and those other guys. I have the right to know.'

'You might, mate, but we don't.'

They went away. A doctor had seen Jake that morning and said he could be discharged the following morning if the night went well with no fever. Jake felt sure there would be no fever. He was enjoying this lazy day and the one that had preceded it, but he knew that shortly he wanted to be up and doing. He had a life to rebuild. Somehow that didn't seem so bad now. Many people had a life to rebuild, homes, work, everything. He was one of a crowd. He needn't be lonely.

It might even be exciting.

After lunch during the period when patients were supposed to nap he had another visitor. He was in a private room and less subject to the hospital's authority than were those in the public wards.

She came in unannounced. She opened the door and slid round it, closing it behind her. Then she stood.

Jake didn't say a word. He allowed his eyes to feast slowly up and down the gorgeous length of her.

She looked dynamite. She was loaded with mischief. She was every ounce his woman, his Lana.

She wore something tight and slinky and dead black that ended just above her beautiful knees. Her dark smoky legs were a poem of slim curve and line. She wore four-inch heels and she had the style of a movie star.

On her top half she wore a little fur jacket that snuggled close under her chin. Its wisps and feathers of fur framed her lovely face. She had on a black hat with a wide brim pulled down to one side. He could see coral lipstick. She was packaged to slay 'em dead and Jake was on his back already, not even wanting to fight.

She took a step towards him.

'No,' said Jake, his eyes dancing. 'Why don't you just take a walk up and down a little, so's I can see you move.'

Her lips curved into an appreciative smile. She began to walk towards the window. Jake watched her swaying hips, her leopard grace. She turned and walked back towards the door. She peeked at him from under the brim of her hat.

'Paris chic, American-style,' said Jake.

'We aim to please.'

Those were her first words. They caught Jake like a blow on his heart. Her throaty, husky voice stroked him like fingertips stroking the length of his cock.

On the next trip to the window she shed her jacket, letting it slide off her shoulders and arms till she could throw it over a chair. Her dress had no sleeves. She wore gloves clear up to and over her elbows.

Jake looked at her milk-white upper arms, softly rounded. The black dress, the black gloves were a startling contrast. He looked down her curving length. The clinging dress showed every part of her figure in sumptuous perfection. He thought about milk-white thighs over black stocking tops.

She had on a pearl choker round her neck, and pearl drops set in gold hung from her ears.

She took a swing back to the door. She began, in a leisurely fashion, to peel one glove. Jake saw her fingernails were coral, the same shade as her lips. Again he saw the lips curve into a smile in that shadowed half-hidden face.

'You witch,' he said helplessly.

She laughed. She reached behind her and with one deft movement she unzipped her dress.

'A nurse might come in,' said Jake weakly.

She slid the dress off. 'I bribe nurses, pussycat,' she said.

She stood still, letting Jake absorb every detail. She wore that hat still. She wore a little écru satin chemmy with heavy café-au-lait lace. Jake could see the colour of the nipples on her high firm breasts through it. The dark hair at the base of her belly was slightly masked by a similar scrap of satin and lace. The dark stockings came up around those milky rounded thighs just as he had imagined. Even better, in fact.

The hand that was still gloved rested on one hip. The pearls shone with a dull lustre at her neck.

'Take your hat off,' said Jake. He was conscious of a constriction in his throat.

She swept it off and shook her luxurious hair free.

'Oh baby,' said Jake huskily. 'I've missed you.'

She came to him and sat on the edge of his bed, kicking off her shoes. She tucked her legs up and leaned forward. She touched his mouth with hers.

Her fragrance enveloped him. Jake brought up his hands and took Lana with them.

'You've hurt your hand,' she whispered. Her lips brushed his skin as she did so.

'Playing with fire.'

She laughed. 'You just don't learn.'

'No,' said Jake and kissed her.

She was alive, independent and totally wicked. She was his woman, she'd chosen him, and he adored her. She was in his arms.

His hands slid under the lace and satin of her garment. Her skin was clear and warm against his. It was soft and yielding. She kissed his chest and he felt her hair spill over his shoulders. He touched her thigh and then ran his hand up and over her buttock.

She leant back slightly. Her eyes were smoky with passion.

'Screw me, Jake. I'm begging you.'

'Lana.'

'Don't say anything. There's nothing to say. Sweetheart, I want to feel your muscle in me. Jake, I'm so lonely down there. My pussy's calling, darling. It's calling to you. I want you in me.'

She pulled down the lace at one breast. It spilled out. She took it herself and lifted the nipple to her own mouth. When she offered it to Jake, it was coral from her lips.

'Suck me, darling. Make it hard.'

Jake made it hard. He sucked hard, her nipple came hard in his mouth like a tiny soldier. Like her clit. He released the breast. 'There's more of you I want in my mouth,' he whispered. 'There's more of you to come up when I call.' His fingers found where her panties went between her legs. He ran his nails across the warm satin there. Lana groaned. Jake slid his fingers under the slip of material.

Her pussy was warm and soft, as yielding as her mouth, as welcoming. She wanted him to come in, she wanted him right there in the quick of her. As his fingers moved she arched her back, almost purring. He found her clitoris and touched it. She jerked against him. 'That's my on button,' she breathed in his ear.

'I know. I'm going to press it some more.'

'Is that a warning or is that a promise?'

'It's a plea and promise and a thank you, all rolled into one.'

His fingers were inside her now. She kissed his eyes and his mouth, pressing her breasts against him, trying to squeeze his fingers with her pussy. Trying and succeeding.

'Let me see you,' begged Jake. 'Honey, I want to see you down there.'

She rolled onto her back and opened her legs wide. She arched back so he saw her fan of dark hair, the pretty choker about her neck, her two breasts, one partly hidden in its lace enclosure, one provocatively pouting out at him.

Her belly was flat under the flimsy satin nonsense that still covered it. He saw her two arms, one black in its long glove, one white. He saw her beautiful thighs divided wide before him, the long dark legs spread for his pleasure.

Delicately he hooked aside the thin strip of damp satin that went between her legs. Wisps of dark hair curled provocatively. His fingers stirred her. Pink and wriggling, long and luscious, peachy and moist, her sex winked out at him.

'Lana, you are the best,' he said. He meant it. She had no peer.

'Kiss me, Jake. Like I like it.'

He bent and licked the satin first. It was musky with her body's juices. He bit it. Then he tore it and her whole pussy was laid bare before his greedy eyes.

He ran his tongue, just its tip, along her. He felt her shiver in excitement. He fingered her little clitoris till it stood free and then he placed his lips over it and sucked.

'I'll come, I'll come,' she protested, wriggling under

him and pushing into his face.

He stuck his tongue deep into her quivering pussy. He ran it round. He put his lips over her vulva and sucked hard. He felt her shake and pulsate and then he tasted her nectar.

She came up the bed and put her arms round him. She kissed him long and slow and deep. She wanted to taste herself in him.

'How come,' she murmured low, her eyes drowsy with desire, 'you're so damned good at this?'

'Take me, Lana. I need you.'

She folded down the covers. Her gloved hand came creeping down his belly, through the dark hair there, to where his flesh bulged. She took the thick arrogant stalk in her hand. She slid her hand down till the hot tip was exposed. Jake watched her head go down. He felt her hair on his belly and thighs. He felt the heat and wetness of her mouth. He felt her kiss. He felt her suck.

When she lifted her head he saw coral lipstick on his sex.

'I need to be inside you,' he said. She smiled. 'I guess you do an' all,' she said with a slow drawling intonation. 'I guess it's about time.'

She opened her body over Jake's. She held his shaft and as she impaled herself on him, as his muscle filled her hot inner quilting, as her muscles expanded to absorb his and then cling, she purred with joy.

Jake felt the whole hot live woman suck his sex into her pussy and then stroke it tight and stroke it soft with slippery elastic skill. His hands went everywhere. She fucked him so slow it was almost painful, the luxurious dragging out of extreme pleasure. His hands went into her breasts, under and outside of satin. His hands held her thighs above the black slash of her stockings. His hands went round and under her so that his fingers slid into the crevice between her buttocks and felt for her little strawberry place there. It made her pussy convulse tightly when he felt it so he felt it again and again.

This lady was a box of the most sophisticated sweets. Each trick she had was a new delight to melt on the tongue and fill a man's soul with sweetness. She could not cloy.

As for Sonia, she became so biologically inert they froze her. She would be a problem for the future. They could do nothing with her now. Jake had his hands too full to worry. He had his life and work to rebuild. There was Peta to consider. It was his feeling that Lana could keep a man occupied for a whole lot a time to come. That was no bad thing to look forward to.

Epilogue

Some months later Jake was sitting on a park bench with an open packet of sandwiches for his lunch, reading a journal and absently throwing crumbs to the birds. A whole hunk of sly fox-red womanhood eased herself onto the bench beside him and slid one long silk-clad leg sensuously over the other.

Jake found his eyes on the neat ankles. Keeping his head still he let his eyes slide up the smoothly curving legs. There was no woman to equal Lana but it remained a pleasant occupation to load his eyesight with a goodlooking piece of femininity.

She wore a short straight skirt that revealed a pleasing amount of thigh. Jake let his eyes slide higher and higher. There was plenty up top to see too, the low neckline revealing the beginnings of the rich cleft between the breasts.

Green eyes met his mockingly.

'Sally,' said Jake coldly.

She pouted. 'Don't be nasty, Jake.'

'Sally. I'm not an important man and I can offer you no information. Run along, dear. You'll get better copy elsewhere.'

She wasn't offended. 'I'm not like that any more,' she said, her eyes sliding down him to absorb details like how much his suit cost.

'And what are you like?'

'I've reformed. I'm a good girl. I do charity work.' She ran the tip of a pink tongue over her glossy lips and smiled.

'And I'm the new lion-tamer at the zoo.'

'Grrr,' said Sally softly.

Jake looked at his watch. 'I have to go, sweetheart. You pop back to skid row and hand out tracts or whatever it is you do.'

She was cross. 'I mean it. I don't put out any more. I have a permanent meaningful relationship in my life.'

'You've found a male black widow spider?'

She looked distinctly sulky. 'You know him,' she said. 'I've reformed him. He says so. And I'm not one of those spider things. I do him good.'

'I think I prefer the old Sally, wicked as sin and selling sex for copy. At least that had a basic honesty about it.'

'It's Sam Riley. You know him. He doesn't drink any more.' Despite his insults she achieved a creamy satisfied smile. 'I make it worth his while not to drink.'

She eased her body slightly and smiled under her lashes at Jake.

Sam Riley. It took Jake a minute to place the name. The drunken journalist who had had enough newspaperman left in his drink-sodden soul to smell the truth of what was happening long before anyone else had made the right connections.

Sam and Sally? That crumbling seedy man the wrong side of middle age and this turbulent young nympho? Jake came close to goggling.

Sally leant towards him. He smelled her fragrance. The neck of her top was loose and for a moment he could gaze deep into her curving bosom. 'Sam and I do it all the time,' she whispered. 'He's a new man since all the trouble. He teaches me all about newspaper work. I teach him about sex.' She licked her lips. 'He doesn't booze, I don't screw around, that's the deal. I told you, I'm a good girl now. I've reformed.'

'Bully for you,' said Jake faintly.

'Of course, you were always special.' She put a hand on his thigh. Her long nails were painted an opalescent pink. 'I adored being in bed with you. You gave me the best fuck of my life.'

Her green eyes bored into him. 'Sam's a big cuddly darling with a cock the size of a cruise missile,' she whispered. 'But you have magic between the thighs. When I saw you on the bench I had to come over. Here's my number at work. Any time you feel like a repeat, magic man, you give me a bell.'

'You call this being reformed?'

'You're the only one, lover. Come up and see me sometime.' Her lips almost touched his ear. 'Fill my pussy. It misses you.'

She bit his ear.

In his house that evening Jake loosened his tie and poured himself a drink. Lana came in from the sun-lounger in the garden.

'So how was it today, lover?' she asked, putting her arms round his neck and kissing him on the corner of his mouth.

'I met an old friend in the park.'

'Mmm?'

'That girl reporter. Sally Trenning.'

'Little Miss Pillow Talk?'

'That's the one.'

'So how'd it go?'

'She offered me sex. I said no.'

'Jake,' sighed Lana. 'You're so strong.'

'Morally upright,' murmured Jake, sliding his hand under her bikini so that the warm rounded flesh of her bottom filled his palm. He kissed her neck. 'She told me she had reformed, though.'

'Reformed?' Lana took her bikini top off and admired her nipples pressed against Jake's shirt.

'Apart from me and her live-in lover, she doesn't put out any more.'

Lana began to undo the buttons of Jake's shirt. He had been horny ever since Sally had propositioned him. Lana rubbing herself catlike against his body when she was all but naked was having a very dramatic effect.

'We're all moral now,' said Lana. She smiled. 'All of us ladies. All anxious to show what an aberration all that sex was. We don't really get that hot. It was a disease.' She scratched the front of Jake's trousers. Then she trailed her fingers over the distended contours of his body there.

Jake's hands were on her hips, clasping her warm golden flesh. She took his face between her hands and began to kiss him on the mouth.

His buttons were undone. His jacket slid off. His tie was removed. His shirt vanished. Slowly, all the time with Lana kissing him, his body was stripped naked.

'You feel like a sandwich?' murmured Lana. She had stepped out of her bikini. Now she pressed her voluptuous naked body against Jake, her breast to his chest, her belly to his groin, her thighs to his.

Jake looked up. His chin was in her hair. Her scent was in his nostrils.

Breasts pressed against his back. Fingers trailed between his buttocks. He gasped. A hand came between his legs and grasped his aching column of manhood. It held him between Lana's thighs and rubbed him there.

Jake groaned. 'You sweet witches,' he said.

'Very moral witches,' said Lana, laughing. 'Aren't we, Peta?'

They pressed their naked bodies so that Jake was crushed between them. Peta took one of his hands and slid it between her thighs. Jake felt her warm, gently throbbing vulva, the silk of her fleece.

'Who's first?' whispered Lana.

'Me,' said Peta greedily.

'Who was first last time?' asked Jake faintly.

'Let's toss for it,' suggested Peta. 'Heads you get into me first, tails you get into Lana.'

'I don't see how I can lose,' said Jake.

'You aren't meant to,' said Lana.

Peta came round in front of Jake and he stood for a moment, his arms full of the two naked women, aroused and willing for him to satisfy them. They each had an arm round each other. He loved to see them like this, their four breasts, their two sweet pussies. At first he had been incredulous when Lana welcomed Peta into their bed but he knew she got a kick out of it, it wasn't just for him that she did this thing. Peta preferred it with Lana present, frankly preferred it to sex with Jake alone.

He didn't mind. How could he?

He stood in his house looking out into the sun-filled garden. Both women sank to their knees. Two sets of lips began to caress his sex. His only problem was in keeping upright.

Lips, fingers, tongues, teeth, all pursued ways of making him prefer to be flat on his back.

It wasn't going to bother him, rejecting Sally Trenning, however hot she came on.

His knees went weak. He began to allow himself to slip down between his ladies. There were times when even a strong man had to give way.

This was one of them.

A selection of Erotica
from Headline

FONDLE ON TOP	Nadia Adamant	£4.99 □
EROS AT PLAY	Anonymous	£4.99 □
THE GIRLS' BOARDING SCHOOL	Anonymous	£4.99 □
HOTEL D'AMOUR	Anonymous	£4.99 □
A MAN WITH THREE MAIDS	Anonymous	£4.99 □
RELUCTANT LUST	Lesley Asquith	£4.50 □
SEX AND MRS SAXON	Lesley Asquith	£4.50 □
THE BLUE LANTERN	Nick Bancroft	£4.99 □
AMATEUR NIGHTS	Becky Bell	£4.99 □
BIANCA	Maria Caprio	£4.50 □
THE GIRLS OF LAZY DAISY'S	Faye Rossignol	£4.50 □

All Headline books are available at your local bookshop or newsagent, or can be ordered direct from the publisher. Just tick the titles you want and fill in the form below. Prices and availability subject to change without notice.

Headline Book Publishing PLC, Cash Sales Department, Bookpoint, 39 Milton Park, Abingdon, OXON, OX14 4TD, UK. If you have a credit card you may order by telephone — 0235 831700.

Please enclose a cheque or postal order made payable to Bookpoint Ltd to the value of the cover price and allow the following for postage and packing:

UK & BFPO: £1.00 for the first book, 50p for the second book and 30p for each additional book ordered up to a maximum charge of £3.00.

OVERSEAS & EIRE: £2.00 for the first book, £1.00 for the second book and 50p for each additional book.

Name ....

Address ....

....

....

If you would prefer to pay by credit card, please complete:

Please debit my Visa/Access/Diner's Card/American Express (delete as applicable) card no:

Signature ....Expiry Date ....